Luke cleared his throat. "You ready?"

"Sure."

He and Bruno followed Sophie to the front door of her unit.

Which was cracked open.

She gasped and stepped back.

"That's not supposed to be open, I'm guessing?" Luke whispered.

"No."

"Stand back against the wall. Bruno, stay." In the blink of an eye, the dog's demeanor changed at Luke's command. His ears went up and he was in instant work mode, waiting for the next order.

A loud crash came from the bedroom area and Luke headed down the hallway. "NYPD! Come out of the room! Hands where I can see them! Now!"

Lynette Eason
and
Dana Mentink

In the Crosshairs

Previously published as *Justice Mission* and *Act of Valor*

LOVE INSPIRED
INSPIRATIONAL ROMANCE

Special thanks and acknowledgment are given to
Lynette Eason and Dana Mentink for their contributions
to the True Blue K-9 Unit miniseries.

LOVE INSPIRED®

INSPIRATIONAL ROMANCE

ISBN-13: 978-1-335-20962-7

In the Crosshairs

Copyright © 2020 by Harlequin Books S.A.

Justice Mission
First published in 2019. This edition published in 2020.
Copyright © 2019 by Harlequin Books S.A.

Act of Valor
First published in 2019. This edition published in 2020.
Copyright © 2019 by Harlequin Books S.A.

Recycling programs
for this product may
not exist in your area.

This edition published by arrangement with Harlequin Books S.A.

For questions and comments about the quality of this book,
please contact us at CustomerService@Harlequin.com.

Love Inspired
22 Adelaide St. West, 40th Floor
Toronto, Ontario M5H 4E3, Canada
www.Harlequin.com

Printed in U.S.A.

CONTENTS

Lynette Eason is a bestselling, award-winning author who makes her home in South Carolina with her husband and two teenage children. She enjoys traveling, spending time with her family and teaching at various writing conferences around the country. She is a member of Romance Writers of America and American Christian Fiction Writers. Lynette can often be found online interacting with her readers. You can find her at Facebook.com/lynette.eason and on Twitter, @lynetteeason.

JUSTICE MISSION

Lynette Eason

ONE

Sophie Walters stood back to count the rows of chairs and relished the thought of the upcoming graduation ceremony that would take place shortly in the auditorium near the NYC K-9 Command Unit headquarters where she worked in Forest Hills, Queens. Today, several new four-legged recruits and their handlers would graduate and join the force in keeping New York City safe.

The unit was made up of officers who handled dogs with a variety of specialties. While based out of their office in Queens, the officers were assigned to divisions of the NYPD throughout the five boroughs of New York City where needed.

As the administrative assistant to Chief Jordan Jameson, who headed up the NYC K-9 Command Unit, Sophie had a wide range of duties, but she'd be the first to admit, she loved the graduation ceremonies most.

Hands down, she loved her job and took pride in the fact that she was very good at it. Something the chief often praised her for. "You have an eye for detail and organization, Sophie," he'd said on more than one occasion. "I don't know what this place would do without you."

If only he knew how hard she'd worked to develop that eye for detail. Sophie smiled, her heart grateful for the man who'd taken a chance on a young green college graduate three years ago.

A thud from the back of the auditorium drew her attention to the left-hand corner and she frowned. "Hello? Is someone there?"

Stillness settled over the large room. When nothing more happened and no one announced their presence, she returned her attention to the ceremony preparations.

Something was wrong. Off. But what?

A little prickle at the base of her neck sent shivers down her spine and she turned to assess the area once more. The auditorium chairs sat empty. She'd unlocked all of the doors in case she had some early arrivals, but the place was quiet for now. Quiet as a tomb. Now, why would she think that? There'd been no more strange noises and nothing that should spark her unease. But she couldn't help feeling like someone was watching.

But why?

And who?

"No one," she muttered. "Quit jumping at shadows." But something still nagged at her.

Sophie scanned the stage trying to put her finger on it. Six chairs aligned just right on the artificial turf. The podium with the chief's notes for his presentation within easy reach, the mic was at exactly the right height, the graduation certificates were laid out in alphabetical order on the table…

The table.

She huffed. She'd placed everything on it without putting the black cloth on. Where was her mind this morning?

Definitely on her brother and the attention-stealing phone call she'd received last night. He'd called to tell her he was quitting college to join the Marines.

Seriously? He was nineteen years old. "What does a nineteen-year-old know?" she muttered. Nothing. Which was probably why he wanted to join the Marines.

But who was she to say it was a bad idea? He was right. They were different people with different lives, but she'd been ten years old when their mother had left and she'd taken on the role of mother figure for Trey. For the past fourteen years, he'd looked at her that way. And now he wanted her to just step aside while he made an important decision without discussing it? A small part of her reminded herself that he was technically an adult.

"But I'm the one who attended the parent/teacher conferences when Dad couldn't get off work," she muttered. "I'm the one who fixed his snacks and washed his clothes and held him when he got his heart broken by the girl who dumped him his sophomore year of high school."

Stop it. Let it go for now and do your job.

Sophie removed the black tablecloth from the supply closet in the hallway, then hurried back toward the auditorium, her mind tuned in to the graduation details now.

She pushed through the auditorium door to the right

of the stage and stumbled to a halt. A man in a base-ball cap and sunglasses stood next to the podium with Chief Jameson's red remarks folder open.

"Excuse me, what are you doing?" Sophie asked. He'd frozen for a slight second when she entered but closed the folder as she strode toward him. Her low heels clicked on the wooden steps and rang through the empty room. She approached him, intent on rescuing Jordan's notes if need be. "The ceremony doesn't start for another forty-five minutes. Did you need help with something?"

"Ah. No." He turned toward her. "Thanks, but—" He kept his head lowered and she couldn't make out a thing about his features.

A little niggle of fear curled in her belly and she remembered the loud noise, the feeling of someone watching her. She stopped so suddenly, she actually slid a couple more inches on the wood floor. Had he been in the auditorium the whole time? Watching her? Waiting for her to leave so he could look through Jordan's folder?

No, of course not. She was being silly.

"But?" She encouraged him to finish his statement even while she could feel his laser-like stare shooting at her from behind the dark glasses. "Were you looking for something in the folder? It's just notes for a speech."

Once again unease shook her. Maybe she wasn't being so silly after all. Something wasn't right with this.

Get away from him.

Goose bumps pebbled her arms, and she turned to run. His left hand shot out and closed around her right bicep as his right hand came up, fingers wrapped around the grip of a gun. Sophie screamed when he placed the barrel of the weapon against her head. "Shut up," he hissed. "Cooperate, and I might let you live."

A gun. He had a gun pointed at her temple. "What are you doing? Why are you doing this? I don't have any money on me." Her shaky voice tumbled from trembling lips. She clamped them down, fighting for control.

His grip tightened. "Go."

Go? "Where?"

"Out the side door and to the parking lot. Now."

"Why don't you go, and I'll forget this ever happened?"

"Too late for that. You're coming with me. Now, move!"

"You're *kidnapping* me?" She squeezed the words out, trying to breathe through her terror.

"I said shut up! I'm not going to prison because of you!"

Still keeping his fingers tight around her upper arm, he gave her a hard shove and Sophie stumbled down the steps of the podium, his grip the only thing that kept her from landing on her face.

Her captor aimed her toward the door, and she had no choice but to follow. Heart thundering in her chest, her gaze jerked around the empty room. No help there. Maybe someone would be in the parking lot?

He pushed the silver bar and the steel door swung out. The gun moved from her head to dig into the center of her back, propelling her out onto the asphalt. His other hand snagged the loose bun at the nape of her neck, yanking her head sideways.

She cried out even while she squinted against the glare of the bright morning sun. Normally, her penchant for being early averted a lot of things that could go wrong and usurp her daily schedule. Today, it had placed her in the hands of a dangerous man—and an empty parking lot in Jackson Heights. Where was everyone?

Think, Sophie, think!

A K-9 SUV turned in and she caught a glimpse of the driver. Officer Luke Hathaway sat behind the wheel of the SUV. "Luke!"

"Shut up!" Her captor jerked her toward a brown sedan with a glance over his shoulder. His grip didn't loosen until he got to the driver's side of the vehicle. "Open the door!"

No way. With a burst of strength, she jabbed back with her left elbow. A yell burst from him along with a string of curses. She slipped from his grip for a brief second until he slammed his weapon against the side of her head.

She screamed as pain raced through her and stars danced, threatening to send her into the approaching blackness. Her captor opened the door and shoved her inside before she could gather her wits. She landed halfway on the middle console and halfway in the passenger seat with the gearshift digging into her hip. Head pounding, heart thudding, the blackness faded and she cried out once again as he gave her another hard push, forcing her awkwardly into the passenger seat.

The door slammed.

"Sophie!"

She heard Luke call her name and tried to ignore the nausea climbing into the back of her throat as she grabbed for the passenger-door handle. Her captor shot out a hand and grasped her by the hair. "Stay still, or I'll shoot you now."

The car roared to life and spun out of the lot.

Luke stared in horror as he realized he'd just witnessed Sophie being kidnapped. He pressed the gas and the SUV shot after the fleeing sedan.

Bruno, his K-9 partner seated safely in his spot in the back, barked. "I know, boy," Luke murmured to the German shepherd. "I'm going after her." Luke grabbed his radio. "Officer needs backup. I have 207 in progress. Repeat, kidnapping in progress. Sophie Walters, Chief Jameson's assistant, is the victim. In pursuit of a brown Buick sedan, license plate Eddie-Larry-Peter-four-seven-five-eight. Closing in on pursuit position." He gave his location and kept a watch for other cars and innocent bystanders.

Unfortunately, Sophie's kidnapper didn't have any such concern. The man swerved to the right and around a parked car, then up on the sidewalk. People scattered like ants. A trash can bounced off the windshield and Luke yanked the wheel to the left to avoid it. Two police cruisers fell in behind him.

Bruno barked again. Luke knew how the dog felt. "Going as fast as I can, buddy." He lifted the radio once again. "Just hit Ninety-Fourth, heading straight for Roosevelt Avenue. Need someone to head him off."

Luke wanted to gun the engine, but he didn't dare. The streets weren't packed, but enough innocent people were there to keep him careful.

In and out of traffic, the man drove, even in the wrong lane several times. Luke stayed with him. Backup stayed behind Luke. "He just took a right on Broadway. I'm guessing he's heading for the Brooklyn-Queens Expressway. Repeat, he's heading toward the BQE."

Luke received confirmation that officers were en route to that area. "Come on, come on. Slow down. Run out of gas. Anything."

But the man kept going. Fortunately, Luke's siren caught people's attention so that they moved out of the way. Sure enough, the man merged from Broadway onto the BQE. "Heading in the direction of the Triborough Bridge. Somebody stop this guy, but be careful, he's got a kidnapping victim with him. Sophie Walters. Civilian employee of the NYPD."

"Copy that," came the response.

The driver continued his game of dodge and somehow managed to avoid crashing into anything.

Luke followed, staying far enough behind so as not to miss a sudden turn, but close enough not to lose the guy. With each turn, Luke gave the directions, knowing backup would try to cut the guy off. Unfortunately, with no clear destination, he couldn't give them clear enough direction.

Where was this guy going? How much longer could he drive like this without killing someone? Tension threaded Luke's shoulders with knots. The kidnapper took another left, heading for one of the more crowded areas of Astoria. The potential for someone to get hurt had just jumped astronomically. Luke requested the area be cleared immediately but knew it wouldn't be in time.

The fleeing suspect missed a city bus by a fraction of an inch and Luke barely squeaked past it himself. A young man on a delivery bike slammed into the side of a parked car in his desperate attempt to keep from barreling in front of the speeding sedan. Briefly, Luke hoped the poor cyclist hadn't broken anything.

Luke braked hard when the sedan swerved. Tires squealing, it headed straight for a fruit stand on the corner. Screams echoed. People ran. The vehicle rammed into the stand, sending produce flying and the owner diving out of the way. Luke screeched to a stop and threw the car into Park. He bolted from the driver's seat and hit the remote button that opened Bruno's area. Bruno leaped out to follow as Luke raced toward the wrecked vehicle in time to see the driver grab Sophie by the arm and pull her from the car.

"Stop! NYPD!" Luke dodged the fleeing crowd and fought his way toward Sophie. "Sophie!"

"Luke!" Her terrified scream spurred him faster. Bruno stayed with him. Backup was right behind him, adding their commands to stop.

Sophie struggled against her captor, and he yanked her hard. She stumbled. Luke closed in, reaching for her. And then the man shoved her away from him. Sophie let out another scream as she flew toward Luke, barreling into him, knocking him off balance.

He fell back, tripping over Bruno, who yelped and scrambled to move out of the way. Luke's back hit the sidewalk with a breath-stealing thud. Sophie landed on top of him and the last of his air left his lungs. From the corner of his eye, he caught sight of the man disappearing into the nearest building. Officers pounded after him.

Gasping, Luke rolled. "You okay?" he wheezed to Sophie.

She groaned and pressed a hand to her head.

Luke staggered to his feet, then helped her up as other officers rushed past them, going after the kidnapper. Two more slowed as though to check on them and Luke waved them on. They took off and Sophie leaned heavily against him. Bystanders crowded around, asking if they were okay while he held her, trying to discern where she was hurt.

Her usually neat bun had fallen, and her long brown hair lay in disarray across her shoulders. He brushed the strands from her eyes and she blinked up at him. "Talk to me, Sophie. You're okay, right?"

"Yes. I… Yes," she whispered. "I… I think so."

He caught sight of the blood on the side of her head. "Wait a minute. You're not okay. We need to get you checked out."

"No, it's all right. Just give me a minute to catch my breath and let my head stop spinning."

"You're hurt. You need a hospital."

She touched her head with a wince. "No, what I *need* is to get back to the auditorium. We've got a graduation that needs to go on."

"Sophie—"

"I'm serious. That guy was only after me because I saw him messing with Chief Jameson's folder on the podium. I want to know what he was doing and if he left something behind that would tell us who he is." She grimaced. "Then you can go after him again."

For a moment Luke could only stare at her. She'd been kidnapped, knocked in the head, driven through the city at breakneck speed, and all she could think about was getting back to see what the guy had been up to? "You're amazing."

She blinked. "No. I'm mad."

"All right. Let's head back to the auditorium, then. While we're riding, you can fill me in on the details."

"Thank you."

Luke caught Bruno's leash, and Sophie followed him—limping slightly—back to his Tahoe, where she climbed into the front seat and fastened her seat belt. Luke settled behind the driver's seat and held the radio to his mouth. "Any sign of the guy who kidnapped Sophie?"

"That's a negative." The voice came back at him through the speaker. "He disappeared after officers chased him through the store. We're still canvassing the area."

"Ten-four."

By the time Luke pulled into the parking lot at the auditorium, Sophie had filled him in on everything that had led to her kidnapping. And Luke was inclined to agree with her. This wasn't just some random snatching. The man at the podium had had a goal—and Luke was itching to figure out what it was.

Another car pulled into the lot.

"Everyone is arriving," she said. "We need to make this fast so we can stay on schedule."

"Sophie—"

But she was already out of the car and hurrying—limping—toward the door she'd been forced from about thirty minutes ago.

"The ceremony can start late, you know," he murmured to her back. With a sigh, he let Bruno out and they followed after Sophie. Inside, he found her surrounded by other officers concerned with her safety. She repeated all of her "I'm shaken up but fine" reassurances until they accepted the answer even if they didn't fully believe it.

"Is she really okay?" Officer Zach Jameson asked. A fellow officer with the NYC K-9 Command Unit, Zach was also the youngest brother to Jordan Jameson, the chief. The family resemblance was startling with his brown hair and blue eyes. Luke noted Carter and Noah, the other two Jameson brothers, standing nearby with their K-9s seated at their sides.

"She says she is," Luke said with a frown. "That's all I have to go on."

The Jamesons had made law enforcement their family business and all had arrived to attend the ceremony, then get back to work. Officer Finn Gallagher, another K-9 Command Unit member, stood nearby, green eyes watching. Usually the jovial, outgoing jokester of the group, he now sported tight features and a tense jaw.

Luke nodded to Chief Jameson's wife, sitting in the front row and glancing at her watch. "Is Katie all right? She looks a little pale."

Jordan's wife had her blond hair in a French braid that fell over her right shoulder. Her blue eyes continued to bounce between her watch and the door her husband should have entered at least fifteen minutes ago.

"I noticed that, too, but when I asked, she said she was fine, just feeling a little under the weather and that she and Jordan had an errand to run after the ceremony so she thought she'd just come watch."

"She's always been crazy about the dogs," Luke said. "And Jordan likes having her here." He glanced around. "Speaking of Jordan, where is he?"

Zach shrugged, blue eyes narrowed as he watched his sister-in-law. "Katie's wondering that, too. He's usually here by now, going over his notes or shaking hands—and paws—with the soon-to-be new graduates."

Sophie broke free of her concerned friends and headed for the stage. Luke and Bruno followed her up the steps and to the podium. "Where's Jordan?" Luke asked. "Did he say anything about running late?"

"No. At least not before I was snatched." Her hand shook slightly as she reached for the red folder. "Let's see what my kidnapper found so fascinating about Jordan's notes." She flipped the folder open and an envelope fell to the floor. Frowning, she retrieved it, slipped a finger under the flap and pulled out the paper inside. Her eyes scanned it and she gasped, the color leeching from her cheeks.

"Sophie?" Luke hurried the last few steps to her side, thinking the knock on her head had finally caught up to her. "Are you okay? You need to sit down?"

"No." She stared at the letter, and Luke frowned. No,

she wasn't okay, or no, she didn't need to sit down? He
stepped behind her to read over her shoulder.

> *I can't go on anymore. Please make sure Katie*
> *is taken care of. Jordan Jameson.*

TWO

Sophie fought to catch her breath. "This reads like a—a—" She couldn't say it.

"Suicide note," Luke finished for her, his brows drawn tightly over the bridge of his nose.

"No," she whispered. "He wouldn't." Her eyes met Katie's. Jordan's wife frowned even though she was too far away to know what was going on.

But one thing was certain. Jordan had too much to live for to take his own life. Just last week Katie had walked into headquarters to meet Jordan for lunch and then suddenly made a mad dash past Sophie's desk and into the restroom. Concerned, Sophie had followed only to hear Katie throwing up.

"Are you all right?" she'd asked when the woman had finally emerged from the stall and finished with the sink.

Katie had checked under each stall, then turned to Sophie and grinned. "We're alone, so I can tell you that I'm absolutely perfect."

At first, Sophie could only blink. Then gasp. "You're pregnant!"

"Shh!" Katie had held a finger to her lips. "I haven't told anyone yet."

"What about Jordan?"

"He knows, but no one else. We're kind of in shock, but it's thrilling and we're really just savoring the moment, you know? We plan to tell everyone soon. Probably after the first trimester."

"Good for you." Sophie had hugged her friend. "I won't tell a soul. What did Jordan say when you told him?"

"He was over-the-moon excited."

"Wouldn't what? Sophie? Hello?" Noah Jameson's voice brought Sophie back to the present.

She blinked away the memory and her gaze lifted to meet Luke's, then slid around the others who'd gathered in front of her, their expressions confused and slightly wary. All except Noah's. She never could read him.

Sophie passed him the note. Noah read it, his expression shutting down even more, then passed it to his brothers. "You're right. He *wouldn't*."

"No, he *definitely* wouldn't," Zach said, pulling his phone from his pocket. "I'll call him, and he'll straighten this out." They waited in silence as Zach stood and punched in his brother's number, blue eyes narrowed. He ran a hand through his hair and pressed the device to his ear, his rising tension adding to the thickness already surrounding them all.

Seconds ticked.

"Answer the phone, Jordan," Sophie whispered.

But Zach was already lowering the device. "It went straight to voice mail."

"No," Sophie said. "That's not possible. He never

turns his phone off. Especially not on a day like this. Straight to voice mail? That scares me a little." A *lot*.

"It's scaring Katie, too," Noah said with a glance at his sister-in-law, who watched them from her first-row seat in the auditorium. Too far away to hear the conversation, yet close enough to know something serious was going on and Sophie knew they were going to have to fill her in.

As though Sophie's gaze compelled her, Katie stood and walked toward them. Noah met her in front of the stage. "What is it? You're all acting weird and being super secretive."

"Can you call Jordan?" Noah asked.

"Why?"

"We need to know where he is and I'm sure if he's got his phone on the Do Not Disturb setting for whatever reason, he'll have it programmed so that you'll ring right through."

A door slammed in the back and laughter reached them.

"Let's move out of the auditorium," Sophie said. "People are starting to arrive and we'll have more privacy in the room next door."

She led the way into a room that held three sofas and a couple of chairs. A full kitchen dominated the back wall to allow for catered events. All of this registered in a nanosecond before they surrounded Katie and waited for her to dial Jordan's number.

With a frown, Katie did as requested, listened for a moment, then hung up. "It went straight to voice mail." Her eyes darted from one brother to the next.

Sophie's nerves tightened, and Katie's gaze landed

on hers. Sophie knew what her friend was thinking. Jordan never turned off his phone. Ever. And if for some reason, he decided to do so, he'd let someone know in advance. Especially in case Katie needed to reach him.

"He's not answering her either," Noah murmured. "I don't believe this. This isn't good."

"I have the password to his phone, so I can track it," Katie said. "He always wants me to be able to locate him if I need to. I've never used it before. I've never had to."

"Then I'd say this would be a good time to do it," Luke said. "Do you mind seeing what you can find out?"

"Of course." She punched in the digits, then lifted her gaze to meet his and the others who'd gathered around her.

"What is it?" Luke asked. "Can you tell us where he is?"

"Something's wrong. It says his phone's offline, but it shouldn't be. He's never offline." Her eyes narrowed. "I'm starting to get really scared. What's going on?"

Carter shook his head. "We don't know, but I've had enough standing around. I'm going to look for him."

"Me, too," Zach said.

"I'm coming, too." Noah shoved his phone back on his clip and planted his hands on his hips. "But before we run out of here all hasty and unorganized, let's get a plan of action together."

Of course that would be Noah's first thought.

"Wait a minute," Katie said.

They froze.

"I don't understand." Katie crossed her arms. "Can someone please explain to me why you're going to look for Jordan when he should have walked through the door way before now?" Katie asked, her voice containing a slightly hysterical edge. "And then tell me why he would have his phone turned off because if you can't, then something's really, really *wrong*." Worry drew lines across her forehead and at the corners of her mouth. Tears shimmered in her eyes. "I know I keep saying that, but I need to know where he is and if he's okay. And you guys know something you're not telling me. Now, please, *what is it*?"

Sophie bit her lip. "We found a note that seems to indicate he's in trouble. Everyone is getting ready to go search for him."

"What kind of trouble?"

"We're not sure, but we're going to find out," Zach said. He put an arm around his sister-in-law's shoulders. "Let's go over here a second so we can talk."

Noah and Carter joined the two off to the side, and Katie gave a sharp cry. Sophie figured they'd told her the contents of the note. Ignoring the need to rush over and comfort her friend, she turned to the others. "Just so I'm clear, I don't believe Jordan wrote that note for one second, but we can't take the chance that it's not real. We have to act as though he did and that he means it."

Luke nodded. "I agree. But where do we start looking?"

Zach and Katie had returned in time to hear her comment. Katie shook her head, tears streaming down her cheeks. "He wouldn't kill himself. He didn't leave that note!"

"We know," Sophie said. She faced Katie and took her friend's hands. "We don't believe it either. Something else is going on and we're going to find out, okay?"

"Yes. Yes, we are." Katie lifted her chin and swiped her hands over her face.

"The guy who snatched me was messing with the folder when I walked in," Sophie said. "Maybe he put the note in there."

"If that's the case, then we need to find Jordan immediately," Luke said.

Katie nodded. "Exactly. So, what's the plan?"

"Was Jordan headed straight here when he left this morning?"

"No," she sniffed. "He was going to take Snapper out to the Vanderbilt Parkway and run part of the bike path, then go to headquarters to shower and change before coming over here."

"Vanderbilt Parkway," Luke said. Also known as the Long Island Motor Parkway. A big part of New York's history, it was a great place to run or ride bikes now that automobiles were banned from it—and he knew it was part of Jordan's daily routine. "Then that's where we'll look first."

"We need to check any of his favorite places, as well," Sophie said.

"He had a lot of favorite places," Katie said. "Not all of them are in Queens."

Luke nodded. "Then we're going to need more manpower. Someone call Gavin and fill him in on what's going on."

"Today's his day off," Sophie said, picturing the tall, dark-haired, brown-eyed handler. Gavin Sutherland was another K-9 officer. His Springer spaniel was well-trained to sniff out explosives. And while they may not need Tommy for that reason, she knew as well as Luke did that Gavin would never forgive them if they didn't include him in the search for their boss. "We'll also need to get a BOLO out on Jordan and get his face in front of people as well as notify officers in all the boroughs to be watching for him."

"No," Katie said.

Carter raised a brow. "No?"

"You know Jordan. He'd hate that. There's got to be some other way."

"But we need to find him fast," Noah said. "In order to do that, we need as many eyes looking for him as possible."

"But—"

"They're right, Katie," Sophie said softly. "I'm sorry, but they are. I'd rather live with his anger than something really be wrong and we not pull out all the stops."

"And besides," Luke said, "that guy was messing with the folder. It's very possible he's the one who put that note there. If so, this could be some kind of setup to make it look like Jordan's going to commit suicide. If that's the case, then speed is of the essence before…"

Before he was killed.

No one wanted to say it, but everyone sure thought it.

Katie swiped another tear and a heavy sigh escaped

her. She finally shook her head and planted her hands on her hips. "Okay. Fine. You're right. We need as many people looking for him as we can get."

The brothers nodded.

"All right," Luke said. "I'm going to see if Dani can trace his vehicle."

"Good idea," Sophie said. Danielle Abbott, one of the department's technical analysts would use the GPS attached to the SUV to get a ping on its location.

"Zach," Luke said, "you get the BOLO out." K-9 Officers Brianne Hayes and Tony Knight stepped forward with Finn. Luke turned to Katie. "Can you make up a list of all of Jordan's favorite places and give it to these guys?"

"Of course."

"Once Katie gives you the list," he said to the others, "divide up. Bruno and I have the Vanderbilt Parkway."

"And me," Sophie said. "We can't have the ceremony without Jordan, so we'll just postpone it until he can be here."

"Postpone the ceremony," Luke said, "but you don't need to go. You've just been through a major trauma."

Sophie straightened her shoulders and lifted her chin. "Jordan's my boss, too. I'm as much a part of this department as the rest of you—"

Luke held up a hand. "I'm not saying you're not."

"Good. And I might even be able to identify the guy in spite of his ballcap and sunglasses. Maybe. So let's not waste any more time debating whether I'm going or not." She headed for the exit, limping slightly.

Luke frowned. "Fine. I'd rather have you with us anyway."

"Thank you," she tossed over her shoulder.

"At least then I'll know you're safe," he muttered.

She grimaced but refused to comment. Instead, she prayed as they raced toward Vanderbilt Parkway. It seemed to take forever to reach it in spite of the sirens that moved traffic out of the way.

Dani had quickly gotten back to them, saying the GPS had been disabled on Jordan's SUV and she wasn't able to get a location on the vehicle.

"What could possibly be going on with him?" Sophie asked. "Jordan wouldn't disable the GPS and he didn't leave that letter, Luke. I think the man who grabbed me did."

"I'd say that's a real possibility, but we have to cover all the bases."

"I know. I'm just saying that I've never seen Jordan so low he'd want to take his own life. Sure, he has struggles, but who doesn't?" She shook her head as she envisioned confronting her brother about his—in her opinion—questionable decision to join the Marines. "But he's not even close to being suicidal." Especially with a baby on the way that he was excited about. But that wasn't her news to share. "There's something else going on and we need to figure out what it is."

"What we need to do is find Jordan and let him tell us."

"Yes. Exactly."

"Keep in mind, though," Luke said, "everyone has a dark side they never show the world. A lot of people have a hidden pain that can sometimes overwhelm them and no one in their lives ever suspects."

Silence fell between them for a moment.

"I know about hidden pain," Sophie finally said, her tone subdued. "But that doesn't mean it always leads to suicide."

"I agree. But sometimes it does—or at least thoughts of it." His low words had her looking at him more closely.

She had a feeling he was speaking from experience. "Did someone you know commit suicide?"

He blinked. "No, nothing like that. I've just worked with a lot of people over the years and I've worked a few suicides. People who've killed themselves, and their families had no idea they were struggling. I guess what I'm saying is that the face a lot of people show the outside world in no way reflects what's really going on inside them."

"Jordan's not like that."

"You know him that well?"

"Yes."

"Huh."

"What does that mean?" she asked.

"I guess I'm just surprised. We've known each other for two years, worked together on a daily basis, and I don't know you like that."

She gaped. "You've never made the effort. Every time you've come into the office, you're like, 'Hi, how are you?' And that's about the extent of it."

He shut his lips and she wondered if she'd spoken out of turn. Asking him about it would have to wait. Luke pulled into the entrance of the park. "Keep going," she said. "You know where the bike trail is, right?"

"Yes."

"I had to come out here on one of Jordan's afternoons off to get his signature on some papers he'd been waiting on. He was running the trail with Snapper and said he'd come in to the office. It was a gorgeous day so I didn't mind getting outside. If it had been raining, I'm not sure I would have offered." She shot him a quick smile.

"Yes, you would have." At her raised brow, he shrugged. "I'm beginning to get to know you a bit, I think."

"It doesn't take long. I'm pretty much an open book."

"Hmm. Somehow, I wonder." He cleared his throat. "Did Jordan have a favorite area out here?"

"Just the Parkway. Sometimes he ran, sometimes he biked, but he always had Snapper with him. And while it's not near here, he also liked to run along the East River."

"Someone else will check there." Luke followed her directions to the entrance. While he drove, she took in the vast landscape unfolding before them. Right in the middle of Queens, the wooded area stretched endlessly. "I don't know, Luke, this place is huge. There's just too much ground to cover."

"That's why so many cops are looking for him."

Already there were a multitude of law enforcement vehicles in the area. No one questioned one more pulling in. Luke got on the radio and reported his position and requested an update. "No one's spotted Jordan yet," he said.

"It's still early." She climbed out of the SUV and waited for Luke to release Bruno and join her. "This doesn't feel right."

"What do you mean?"

"While I know and understand that we're following protocol in the way we're conducting the search, I just feel like we're on the wrong track and wasting precious time. We need to check that letter for fingerprints. Ones that don't match ours."

"It's in an evidence bag. I'll get someone to send it over to the lab immediately. Regardless of where Jordan is, that guy kidnapped you and we need to find out who he is."

"No kidding." She bit her lip and glanced around.

"Jordan likes this path a lot," she said. "Katie says when he needs to be alone, he spends as much time as possible walking, running or biking this trail and praying. She says it calms him and gives him focus."

Officers talked with those enjoying the warm spring day. One held up his phone and showed a young couple the screen. Jordan's picture, no doubt. They both shook their heads and the officer's shoulders slumped slightly, but he nodded and made his way to the next person.

"What is it?" Luke asked her.

"What do you mean?"

"Something's been bothering you—other than the obvious—since we found the letter," Luke said. "So, what is it?"

Sophie pressed her lips together, then looked at him. "The handwriting on the letter was Jordan's."

He stilled. "Are you sure?"

"Of course I'm sure. I see it every day. He's forever writing notes and placing them on my desk."

Luke stared at her. "Why didn't you say something earlier?"

"Because I thought we'd have answers by now. I

thought we would have found Jordan and he would have explained everything. The fact that we haven't found him yet scares me to death, because while I don't believe he's suicidal, I definitely believe he's in some kind of serious trouble and time may be running out for him."

The problem was, Luke mostly agreed with her, although he couldn't deny the little niggling of doubt that wanted to raise its head and demand attention.

He shoved it aside for the moment, slightly ashamed at the flare of uncertainty—and, if he was honest—jealousy of her unwavering loyalty to her boss. It hadn't taken him long to discover there was a depth to Sophie he wouldn't have guessed she possessed.

However, just in the last few hours, she'd proven herself a loyal employee—the kind who worked hard because of her innate integrity, not just because she was earning a paycheck. And she was Jordan's friend as well as his assistant. She would defend those she cared about to the bitter end—including her fierce belief that Jordan wouldn't kill himself. She'd made that abundantly clear.

And yet, Luke hesitated. While he admired that about Sophie, sometimes loyalty and devotion could blind a person to reality. Sometimes. He wasn't saying that was the case with Sophie and their boss, but he wasn't ruling it out either. And a small part of him couldn't help wondering what it would be like to have someone like Sophie in his corner. For someone to have that kind of unshakable devotion to him.

Bruno jerked at the end of the leash, anxious to do

his job. Only Luke didn't have a job for him to do. Bruno was a cadaver K-9, whose specialty was finding dead bodies, and Jordan wasn't dead. Luke's jaw tightened, but he followed after the animal, determined to do his part in locating his boss. He had to keep believing it wasn't too late. That *he* wasn't too late. *Please, God, please let us find him—alive—and let there be a reasonable explanation for his disappearance.*

For the next two hours, he and the other officers searched the area without success. Jordan wasn't there. Or at any of his favorite places according to reports coming in.

"Where could he be?" Sophie finally asked on the verge of tears.

Luke's heart slammed against his chest in empathy with her worry. "I don't know. Maybe you're right, though. Maybe we need to sit down with Katie and talk through everything."

"Like what?"

"Like Jordan's morning. His schedule. What he said to her before he left? Everything. There's no detail too small, but I'm pretty confident about one thing."

"What's that?" Sophie asked.

"Jordan never made it to the Parkway this morning."

"Why?"

"Because Bruno didn't even get a hint of his scent. That means he wasn't there."

"Then let's go." Sophie hurried to the SUV and Luke climbed behind the wheel after making sure Bruno was settled. He paused.

Sophie frowned. "What are you waiting for?"

"Do you have Katie's number?"

"Of course."

"Can you call her? I think we can do this over the phone and it will be faster than going back to the auditorium."

"Sure. I can put her on speaker."

Sophie dialed the number. It only made it through half a ring before Katie answered. "Sophie? Did you find him?"

"No, I'm sorry."

Katie's muffled sob echoed through the phone's speaker, and Luke winced. Katie was one of the sweetest people on the planet and he hated that she was suffering—that they were *all* suffering. "I'm here, too, Katie," Luke said. "Listen, we're not giving up, so just keep hanging in there, okay? But we think you can help."

"Yes. Of course." She sniffed. "Anything. What can I do?"

"Tell me about this morning when you last saw Jordan. What was his mind-set like?"

"Um…nothing unusual. He seemed fine. And by fine, he was joking around about some things, talking about where we'd take our next vacation. He was proud of the graduating K-9s and handlers and said what a great addition they would be to the force. He was looking forward to the future," she said softly. "That note wasn't from him."

"I don't think it was either," Sophie said, "but did you look at it?"

"No, I didn't want to. Why?"

"It was his handwriting."

Katie paused. "Then someone forced him to do it,"

she said, her voice low, but firm. "The only way he would write that note is if someone held a gun to his head." She paused. "Or threatened me."

"I'd agree with that last part," Sophie said.

"What time did Jordan leave this morning?" Luke asked.

"Before I did—around 8:30. He took Snapper with him for their run, then was supposed to go straight to headquarters, where he was going to use the shower, dress, then head to the auditorium to go over his remarks before the ceremony."

Luke paused, lips pursed. "Did you see him actually get in the vehicle and drive away?"

She paused. "Um…no. I didn't."

"I've got an idea," he said.

"What's that?"

"I don't think Jordan ever made it to the park to take Vanderbilt Parkway. I'm going to get Finn to bring Abernathy to your house and see if the dog can pick up Jordan's scent and at least tell us which way he went when he left the house—and whether or not he was on foot or in his vehicle."

"But the SUV is gone."

"I know." That didn't necessarily mean Jordan was driving it. He kept that to himself. "I'll meet you there."

Luke hung up and dialed Finn's number.

"You find him?" the K-9 officer answered.

"No. Sophie thinks we're going about this all wrong and I have to say I kind of agree with her."

"What do you have in mind?"

"Meet me at Jordan's house with Abernathy. Katie's

going to give us one of the chief's shirts and you're going to see how far Abernathy can take you."

"Not a bad idea. I'll meet you there in twenty."

"On the way."

When Luke neared the Jameson home in Rego Park, all he could do was pray Abernathy and Finn would find something that would give the next step in their search for Jordan. The three-story multifamily building was home to the entire Jameson clan.

"We'll need to talk to Alexander and Ivy," Luke said.

Alexander and Ivy Jameson, parents to Noah, Carter, Zach and Jordan, lived on the first floor. Jordan and Katie shared the second floor, and the other brothers, along with Carter's six-year-old daughter, Ellie, had the large third-floor apartment in true *Full House* fashion. Luke knew Carter's wife, Ellie's mother, had died in childbirth, leaving Carter devastated and in need of help with the newborn. The family hadn't hesitated, jumping right in to do whatever Carter needed.

Luke had often envied the tight-knit family that was so very different from his own. With one brother and a father who blamed him for his mother's death, Luke kept his distance from them.

"Mr. and Mrs. Jameson are out of town this week visiting relatives in Florida," Sophie said. "I sure hope we can find Jordan and not have to tell them anything about all of this."

"Okay. Then that's the plan for now."

He parked on the street just as Finn and Abernathy

arrived. Katie's car was already in the driveway. The door opened, and she stepped onto the porch. Luke drew in a deep breath. "All right, let's do this."

THREE

Sophie had prayed the entire drive to the Jameson home. Prayed and kept an eye on her phone. Of course it hadn't rung and no one had called in on the radio to report they'd found Jordan. She climbed out of the SUV and stood beside it while Katie approached Finn, holding a bag in her gloved hands.

"Jordy dropped this shirt on the bathroom floor yesterday when he came in from his run," Katie said. "I'm a little embarrassed to say that I left it there simply to see how long it would take him to pick it up. It was a private joke. He leaves his clothes on the floor, I leave my towels." She sniffed and swiped a stray tear, then waved a hand. "Never mind. I'm chattering. I used gloves to put it in the bag so it wouldn't have my scent on it."

Abernathy, the eager-to-work yellow Lab, stood at Finn's side, tail wagging, ears perked, eyes on the bag. The dog's nose quivered as Finn took the bag. "That was good thinking. Are you sure you aren't part cop?"

Katie offered him a small smile. "Being married to Jordy has taught me a lot," she said softly. Tears stood in her eyes. "Please, just find him. I'll never fuss about him leaving his clothes on the floor again."

"That's the plan. Let's start inside."

Sophie and Luke followed Katie, Finn and Abernathy inside. Finn pulled on a glove, then opened the bag and removed the shirt. He held it out to Abernathy, who shoved his nose in it, over it and around it.

Once he was sure the dog had the scent, Finn let him take the lead even though they knew Jordan wasn't inside. There was always the hope Abernathy would lead them to some sort of clue.

Sophie frowned. It was such a long shot. Were they wasting valuable time searching the house when Jordan could be somewhere needing help? But these guys were the best. They did this on a daily basis and would be hyper diligent now that one of their own was missing. She knew this. She could trust them. Sophie kept her lips shut and let the professionals work.

Finally, Abernathy led them to the back door and out into the backyard. K-9 handlers were required to have an outdoor space for their dogs, and this house couldn't be more perfect. Sophie remembered overhearing a conversation about how Alexander and Ivy bought the multifamily house when their sons were little and rented out the other apartments before giving them to their children when they were ready to live on their own. Even while her mind spun with facts she knew, she kept an eye on Abernathy and Finn.

Finn once again let the dog lead, all of his attention tuned to the canine's body language. Abernathy covered the back area, then returned to Finn and sat.

"Nothing back here," Finn said. "Let's try outside

the fence." The gate opened into the small driveway that ran the length of the house.

The dog led them out into the street and ran a short distance before stopping and looking back at Finn. Sophie and Luke caught up.

"He's lost the scent," Finn said, "but I think this means that Jordan and Snapper definitely got in the vehicle and took off."

"Then where's the car, and where's Snapper?" Sophie asked.

Luke shook his head. "Jordan could park that K-9 SUV anywhere and no one would think anything about it other than there was a cop somewhere close by. At least not for a while. We've got a BOLO out on it, but people will have to be paying close attention to the license plate."

"I don't know," Sophie said. "Seems to me that might make it even easier to find."

"Always looking for that silver lining, aren't you?"

"Keeping hopeful, Luke, that's all."

"Good," Finn said. "We need to stay hopeful. Prayers wouldn't hurt either."

"What about security footage?" Luke asked. "Katie probably knows the route Jordan takes every morning. We could check any cameras along that drive."

"Good idea. As soon as we get that route, I'll call it in."

"I know the route," Sophie said. She rattled it off.

Finn popped his phone from the clip on his belt. "I'll call it in and we'll see what Dani can pull," he said.

While Finn put in the request, Sophie paced. "The longer, he's missing, the chances of finding him drop," she muttered. They knew that as well as she did. But she wasn't really talking to them, just stating a fact and reminding herself that they needed to find him fast. "So, we know he got up, and his plan was to go for a run with Snapper and then go to headquarters to shower and change. On his way to the auditorium, he might have planned to stop somewhere and grab something quick like toast or a bagel."

"That sounds right," Katie said. "Only he never made it to the auditorium."

Actually, they weren't sure he even made it out of the neighborhood.

They all fell silent until Luke rubbed a hand down his cheek. "There's nothing more we can do here," Luke said. "Let's get back to headquarters. Sophie, would you be willing to go through Jordan's office and see if anything strikes you as off?"

"Of course." Sophie looked at Zach, Katie, Noah and Carter. "Do we need to call your parents?"

Noah shook his head. "No, not yet. It's only been a few hours. I'm not ready to sound the alarm yet."

"Katie," Sophie said, "do you want me to come back and stay here with you after I've gone through his office?"

"No. I'll come back to headquarters." Katie rubbed her arms as though chilled. "I can't stay here right now."

"Are you sure?" Sophie stepped forward and pulled the woman out of earshot of the others. "This is super stressful, and you need to rest. Take care of yourself."

"I know. And I will. But I can't…stay here and do nothing."

Sophie understood that. "All right. You can rest on the sofa in Jordan's office if you need to."

"If I need to. I just want to be where everyone else is, so I can know the updates as they come in."

Katie insisted on driving her own vehicle. Sophie didn't blame her but was worried for her friend. Her pregnant friend whose husband was missing. Sophie ran places and people through her mind, desperately searching for someone who might have a clue where Jordan would be.

"Sophie?" Luke asked "You okay?"

Sophie blinked. And realized she'd been lost in thought the entire ride back to headquarters. She drew in a deep breath. "Yes, sorry. I was just…thinking."

"Are you in pain?"

"My head hurts and my leg is bruised, but time and some ibuprofen will take care of those issues. I can ignore the discomfort for now."

"If you're sure."

"I'm sure." With Sophie favoring her bruised leg, they hurried toward the headquarters building. Just inside, her phone rang. She grabbed it from her pocket and checked the screen, then shook her head at Luke. It wasn't Jordan. His shoulders dropped. "It's my dad," she said, lifting the device to her ear. "Hi, Dad."

"Hey, sweetheart, something kind of weird just happened and I wanted to give you a heads-up."

"Okay. What's going on?"

Luke raised a brow and she shrugged.

"Someone just called here looking for you."

"Looking for me? Who?"

"He said he was a friend from college, that he'd

tried calling your number, but when you didn't answer, called me. Then he started asking a lot of personal questions, which I declined to answer, of course. He finally cursed and hung up on me. It's got me worried about you."

Dread curled in the pit of her stomach, adding to the ball of worry for Jordan that was already there. "Okay, thanks for letting me know. I'll take care of it."

"Do you know who it could be?"

"I have an idea." Her gaze locked on Luke's. He stood there listening unabashedly. Sophie didn't care. If she'd wanted privacy, she would have walked into the conference room.

"I have to leave to head for work. It's just an overnight run, but it'll be late tomorrow night before I'm back. You sure it's okay for me to leave?"

A truck driver, he was often gone overnight. As a child, Sophie had wished he could be home more. At this moment, she was glad he was getting out of the city. "I'm sure. I'll talk to you later, Dad. Thanks for letting me know."

"I'm not going to kid you, Sophie, this scares me."

"I know. And I promise I'll take care of it." She paused. "And if I have trouble doing that, I know people who can help."

Her father let out a low laugh. "Yeah, I guess you do. Be careful, hon."

"Always. Have a good trip."

She hung up and stood silent for a moment while she processed.

"What was that all about?" Luke asked.

"My dad is a long-haul trucker and was getting

ready to walk out the door for an overnight run when his phone rang." She told him about the call. "I think it's probably the guy who tried to kidnap me this morning digging for information." She shuddered. "What worries me is that he knows my dad's home telephone number. And in order to find that out, he had to know my name—and my dad's."

Luke definitely didn't like the sound of that. He shook his head. "I don't think you should go home. If he knows your name and number—and your father's—he most likely knows your address, too."

"Of course he does. I share a house with my dad and brother. But how would he find that out?" Sophie ran a shaky hand over her bun, then straightened it.

"He knows you work for the K-9 unit here in Queens. He may have even been in the auditorium watching you set up, just waiting for a chance to make his move."

Sophie shuddered. "I did have an eerie sensation of someone watching me. Like someone else was there but didn't want me to know it." She paused and frowned. "As I told you, I even heard something but didn't think much of it."

"It wouldn't be too hard to figure out who was taken from the auditorium. All he had to do was ask someone."

"Oh. Right. I should have thought of that." She fell silent. "Then that means I definitely can't go home. I have a separate apartment from my brother and father, but it's still the same house." A sigh escaped her. "I mean, I have no choice. It's not like I can afford a hotel."

"I have a better idea," Luke said.

"What?"

"Would you be willing to stay at my place?"

"Oh." She chewed her lip.

"Well?"

"I'm thinking."

"There's really nothing to think about."

"What do you mean?"

"I mean, I don't think you're safe and I'd like you to come home with Bruno and me until we can find the guy who kidnapped you." She blinked at him as though having trouble processing his words. "Sophie?" He gave her a slight shake, eyes narrowed with concern. "Are you listening?" Had she gone into some kind of shock? A mental overload?

She finally blinked and met his gaze. "I think I've had enough for today."

"I agree. I'll take you to your place and you can pack a bag. Then we'll go back to my house."

"I think that would really inconvenience you. Don't you have a couple of roommates?"

"Two. Sam and David. The good thing is Sam's out of the country for a couple of days so you can use his room."

The fact that she simply nodded told him how worn-out she was—and was probably hurting even though she hadn't said a word about being in pain. "How does some ibuprofen sound?"

"Like a really good idea."

"You better keep some in your system. You're going to feel it tomorrow even more."

"I know. Thanks."

Luke led the way to his Tahoe and Bruno jumped into his spot in the back. Sophie settled into the passenger seat and buckled up. Bruno leaned forward and settled his snout on her left shoulder, then licked her cheek with a swipe of his long tongue.

Luke gaped. "Bruno!"

"Don't fuss at him," Sophie said, wiping her cheek on her shoulder. "It's sweet. I think he knows I need comforting and is offering it." She scratched the dog's ears, and Bruno rolled his eyes to Luke as though gloating in his successful attempt to gain Sophie's attention.

Luke scowled at the animal, but it didn't seem to faze the dog. With a huff, Luke pulled from the parking lot and headed for Sophie's home in Woodside.

It didn't take long to reach it and he turned onto her street. "Nice house," he said.

"I like it. It's been in the family forever. My brother and father live upstairs, and I have the downstairs. Someday, I hope to afford something of my own but for now, this works for me." She quirked a small smile at him. The first one he'd seen all day. Then she scratched Bruno under his chin. Again. "I'd like a dog," she said, "but dogs need space to run. I have a yard, but it's too small for the size dog I'd want."

"That's why K-9 officers are required to have a yard." He smiled. She knew that, of course, but it was small talk. Something to keep her mind on anything but the events of the day—and his off the fact that he was jealous of his dog.

He cleared his throat. "You ready?"

"Sure."

He and Bruno followed Sophie to the front door of her duplex-style home.

Which was cracked open.

She gasped and stepped back.

"That's not supposed to be open, I'm guessing?" Luke whispered.

"No."

"Stand back against the wall next to the door. Bruno, stay." In the blink of an eye, the dog's demeanor changed at Luke's command. His ears went up and he was in instant work mode, waiting for the next order. Bruno sat next to Sophie and she placed a hand on his head. Luke pulled his weapon and stood to the side of the door. Using his left hand, he gave the metal door a light shove. It swung inward on well-oiled hinges.

Luke stepped over the threshold and glanced to the right. Kitchen with the stove light on. Living area to the left. Hallway straight ahead with the bathroom at the end and the bedroom to the left. Small and efficient.

And trashed. Sofa cushions lay on the floor along with the lamps that had probably been on the end tables. The intruder hadn't spared the small buffet in the eating area either and the drawers had been yanked out, dishes crushed onto the hardwood floor.

A loud crash came from the bedroom area and Luke headed down the hallway. "NYPD! Come out of the room, hands where I can see them! Now!"

Silence.

"I'm not playing!" Luke said. "Come out with your hands where I can see them!"

A black-clad figure shot out of the room and slammed into Luke hard enough to knock the breath from him. And his gun from his grip. The weapon hit the floor and skittered across the wood out of reach. Gasping, Luke threw a blind punch that grazed a whiskered jaw.

Bruno growled and lunged forward, snapping at the attacker, who stumbled back, tripped and fell with a thud to the wood floor. Only to lurch to his feet and come forward swinging as Bruno moved in. He caught the dog on the ear. Bruno yelped and darted away, shaking his head.

Luke dove after the man and wrapped a hand around an ankle, yanking him back to the floor. Bruno added his displeasure and snapped his teeth in the man's face.

A foot kicked out and landed a hard blow to Luke's temple, stunning him. Stars spun in front of his eyes.

Again, the assailant managed to find his feet—and headed for Sophie. She darted away. Bruno barked and launched himself at the man once more, this time closing his teeth around an arm. The pained scream echoed through the apartment.

Luke rolled in time to see Sophie swing a lamp into the man's chest. The lamp fell, hitting Bruno's snout before crashing to the floor. The dog flinched and released the attacker, who rushed out the door.

Then Bruno was beside Luke, nudging him and whining.

Luke shook his head. While everything had happened in mere seconds, Luke raged that he couldn't move fast enough. Finally, he made it to his feet while his head spun and nausea curled in his gut. "Sophie!"

"I'm okay." She rushed to him. "Are you?"

"Fine. I've just got to learn to duck." He grabbed

his weapon and raced to the front door in time to see the man hop into a light gray Jeep he'd had double-parked four doors down and peel away from the building. Luke slapped a hand against his thigh. He couldn't see the license plate.

He snagged his phone and called it in with what little information he had. When he hung up, he drew in a deep breath and pressed a hand to his aching head, then turned to Sophie, who now sat on the sofa with Bruno's big head resting on her knee. She examined the animal's ear and nose with gentle fingers.

"Is he okay?" Luke asked. "Do I need to get him to the vet?"

"I think he was just stunned, but if you would feel better taking him to the vet, we can do that."

Luke looked his partner over and sighed with relief when he found nothing concerning. "Good boy, Bruno." The dog licked his hand, then turned back to Sophie and nudged her hand.

With the danger past, Luke allowed himself to take a moment to simply watch her. She continued to scratch Bruno's ears, and Luke was hit with the longing to take the dog's place. A brief flash of the two of them sitting on the couch, watching a movie and sharing a bowl of popcorn held him frozen for a second.

"Luke?" she asked. "You okay?"

He blinked. "Yeah, fine. Officers are on the way."

"I'm sorry."

"About what?" He stilled and frowned.

"For not finding a weapon or some way to help you."

Luke went to her and pulled her into a hug. "It's okay. I was just worried about you." And because the feel of her in his arms made his head spin way too much, he released her and stepped back.

"I'm going to call my dad," she said. "I need to let him know what happened. And I need to call Trey."

"Of course."

She dialed her brother's number, waited, then hung up. "He's not answering."

"Try your dad."

She did, and Luke couldn't help notice her sigh of relief when he answered on the first ring. "Hey, Dad, I know you're on the road, but I need to let you know someone broke into my place." Pause. "No, I'm fine. I'm with a friend from the station. Do you know where Trey is?" She shook her head at Luke. "Trey went hiking with friends and won't be back until Saturday," she said, then went back to the phone and explained the fact that she was going to stay with Luke and his roommates for a while.

Her father said something, and she nodded with a glance at Luke. "I'm sure, Dad. I'll be safe there and, hopefully, whoever broke in won't be back. You still have several dinners in the freezer for when you get back from your run and most of the clothes are washed. Hopefully, by the time you and Trey get back, all of this will be over."

Luke watched her, considering her words and what they meant.

She hung up and caught his gaze. "What? Why are you looking at me like that?"

"You do a lot for them, don't you?"

She shrugged. "My dad's done a lot for me." She

paused. "Don't you help your family out when they need it?"

"Not really. We don't talk much."

"Oh. That's…sad."

"I know." He cleared his throat. "But forget about that. While I want to hear more about your family, why don't you start taking inventory? Just don't touch anything. When the officers get here, they'll take prints. Ours are on file so they'll be able to eliminate those."

She shook her head as her gaze swept the area. "I don't think he took anything. He just broke everything."

Luke noticed the shattered flat screen television on the floor. Her iPad and Blu-ray player lay in front of the television stand. Also broken.

"He stomped on them," she whispered. "Why?" Tears leaked from her eyes and she swiped them away with an angry brush of her fingers. Before Luke could answer or offer more comfort, she leaned over and picked up a figurine from the floor. "This was on my coffee table. He swept it to the floor, but it didn't break, which is a relief. A friend gave it to me." She paused, studying it. "Although, it's worth several hundred dollars. And yet, he left it."

"Which means he was probably looking for something and this wasn't a random criminal simply after items to sell for easy money."

She frowned. "But what?"

He nodded to the corner of the room. "Your desk is turned upside down. If this was the same guy who called your father looking for you, then maybe he was searching for something that would tell him how to find you. And when he couldn't, he took his frustration out on your stuff."

"Why didn't he just wait until I got home?" A pause. "Then again, maybe he did. Maybe he was in my bedroom just waiting to..." She shuddered. "I'm so glad you were here."

Luke's heart twisted. He went to her again and wrapped his arms around her to pull her into a hug once more. He could put his own feelings on hold and simply offer her comfort. For a moment, she stiffened, then leaned against him.

"I'm sorry, Sophie," he said softly. "I know this has been a rotten day for you."

"It's been even more rotten for Katie," she mumbled.

"Yeah. I can't argue with that." He sighed. And realized he didn't want to let her go. While he could tell she was finding comfort in the embrace, he realized he was, too. Which made him frown. While she was changing his perception of her, he reminded himself she was still young. Very young.

Bruno nosed in between them and Sophie let out a watery laugh.

"I think he's feeling left out." She scratched his neck and the dog sighed his contentment. "All's right with his world, isn't it? He's just happy to be with those he loves and having his ears scratched."

"Yes, he's pretty easy to please. Ear scratches, belly rubs and a hug every once in a while."

"I think everyone could learn a few lessons from this guy," she said softly.

"Amen to that."

"Did you know we're getting a new dog?"

"Who? You and your family?"

She laughed. "No, the department. Her name's Stella and she's a gift from the Czech Republic. She's supposed to be really special." Bruno licked her cheek and she huffed another choked laugh. "But not as special as you, Bruno, I promise."

Luke's phone buzzed, and he snatched it to check the screen.

"Who is it?" Sophie asked.

"A group text from Katie. Just wanting an update."

"Oh."

While all was right with Bruno's world, Luke's was standing on its head. And Katie was growing more and more desperate as time passed without hearing from her husband. Frankly, he couldn't blame her. Luke closed his eyes and hugged Sophie once again, this time allowing himself to take comfort from her. He said a silent prayer that Katie would get to hold Jordan in the near future.

Please let us find him.

FOUR

Sophie decided she could stay right there in Luke's arms for the rest of eternity. However, that wouldn't be very productive when it came to finding Jordan. And not only that, she had no business letting her attraction for the man influence her into letting a romance develop. But she had her brother and her father to look after. Romance wasn't in the near future for her.

Before the thought could depress her, a knock on the door had her slipping from his embrace. "I guess I should pack a bag after they process this place, huh?"

"I think that would be a good idea."

Luke let the two officers inside and made the introductions. Sophie forced a smile. "Thank you for coming so quickly."

"Of course," the one nearest her said. "We're just going to do our thing."

"Perfect," Sophie said.

It didn't take long for them to finish. Once they were gone, she forced herself to face the destruction in her bedroom. Slashed pillows spilled their filling and her blinds had been ripped from the windows. Drawers had been overturned and the contents littered the floor next to the dresser. What bothered her the most was the fact that her bedside lamp had been thrown against her mirror, shattering both items. What reason could he have had for such wanton destruction in here?

It was almost like the person was mad at her and wanted her to know it. He'd made the whole break-in personal. Which probably meant that he hadn't gotten what he'd come for.

Her.

With a shudder, she ignored the mess and pulled three outfits for work from her closet, some jeans and T-shirts and anything else she thought she might need. Next, she added toiletries from the bathroom. Thankfully, it didn't look like he'd touched that room.

Rolling her small suitcase behind her, she walked back into the living area where Luke and Bruno waited. "I think I've got everything I'll need for a few days. With access to a laundromat, I can even stretch that."

"Good," Luke said. He led the way back to his vehicle, Bruno trotting along beside him. Once Sophie was buckled and Bruno was settled in his area, she drew in a deep breath and closed her eyes for a brief moment.

"How are you holding up?" Luke asked.

"My head is pounding, and every muscle feels like it's been through a rigorous workout, but I'm alive and I'm grateful. What about you? How's your head?"

"Pounding a bit like yours, I imagine, but I'll be okay."

When his right hand curled around her left, Sophie took comfort once again from his touch. "Thank you for staying with me," she said softly. "I can't tell you how much I appreciate it. I don't know what I'd do if I had to face all of this alone."

"Of course." With a gentle squeeze of her fingers, he released her hand and turned the key. The Tahoe purred to life and Luke headed toward his apartment.

"Are you sure this is going to be okay?" she asked. "I really don't want to put you out or cause any inconvenience."

"I'm positive it's all right. Like I said, Sam is out of the country on business and David is working the late shift. He'll be home around midnight."

"Tell me what they do again?"

"Sam's a consultant for a software company. David is a fireman. He works out of the station near our home."

"You like them. I can hear it in your voice."

"I do. They're great guys—and even fun to hang out with occasionally in spite of the fact that they're not cops." He quirked a smile and slid a glance at her. She bit her lip, still concerned she might be in the way. "Don't worry," he said. "We don't live in a pigsty or anything. The place is almost ridiculously neat."

"That hadn't even crossed my mind, but why do I sense a story behind that?"

"Sam's mother has adopted David and me. She comes by twice a week to clean and drop off food."

"Wow."

"Yeah, no kidding. But we don't mind. Sam's father passed away about six months ago, so we let his mom do what she wants. It keeps her busy and helps us out at the same time."

"I'd say that's a wonderful arrangement for everyone involved."

A short time later, he parked in a free spot and they walked down the block to a three-family house. The houses were packed together along the narrow street. He had told her that he and his roommates rented the apartment on the first floor.

Sophie hadn't been to his home before and she couldn't help admiring the small, well-kept front area around the steps leading up to the door. She spotted roses and daffodils and a few other colorful bulbs she couldn't identify. "The flowers are beautiful. Really gorgeous. Who's the green thumb?"

"Thanks. All three of us enjoy the work when we have a day off. It's kind of a stress reliever."

Stress reliever. She could use one of those. Tears flooded her eyes, the surge of emotion taking her by surprise.

"Sophie?"

"I can't believe this is happening," she whispered. "Where can Jordy be, Luke?"

With a heavy sigh, he shook his head. "I don't know, but we'll find him." A pause. "You call him Jordy?"

She shrugged and shoved the tears away. "He said it was okay one afternoon when I was eating with him and Katie. She called him Jordy and told me I'd graduated to that of trusted friend and had the honor of using his family name." Her gaze met his. "It's been too long. Too many hours are passing with no word. You know as well as I the longer we go without hearing from him, the more likely it is we—" She bit her lip.

"Won't," he finished for her. "I know. I'm worried,

too, but we won't give up. Hopefully, Jordan will call before too long and we can all get back to business as usual."

"Yeah." She slipped out of the seat and followed him up the steps and inside to the shared foyer.

The wood floors gleamed. He led her to the far end of the short hallway and opened the door to his apartment. Once inside, she looked around. It sparkled. "Wow, you weren't kidding. It's super clean."

"Yep. And since Sam's mom was here this morning, his room should be nice and shiny, too. Clean sheets, clean towels, the works. He has a bathroom attached so you'll have all the privacy you need."

He pulled her suitcase behind him and she soon found herself in a bright, if masculine, bedroom. "It's lovely," she said, forcing a smile to her lips. She loved the room. She hated the reason she was using it.

"I'll just leave you to get settled while I go inspect the refrigerator," he said. "Are you hungry?"

"Starving."

"Give me a few minutes and we'll eat."

Fifteen minutes later, dressed in yoga pants and a long sweatshirt, she padded into the kitchen, where she found Luke dishing up something that smelled delicious. "Chicken cordon bleu?"

"I think so. Sometimes I'm not sure what she brings, but it's always good."

"Do you eat like this every night?"

He flushed. "Well, not *every* night."

"You guys are spoiled completely rotten. I feel sorry for your future wives. If you even *want* to get married."

"Hey, now, what's that supposed to mean?"

She giggled at his affront. "Well, really, take a look around. You have a spotless apartment, gourmet food at the push of a button and no one to nag you about taking the trash out. Why would you need to get married?"

His eyes locked on hers. "Maybe I wouldn't mind too much about being nagged to take out the trash."

Her breath caught somewhere between her lungs and her throat. "Oh. Well. Okay, then."

A slight smile tilted the corners of his lips, then he frowned. A sad one. "But I don't know that it'll ever happen for me."

"Why not?" Frankly, she would have thought he'd have plenty of opportunities to find himself engaged and married. A twinge of jealousy flashed, and she shoved it away.

He shook his head. "I'm not really marriage material. At least that's what I've been told."

She blinked. "Who told you that?"

"An ex-girlfriend." His lips tightened, then relaxed as though he'd forced it. "What about you? You have any plans for marriage in the future?"

"In the future, maybe. Not necessarily the *near* future, but yes, I think I'd like to get married. One day. To the right person, of course."

"Of course. So, you haven't met Mr. Right yet?"

Sophie laughed. "I don't know. There's no one on my radar right now." Except…she had a feeling if she looked close at that radar, she might see Luke right there—a little blip on her screen. As a potential boyfriend. Should she be looking. Which she wasn't. Her father and brother needed her. Well, her father did anyway. Being married or even dating would severely cut into the time that she would have to be there for her dad. The thought hadn't bothered her much before. But now, looking at Luke, she had to admit, she almost wished things could be different. But she couldn't help wondering… "What was it that made you 'not marriage material'?"

His jaw tightened. "Ah, well, according to the ex, I'm too serious, need to loosen up and learn how to have a good time." He grimaced. "And I work too much. She let me know in no uncertain terms that I would never be Mr. Right for her."

"She sounds terribly immature. I'm glad you got out of that relationship."

"I am, too." He studied her with a look that sent heat surging into her cheeks. She cleared her throat and shrugged. Then winced when the action tugged at sore muscles. She used her opposite hand to massage the area. "I sure met Mr. Wrong today." A shudder shook her.

"I'll say. But you have time. You're young."

"And what are you?" She lifted a brow, shaking off the remembered terror. "A stodgy old bachelor?"

A light snort escaped him, and he offered another grin, but she thought she saw something different in his gaze. Something…interesting and worth exploring.

"That's me. Old and set in my ways."

But he might be willing to change some of those ways. For Sophie anyway. Right now, Luke found himself wishing he wasn't quite so old. Not that thirty-three was ancient, but the nine-year age difference made him grimace. And what was up with him blurting out that he wasn't marriage material anyway? He might think that, but he didn't need to pass that on to her. She'd thrown up a few walls as soon as the words had passed his lips. One thing she was right about, though, was the more time that passed without finding Jordan, the more his nerves tightened.

"How about a change of subject while we eat?" he asked.

"Sure." She took a bite of the chicken and closed her eyes. "This is wonderful."

He waited for her to look at him before nodding. "I can't stop thinking about Jordan."

"I know. Same here," she said softly. "And Katie. My heart hurts for her."

"Which is why we've got to keep thinking. Can you recall anything that would suggest Jordan has any enemies?"

Sophie set her fork on the table and rubbed her eyes. "No, not right offhand. I mean, he was mostly behind a desk these days, but before he was chief, he worked the streets just like you guys. I'm sure there are some criminals he arrested who still hold a grudge, but there've been no threats, no weird phone calls, *nothing.*"

"Unless he just didn't tell you about them."

"True, but I would think I would have noticed *something* if that was going on."

"What about any problems at headquarters? With other officers or anyone else who works there?"

"There are the usual complaints, but nothing we haven't dealt with before and nothing stands out at all. This is so frustrating!"

"I know." Her facial expressions fascinated him. He

found himself thinking he could watch her indefinitely. "I admire you, Sophie."

She blinked and some of the ire faded from her eyes. "What makes you say that?"

"I've known you for a couple of years now, right?"

"Yes. I started working at the K-9 unit right out of college, and we met my second day on the job."

She remembered that? "But we've never really gotten to know each other on a personal basis."

"No, just pretty much in passing. Why?"

"Because you're just not what I expected or would have imagined."

She raised a brow. "What does that mean?"

"Don't take this the wrong way, but you're so young and yet so mature." And so attractive. Her youth had kept him from looking at her twice in the past and now he found himself regretting his quick judgment.

"Chalk it up to life experiences," she said. "I had to grow up pretty fast after my mother walked out."

Whoa. He hadn't been expecting that. "How old were you when she left?"

"I'd just turned ten. One day she was there, the next she wasn't." She shrugged, but he sensed the hurt beneath the gesture.

"I'm so sorry."

"I am, too. For a long time I wondered if it was my fault."

"What? Why?"

"I...wasn't the best or brightest student and my parents fought a lot about me. Later, I was diagnosed with a learning disability and things changed dramatically for me after that, but Mom was already gone." She shook her head. "Anyway, as you can imagine, my dad was thrown for a while. He struggled with depression, but later told me that my brother and I were his world and his reason to keep going. I didn't realize how rough it was on him at the time, but now I look back and can see how hard he worked to be there for us."

"Well, if you're any indication of the type of dad he was, then he must have been pretty amazing."

Her flush made him smile.

"He was super amazing, so thank you," she said softly. "Still is. He's always looking out for me and my brother."

"And you look out for them, don't you?"

"I do. After Mom left, I knew I had to be the one to pick up the pieces." She shrugged. "It was hard, but we managed."

"Do you know where your mom is now?"

"I think she was in Texas the last time I heard. I don't talk to her very often."

"You don't hold a grudge?"

Sophie sighed. "I was angry for a long time. A very long time. But I came to realize that she just wasn't cut out to be a mother and Trey and I were probably better off without her. My grandmother—Dad's mom—stepped in and helped quite a bit when she could, so she was a good influence."

"But not the mom you needed."

"No."

"You became that for Trey, didn't you?"

"How could you tell?"

"Just a hunch."

"I'm five years older than Trey. He was still a baby

when she left, and even though I was only ten, I suppose it was only natural that I would mother him. But," she sighed, "he's nineteen now and trying to stretch his wings and figure life out."

"Kids do that."

"I know, but..."

"What?" he asked.

"It's hard to let go."

"Lots of things are hard to let go of, but sometimes it's better for everyone if we can manage to do that."

She went still, her eyes studying him with an intensity that had him working hard not to squirm.

"What is it?" he finally blurted.

"Tell me about her," Sophie said.

"Who?"

"The woman who hurt you so terribly. I know she said you weren't marriage material but tell me more. That's who you were thinking of just now when you talked about letting go, wasn't it?"

Luke flinched. He couldn't help it. "Yes. She was young like you—which is what made me so surprised at your maturity—and she had a crush on me. At least I thought so." He shrugged. "I was new to the K-9 unit and she liked the idea of dating a cop. And I wasn't opposed to dating a pretty woman who had the ability to make me laugh."

"Pretty, huh?"

"She was. But I'm not completely shallow. I genuinely liked her." He shrugged. "Or thought I did."

"But?"

"But she wasn't serious about the relationship. At first that was okay, but then she decided she didn't like all the hours I was putting in. She wanted to go out, have fun, not catch meals during breaks and at odd hours."

"So, you weren't marriage material because you were dedicated to your job and chose to honor the commitment you made instead of blowing it off to make her happy?"

He hesitated then gave a low laugh. "Yes. Exactly."

"I'm sorry, but it sounds to me like she was the one who wasn't marriage material. I didn't exactly have the best role models, but even I know marriage is more than just fun and games. It's teamwork, hard work and it takes commitment. Honestly, she sounds a lot like my mother. You were wise to let her go."

"I know." His jaw tightened at the memories. "But trust me, I won't make that mistake again."

She continued to eye him, curiosity and sympathy coating her gaze. "What was it about her that you fell for?"

He flushed.

"What?" she pressed.

"I had a bit of an ego, and she made me feel like I was someone important. Unfortunately, as time went on, her immaturity was something that I just couldn't deal with—especially when it came to my job. If I had to leave in the middle of dinner or had to cancel a date due to a case, then she would pout for days. We had a pretty big blowup when I called her on her immaturity. She didn't like it."

"I'm sure that was difficult."

"Very." He rubbed a hand over his chin.

"I'm sorry."

"For?"

"For her. For you. For a lot of things." She touched his cheek. "She lost out on a lot, but I'm glad you figured it out before it went any further."

"Yeah. Me, too."

"The experience has made you distrustful," she said softly.

"I don't know if *distrustful* is the right word. *Careful* might be a better description."

"Hmm…"

"What's that mean?"

Sophie shrugged and grimaced. She reached up to rub her shoulder and Luke frowned. "Are you okay?"

"Just sore."

"Here. Let me help." His hand replaced hers and he began a gentle massage of the tight muscles. "Your shoulders are like rocks."

"I know. It's the worry for Jordan, I'm sure."

"That's probably part of it, but the wreck didn't help. Nor the break-in. You're going to really feel this tomorrow."

She glanced up at him with a smile. "I'll survive."

He found himself ensnared in her innocent gaze. When his eyes dropped to her lips and the desire to close the distance hit him, he pulled in a deep breath and stood. "I'd better let you get some sleep."

A flush heated her cheeks and she nodded. "That's a good idea."

"If you hear noises and footsteps, it's just David coming in from his shift."

"Okay."

"Unless you hear me yell and tell you differently."

"Hopefully, that won't happen."

"Hopefully," he echoed. She didn't move, and Luke lifted a hand to touch her cheek. "I haven't talked to anyone like that in a long time," he said. "It was nice."

"I thought so, too."

Her pulse fluttered in her throat and he stepped back. "Good night, Sophie."

"Night, Luke."

She disappeared down the hall and he waited until the door shut with a soft snick before letting out the breath he'd been holding. "Whoa," he said softly to the empty room. "What just happened?"

The silence had no answer for him, but one thing was for sure. It couldn't happen again.

She was too young, too sweet, too innocent. He'd fallen for that before and look where that had gotten him.

No, from now on, he'd keep things strictly professional between them. Certainly no kissing—or even *wanting* to kiss her. *That* had come out of nowhere. And now he couldn't stop thinking about it.

But he had to.

Because he was going to keep things strictly professional.

Because if he didn't, his heart wouldn't survive. And he didn't have time for distractions no matter how pretty she was. He had a boss—and friend—to find. He just prayed he would find him alive.

FIVE

Sophie couldn't help but think about the conversation with Luke from last night even while she hurried to get ready for work. Something had clicked between them and while she wouldn't lie to herself and pretend she wasn't interested in him, she couldn't pursue anything either. Not that he would be welcome to her interest.

He'd already said he wouldn't make the mistake of falling for someone so much younger than him. She almost had to smile at the irony. She'd had to grow up so fast, she never really thought about her age as a number. There'd been some days growing up she'd felt as ancient as dirt.

Her age notwithstanding, she just couldn't get involved with anyone right now. Not when her father and brother needed and counted on her so much. So she could just stop thinking about it—and Luke. Her top priority was finding her boss—and Snapper. Because if she found one, the other had to be close by.

A knock on the door jolted her. "Yes?"

"I heard you moving around," Luke said from the other side. "I thought I'd tell you to dress comfortable.

We're taking over the next shift in looking for Jordan. I'll explain more in the car."

"I'll be out in just a few minutes."

"I'll have coffee and a bagel ready. That okay?"

"Perfect."

She found her phone and voice texted Katie. How are you holding up?

Not well. He's never gone this long without contacting me. He's certainly never gone all night. I'm so scared, Sophie. The fact that the reply came so quick said Katie was sitting by her phone.

I know. I am, too. Hang in there, Katie, we'll find him. We have to.

I'm trying hard to believe that and not listen to the little voice that knows all the statistics for missing people. I'm praying. It's all I can do.

I'm adding my prayers to yours. Text or call if you need anything. Even if it's to have a momentary breakdown. I'll listen. And probably join you.

Thank you, Sophie. Just knowing you're out there looking for him helps so much. I can't tell you how much I appreciate that everyone is going all out in trying to find him.

Absolutely. We love him, too.

Sophie tucked her phone away and drew in a steadying breath. She went into the kitchen to find Luke and the young man she assumed to be David, one of his roommates. "Good morning."

"Morning," Luke said. He made the introductions.

Bruno lay stretched on a rug in the corner. He lifted his head and popped to his feet to amble over and give her hand a nudge, silently asking for some attention. She scratched his ears while she inhaled the smell of fresh-brewed coffee. Her mouth watered.

David drained his mug and stood. "Sorry to meet you and run, but I promised to cover part of a shift this morning. Pleasure to have you staying here, though."

"Thank you. You're very kind."

"I'll be home to crash later, though. I hope you find Jordan," he said softly. "I'll be keeping my eyes and ears open, too."

He left, and Luke handed her a to-go cup of coffee and a bagel. "We don't want to be late. So how'd you sleep?" he asked and motioned for Bruno to come. The dog loped over to the door and sat, tail thumping his eagerness to get the day started.

"Pretty well, all things considering," Sophie said.

"Yeah."

"Have you heard anything more about Jordan?"

"That was one of the things I was going to fill you in on. Zach called his parents last night when Jordan didn't turn up. They're on their way home. I think they land sometime within the hour."

"Good, I'm glad they told them. And sad, too, because it means they felt they had to."

"And that's not all."

"Okay." Her gut tightened.

"They found his vehicle," Luke said. He opened the

door and a soft breeze blew across her face, letting her know it was going to be a warm day.

"Where?" Katie hadn't said anything in their short text exchange so she must not know. "And when?"

"At the biking trail about five minutes before you walked in the kitchen."

"Wait a minute. They found his car near the biking trail we searched yesterday? At the Vanderbilt Parkway?"

He glanced at his watch and frowned, silently urging her toward the vehicle. "That's right. Officers found it on a routine check of the area. A check they were doing more often in hopes that Jordan would show up. Instead, they found his vehicle."

Sophie planted herself in front of him and he stopped. "That wasn't there yesterday," she said. "We—and other officers—searched every square inch of that bike trail."

"I know. It had to have been left there during the night. Danielle's working on pulling surveillance footage." He continued toward the SUV and Sophie hurried after him and Bruno.

Luke started the SUV and backed out of the short drive. "I don't get it. Why leave the vehicle there?"

"Lots of reasons."

"Like what?"

"I don't know, but there has to be something."

They fell silent, and he drove for the next few minutes while they contemplated why Jordan would leave his vehicle there—but not call in to let anyone know where he was or what he was doing.

Finally, Luke sighed. "I don't know. I can't figure it

out." A pause. "You mind answering a couple of questions for me?"

"Of course not."

"What was school like for you?"

She bit her lip and looked away. "That's your question?"

"Is it weird?"

"A bit."

"Humor me. I have a reason for asking."

Sophie hesitated, and he thought she might refuse to answer before she gave a slight shrug. "School was a nightmare before the diagnosis. Mom and Dad had some knock-down, drag-out fights about my grades and Mom used to yell at me that I wasn't trying and that I was stupid. Dad would yell at her for yelling at me and Trey would just cry."

Luke drew in a harsh breath. "That's awful. I had a feeling it was. Which leads me to my biggest question."

"What?"

"How did you turn out so…?"

"So what?"

"Great. Grounded. Self-confident. I could go on, but you get the idea."

A smile tilted her lips in spite of the memories. "My dad. He was my rock. My brother's, too, although Trey had a harder time of it. I don't think he's ever really dealt with Mom's desertion. He was always a quiet kid, but after Mom left, he really withdrew. It's only lately that he's starting to come into his own." By joining the Marines, though? She still hadn't talked to him about that. And truly, if she thought that's what he really needed to do, she wouldn't fight him on it, but he'd always dreamed of becoming an engineer and she didn't want to see him throw that dream away. Then again, he could always study that while in the service. Maybe she just needed to admit she was having a hard time letting go.

"I'm sorry," Luke said.

What? Oh. "Me, too. But Dad's always been there for us. When I was first diagnosed with the learning disability, I was crushed, but Dad raised me to understand that I'm more than a label. He helped me come to know and believe that I have a purpose in life, that I have choices. And if I make the *right* choices, I can overcome and do pretty much anything I set my mind to."

"I think I'd really like your dad."

"You would. I'll have to introduce you sometime." She snapped her mouth shut. Now, what had made her say that? "I mean, if you—" She needed to zip her lips. He had no interest in meeting her father. Worry for Jordan was making her grasp at anything that might serve as a distraction. Was that where the attraction for Luke was stemming from? As a way to distract herself?

Maybe.

But she didn't think so.

"I'd love to meet your dad sometime, Sophie."

His soft response had her swallowing.

So…what did that mean?

Nothing. It meant nothing. He was being polite and kind and doing his best to keep things from being awkward. She appreciated that but reminded herself that she needed to keep her focus and not let Luke distract her.

At least not yet. She still had a brother to put through college and a father to take care of. And she needed to keep her attention on finding Jordan until he was safely home with Katie and all was right with the world again.

Please, God, let us find Jordan.

Luke had to admit he wasn't sure what to think about Sophie anymore. She was smart and beautiful and had thrown his whole mental and emotional well-being into confusion. Generally, he stayed away from the idea of dating anyone who even seemed like they wanted to play head games with him—no matter what age, but especially younger women.

But he had a gut feeling that he wouldn't have to worry about any of that kind of thing with Sophie. He was almost convinced that she didn't know anything about playing head games, and if she did, she was above doing it.

He'd spent two years seeing Sophie on a daily basis. How had he been so blind to her true personality? How had he missed that she apparently had more layers than an onion? Because he'd made a snap judgment effectively limiting his ability to see past the exterior. The more he learned about Sophie, the more he wanted to know.

But right now, he needed to keep his focus. What he wanted most was to find Jordan alive and well with some kind of rational explanation for his disappearing act.

Luke wheeled in to the parking area of the walking trail, dodging one of the park's many landscaping trucks that was being ordered from the area. The man shut the tailgate and climbed into the cab of the truck. With a salute, he vacated the parking lot.

Finn and his dog, Abernathy, along with the Jameson brothers, Noah, Carter and Zach, had gathered in a huddle. Probably discussing the best course of action to take from this point. First thing would be to make sure the vehicle was secured, then decide if the crime scene unit needed to be called. If Jordan had driven the vehicle here himself, then all would end well.

If not, then...

They would fan out and let Finn and Abernathy take the lead searching the area for Jordan. The others had left their dogs in their respective vehicles so as not to be a distraction to Abernathy.

Luke debated about bringing Bruno. For now, he left him in the SUV. He and Sophie approached Noah, who stood next to the abandoned K-9 vehicle. The two officers who'd found it had already taped it off. Just in case. The visible declaration that this was a possible crime scene sent a wave of nausea through Luke.

Please don't let this be for real. The thought blipped through his mind before he could snuff it. There had been a few crime scenes where he'd simply wanted to turn around and leave, call it a bad nightmare and forget about it. Unfortunately, he'd had to work every one of those. Just like he'd work this one. For Jordan.

Sophie stopped outside the perimeter of the yellow tape while Luke ducked under it.

K-9 officer Gavin Sutherland had Tommy, his bomb detection Springer spaniel, sniffing at the back of the SUV. Gavin looked up and Luke raised a brow. The other officer shrugged. "Didn't figure it would hurt to be cautious the way things were playing out. No one believes Jordan killed himself, which means foul play is most likely involved in his disappearance."

Gavin nodded to Sophie. "Someone tried to snatch her because she caught him planting that note in the folder. And now Jordan's vehicle is found in plain sight exactly where Jordan was planning to go, but Jordan's not with it?" He shook his head. "Tommy and I were here. I figured we might as well make sure there aren't any explosives around."

That was so like Gavin and his "better safe than sorry" motto that Luke didn't even blink. "And?"

"We're all good. It's clear." Gavin stepped aside with Tommy. Luke drew in a deep breath and slipped on a pair of gloves. At the driver's side, he opened the door. He'd look for clues about Jordan's possible whereabouts—and determine if the crime scene unit needed to be called.

Finn opened the passenger door and shot him a frown. "What'd you bring Sophie for? This isn't exactly her beat."

Luke met his friend's gaze. "She was kidnapped yesterday. Then when I took her home, her place was trashed."

Finn's right brow rose. "I knew about the kidnapping, of course. Didn't know about the break-in. That's not a coincidence."

"I don't think so either. I figure she's safer with me than on her own where someone can have another go at her." Luke paused. "Besides, think about it. Other than Katie, Sophie probably spends the most time with Jordan. She handles his business calendar as well as some of his personal stuff. If she can give us information we don't have to bother Katie with, then I'm all for that."

"You've convinced me." Finn drew in a deep breath. "Let's see what we can find."

Together, they searched, looking for anything that would give them information about Jordan. All officers had been trained in forensic evidence handling, so searching the car wouldn't be called into question should a court case result.

Which Luke prayed wouldn't happen. His gut was screaming otherwise and ignoring it was taking a lot of willpower.

A glance over his shoulder sent determination through him. Jordan's solemn brothers stayed back without being asked. They must have come to the same conclusion. Finding Jordan's empty vehicle wasn't good and, as much as they might wish otherwise, had the potential to be very, very bad.

If Jordan was a victim of a crime, they could have no part in the investigation or they would risk the evidence being thrown out should anything come of it. But they would watch and listen and try to help in every other way possible, offering suggestions and advice.

Carter said something, and Noah nodded while Zach frowned then pointed to Jordan's vehicle. Carter and Noah headed for the trail, dogs trotting along beside them while Zach jutted his jaw and kept his eyes trained on the action around the vehicle. Luke figured the two brothers were going to keep searching for Jordan while Zach wanted to see what he and Finn uncovered.

Sophie stepped up to Zach and squeezed his forearm. He shot her a tight smile that faded quickly. A dart of jealousy flashed through Luke. Not at the interaction between the two. Sophie's actions were those of a concerned friend, nothing more.

Instead, the jealousy—and slight bit of shame—came from the fact that she *was* Zach's friend. Before yesterday, Luke wouldn't have been able to say that she was anything more than a passing acquaintance. Someone he'd known on a professional basis. Although, if he was honest, he'd admit he found her attractive and had had a few wishful thoughts about her being closer to his age. But he wouldn't have called her a friend. Before today.

"Luke?" Finn said. "What are you thinking?"

Luke blinked and focused. "It's been wiped clean," he said softly.

"Looks like it. Someone trying to hide prints? Evidence?"

"That's what my gut says. But I want to let Bruno take a sniff. He's been trained in more than just finding dead bodies. Let's see if he alerts to anything."

"Like what?"

Luke shrugged. "I don't know. If it's been wiped clean, there may be traces of evidence left that we can't see, but Bruno can smell."

"Like blood," Finn said flatly.

"Yeah."

Finn nodded. Luke avoided eye contact with those watching, got Bruno and brought him over to the vehicle. "Go, boy," he said softly. "Search."

Bruno hopped into the vehicle and went to work. His head bobbed and weaved as he examined the front seat, then Luke let him out and into the very back where Snapper would have been in the kennel box. Bruno took one sniff near the front of the box and sat.

"He found something," Luke said.

"What?"

Luke climbed in and used the light on his phone to illuminate the area Bruno had alerted to. He sucked in an audible breath.

"What is it?" Finn asked.

"A dark stain. On the bottom of the door. It's dried, but it could be blood. Let me get the luminol and we'll find out for sure, then see if there's any evidence of more and whether someone tried to clean it up. We'll get this sent off to the lab and processed ASAP. If it's blood, I want it compared to Jordan's."

Luke climbed out of the vehicle and shot another look over his shoulder. All three brothers stood silent, arms crossed, eyes intense. He sighed and rose. Zach raised a brow, questions all over his expression.

"Just getting something from my trunk," Luke said.

"What?" Sophie asked.

Luke hesitated.

"Spit it out, man," Zach said. "There's no way we're having secrets."

"I'm going to get some luminol to take a sample of something that could possibly be blood." Zach paled. Luke held up a hand. "It's only a small dark stain. Could be from anything. It's not enough to scare me, but we've got to process it and the rest of the vehicle."

Zach swallowed hard. Sophie's fingers curled into fists. Luke retrieved the luminol and other items he needed for the sample and passed them to Finn. If someone had cleaned up the vehicle and tried to get rid of any other blood that had spilled, Finn would find it and then CSU would take over when they arrived.

"When you're finished, we'll let one of the officers run it to the lab so they can get started on it ASAP."

"Good idea."

Ten minutes later, a uniformed officer sped away, siren wailing. Luke drew in a deep breath. "Have Noah or Carter found anything?" he asked Zach. The young man shook his head. "All right, then. I think it's time to join in with Carter and Noah and search this area again. If his vehicle is here, maybe Jordan is, too."

Unfortunately, he was deathly afraid that if Jordan was here, they were way too late to be of any help.

SIX

Sophie bit her lip and watched as the cruiser took the evidence away, then turned her attention back to the action in front of her. Luke's phone rang, and he answered it while Finn readied Abernathy to start searching.

"Right. Okay," Luke said into the phone. "Thanks, Dani." He hung up and turned to them. "Dani's gotten some surveillance video from the guy who kidnapped Sophie and says she knows how he managed to disappear after the wreck." He nodded to Finn. "We'll check it out after we're finished here."

Finn held Jordan's shirt from yesterday so Abernathy could get a good whiff of it. The dog sniffed it and stuck his nose to the ground, then in the air as he paced back and forth near Jordan's SUV.

When he caught the scent, he took off down the trail weaving back and forth on the asphalt but heading deeper into the wooded area away from the trail's entrance. Finn hoofed it after the dog, followed by Jordan's brothers.

Sophie hurried over to Luke, who stood still and silent. Watching. "What is it? Aren't we going?"

He blinked as though she'd pulled him from some deep mental place. "Yes." But instead of following the others, he walked to his vehicle, grabbed his evidence duffel from the back and let Bruno out.

"What are you doing?" she asked. "This isn't a job for Bruno. He finds dead people, not living ones."

"He needs to walk and find a tree. We'll stay far enough behind that he won't be a distraction to Abernathy."

Sophie frowned, anxiety notching up. "You think we're going to need Bruno, don't you?" she asked quietly. Tears and hysteria welled, and she squelched both with a massive dose of willpower.

"I sincerely hope not," Luke said, "but I can't deny that I have a feeling—"

"What? What kind of feeling?" Why was she asking? She already knew the answer. She supposed she wanted him to deny it.

He glanced at the trail and shook his head. "Never mind. You ready?"

"I am." The three started off at a fast clip with Bruno leading the way. "What kind of feeling?" Sophie asked again, unable to resist pressing for an answer.

"It's probably nothing."

"You don't believe that."

He shrugged.

"Fine. I don't want to speculate on that either, so let me run this by you."

"Sure. What?"

"I've been thinking," Sophie said.

"About?"

"The reason that guy decided to kidnap me. I think

Gavin's right. I was in the wrong place at the wrong time. I think the guy planted that suicide note in Jordan's folder and when I walked in to question him, he realized he was caught. Kidnapping me was a spur-of-the-moment, desperate act of someone who didn't want it found out that he was there. Thankfully, you came along when you did."

"It's a little soon right now, but I'll follow up on the letter in a couple of hours and see if the lab was able to find any prints."

"Please."

She dodged a tree limb as Bruno continued to mirror a similar path that Abernathy had taken, weaving and sniffing. It didn't take long to catch up to the others, who'd stopped.

Finn looked up when they approached and shook his head. "Abernathy's lost the scent. I'll need a minute to help him get it back."

Luke held Bruno back when the dog wanted to lurch forward. "Easy, boy."

Sophie frowned, watching, keeping her thoughts to herself.

Noah sighed. "We'll keep going and see if we find anything out of the ordinary. Radio us if Abernathy catches the scent again."

Finn nodded, and Noah, Carter and Zach continued to trek the path, leaving Finn, Sophie, Luke and the dogs alone. The whomp-whomp-whomp of blades cutting through the air reached her and she looked up through a break in the trees just in time to see a helicopter make a pass.

"The media's here," she said.

"How'd they find out so fast?" Luke muttered.

"There are a lot of cop cars here," Sophie said. "They know something's going on, but probably not the details."

"Then we need to get going on this. It won't be a secret for much longer." Finn held the bag with the shirt out to Abernathy once more.

"I think that Jordan was forced to write that note," Sophie said, picking up her earlier train of thought. "Katie was absolutely right. If someone threatened her or someone he loved, Jordan would have just written the note with the intention of tearing it up later after he explained what happened."

"I agree," Luke said, "but my question is why? What's the reason behind it? The motive?"

Finn glanced at her, started to say something, then went silent.

"What?" she asked. "Now's not the time to withhold your thoughts."

"Could I say something without you two thinking the worst of me or getting mad?" he asked.

She glanced at Luke, who shrugged, then studied Finn for a second before nodding. "Okay."

"While I think that what you've just described is a likely scenario, how well do we know Jordan? Any of us? After all, he wouldn't be the first cop to hide his emotions, his true feelings, under a layer of professionalism."

Sophie scowled. "Not Jordan. I saw him day in and day out. If he was depressed or struggling with something, I would have noticed." She paused. "Or Katie would have mentioned it. We're good friends and she wouldn't keep something like that from me."

"I agree with Sophie," Luke said. "If she says Jordan was fine emotionally, then he was." He swept an arm out. "And besides, all of this screams foul play."

Sophie shot Luke a grateful smile. She appreciated his support and faith in her. It drew her like a magnet, but she couldn't help a small silent caution to her heart. Luke acted like he took her seriously, but not many men did because of her age and appearance that made her seem even younger. So, for now, while she had hope that Luke saw her as someone who knew what she was talking about professionally, she'd keep her guard up on the personal front.

Finn nodded and controlled the suddenly eager dog pulling at the lead. "I'm just trying to cover all the bases. Truly, I don't think Jordan killed himself. I just think, as cops, we need to look at all angles."

"I know," Sophie muttered. "But not this time. I was kidnapped by the guy who planted the note, remember?"

Abernathy pulled harder and Finn gave a grin of satisfaction. "We're back on the scent. Let's go find our boss and bring him home."

Sophie and Luke let Finn and Abernathy get a short lead before following after them. Sophie sent up silent prayers and kept her eyes open for anything that might lead them to Jordan. Abernathy led them off the jogging trail, his tail wagging.

Bruno lifted his head and swiveled left. He pulled on his lead and Luke sucked in a breath. "No," he whispered. Sophie's heart clenched. She met Luke's gaze and the stark agony there terrified her.

"Luke?"

Without a word, he followed Bruno off the trail, stepping over the underbrush and around a dense set of trees. Sophie followed, doing her best to ignore her pounding heart.

And then Bruno found a small path that led around another thick copse of bushes and trees. He followed it and disappeared from sight. And the leash went slack.

Luke pulled up short. "Stay back, Sophie."

"What does that mean, Luke? Why isn't he moving?" But she knew why. Bruno wasn't moving because he was sitting—his alert that he'd found a body. She caught up to Luke and grasped his arm. "It doesn't mean it's Jordan."

"I know. I'm going to find out. Just stay put." Luke vanished.

But she couldn't. She followed him, her eyes landing first on Bruno, who sat facing them. When she looked behind him, she let out a small cry. Dressed in his jogging clothes, Jordan sat back against a tree trunk, eyes open, staring at nothing.

Luke bit back his own cry but couldn't suppress the low moan of grief.

"Jordy!"

Sophie's piercing cry turned him around just in time to catch her around the waist as she hurled herself toward Jordan's body. "No, Sophie, you can't do anything. He's gone." He pulled her into a hug, holding her against his chest while she wailed. "He's gone," he whispered against her ear.

And had been for a while judging from the color of his skin and sightless gaze. But Luke would check. He had to. He pressed Sophie's face into his chest, feeling the shudders wracking her. "I'm going to see if there's a pulse." Even though he knew there wouldn't be, but some small sliver of hope urged him to try. "Stay here for a second, please? I mean it. We can't mess up the scene. And...call the others, will you?"

She nodded, and he released her, pressing Bruno's leash into her hand. From his bag, he pulled little blue booties and slipped them over his shoes to prevent tracking any foreign evidence into the area. With one last look at the trail, expecting to see Jordan's brothers appear any moment, he turned to make his way to his boss, noting the landscape, the trampled undergrowth and broken tree limbs.

It looked like Jordan had just walked over, sat down...and died. A long groove in the ground looked like someone had dragged a stick, then stopped at Jordan's resting place.

Kneeling in front of the man who'd been more than a boss, one he'd considered a friend, Luke clamped his lips together and pressed his fingers against Jordan's neck, then his limp wrist.

Nothing.

The fact that his skin was cold to the touch told him Jordan had been dead for a while. Lividity had come and gone, which meant he'd probably been dead shortly after they realized he'd gone missing.

Luke dropped his chin to his chest to get his raging

emotions under control. Once again, he was too late. His mother had died because he'd been late—killed by a carjacker when he was eight years old. He still blamed himself when he thought about it too long. And now Jordan. *Too late, too late, too late.*

"Luke?"

Sophie's wavering voice brought him to his feet. He turned to find Zach, Noah and Carter standing back, faces twisted in stunned grief, but with faint hope that Luke would find a pulse. Finn held Abernathy back, ordering the dog to sit, his own anxious gaze matching those of Jordan's brothers.

Luke met Sophie's eyes, then the brothers', and gave a slight shake of his head.

"No!" Zach's wail echoed through the trees. He turned and punched the nearest trunk. Then clasped it and pressed his forehead against it. Noah wrapped his arms around his younger brother. Carter didn't move, his gaze locked on Jordan's body. His mouth worked, but no sound emerged. He took a step toward Jordan.

Luke went to Carter and gripped his friend's bicep, stopping his forward momentum. "I can't let you go to him," Luke said hoarsely. "We have to protect the scene." He left out the word *crime* but knew it was implied.

Carter spun away to drop his head. His shoulders gave a violent shudder, then went still. When he turned back, his reddened eyes burned into Luke's. "Get this investigation going, Luke. Please," he whispered, the raw anguish searing Luke's heart.

Noah stepped forward, jaw hard, eyes harder. "I

don't know what happened, but my brother didn't kill himself and we need you to help prove it."

"Of course." Luke nodded and cleared his throat. "Finn, secure the scene." He didn't recognize his own grief-ravaged voice, but they needed to act. Jordan deserved it.

All three brothers now stood next to one another, their eyes on Jordan. And all three held themselves back from rushing to the man, knowing they'd destroy any evidence that might be there to tell them what happened. "Carter?" Luke asked. The man shifted his gaze to Luke. "Can you, Noah and Zach search for Snapper? If Jordan's here, so's Snapper."

With a jerky nod, Carter turned. He directed his other two brothers to follow.

Zach shook his head. "I'm not leaving him." He crossed his arms and kept his eyes locked on Jordan.

Carter started to say something, but Noah put out a hand. "It's okay."

Noah and Carter took off down the trail, seemingly grateful to be able to focus on something other than the soul-crushing despair. Zach stayed put, still as a statue, his eyes locked on his brother.

Sliding his hands around Sophie's biceps, Luke grasped them in a gentle grip. "Sophie?"

She looked up, tears streaking her ashen cheeks.

"I'm going to call it in," he said. "Okay?"

She nodded. "Yes. You have to call it in."

Her automated response came from shock and he gave her a second before he squeezed her arms. She drew in a shuddering breath.

"I need you to wait on the trail," he said, "and direct

the medical examiner and crime scene unit this way when they get here," he said. "It shouldn't take CSU long since they're working on the vehicle, but the ME has to have a first look. Okay?"

She nodded again, her eyes fixed on his. Trusting him. Willing to follow his lead. His throat tightened. He didn't deserve that look. Shoving aside the unwelcome wave of self-pity, he cleared the lump from his throat. "We've got to keep it together for Jordan, okay? Can you do that? Can you help me?" He paused and drew in a steadying breath. "Because if you lose it, I will, too."

With a slow nod, Sophie straightened her shoulders and swiped her cheeks. "I can do that. For Jordan—and you." She functioned on autopilot, her mind grappling with disbelief and sorrow.

But she'd keep it together. For now. Time passed in a blur of crime scene tape, pictures, the medical examiner's appearance and the subsequent removal of Jordan's body in the black bag. Sophie watched them go. So many questions—very few answers.

"Anyone find Snapper?" Luke asked her as Finn stepped up to join them. The crime scene unit had appeared to do their job and Sophie watched them carefully—as though just her presence would ensure their accuracy and professionalism.

"No," Sophie said. The three of them stood about ten yards away from where the CSU worked, surrounded by trees and other spring greenery. But for her, the place had lost its beauty and it would forever have the dark stench of death stamped on it. "Which means someone took him," she added. Finn raised a brow and she shrugged. "Snapper was Jordan's shadow. That dog would have stayed by Jordan and probably barked his head off until someone came to investigate. You know that as well as I do. If Snapper isn't here, then someone took him. It's as simple as that."

"And just as complicated," Luke said softly.

"Yeah."

Finn sighed. "I'll go talk to Jordan's brothers and fill them in."

He left, and Luke turned a concerned gaze on her. "Are you going to be okay?"

"In time." She rubbed her arms, the goose bumps there having nothing to do with the weather. "I'll grieve like we all will and I know eventually, his loss will hurt less, but for now..."

"Yeah."

"The healing process will go faster if we could catch Jordan's killer."

"We don't know that there is a killer," he reminded her gently.

Meeting his gaze, she offered him a sad smile. "Yes, we do."

He looked away with a short nod. "The medical examiner said she couldn't see any outward reason for Jordan's death. No bullet holes, no trauma, nothing. So, let's wait for the official word before we call it murder, okay?"

"Okay."

"But," he said with a sidelong glance at her, "we're going to start investigating like it's a murder. Just in case. We don't want to lose any time or momentum. If it turns out not to be, then so be it."

"Good."

"And we need to find Snapper. We'll get some flyers printed and posted. Maybe offer a reward for his return."

"Good idea," she said softly.

"Hey, Luke?" Finn called. "Can you come over here a second?"

"Sure." Luke squeezed her shoulder and left to join Finn.

Sophie stayed put, thinking. What was she missing? Did she know something that would help find Jordan's killer and she just didn't know she knew? When racking her brain produced nothing, she spun to head back to the vehicle. There was nothing more she could do here.

A loud crack echoed through the air and a puff of wooded undergrowth littered her ankles. Sophie jerked to a stop.

"Sophie! Get down!"

She dropped just as another bullet slammed into the tree trunk beside her. And then Luke was there, his body covering hers, his weapon in hand, looking for a target.

Officers swarmed past, each one taking care to use the trees as cover while searching for the shooter.

Luke's hand closed over hers and pulled. "Stay behind a tree!"

Sophie ducked, heart pounding. She grasped the trunk and knelt, trying to make herself as small a target as possible. Shouts from the other officers reached her as they quickly formulated a plan to catch the shooter.

And then Luke was beside her, his hand on her shoulder. "Head to the vehicle, Sophie. Bruno, heel!"

A motorcycle roared, then the engine faded as the three of them raced down the path toward the SUV. With a click of the remote, the back door opened. Bruno shot into his area and Luke reached around Sophie to shove her into the passenger side. When he landed in the driver's seat with a grunt, Sophie turned, heart thudding, hands shaking.

"Are you okay?" he demanded.

"Yes. I… I think so. Someone was shooting at me… or us?"

"He was definitely shooting at someone, but you're safe now. There's no way he's still around here with so many officers on his tail. They'll catch him."

"And if they don't?" She couldn't help the small squeak that slipped from her throat.

Reaching across the console, he pulled her into a hug and she buried her face into his shoulder for the second time that day.

"They will. I'm so sorry this is happening to you. You don't deserve this, Sophie."

She sniffed and squeezed her eyes against the flood of tears that wanted to fall. Crying could come later. Right now, she had to think. "Why does he keep coming back?"

"Because you saw him."

"But I didn't get a good look! Even when we were in the car racing through the streets, he had the baseball hat and sunglasses on. I don't think I could even pick him out of a lineup."

"Yeah, same here. But either he doesn't realize that, or it doesn't matter to him." He held her tighter. "I'll protect you, Sophie, I promise."

"But who's going to protect you?"

A knock on the window pulled them apart. Finn stood there. Luke lowered the window.

"We spotted him, but he got away," Finn said, his gaze bouncing between the two of them.

"The motorcycle?"

"Yeah. We couldn't pinpoint exactly where he was shooting from, but after he took his shots and realized we were coming, he hopped on and hightailed it out of here. I've already released a description, but it's not much so I'm not holding out too much hope."

Luke nodded. "All right, I'm going to take Sophie home. Keep me updated."

"Of course."

Once Finn was gone, Sophie shook her head. "You can't take me home yet."

"Why not?"

"I need to at least be there when Katie gets the news."

Luke took her hand. "Of course. I'll take you to see her."

Her phone rang. "Hello?"

"It's Noah, Sophie. We're headed to Katie's and were wondering if you could be there."

"I was just heading that way."

"I think the media is heading for the house. See if

you can beat them there and keep her from hearing it from anyone but one of us."

"Me? But—" How would she manage to do that?

"She'll need you," Noah said, his voice hoarse."

"I... Okay. I'll do my best."

"Thank you."

Frankly, she wondered if she'd be able to even look Katie in the eye when she saw her, but she'd have to try. For Katie.

SEVEN

Luke's heart still pounded with shock and grief and he had to wonder if the feelings would ease anytime soon. He doubted it but did his best to focus on Sophie. "Tell me how you and Katie came to be such good friends?" he asked as he headed toward the Jamesons' house in Rego Park.

"When I started working for Jordan, he introduced me to Katie right away, said he had a feeling we'd be good friends." She gave him a half smile. "He took us both to lunch one day and we hit it off immediately."

"He had good intuition about a lot of things."

"True. Anyway, sometimes when Katie would come in to the office to see Jordan, she'd have to wait if he was on the phone or in a meeting that went long. We'd wind up chatting, and eventually, we started going to lunch together a few times a week—especially if Jordan couldn't go."

"Sounds nice."

"It was." She blinked at the sudden rush of tears once again. "I can't believe the timing of this. It's unbelievable."

He frowned at her and she pressed her fingers against her lips. What did the timing of Jordan's death have to do with anything? It's not like there would be a better time for him to die, would there? Luke had the feeling that wasn't the way she meant her words to sound. Instead, he figured she knew something she wasn't telling and he didn't like it. Instead of pressing her, he drove through the streets of Rego Park, turning onto Furmanville Avenue and past the St. John Cemetery, then onto Woodhaven Boulevard, all the while looking for a parking spot. He could use the BFK parking garage, but that was about a mile and a half from the Jamesons' home and he didn't want Sophie exposed for the length of time it would take to walk from the garage. Then again, he could just drop her at the door of the house and go find a spot, but that would entail leaving her.

Finally, he wedged the SUV at the end of the block on Fitchett Street and cut the engine. When he turned to look at her, the devastation on her face grabbed his heart in a vice grip. He took her hand in his. "I'll be there, too, okay? We'll all be there and be her support. Whatever she needs."

Sophie nodded, opened her door and stepped out of the vehicle. Luke did the same and released Bruno from his area. The dog trotted beside them as they worked their way up the sidewalk. Luke kept his eyes open, watching the surrounding area. He hadn't mentioned it to Sophie, but he'd been looking for more than a parking spot while he'd been driving up and down the streets.

And while he saw nothing that set off his alarm

bells, he couldn't help the feeling that someone was out there. Watching and waiting for the chance to get to Sophie. The thought propelled him closer to her and he wrapped an arm around her shoulders.

She glanced up but didn't pull away. Seconds later, they approached the front door. Officers stood outside the home. A protective measure for Katie just in case whatever caused Jordan to disappear—and die—was a threat to Katie. Luke knew they were there, as well, out of concern and support for the wife of their chief.

He nodded to each of them.

"Any word on the chief?" one asked.

"I can't say anything right now," Luke said, "but you'll be hearing something soon." No way was anyone else finding out about Jordan's death before the man's wife.

"Luke. Sophie!"

He turned to see Noah, Carter and Zach hurrying toward them. Luke stepped back and allowed the brothers to take the lead. Noah opened the door and they made their way to Katie and Jordan's apartment.

Zach knocked.

When Katie opened the door, her red-rimmed eyes met Zach's, then bounced from person to person until they finally landed on Sophie, who stood slightly in front of the brothers. Luke frowned at Katie's almost translucent appearance.

"What is it?" she asked. "Did you find him?"

Zach drew in a deep breath and nodded.

"Well, what?"

No one spoke. Finally, Sophie took her friend's hand

in hers and led her back through the foyer and into the den. "Let's sit down."

Katie obediently followed Sophie to the couch and sank onto it. "It's obviously not good. So, what? Which hospital is he in? How bad is it?"

Noah stepped forward and cleared his throat. "He's gone, Katie," Noah said.

"He's..." Sophie glanced at Luke and the others. She swallowed. For a moment, Katie simply stared at her brother-in-law. "Gone? Gone where?"

Sophie shook her head and Noah gripped her fingers. "He's dead, Katie. He's...dead." He choked on the last word and turned away.

Again, Katie stayed rock still for a good ten seconds, then tears filled her eyes to spill over her lashes and streak her cheeks. "No," she whispered. Her face crumpled, and Sophie leaped forward to pull her friend into an embrace while Luke looked away and pressed fingers to his burning eyes.

This wasn't the first time he'd had to be present or tell someone a family member had died, but it sure was the hardest. "I'm sorry, Katie," he whispered.

Katie sobbed into Sophie's shoulder for what seemed like an eternity. Finally, she pulled back and Sophie pressed tissues into the woman's hand. Luke didn't know where she'd gotten them, but he was beginning to understand that that was Sophie. Always prepared. Even for this.

"It's on the news," Zach said, his voice rough. He glanced up from his phone. "Someone leaked it." He looked ready to find the person responsible and let them have it.

"We were worried about that and got here as fast as we could," Luke said. "How far away are your parents?" he asked.

"They should be here anytime now," Carter said.

"Do they know?"

"Yes." Noah raked a hand over his head. "Once we realized it was on the news, we had no choice but to break it to them over the phone."

"I'm sorry."

A sharp cry escaped Katie and she broke away from Sophie to dart down the hallway.

"Katie?" Zach called. His sister-in-law ignored him.

Sophie's tear-filled eyes met Luke's for a brief second, then she hurried after her friend.

Sophie stopped at the bathroom door. The sounds of Katie being sick reached her and she closed her eyes to offer up a silent prayer for her grieving friend. When it sounded as if the episode was over, Sophie knocked.

"Come in."

Katie sat on the floor, her back against the wall, eyes closed. "What am I going to do without him?" she whispered as another tear slid down to drop off her jaw.

Sophie sighed and lowered herself beside her friend. "You'll go on and you'll raise his baby to know that his or her daddy was a hero."

Katie gave a slight nod, but her tears never stopped flowing.

"And," Sophie said, "it might be a good idea to tell everyone about the baby. Not only will it give everyone hope that Jordy will live on in his child, but you need the support, someone to go to your doctor's appointments with you and hold your hand through all of this."

"You haven't mentioned it?"

"Of course not. That's not my news to share."

"No. It was *ours*." Her eyes opened, and anger flashed. "Mine and Jordy's. And now that's been ripped away from us. Why?"

Sophie gripped her friend's cold fingers and squeezed. "I don't know, Katie. It's not fair."

"No, it's not." She sighed, and her shoulders drooped, surprising Sophie that the sudden surge of anger vanished in a flash to be replaced with raw grief once more. "I'll tell them after the funeral," Katie said. "But…if it becomes necessary for someone to know, then you have my blessing."

"Thanks. It might very well be necessary." She really thought Luke should know if only to fully convince him that Jordan would never take his own life. "But why not tell everyone now? It would be such joyous news in the midst of all of this tragedy." Wouldn't it?

Katie swiped a tear. "I don't know. Do you really think so? That it will bring them joy or just heighten the loss and the grief because they all know how much Jordan would have loved this baby and now he'll never get to—" She pressed the heels of her hands to her eyes.

Sophie bit her lip. "I truly don't know."

"Jordy and I wanted to keep this just between us for a while," Katie said, dropping her hands into her lap. "So we could savor the idea—and make sure the pregnancy was going like it should—not that we had any reason to think otherwise." She gave a small shrug. "But it was fun. It was our secret." Another tear dripped off her chin and she nodded. "All right. I'll tell them in a few minutes."

Silence fell between them and for several minutes they sat there while Katie worked on getting her tears under control and Sophie wondered what the future would hold for her friend.

"How did he die?" Katie finally asked. "Who killed him? Because I know it wasn't self-inflicted."

"I don't know. I saw him," Sophie said softly. "And…"

"Tell me. Please."

"He looked peaceful. Like he'd taken a walk in the woods and found a comfortable spot to sit while he contemplated the future." No need to mention his open, staring eyes. "There wasn't a bullet hole or any blood except for a trace amount found in his vehicle. And it's very possible it wasn't his. The medical examiner will know more once she's finished with the…everything."

"The autopsy."

"Yes." Sophie didn't want to say the word in relation to Jordan. The fact that Katie had done so was a testament to her strength. Strength that Sophie was going to have to find and emulate.

"Where's Snapper?" Katie asked. "Did you find him?"

"No."

Katie groaned and lowered her forehead to her knees. "He should have been right there with Jordy. He wouldn't have left him willingly."

"I agree. We've already talked about that. Everyone's searching for him now. And now that it's all over the news, I think they're going to print up some flyers and put them out along the biking trail and around the park."

A knock on the door pulled them to their feet.

"Everything okay in there?" Zach asked. "Sorry, that's a dumb question. I know everything's not okay. Is there anything you need? Anything we can do?"

"They must be feeling pretty helpless out there," Katie said.

"Probably, but you deal with this however you need to. They'll wait," Sophie said.

"No, it's okay." Katie swiped her face, then rose to wash her hands. Taking a deep breath, she faced the door. "We're coming," she called. She opened the door and Sophie followed her and Zach down the hall to the kitchen, where an older couple sat at the table, expressions drawn, cheeks wet with their tears. They rose.

"Hello, Mr. and Mrs. Jameson," Sophie said while Katie slipped into her mother-in-law's arms.

"Hello, Sophie." Mr. Jameson hugged her. Hard. His desperate grief reached inside her and ripped at the fragile hold she had on her emotions.

One by one, Jordan's brothers hugged Katie, then led their parents and Katie into the living area.

Luke stayed behind. "Can I help do something?"

"You can make all of this go away or wake me up from the nightmare," Sophie said softly, pulling plastic cups and plates from under the cabinet near the refrigerator.

"I wish I could."

"I know."

She rummaged through the refrigerator, pulling

leftover containers and lifting the lids, sniffing…and mostly tossing into the trash.

"What are you doing?" he asked, mystified.

"As soon as people hear, they're going to be arriving in droves. Jordy and Katie are…were…a part of a large couples Bible study. They'll come to offer their sympathy and they'll bring food. We'll need room for it. There's another refrigerator and freezer outside on the porch, as well."

Luke stood, held silent by her resilience and her thoughtfulness. "You're amazing," he finally said softly. She was hurting, grieving, just like the rest of them—and yet she was putting everyone else first.

She paused and offered him a small smile. "I'm not that amazing. It helps to stay busy, to focus on something besides my shattered heart."

"Yeah." He paused. "What can I do to help?"

From the pantry, she pulled out a few water bottles and set them on the counter. "I don't know. Nothing, really."

"Sophie?"

She turned to see Katie in the doorway. The woman hurried over to her and grabbed her in a hug much like the one Mr. Jameson had given Sophie earlier.

Luke nodded to the door, indicating he was going to give them privacy.

Sophie hugged Katie back. "What is it? Here, take a water bottle. As many tears as you've cried, you need to hydrate."

A giggle slipped from Katie and she slapped a hand

over her mouth. "How can I laugh at that? Something is wrong with me if I can laugh at a time like this."

"Nothing is wrong with you other than elevated hormones. And dare I say it, but Jordy would be the first one to tell you to laugh."

"Thank you," Katie whispered and gave her another hug. "I can't thank you enough for just being here. I love my in-laws, but sometimes they can overwhelm a girl a bit."

"I'm here anytime you need me, Katie. You'll get through this. It's going to be hard and there are going to be some dark days ahead, but we'll get there. We have to," she whispered, releasing her friend and gripping her hands once more. "It's what Jordy would want."

Katie nodded. "You're right. It is what he'd want. He'd want us to be happy and to enjoy life and laughter again. Just keep reminding me of that when I'm deep in the pit of despair and missing him desperately, okay?"

"I promise." It would be a good reminder for Sophie, too.

"Okay, I'm going to put on my strong face and go back into the den and tell them about the baby."

"Good."

After yet another hug, Katie left, and Sophie grabbed two water bottles and went in search of Luke. She found him in the sunroom, hands shoved into his pockets, staring out into the backyard. Bruno lay stretched out on the large throw rug, his watchful eyes following her.

"Katie's with her in-laws now. I think she's going to be all right. Eventually."

"She will. It'll be hard, but she'll get there. It may

not seem like it now, but we all will." A pause. "I don't understand," he said softly.

"Understand what?"

"This whole thing. I keep thinking about him. Just sitting there under the tree. No sign of foul play, nothing."

"Have they found his phone?"

"No, but that doesn't mean he didn't leave it somewhere."

"Not Jordan. And especially not now."

He turned. "Where does this unwavering faith come from? How are you so sure?"

"I…just know. Without a doubt."

Luke ran a hand over his chin. "Okay, well, let's say you're right and Jordan didn't kill himself. I truly don't think so, but I'll admit to some lingering doubts. However…"

"However…?" she asked.

"If it wasn't suicide then that means his death was either due to some crazy undiagnosed medical issue, like a heart condition or a brain aneurysm or—"

"Or it was murder," she said. "And since he'd just had a checkup not too long ago, I'm going with murder." Although, she admitted silently, some things could be missed even in a thorough checkup. But still… something in her said Jordan's death wasn't an accident or a medical mishap.

Luke nodded. "I was inclined to believe that, too—until I saw him. I took a good look at him, Sophie. There were no wounds or any evidence of a traumatic injury."

She sighed and rubbed her eyes. "Well, I guess we'll

just have to wait and see what the medical examiner says." She paused and handed him one of the bottles of water.

"Thanks."

"Sure. So, what's next?"

"What's next is," Luke said with a heaviness that made her heart hurt even more, "they plan a funeral and we find out why our healthy, happy friend died."

He twisted the cap off the bottle and took a long swig. She could tell he was still troubled and even knowing she couldn't really help, she had to try. "Tell me," she said softly.

"I'm just thinking."

"About Jordan, of course."

"Of course." He gave a short laugh, one without humor. "I can't stop thinking about him. I keep running everything through my mind over and over. It's like a loop and I can't seem to find the stop button."

"You're wondering if you could have saved him."

Luke jerked, his eyes locked on hers. "Yes, but how…?"

"Because I'm wondering the same thing. Well, not if you personally could have, but if any of us could have. What did we miss? If it was murder, who had it in for him?" She glanced into the den, where Katie and her brothers-in-law sat speaking in low tones. "And does someone now have it in for Katie?"

Luke took her hands in his. "I know you're worried for Katie. I am, too. But she has four male protectors in there and a mother-in-law who thinks of her as her own daughter. I think we need to turn our focus on you—and who has it in for you."

EIGHT

Sophie shivered at his ominous reminder and he grimaced. He knew she'd been working hard to put the incidents aside in order to be there for Katie, but he also needed her to stay alert and watchful. "Are you ready to go?"

She nodded. "I'll check with Katie and make sure she's all right with me leaving."

While Sophie was doing that, Luke stepped into the foyer and called their tech guru, breathing a sigh of relief when she answered on the first ring. "Hi, Dani."

"Hi, Luke."

"Any news?"

"Like what?"

"Like security footage of Vanderbilt Parkway."

Keyboard keys clicked in the background. "I just got it in, believe it or not. I haven't really had a chance to go through it yet."

"Want an extra pair of eyes?"

"Always. But I'll be reviewing it while you're on the way."

"Thirty minutes?"

"I'll be here. Gotta go. Bye." She hung up.

Dani was fabulously good at her job even if her phone etiquette could use a little work. He went looking for Sophie to let her know he was ready and found her in the kitchen with Katie. The two had their heads bent together and were whispering. He cleared his throat and they both jumped as though guilty of some conspiracy. "Uh, sorry. If you need more time."

"No," Katie said. "It's okay. I was just explaining something to Sophie. Thank you for everything."

"Sure."

She headed back to join her family and Sophie turned her gaze on him. "So, we're headed to headquarters?" Sophie asked, her brow still furrowed from the conversation he'd just interrupted.

"If that's all right."

"It's more than all right. At least I feel like we're doing something proactive that might lead us to discover what happened to Jordan instead of sitting around waiting on...everything."

They found the others and said their goodbyes with Katie promising to call should she need anything. Zach, Noah and Carter all wanted to go, too, when they realized the footage was available.

"It's better if you don't," Luke said. "You three can't be anywhere near the investigation on this. Should Jordan's death be due to something other than an accident or a health-related issue—"

"Like murder?" Carter snapped.

"Yes," Luke said evenly. "Like murder. If that's the case, you don't want to do anything that would jeopardize us getting a conviction once we catch the person responsible."

Zach's jaw tightened, and Noah laid a hand on his shoulder without taking his eyes from Luke. "You'll let us know what you know?"

"As soon as I know it."

Noah gave a short nod and Sophie followed Luke out to the SUV. A light rain misted them. "I hope this doesn't interfere with gathering any evidence around the crime scene."

"They'll have known it was coming and prepared for it." And worked fast.

Luke drove to headquarters and found a spot on the street, thankfully not too far from the entrance. "You ready?" he asked Sophie.

"I guess so." She bit her lip and sighed. He didn't have to be a genius to know it was going to be devastating walking into that building when Jordan never would again.

When he let Bruno out, the dog shook himself and trotted toward the three-story building. Luke and Sophie followed. Luke kept her between him and the suite of offices to their left as they walked down the sidewalk.

If there had been a better way to get into headquarters without exposing Sophie to the outside, he would have used it. Having no choice, he did his best to use his body as a shield, although he'd admit to breathing a sigh of relief when they reached the double glass doors that led into the main lobby area. He punched in the code that allowed them access and stepped inside.

Luke was almost as comfortable in this building as

he was in his own home. Bruno was, too. Mostly because of the treats Luke kept in the bottom drawer of his desk. Since his reward for finding a cadaver was playtime with a tennis ball, the treats wouldn't confuse him.

The receptionist, Officer Patricia Knowles, sat behind the large U-shaped desk where she kept tabs on the comings and goings of the handlers and their K-9s—and answered the never-ending ringing phone.

Once inside the lobby, Luke nodded to Patricia, whose eyes went wide at their entrance, but she simply threw them a wave before pressing the button on her headset to answer the phone.

"She was surprised to see us," Sophie said.

"Jordan was just found a few hours ago. No doubt she thought we'd still be with the others."

"Which is where I'd love to be, but if this can help us find Jordan's killer, then this is where I need to be."

"Exactly."

Luke headed for the large open area with cubicles that separated the handlers' desks and gave them a modicum of privacy.

Somber eyes followed him, and he knew each person wanted to stop him and ask him about Jordan, but they respected his body language and turned their attention to Sophie. One by one, she hugged each officer.

While she spent time giving and receiving condolences and fielding questions that had no answers, Luke stopped at his desk to retrieve a treat for Bruno, who wolfed it down. For a moment, he leaned against his desk and closed his eyes. He wanted to pray, but the heaviness in his soul had no words. Instead, he drew in a deep breath and found Bruno had settled onto the dog bed in the corner and was watching him with sympathetic dark eyes.

When he had his emotions under control, Luke exited the cubicle and nodded to Sophie, who extricated herself from the others. She walked with him past the small connecting hallway that led to Jordan's office. Just outside Jordan's office was Sophie's area. Her desk was tidy, the chair pushed in. It looked ready for her to return. He averted his eyes from Jordan's door as emotion welled once more and couldn't help noticing that Sophie did the same.

Luke led the way down the stairs. The large training center was to the left. Dani's office to the right. The door stood open and she motioned them inside. Her red-rimmed hazel eyes behind the large-framed glasses perched on her nose attested to her own emotional state. She had her curly blond hair pulled up into a messy ponytail. "How's Katie?" she asked.

"Not good, as you can imagine," Sophie said, "but she's strong. With support and love from her family and friends, she'll get through this. We all will." She felt like a broken record, but it was the only answer that fit—and offered the hope everyone needed right now. Including herself. Maybe if she said it enough, she'd start to believe it.

Dani nodded and moved behind her desk. Monitors lined the wall in front of her. "All right, just so you know, I managed to grab the footage from the ATM across the street from where your wreck happened and your kidnapper bolted. But first, let's look at the park-way footage."

"Great," Luke said. "How'd you get it so fast?"

"I pulled in a few favors I'd been saving for the right case." She shook her head. "I didn't expect to be re-deeming them on a case like this."

"I know." Luke leaned in. "Show us."

"So, here's what I managed to get from some of the surrounding security cameras. There's one right be-fore you enter the trail. Once they were on the path, it gets a little trickier. Fortunately, there's a study being done on the feasibility of expanding the parkway, so I've got a bit more to work with. They'd placed some counters along the pathway that are triggered every time someone passes by. I don't know how accurate they are, but I think it gives a good idea of the use of the place. Anyway, I've paused it at the place where things get interesting. In spite of the darkness, you can make out what's going on pretty well. Just not who the person is in the video, unfortunately."

A few clicks on the keyboard brought images up on the monitor closest to Luke. "This is the footage from this morning," Dani said. "There wasn't any sign of him on the camera the day he actually disappeared." The footage began to play. For a moment, there was nothing, then Jordan's SUV came into view, just barely on the side of the screen. The driver exited, wearing a hoodie over a baseball cap, along with dark sunglasses. "How can he see with those on?" Sophie whispered.

"Probably put them on just before exiting the ve-hicle," Dani said.

The driver went to the back and pulled out a long pole. "What's he doing?" Luke asked.

"You'll see."

He attached a piece of cloth to the end, turned and lifted the pole toward the camera. The man's sleeve rode up and Luke caught sight of something on the person's arm. Then the camera went blank.

"What's the point of that?" Sophie asked. "Why try to make it look like a suicide if you're going to let yourself get caught on camera covering the lens? That doesn't make sense."

"Unless it was Jordan," Dani said. "But I'm pretty sure it wasn't him." She returned to the part where the man lifted the pole. "There. See that?" Dani zoomed in. "A tattoo of some sort. I can't make out the design, though, so there's no way to run it through the tattoo-ID software."

"It's not Jordan," Sophie said. "He doesn't have a tattoo. So, again, why would this guy allow himself to get caught on camera?"

"I don't think he realized he was within camera range," Dani said. "See where he parked?" She rewound the footage. "That's right on the edge of the parking lot. He approached the camera off to the side when he covered it. These cameras are wide-angle, though. I think he just miscalculated."

"You may be right," Luke said. "I know we need to wait for the autopsy results for an official cause of death, but this is clearly a murder however it was done. It's obvious from the note that he's trying to set up Jordan's death as a suicide, but he sure did a lousy job. Other than the token action of leaving Jordan's vehicle there to make it look like he drove himself to the park, there's no other sign that this is a suicide. What did he kill himself with? There are no pills, no evidence of any drugs, nothing."

"No one ever said criminals had to be smart," Sophie muttered.

"True enough." He glanced at Dani. "Is that it?"

"No, not totally. Take a look at this."

Another monitor blipped to life. "Like I said, there's a study being done on the path. These are the monitors that track how many people are using the path. Last night, there was nothing from 1:00 a.m. until movement at 3:20 a.m. Then at 3:25 a.m., more movement, then nothing until around 5:16 when two joggers went for their morning run."

"So, what does that tell us?" Luke asked.

"I cross-referenced that information against the security footage at the entrance to the parkway. There's no record of anyone entering around that 3:20 time on foot other than the guy who covered up the camera."

"Anyone could have entered from anywhere along the path."

"I know. But then one person exited at 3:40 at this point of the trail and this is what I got from one of the security cameras along the overpass." She clicked a few more keys. "It's two miles away from where Jordan and his SUV were found." She froze the frame to allow them a good look at the person. "He's also dressed just like the guy who got out of Jordan's SUV."

"Did he get into a vehicle?"

"I can't tell. He kept going until he was out of camera range."

"This doesn't tell us much," Sophie said. "It's terribly disappointing."

"Let's not be so hasty to assume that," Luke said. "Let's take another look. See if you spot anything that stands out. Is there anything on his clothing, shoes, hands, that could be identifiable later? Does he have a limp? A habit. Anything?"

Dani played the footage again.

"He's wearing gloves," Sophie said. "This time of year that wouldn't be too suspect except maybe in the middle of the day when it warms up."

"But at night, with the temps getting into the mid-forties, they make sense. But that's not why he's wearing them."

Sophie shook her head. "We need to know when Jordan died," she said. "Any word about what his time of death was?"

"The ME's working on that. We should have a preliminary report soon."

"How did he get Jordan's body out there?" Sophie asked. "Jordan was a big guy. A little over six feet and all muscle. He would have weighed too much for someone to carry for very long—even for a person similar in size to Jordan."

"Good point," Luke said. "Either Jordan walked and he was killed there at the spot, or the killer had help."

"Or the killer had something to transport him in," Sophie said.

"Yeah," Luke sighed. "Or that."

Sophie shook her head. "I don't understand, though. Why put his body here where it's sure to be found rather than leaving him in a river or someplace harder to find him?"

"The killer wanted Jordan found," Luke said. "I mean, it all kind of fits with leaving the suicide note, don't you think?"

"Of course, but wait a minute," Sophie said.

"What is it?"

"Just that I think I know why he would put Jordan in that particular place. The killer thought he was being clever. Smart."

Luke tilted his head. "How so?"

"He had to be watching Jordan. Following him," she said, her voice low, thoughtful. "How else would he know what time Jordan left his home or that Jordan went running just about every single morning in that particular park?"

"He'd been spying," Luke said. "You have to be right."

"If so, then he's been planning this awhile." Sophie swallowed, suddenly nauseated at the thought. "Watching and waiting for the opportunity to strike."

"And when he got it, he took it. By planting the suicide note, then having Jordan found in a place that he was known to love…" She shrugged and swiped a tear from her cheek.

"It would back up the whole idea that he really did kill himself." His gaze snagged hers. "If you hadn't caught him planting the note, we might still be considering that it was a suicide."

"And not looking for a killer," she whispered.

"Exactly."

Luke's phone rang, and he glanced at the screen. "It's Elena, the medical examiner, I need to take it."

Luke stepped into the farthest corner of the small room and pressed the phone to his ear. "Hi, Elena. What have you got?"

"I've finished the autopsy. An initial examination of Chief Jameson shows no outward trauma. It looks like there was some damage to his heart, so I've sent off samples to be tested for various drugs, et cetera, but those won't be back for a while."

"Are you saying he had a heart attack?"

"I'm saying it's possible. There's definitely damage, but until I get the results of the tox report back, I can't say for sure what caused it."

"You can't put a rush on those results?"

A sigh reached him. "I knew Jordan, too, Luke," she said. "I'll do the best I can to hurry things along, but you know this lab stays backed up." She paused. "I'll do my best to get this expedited. He was a good man and served this city well. If he goes to the front of the line, I don't think anyone's going to argue about it."

Luke closed his eyes, grateful for the woman who would get it done even though she made no promises. "Anything you can do would be appreciated."

"Of course."

He hung up and rubbed his eyes, then returned to Dani and Sophie, who were watching the footage one more time.

"I don't see Snapper," Sophie said.

"No, I noticed that right off," Dani said. "He could

still be in the vehicle at this point, but we won't be able to know for sure since the camera's blocked."

"Anything else?" Luke asked.

"That's it for now on that one." Dani clicked a few keys on her keyboard and another file with security footage popped up onto her screen. "Okay, now, this is from the ATM across the street from where Sophie was pulled from the car by the kidnapper. You can't see the crash, but you can see the guy running away from it." She played the video. The sedan carrying Sophie and her kidnapper zipped past. A moment later, Luke pulled to a stop just past the ATM.

Dani looked at him. "Good thing you didn't park in front of it."

"I wasn't thinking about that, to be honest. I just wanted to get to Sophie."

"I know, but we're fortunate to have this." She pointed. "Okay, see that? He ran from the car and darted into the store directly across the street."

"I saw him go in there," Luke said, "and officers went after him while others traced the plates. The car was stolen, which came as a huge surprise." He couldn't help the sarcasm. He could have almost said it had been stolen without the need to run the plates. "Officers covered all the entrances and couldn't discern how he basically just disappeared."

"I think I figured that out," Dani said. She clicked a few more keys. "I looked around for some more cameras and found one inside the store. The owner was gracious enough to email me a copy of the footage. It looks like your kidnapper went into the back where the storage area is and climbed out the window and up the fire escape, then hauled himself onto the roof. I know the place was searched, but by the time officers were in the store, your guy was long gone."

She switched to another camera. "This camera was on a building opposite the one the guy ran into. Fortunately, it's at a higher level, aimed down toward the back alley—and it allows us to see a portion of the room along those connected buildings." She hit Play. "And, there he goes across the rooftops and then down the fire escape when he's almost to the end. I don't have any more footage of it, but I called the business in that last building and asked for a description of the place. From the way he described it, it's not hard to guess that the guy simply swung over the edge of the roof, planted his feet on the wrought-iron ladder and climbed down the fire escape to hit the asphalt running."

Sophie shook her head. "Well, at least we know how he got away." She looked at Luke. "So, what now?"

"Now, we bury our boss and friend and find out exactly why and how he died—and who's responsible."

Luke escorted Sophie and Bruno to the Tahoe, then climbed into the driver's seat. Something niggled at the back of his mind, but he couldn't quite put his finger on what was bothering him.

"You said something that I think we need an answer to," he said.

She turned to him. "What?"

"About Jordan and how someone managed to haul his body out to the spot where he was left. And using something to transport him."

"Yes. I can't see Jordan just walking in there and having a seat against the tree."

"He didn't."

She raised a brow and he sighed. "He'd been dead for a while by the time we found him."

"How do you know?"

"Rigor had already left his body. He wasn't stiff."

"Maybe it hadn't set in yet."

Luke shook his head. "He had on short sleeves," he said softly. "Blood had pooled under the arm that I got a good look at. That means he'd been gone awhile."

She bit her lip and looked away. "I wanted to believe we could have saved him."

"I know. We all did." He drew in a deep breath and refocused. "But what I was getting at is this. When we found Jordan, I noticed a long groove in the dirt, like someone had pulled a heavy stick through the area."

"Okay." She frowned at him. "What are you getting at?"

"What if someone used a wheelbarrow to get Jordan from his vehicle to that spot in the woods?"

Sophie tilted her head, studying him. Then gave a slow nod. "That makes sense, but there was no wheelbarrow sitting around the scene that I saw. Did you notice one?"

"No."

"And Dani showed us where the guy walked out of the area later. What did he do with the wheelbarrow?"

"Good question."

"And if he had it in the back of Jordan's vehicle, I would have thought you and Finn would have found some evidence that it had been there."

"And we didn't. Then again, the Tahoe was practically spotless except for that bit of blood and few dog hairs, which most likely belong to Snapper."

"True."

"So where would the wheelbarrow have come from and where did it go after he used it?"

They fell silent, still sitting in the running vehicle outside of headquarters. Bruno shifted so he could place his head on her shoulder with a sigh. She reached back to scratch his head and his eyes closed halfway. "He's such a good-natured dog."

"Yeah. And I made a huge goof with him the other day."

"What was that?"

"I didn't reward him for finding Jordan," he said, his voice gruff. "I didn't even think about it."

"You had other matters on your mind."

"I've never, in all my years of training and working with dogs, forgotten to reward one." Her hand closed over his and Luke let the comfort of her presence wash over him. He liked having her with him. She made the burden lighter.

"Don't beat yourself up, Luke. It's not going to ruin Bruno."

"I know, I just..." He shook his head, then met her gaze. "This has thrown me, Sophie, I'll admit it."

She nodded. "I think this has thrown everyone. I know I feel like I've been sucker punched and haven't been able to get my breath back."

"That's the most accurate description I've heard someone come up with. You're right. That's exactly how I feel. Like I haven't been able to take a deep breath since finding Jordan in the—" A memory flashed. "The vehicle at the entrance to the parkway."

"What are you talking about?"

"Maybe nothing, but I'm going to give it a shot." He grabbed his phone and called Dani while Sophie frowned her confusion. "Can you get me the number for whoever's in charge of the park maintenance and operations vehicles?"

"Vanderbilt Parkway?" Dani asked.

"Yes."

"Hold on a sec." Her keyboard clicked. "Walter Love. I'll text you the number."

His phone chimed. "Got it. Thanks."

"You think the person in that vehicle had something to do with Jordan's death?" Sophie asked.

"I don't know, but do you remember seeing it on the surveillance video?"

"No, I don't."

"That's because it was parked away from the parking lot, almost behind the camera." He dialed the number Dani had texted him, identified himself to the person who answered the phone and was put directly through to Walter Love.

"Mr. Love, this is Officer Luke Hathaway. I'm investigating an incident that happened with one of our other officers out at the Vanderbilt Parkway. This morning, there was a maintenance and operations vehicle with a trailer out there and I was wondering if you could tell me who was driving it. I'd like to question him and see if he saw anything that might help us out."

"The guy who was driving it this morning was sent

out to get it because it disappeared from a work site day before yesterday."

"Disappeared?"

Sophie's gaze swiveled to his, her expression questioning.

"Yep. One of my other workers was spreading mulch and took a quick break to run to the restroom. When he came back, the truck and trailer were gone."

Luke raised a brow. "He left the keys in the ignition?"

The man coughed and cleared his throat. "Well, yeah, he did. They're not supposed to, but sometimes our guys leave them running when they're only going to be a couple of minutes—whether it's to grab a snack from a machine or whatever. I have a feeling that things are going to be changing around here after this theft incident—the only one that's ever happened, by the way. Anyway, we looked all over for it and then someone spotted it this morning, so I sent my guy out to get it about the time the cops were pulling in."

"Yeah, I remember seeing him. Listen, can you tell me if there was a wheelbarrow in the back of it?"

"Yep, sure was."

Luke nodded, his pulse pounding a bit faster. "Great. I'm going to have officers who are in close proximity come out there and secure it. Until they get there, I'm going to need you to keep that truck and trailer under lock and key. Make sure no one touches it or uses it anymore."

"Carlos brought it back and parked it before his shift ended this morning. I'll have it secured. No one will touch it until your officers arrive."

"I'll need to speak to Carlos. Is he available?"

"I can have him in the office when you get here, or you can find him at home."

"Are you willing to give me an address over the phone?"

"If it can help catch a killer." Walter rattled it off. Then added Carlos's cell number. "See if he's home. You'll probably wake him up. But if he's not there, he's at the gym."

"Thank you so much." Luke hung up and made the arrangements for local officers and the forensics team to head out to the maintenance garage. He touched base with the other detectives working the case and filled them in. They promised to keep him in the loop if anything was discovered. When he hung up, he turned to Sophie. "I need to make a quick stop before we head back to my place."

"Of course. What's going on?"

He told her everything Walter Love had said.

"And you think Carlos might have seen something?"

"Only one way to find out."

NINE

Carlos had said he'd be home and to come on over. As she and Luke pulled to the curb of an apartment complex, Sophie sighed and rubbed her arms.

The neighborhood park across the street sat empty, devoid of children's laughter and running feet thanks to the recent surge of gang violence in the area. She'd recognized the street name from the case files sitting on Jordan's desk. Sophie shook her head and pursed her lips. Sometimes it seemed as if all of their efforts to fight crime and keep the city safe for the residents were for naught. Then again, what else were they going to do? Sit back and let the bad guys win?

Not hardly. It was an uphill battle, but one that was worth fighting.

Luke let Bruno out of his area and paused to scan his surroundings before coming around to the passenger side and opening her door.

"You see anything?" she asked.

"Nothing out of the ordinary."

He hovered close as he led the way to the glass front door. Since there was no buzzer or gate, he pulled the door open and ushered her inside with a glance back over his shoulder.

"What is it?" she asked. "You're acting nervous."

"Not nervous, just aware. And it's a feeling."

"Of?"

"Being watched, but I don't see anyone."

He'd had a feeling about Jordan, too. She shivered in spite of the warmth of the day and didn't want to admit she was almost surprised no bullets had come their way.

The interior door that led to the elevator required a tenant buzz them in. Luke pressed it. "Officer Luke Hathaway here to see Mr. Hernandez," he said in answer to the greeting.

The door clicked, and Luke pulled it open.

They rode the elevator to the twelfth floor and found apartment 12B. Luke knocked. Footsteps sounded, and the door opened.

"Carlos Hernandez?" Luke asked.

"Sí." Mr. Hernandez stood around six feet tall and had a dark complexion and kind eyes. His jet-black hair was neatly combed, and the pleasant scent of some kind of spicy soap wafted toward her.

Luke introduced them, and Carlos stepped back. "Come in," he said. His light accent held a warm welcome even as his brows dipped in concern. "I am so sorry to hear of the death of Chief Jameson. It's terrible."

"Thank you," Sophie said.

Once they were seated on the sofa under the window, Carlos settled into the recliner opposite them. "What can I do for you?"

"You work the 7 p.m. to 7 a.m. shift, right?" Luke asked.

"Yes, I work on any vehicles that need repairs for the next day."

"Did you see anything last night near the parkway?"

Carlos shook his head. "No, I was in the building all night like usual."

"What about when you went to pick up the truck this morning? The one that had been stolen?"

"No, nothing. I was told the truck was there and to go pick it up and examine it to make sure no damage had been done to it. I got there shortly before the police officers arrived and the keys were in the ignition. I checked the truck over and all seemed to be in order. Then the police started arriving, and I was told to leave the area. So, I did."

Sophie wanted to let out a huge sigh. She hated dead ends.

"But," Carlos said, "the worker who was driving the truck when it was stolen said he searched everywhere for it and couldn't find it. We watched the security footage and saw how the thief left but didn't see how the truck was returned to the property."

"We'll get those pulled and see if our technical analyst can find something. Anything else you can think of?"

"Nothing, I'm sorry. I'm not much help, am I?"

"It's not your fault," Sophie said. "Thank you for speaking with us."

"Of course."

Carlos saw them out of the apartment and they made their way to the elevator once more. Sophie pressed the down button and pointed to the Out of Order sign on the second elevator. "Was that there earlier?"

"I didn't notice."

"Me either." She sighed. And it really didn't matter. "Do you think we'll really find who killed Jordan?" Sophie asked softly. "Time is passing quickly. Just like the longer Jordan was missing, the less likely it was to find him alive. And we didn't. Now, the more time that passes and his killer isn't caught, the more likely it is that he won't be."

"Don't think like that, Sophie. You can't."

"Why? You are."

He cut his eyes at her. "I'm not sure I like that you can read me that well."

"I've had a couple of years to study you."

He raised a brow and shook his head.

"What?" she asked.

"I guess it's just becoming clear to me how closed-minded I can be. I judged you based strictly on your age, not on who you are. I don't really like learning that about myself."

She smiled. "But you're willing to change, right?"

"I'm willing."

The doors slid open and Luke placed his hand at the small of her back to guide her into the elevator. Bruno followed and sat next to Luke even while he nudged her hand for a scratch.

She obliged, thinking about Luke's confession. He'd judged her without knowing her. Well, at least she now knew why he never gave her a second look or bothered to talk about anything besides work.

Once they were on the way down, he got very quiet

and seemed lost in thought. "I still look for my mother's killer."

Her breath caught. "What?"

"I was thinking about Jordan and the fact that his killer is out there somewhere. This is hitting home with me in a way no other case has, and it has to do with my mother's death. It's a long story. I'll tell you about it sometime, but for now, I need to concentrate on getting you back into the car without a sniper taking a shot at you."

His mother's killer? How had she not known about that?

Then again, their conversations for the past few years had been strictly professional and surface-level. Still. She would have thought she'd have heard something in regard to his mother's murder just by being in the office with everyone he worked with and was close to.

Or maybe it was a taboo topic, and everyone respected that.

So, she would, too. She wouldn't speak of it unless he brought it up.

The elevator jerked, and Sophie grabbed the rail to keep from falling to her knees. Luke slipped an arm around her and pulled her against his chest while Bruno barked and lowered himself to the floor.

A loud screech sounded, and the car raced down, then slammed to a stop. Only Luke's grip on her kept her from losing her balance. "What was that? What's going on?" she asked.

He grabbed the phone from the box on the wall and

held it to his ear. Then let go of the handset. "It's not working. Try your cell."

Before she could pull the device from her pocket, the elevator jerked once more into a rapid descent. This time she clutched the rail and sank to the floor. Luke fell beside her, one arm wrapping her tight against him while he held on to the rail with the other.

"Luke!"

The car picked up speed.

Luke's hold tightened. "Hang on!"

Panic attacked her, and she dipped her head against his chest to pray. Then the free fall stopped, yanking the car hard. She slammed against Luke and he fell into the wall. Bruno barked and leaped on top of Luke.

"Why does it keep doing that?" she cried.

"I don't know," he said with a grunt as he moved the dog off of him with a comforting pat, "but the safety features are keeping it from plunging all the way to the ground—and keeping the car from going down as fast as it could—which is why we're not being tossed around like rag dolls. Regardless, we need to get out of here."

"Yes, getting out sounds really good," she said, heart thundering, fear choking her.

While he waited a few seconds as though trying to decide if they were going down again, Sophie dialed 911 with shaking fingers. Luke moved away from her to the doors, slid his fingers into the narrow opening and pulled. Nothing. "Stay on the floor and hold Bruno in case we fall again."

"911. What's your emergency?"

Sophie rattled off the situation.

"What are you going to do?" she whispered to Luke.

He looked up. "I need to find something to pry these doors open with."

Sophie turned her attention back to the dispatcher, who assured her someone was on the way.

The sudden pounding on those doors elicited a squeaky scream from her tight throat before she realized it was someone who might want to help. "We're in here!"

"I'm the building super," the deep bass voice called out. "We're going to get you out. Just hold tight."

"Hold tight," she muttered, but she did dig her fingers into the dog's fur. He licked her face and she settled her forehead against his, still holding the phone while the dispatcher continued to update her as to where the nearest police cruiser was.

The car dropped once more—the high-pitched squealing said the brakes and cables were trying hard to do their job, but something was working against them.

When they finally came to yet another abrupt halt, Luke scrambled to his knees and moved to the door. "Someone's at the control box, trying to override the safety features!"

Sophie stared at him. "You think someone's doing this on purpose?"

"You have a better explanation?"

"But how?"

"He followed us here, knew we'd be on the elevator and decided to take it out with us on it."

"Anyone could have been on it. How would they know when to try to send the car plummeting?"

"All he had to do was watch the floors. When the

elevator was called to the twelfth floor after we'd been up there awhile, he figured it would be us going back down."

"But what if it wasn't?"

"Doesn't matter. It was."

"And he just happened to have an Out of Order sign to make sure we took the right elevator?"

Luke shrugged. "Maybe he saw it somewhere else and grabbed it."

A screech came from the doors. Sophie flinched and ducked, preparing for another drop. When it didn't come, she opened her eyes to see the doors slide open.

A pair of brown eyes stared down at them. "Are you two okay?" the man asked.

Luke grabbed Sophie's hand and Bruno's leash and helped them out of the car. Sophie sank to the floor, not even realizing she was crying.

"I think so," Luke said. "Thanks for coming to the rescue." Luke dropped beside her. "It's okay, Sophie."

"I'm Cliff, the super. She going to be all right?"

"Yes, thanks."

Sophie sniffed. "I'll decide if I'm going to be all right or not, thank you." She pressed her fingers against her eyes. "He could have killed us."

"I think that was the plan, but he wasn't counting on all of the safety features."

"I thought he was bold before," she said, dropping her hands from her face, "snatching me right out of the auditorium, but at least no one else was in danger. This could have seriously hurt someone else." She met his gaze. "You."

"Guy was in the elevator control room like you

thought," Cliff said. "I had one of my workers try to grab him, but the guy fled. I called the cops."

"I called them, too."

His radio crackled, and he listened, then nodded. "Cops are on the way up."

Two uniformed officers arrived and Sophie rubbed her eyes. "He's not going to stop," she told Luke. "He's going to keep trying to get to me until he finally does."

Luke pulled her close. "No way, Sophie. That's not going to happen."

She took comfort in his words even while she wished she could believe them.

The next two hours passed in a blur for Sophie as she gave her statement and learned that a man dressed in a baseball cap and sunglasses had used a gun with a suppressor to shoot out the lock on the elevator control room door, then had done his best to sabotage the car. The only witness was a scared fourteen-year-old girl who saw him do it, then ran to her apartment to tell her mother. After a debate with her husband about whether or not to get involved, the mother had finally called the police.

"We'll get the description out," the young female officer said, "and see if anyone else comes forward. I wouldn't count on it, though. The fact that the mother did is a rare occurrence around here."

And then it was over. Sophie let Luke get her back into the SUV. As though he could sense her distress, Bruno put his head on her shoulder and she gave his ears another scratch.

Luke's mood had taken a turn for the silent and she figured he was probably processing the conversation they'd had with Carlos, not to mention the adventure in the elevator.

She shuddered and refused to think about that. She'd simply do her best to block the entire incident from her mind and if Luke didn't want to talk, she'd think about his previous words. The ones where he mentioned that his mother had been killed—and her killer had never been caught. It was a hard thing to digest, but she knew one thing. Luke was more determined than ever that another killer not go free.

Please, God, let us find the person responsible for Jordan's death.

Because she didn't know how his brothers and Katie would be able to move on without justice for the one they all loved.

TEN

The morning of Jordan's funeral dawned bright and sunny. Sophie would have thought nature was mocking their heavy hearts if she didn't know that Jordan would have chosen a day just like this for his final goodbye.

He'd been a cop and he'd had no problem facing the reality that every day could be his last, but he hadn't been morbid about it. Instead of scowling at the weather for its cheerful disposition, she thanked God for sending it. She chose to believe He'd done so in honor of Jordan.

The twenty-four-seven protection seemed to have staved off any more attacks and while she was grateful for it, it was driving her crazy, too. She wanted her life back. She wanted to wake up and realize everything was just a nightmare and Jordan wasn't really dead.

She sighed and pressed fingers to her eyes. She needed to stop wishing for the impossible and deal with reality, no matter how much she was struggling.

And then there was the fact that she couldn't dispel the guilt of taking over Sam's bedroom, but for the life of her, she couldn't figure out what to do about it. Sam had come home and taken the couch or used David's room when the other man was gone. Both men were gracious and welcoming, never making her feel like an interloper. Unfortunately, her situation was what it was for the time being.

"So, quit thinking about it," she said. But honestly, she'd rather think about that than what lay ahead.

The funeral.

Jordy's funeral.

She grabbed her phone and texted her dad. You and Trey okay?

Her phone buzzed, but it wasn't her father answering. Katie had texted. Sit with me today, please. With the family. If you're comfortable doing that.

Her poor, heartbroken friend. Sophie texted back. Of course. I'd be honored.

And she would be. While she styled her hair for the funeral, her mind tumbled back to that conversation with Luke as they'd left Carlos's home. Luke's mother had been murdered and he still hadn't told her how or when. She could do the digging on the story herself, but she wanted to hear it from him.

Over the last three days, he'd stayed busy while keeping her near. However, he'd seemed to pull away, distancing himself from her emotionally and she wasn't sure why. As a result, they'd had very little time to talk about anything not related to the case. Or Jordan's funeral.

He'd tell her when he was ready. Obviously, he wasn't there yet.

Her phone vibrated.

We're fine, Sophie. You just take care of yourself right now. Give my regards to the Jamesons and tell them I'm sorry I won't be able to be there. I can't get off of work.

They'll understand. It's okay. You need anything?

Nothing. Love you, hon.

You too, Dad.

Maybe her father wasn't as helpless as she'd thought.

A text from Trey. What kind of fabric softener do we use?

But Trey was. She answered him and he, too, expressed his sorrow for the Jameson family.

With one last push on a bobby pin that held her hair in a bun, she started when a shadow outside the window caught her eye. The motion jerked her hair down, ruining the work she'd put into creating the professional bun.

Sheer curtains covered the windows, but the way the sun was shining, she could make out the silhouette of someone wearing a baseball cap standing just outside her bedroom.

She strode forward to the side of the window and threw aside the fabric. The person stumbled back, caught his balance and took off.

"Luke!"

Her cry brought him running. "What is it?"

"Someone was outside the window! He just ran off."

Luke whirled and headed for the front door. "Stay here."

Pressing a hand against her chest as though it would help calm her racing heart, Sophie peered out the window to see Luke step into her line of sight, weapon held in his right hand. She waited, watching him search the area, ready to leap out the window to offer whatever meager assistance she could if it appeared he needed it.

It didn't take him long to finish searching the yard. He even went out the back gate to check. Having him out of her line of sight didn't sit well with her, and she was on the verge of going after him when he stepped back into the yard and shut the gate behind him. He looked up and caught her eye. With a shake of his head, he walked toward the door.

Trembling, she checked the lock on the window, grateful to find it securely in place.

Several heart-thumping seconds passed before the sound of the front door opening sent her hurrying from the bedroom to find Luke tucking his weapon back into his holster. Bruno flopped onto the kitchen floor.

"Did you see him?" she asked.

"No. I saw his footprints, though."

Sophie pressed her palms to her eyes. "I think it was the same guy who kidnapped me from headquarters. It looked like the same ball cap."

"Okay, I guess this guy is back. He might have been watching the place trying to get you alone."

"But you're here."

"I went out the front door a little while ago to take Bruno for a quick walk just as David was leaving for work. I knew you would be all right. I didn't come back in the front. I took a shortcut through the back and came in that way."

"So anyone watching the house would have seen both of you leave," Sophie said, "not realizing you'd come back in, and thought I was here alone."

"Exactly."

"That's just awesome." Her tone clearly conveyed that it was anything but. "I'm going to go fix my hair again, then I'm going to need some coffee."

"I'm going to change out of these sweats and I'll meet you in the kitchen."

Fifteen minutes later, she returned to the kitchen to find Luke sitting at the table sipping coffee. Bruno lay stretched on his side, eyes at half-mast. At her entrance, his ears twitched, and his tail thumped once as though saying, "Welcome back." Then his eyes shut, and a light snore reached her.

Her gaze snagged Luke's and her breath stilled in her lungs. Dressed in his ceremonial blues, he was incredibly handsome. Although the days had passed in a blur of work, the evenings had been spent talking. About everything and nothing. Certainly not his mother's death. However, they *had* discovered a mutual love of Scrabble and chess, and so far were neck and neck on wins and losses.

And yet, even with the competition and light laughter as they played and teased one another, she couldn't help feeling like Luke was holding a piece of himself back. Like he felt like he had to keep her at arm's length. She didn't like it but wasn't sure what to do about it. Or if there even was anything she *could* do.

"Sophie?" Luke raised a brow.

"Sorry. I was just thinking." Ignoring the flush creeping into her cheeks, she grabbed a mug and placed the coffee pod into the maker and shut the lid.

"Are you okay?"

"As okay as I can be. I can't believe we'll bury our boss today. It's surreal."

"I know. Did you get some sleep at least?" he asked.

"Not really."

"Yeah."

The wealth of understanding in his voice vaporized all thoughts of her crazy attraction to the man and the fact that she knew he was attracted to her even though he was fighting it.

Today was about Jordy, not about what was possibly developing between her and Luke. "Katie texted me," she said. "She wants me to sit with the family."

"That doesn't surprise me. She thinks of you as a sister."

Sophie nodded. The tightness in her throat blocked any words she might have.

He stood and wrapped his arms around her, his lips next to her ear. "It's okay, Sophie."

"What is?" For the moment, his barriers were down and she closed her eyes, allowing herself to take comfort in his embrace.

"The fact that we want to smile. Or laugh. Don't feel guilty because you have flashes of joy."

His spot-on assessment of her feelings sent her emotions reeling. The fact that he was willing to go that deep into a conversation gave her hope. "My mind knows you're right. Maybe after the funeral—or after we find his killer—my heart will allow the smiles and laughter without the accompanying guilt."

"It'll come," he said, stepping back. "It may take a while, but it'll come."

"You speak from experience."

"Yes."

"Tell me." She'd vowed not to bring it up but felt compelled to do so.

He stared into his coffee as though he'd find the answer. Sophie stayed still, sensing if she moved, the moment would vanish.

"My mother was killed when I was eight years old," he finally said. "I know I mentioned it. I'm sorry I haven't explained sooner. The truth is I hate talking about it. Because with the telling and remembering, the grief and regret comes back."

"What happened?" she asked softly.

"A carjacking." His words, so quiet they barely reached her ears, held a wealth of emotion.

"Oh, Luke," she whispered. "I'm so sorry. How awful."

"I was at a martial arts class one evening. I was at the dojo five days a week for their after-school program and I loved it because I got to take karate, too. I saw Mom drive up on time like always, but I wasn't ready to leave yet because I had a belt test coming up the next day and wanted to go through the forms one more time. So, I pretended I didn't see her."

"What happened?"

"Halfway through my routine, a loud crack broke through my concentration. I spun to see a man in a ski mask pull my mother from the driver's seat and throw her to the asphalt." He pressed fingers to his eyes. "He got in the car and drove off, leaving my mother dying on the ground. He'd shot her in the head. She'd lowered her window because it was a beautiful fall evening, her favorite time of year. And he just walked up and shot her." He lowered his hand from his eyes and looked at her. "If I hadn't made her wait, if I had walked out of there on time, we would have left and she would still be alive."

"You were a kid, Luke," Sophie said, covering his hand with hers. "You can't shoulder that blame. That belongs to the man who killed her."

He offered her a small sad smile. "I know. Mentally, I do. I just…" He shook his head. "I've been thinking about her a lot since we found Jordan."

"Because her killer was never found?"

"Yeah." He stood and dumped the remainder of his coffee in the sink, then turned. "I can't let another killer get away, Sophie, I can't."

"We won't," she said, her words a promise. "We won't."

ELEVEN

Luke gave himself a mental shake. Once again, he'd spilled his guts about a topic he never talked about. And spilled them all over Sophie. A woman he was extremely attracted to and needed to keep his distance from. Emotionally, if not physically since he was determined to protect her. And yet, he couldn't seem to rein in his tongue. She was such a good, active listener that he could almost feel her compassion soothing his wounded childhood self. It was like he craved that.

Well, it had to stop. Period. "Are you ready? I don't want to be late." She flinched at his snapped words and he cleared his throat. "Sorry. I'm just... I didn't mean to be abrupt. I'm sorry."

Sophie stood. "It's okay, Luke. We're all on edge. Let's go."

With Bruno in his area and Sophie once again in the passenger seat, Luke started the vehicle and headed for the church. His eyes alternated between the road and the rearview mirror. The fact that someone had been at her window—and *knew* that it was hers—had his nerves on edge. Sophie's, too, apparently, as he caught her watching the mirrors, as well. Good. She needed to be on guard.

When they turned into the parking lot, it was already overflowing with cars parked anywhere they could find a spot. Police cars and SUVs lined one side of the lot and down the street and around the block. News helicopters cluttered the air, sharing space with the police choppers.

"I've been to more police funerals than I would like to remember, but I've never seen a turnout like this. Are there any officers left to guard the city?" she asked. Her wide eyes bounced from one area to the next.

He smiled. At least he hoped it was a smile. "Plenty." She knew it as well as he, but he had to admit that it looked like every officer in the state had come out to pay their respects to a man who had sparked admiration in each person he'd ever met or worked with.

"Do you think he's here?" she asked. "The person who killed him?"

Instant tension threaded across his shoulders and the base of his neck. "It's definitely possible."

"Have you heard anything more about what killed him? I know the toxicology report won't be back for a while, but it seems like there should be some kind of news."

"That was Elena on the phone earlier, calling to tell me her initial assessment that his death is somehow related to his heart was correct, but that's pretty much all she can tell us right now."

Sophie sighed. "I want answers, and I want them yesterday."

"We all do." She was stalling. Asking questions she already knew the answers to. He didn't blame her, but… "We have to go in, Sophie."

With her eyes on the front door of the large church, she gave a short nod. "I know."

"Sitting here dreading it isn't going to make it any easier."

"I know that, too."

"Then I'm going to pull as close as I can to the back door, let Bruno out, and come around and open your door. Once you're safely inside with some officer friends, I'll move the SUV and join you. Bruno can stay with you until I return and then we'll find Katie and the others."

"You think he would take a shot at me here?"

"I'm not putting anything past this guy."

She nodded. "Okay. Thanks. I'm ready."

Once she was inside, Luke parked and returned to find her right where he'd left her. With three other K-9 officers and Bruno standing guard. She sent him a small, tight smile when he stepped through the door, and he gave a nod of thanks to the other officers. Cupping her elbow, he escorted Sophie to the front row and seated her next to Katie.

Katie's gaze met his. "Thank you, Luke."

He hugged her. "I'm so sorry, Katie. I can't even tell you how sorry."

"You don't have to."

The brothers nodded, and six-year-old Ellie sat in Carter's lap, holding her father's hand and looking confused with the whole proceeding.

When Katie reached over to grasp Sophie's hand,

Luke swallowed hard, clicked to Bruno and took his place, back against the wall so he had a good view of the room. He stood next to Gavin Sutherland and his K-9, Tommy. The dog glanced at him then settled his snout on his front paws.

"Hey, man," Gavin said. "Wondered if you were going to make it on time."

"Had to make a special delivery first."

"Sophie?"

"Yeah."

The music started, and they fell silent, but Luke's thoughts continued to swirl even as his eyes landed on the coffin at the front. Instantly, his throat went tight, and he noticed he wasn't the only officer in the room desperately fighting to keep his emotions under control.

Luke looked away, focused his mind elsewhere even as the soloist hit each note with a purity that sent chills down his spine.

Or were the chills from the fact that he couldn't be sure someone hadn't followed them to the church? Then again, someone wouldn't have to follow them. It wouldn't take a genius to figure out where they'd be. Where Sophie would be. But would someone really be brazen enough to try to attack her in the middle of a funeral with hundreds of cops around? Maybe. If he thought he could stay hidden—or escape in the midst of the chaos it would generate. Luke thought the last one might be the key.

He could see the back of Sophie's head from his stance against the wall. And if he could see it, so could everyone else. It just occurred to him that the balcony would be the perfect spot for a sniper to draw a bead on Sophie's carefully pinned bun.

Sophie held Katie's hand through the service, barely registering the songs or the message. Memories of Jordan spun through her mind like a movie reel set to the greatest hits. Fun times, his laughter, his love. So much love. For his job, his family, the people who worked for him, the dogs...and most of all, for Katie and his unborn child.

But second only to Katie and his family were his love of justice and his desire to right the wrongs perpetrated on others. Sophie ground her molars to keep her tears at bay.

Justice.

The word seared itself into her heart. "We'll get you justice, Jordan," she whispered. "We will."

Katie's hand squeezed hers, and Sophie realized she'd spoken the words aloud.

And then the church service was over. Now she had to make it through the graveside part without having a complete meltdown. But if Katie could do it, so could she.

The family stood and filed from the church. It was just a short drive to the cemetery and for a moment Sophie and the family were the only ones outside at the gravesite as they waited for the limos to pull around.

The hair on her neck prickled and she swept her gaze around the area before landing on the lone figure leaning against one of the large mausoleums. Sunglasses covered his eyes and he had a baseball cap pulled low.

She gasped and stumbled to a halt.

Katie stopped, too. "Are you okay?"

Sophie glanced at her friend, then back at the spot where she'd seen the man.

Only to find it empty.

"What is it?" Zach asked. Carter and Noah shot her concerned looks.

Chills danced over her skin in spite of the warm weather. "Nothing," she said slowly. "I'm okay. I just thought I saw the guy who'd kidnapped me over by the tree, but he's not there now."

"Someone we need to be watchful of or worried about?" Katie asked, her red-rimmed eyes narrowing.

"I'm not sure." Her friend had enough to worry about and the last thing she wanted to do was to take attention away from Jordan. Not today. She rubbed Katie's shoulder and shot Jordy's brothers a tense smile. "It's probably nothing but my recent paranoia. Please, let's keep going."

"No," Zach said, "we'll check it out. They won't start the service without us."

He and Carter took off to check out the area while Noah stood guard next to them.

The minutes stretched. Finally, Noah and Carter returned, mouths tight. Noah shook his head. "We didn't see any sign of anyone, but that doesn't mean he wasn't there."

"Let's keep going," Noah said. "Everyone's on the alert."

Katie nodded, and they all fell silent.

Ellie stepped up to her and slipped her small hand into Sophie's. "My uncle Jordy died, Ms. Sophie."

"I know, honey."

"He's in heaven. Daddy said he's with my mom."

Sophie could only nod, her throat tight. "Yes. I know he's in heaven. He loved God very much."

"I do, too. I'm going to heaven when I die."

"Well, hopefully, that won't be for a very long time."

And now, Sophie couldn't help wondering if she was putting the family in danger just by being at the service. She turned to Carter and gave him the little girl's hand. He raised a brow, but she shook her head.

The limos finally pulled to a stop next to them and Katie slid in the back seat. Sophie joined her. While the others' attention was diverted as they loaded into the vehicles, Sophie leaned over to her friend. "I think I should leave," she whispered.

"Leave? Why?"

"I don't want to put any of you in danger by being close to you. Someone is after me." She swallowed. "And I don't think he cares who he hurts. I also don't want to be the cause of any disruptions on this day."

Katie linked her arm through Sophie's. "You're not going anywhere." Her eyes narrowed. "If Jordan's killer is here, then he's going to see that we have you surrounded and he's going to have to go through us to get to you. He's not getting another one of us." She kept her voice low, but her vehemence came through loud and clear.

Insisting she leave would only cause Katie more distress so all Sophie could do was nod and squeeze her friend's hand. And then the limos were pulling up next to the two tents.

The first one held a K-9 SUV like the one Jordan had driven. Covered in roses, it was a stark reminder that her friend would never again climb behind the wheel. The second tent held several rows of chairs for the family. Jordan's casket had been wheeled front and center.

Sophie tightened her lips and darted frantic glances around the scene. Where was Luke? As part of Jordan's unit, he should be near the family during the next part of the service.

She stepped under the tent and sat in the end row seat so that Katie could sit next to her mother-in-law followed by Jordan's father and brothers. As soon as they were all seated, a soulful bagpipe solo started, the clear mournful notes of "Amazing Grace" lifting and sweeping around her, causing that ever-present tension in her throat to grow into a near-strangling lump.

Sophie lifted her gaze to the coffin directly in front of her and swallowed hard, hoping the knot would lessen while refusing to let the tears fall. She blinked and drew in a deep breath, needing her vision clear.

Surrounded by police officers, she should be able to focus on being there for Katie and getting through the day without a complete meltdown, but her nerves wouldn't settle. That feeling of being watched crept over her once more and she started studying faces, trying to catch the eyes of whoever seemed to be triggering the sensation. No one stood out and she shook her head, wondering if she truly was just being paranoid. Not that she didn't have reason to be.

And yet there was nothing she could see that should have her nerves gathered so tight. It was what she couldn't see that worried her.

When Jordan's family was seated, the others gathered around the tent, forming a protective circle around them just as the song faded to a doleful end.

The only sounds were the occasional cough, sniff or shuffle from those attending.

Once again, Sophie swept the crowd and easily found Luke about ten yards away in the line of blue. No blending in for him. Everything about him stood out to her. Sorrow and grief had etched his face into hard lines, but his chin jutted, and his shoulders never sagged. She drew comfort from his strength.

His gaze locked on hers and his brow rose as though asking her if she was all right. She gave a slight nod. He returned it.

The rest of the service passed in a blur only to come into sharp focus when everyone fell into an expectant hush.

Sophie's gut twisted. She wasn't ready for this part.

The final call.

Radio static sounded over the loudspeakers and a sob slipped from Katie's lips. Sophie reached over to clasp her friend's hand as dispatch came on.

"Central to Officer 75990."

Silence. Waiting.

"Central to Officer 75990."

More silence. More waiting for the answer that would never come again.

"Chief Jordan Jameson, please respond."

Tears flowed freely now for Sophie. She simply couldn't control them. Katie's grip tightened.

"Chief Jameson," dispatch said, "no response. Officer 75990, Jordan Jameson, is end of watch. He has gone home for the final time."

A long, loud beep resembling that of a flatlining patient pierced the air. Gasping sobs came from all directions.

Then dispatch finished the End of Watch Call by saying, "Chief Jameson, the city of New York and the K-9 unit thank you for your service and your sacrifices. May you rest in peace with your eternal Savior. We will miss you."

Sophie thought the dispatcher may have smothered a sob on the last word.

More radio static. More muffled sounds of grief.

Then a heavy, misery-laden silence surrounded them, pressing in on her. Sophie likened it to suffocating. Could one actually die from grief? She drew in a deep breath and used the tissues she finally remembered she had to wipe her cheeks.

The bagpipes broke into the stillness once more and the strands of "It Is Well with My Soul" nearly undid her.

She couldn't do this. Jordy had been her friend, her boss, her support when she'd needed it. He'd given a green kid fresh out of college a chance because he said he saw great potential in her. He'd believed in her like her own father and it had left a permanent impression on her heart.

"I know he's with you, God, but we're going to miss him like crazy," she whispered so low not even Katie noticed.

Luke's gaze touched hers again and for a moment, it was just the two of them, drawn together by their shared sorrow, somehow finding strength in the visual connection.

When the song ended, Zach stood and walked toward the podium. His jaw like granite, he looked out over those who'd come to say goodbye to Jordan.

Sophie swallowed and glanced around, still on edge after seeing the man in front of the mausoleum.

"I have a lot of memories of Jordan," Zach said. "Good times, bad times, crazy times. Times we swore each other to secrecy over. But one memory that stands out the most is… Well, Jordy's the reason I'm a cop." His voice broke and he took a moment to gather his composure. "You see, I'm dyslexic, which means school was never fun for me, but I graduated high school and decided to go to the police academy. About halfway through it, I was ready to give up."

Sophie stared. Oh, how she could relate.

"But Jordy wouldn't let me." Zach cleared his throat again and drew in another steadying breath. "He helped me study, he figured out how to channel my attention by using short spurts of study time followed by some kind of exercise. Whether it was running with the dogs or going to get ice cream." A tear slipped down his cheek and dripped off his chin. He looked up. "Jordy was one of the most unselfish people I've ever met. Even as a kid, he always put others first."

Sophie's heart thudded even harder, beating in sympathy with the man whose struggles had been her own. No wonder she'd been so drawn to Jordan, looking up to him like she had her own father. He'd done for Zach what her dad had done for her—and she now understood why he never mentioned any mistakes she made in her scribbled notes. She clutched her tissue.

To her left, someone coughed. Then coughed again.

Sophie saw the woman slip a cough drop into her mouth, then whisper something to the man next to her. She turned to leave, weaving her way toward the back.

The movement distracted Sophie, and she found her eyes drawn to another man in the crowd. She paused, letting her gaze linger. He reminded her of the man she'd seen near the mausoleum. The one who'd kidnapped her. But no, that couldn't be him. Could it? The man she'd seen had been wearing sunglasses and that hideous baseball cap.

This guy was wearing a navy blazer, but no ball cap even though he had on sunglasses—like so many of the men standing outside the tent in the direct sunlight. But for some reason she thought he watched her from a small opening in the mass of bodies. At first, she was unsure why she was so leery of him.

Until he turned his head slightly and she caught a glimpse of his profile. She sucked in a breath. It was the man from the podium. The man who'd been by the mausoleum—the same profile she'd stared at when she'd been in the passenger seat of his speeding car.

She swung her gaze back to Luke.

TWELVE

Luke frowned. Something was wrong. Sophie looked ready to burst from her seat. She slid her gaze from his to her left. Then back to him. Then to her left and back to him.

She was trying to tell him something. And it was urgent.

The next time she slid her eyes to the left, he followed her line of sight. And there was the man who'd kidnapped her from the auditorium. While the family sat, there was standing room only for the others—a wall of bodies surrounding the family. Luke didn't miss the symbolic gesture. Nor did he miss the fact that the man had started moving, slowly slipping through the spaces until he was about ten yards away from Sophie. And then he paused glancing at the podium, acting as though he belonged there.

Luke held still even though the man didn't notice him. What did the guy think he was going to do? Grab her with hundreds of officers around?

Or simply shoot her where she sat and run?

Impossible. He'd be caught immediately. Then what?

The guy turned his gaze back to Sophie. Watching her. Waiting? For what?

For the right moment that he could reach her. For the break in the crowd that would allow him to act.

Luke nudged Finn. When the man leaned in, Luke said, "That's the guy who kidnapped Sophie the other day. I don't know what he's doing here, but it can't be good."

"Here?" Finn placed a hand on his weapon.

"I don't want to disrupt Jordan's funeral, but we may have to."

"See if you can get between him and Sophie," Gavin said. "I'll go behind him."

As one, they began to move, the dogs staying at their respective sides. They drew some notice as well as frowns, but Luke ignored them, his focus on the man whose attention hadn't swerved from Sophie. The service was coming to an end. Soon, people would begin milling, the crowd would pack in around the family—and Sophie. When would he make his move? Luke played out several possible scenarios even while he rushed to prevent it. Shoot her? Too obvious. Stab her? Quiet and easy but might not provide him with the ability to get away. Then what?

Sitting on the end of the front row, Sophie would be easier to get to than if she'd been in the middle. Or on the back row where the crowd offered a buffer against anyone approaching from the rear.

The need to reach her pushed him faster—which was like trying to hurry through quicksand. The crowd was thick but thankfully not packed tight. Still, it made rushing impossible. For a moment, he lost sight of the man. His attire allowed him to blend in easily.

"He lived well," Zach was saying from the podium. "He knew how to have fun and he knew when to be serious. He was a shining example for all of us who loved him and looked up to him. Despite what the newspapers are reporting, Jordan did not kill himself. He was murdered, and you'd better believe that my family will do whatever it takes to bring his killer to justice." Zach's grief-ravaged voice rose in his passion to convey his feelings about his brother.

*Amen*s echoed through the crowd and Zach nodded to the minister, who returned to the podium to start the closing prayer.

Luke listened with half an ear as he once more caught sight of the man stalking Sophie. Still far enough away, but closing in.

Then the service was over, and people stood. Luke maneuvered Bruno so he could slip between Sophie and the man who'd just now noticed him.

With a scowl, the guy froze, spun and started weaving back through the crowd. Luke gripped Sophie's arm. "Stay with Katie and the family." Then he was on his radio, giving a description of the fleeing man. Officers immediately responded, but Luke had lost sight of him. He radioed in the last place he'd seen him even as he continued to follow in that general direction.

Finn closed in behind Luke. "There!" Luke caught a glimpse of a figure heading toward a line of vehicles at a fast jog. Something fell from his navy blue blazer just before he slipped around a massive mausoleum and disappeared. Other officers raced past Luke, who drew to a stop and knelt.

A syringe.

Meant for Sophie, no doubt. Well, that explained his attempt to get as close as possible. And he would have if she hadn't spotted him.

Gavin reached him. "What is it?"

"Do you have an evidence bag on you?"

"No. I'll get one." Gavin hurried off, his K-9, Tommy, loping along beside him.

Luke's radio crackled, and Finn's voice came through. "We lost him. He jumped onto the back of a motorcycle and sped off. We've got it called in and they're sending a chopper to look for him."

"Ten-four."

When Gavin returned with the bag and a pair of gloves, Luke collected the syringe, dropped it in the bag, then sealed it. He pulled a pen from his vest and labeled the bag.

"Was he wearing gloves?" Gavin asked.

"I don't know. I didn't get close enough to see." Luke met Gavin's eyes. "He was trying to get close enough to inject her. It's quiet, subtle. A quick sting. And she might not have realized what happened right away."

"Giving him time to slip away, blending in just like he did anyway."

"Yeah. At least Sophie was spared, though." A shudder ripped through him. Handing the bag to Gavin, he said, "I'm going to get back to Sophie. I don't think that guy will show himself again today, but I don't want to take a chance on being wrong."

Gavin glanced at the evidence bag. "Sure. I'll just get this sent off to the lab."

That reminded Luke he still hadn't heard if any prints had been found in Sophie's apartment. He made a mental note to check on that tomorrow and clicked to Bruno. "Heel, boy."

The dog rolled to his feet in an agile move and slipped up next to Luke's left side. When Luke returned to the tent, Katie and Sophie were wrapped in a hug. He stepped up beside them and Sophie's eyes met his, but her words were for Katie.

"You promise to call me if you need anything?"

"I promise. Now that Jordan's parents are here, I promise not to be so clingy."

"You're a far cry from clingy," Sophie told her friend. "You know I don't mind helping or just sitting. Or whatever."

"I know," Katie said softly. "Thank you."

Carter approached, his eyes and nose red, but his jaw firm. "We're going to Griffin's," he told Luke. "In honor of Jordan. He'd insist on it."

Griffin's Diner was owned by Louis and Barbara Griffin. Since they served top-notch food and had a premium location near the K-9 Headquarters, it hadn't taken long for it to become *the* hangout for officers and their dogs. Thanks to the Griffins' love of all things law enforcement, they'd built a specific area called the Dog House. Officers could eat in that area with their K-9s without the restaurant being in any violation of health codes.

Luke nodded. "Sophie, that all right with you?"

"Sure. Carter's right. Jordan would insist."

"We'll meet you there."

When they all walked into Griffin's, Sophie noticed every eye in the place turned to them. "We'll be in the Dog House, Lou," Carter said, his voice rough.

"Violet'll be right out," Lou said. "Sorry I couldn't make it to the service."

"It's okay," Luke said, shaking the man's hand. "We understand. And so would Jordan."

"Yeah." The man's nose reddened and he turned away. "Free burgers in the Dog House!" His holler carried to the back.

"Dog House burgers coming up!" The cook's answer had Lou nodding.

"For Jordan," he told Luke.

Sophie cleared her throat and hurried to find a seat before she burst into tears. Coming here was a mistake. Jordan had loved this place, and his presence practically bounced off the walls. The Griffins had dedicated this room to fallen NYPD officers—many of them K-9 handlers and K-9s themselves. Bruno had been named for Alan Brunowski, killed in the line of duty. The officer's picture hung on the wall opposite the chair she slid into.

Luke seated himself next to her. "You okay?" he asked softly.

"What was he doing there?" she asked, her voice equally low. When Luke didn't answer right away, she nudged him. "Luke?"

"He was up to no good, let's put it that way."

"He was coming back for me, I suppose?"

"Looks like it. You're the one who saw him at the podium. He obviously thinks you can identify him."

"But you can, too."

"I'm not sure he realized that. Before now anyway. You can better believe I'll be watching my back from now on, though."

"Good." She nodded and sighed. "Well, thank you for keeping me safe from him."

He sighed as Carter, Noah and Zach settled their dogs, then took their seats at a nearby table. Luke shot her a tight smile and squeezed her hands. "Let's forget about him for now. You're safe here."

She swallowed and picked up the menu she didn't need to look at. "You're not telling me everything." She paused. "Was he going to shoot me? Strangle me? What?"

"Inject you," Luke said. "He had a syringe and it fell out of his pocket when he was running away. We sent it off to the lab so, hopefully, we'll know something soon."

She flinched. Well, she'd asked. "Thank you. I want to know everything. At least the stuff that pertains to me. It's the only way I feel like I can be prepared for… whatever." Sophie held his gaze. "Promise me."

He gave a slow nod. "Okay."

"You two telling secrets?" Reed Branson asked. Reed was tall with dark brown hair and eyes. Part of the K-9 unit, he and his bloodhound partner, Jessie, like Finn and Abernathy, could track just about anything. Reed, Brianne, Tony, Finn and Gavin rounded out Luke and Sophie's table.

"No secrets," Luke answered. "Just discussing something that *pertains* to Sophie."

"Hi, everyone," a voice next to Sophie said. She looked up to see Violet Griffin, daughter of Louis and Barb, standing behind her, notepad ready to take their drink order. The burgers would be free, but they'd pay for anything extra. Violet had her long curly brown hair pulled into a ponytail. Her dark eyes were cast slightly over her shoulder to rest on Zach, who was seated behind Sophie. "I'm so sorry about Jordan."

"Thanks, Violet," Luke said.

Violet's gaze continued to linger on Zach for a few more seconds before turning her attention back to them. "I'm really worried how his death is going to affect Zach," she said, keeping her voice low. "He and Jordan were really close."

"The Jamesons are strong people," Luke said. "They'll stick together and get through this as a family."

"Of course. Sorry. I guess it's really not my business." Her gaze slid back to Zach, then she bit her lip and shook her head. "So, what can I get everyone to drink?"

Sophie raised a brow but ordered a water with lemon without commenting.

Luke and the others gave their requests, then Luke tilted his head and asked, "How's the airport business?"

Violet's lips curved. "It's going well. There's never a dull moment and it keeps me on my toes, that's for sure."

"Oh, that's right," Sophie said. "I always just see you in here. I forget that you work at the airport, too."

Violet's full-time job as a ticket agent at the airport kept her busy. But when her hours allowed, she could be found helping at the restaurant.

Violet shrugged. "It pays the bills, but I can't seem to completely give up working here. I love the customers and Mom and Dad need the help. Plus, it helps pay for the night class I signed up for."

"Night classes, too?" Sophie said. "Wow, you're incredibly busy."

"I like it that way, I guess."

"Doesn't leave much time for a social life, does it?" Luke asked.

Once again, Violet's gaze slipped to Zach. "No, not much of one, but that's okay. Maybe one day things will change."

"Maybe."

"Hey, Sophie," Gavin said, "I heard about the dog coming from the Czech Republic. She's supposed to be getting here soon, isn't she?"

"Any day now." Sophie sighed. "She's a Labrador retriever, and her name is Stella. Jordan was instrumental in getting her here because of a favor he did for the prime minister when he and his family were visiting last summer."

"What kind of favor?" Brianne asked. "How'd I miss that?"

"Jordan kept it quiet, but the PM's daughter went missing for a short time. She snuck away from her security detail. Jordan and Snapper tracked her down." She sighed. "I hate that he's not going to be here to see Stella arrive." The table fell silent and Sophie cleared her throat. "Sorry, I didn't mean to…" What could she say?

"No, it's okay," Luke said. "We're going to talk about Jordan and remember him. He'd want that. And Stella… Well, she's going to generate quite a bit of publicity for the department, so we definitely have to put our best foot forward."

"And make Jordan proud," Sophie said softly.

"Exactly."

"Brianne's going to be working with her." Sophie smiled at the woman. Brianne's big brown eyes gleamed with anticipation at the thought of the challenge. "I know you'll have her working right up there with the best of them in no time."

"That's the plan."

While Luke ate, he observed Sophie from the corner of his eye. She might be young, but she was strong. And pretty. And smart. And—

And nothing. As long as he was her protector, she was off-limits. Not to mention the fact that she was so much younger than he. Only that didn't seem to be such a big deal anymore. But it should, right?

"Everyone okay here?" Violet asked. She refilled glasses while she spoke. "Can I get anyone anything? Dessert?"

Groans answered her.

She laughed and left to wait on the next table—the one where Zach sat—and Finn pushed his silverware to the side. He leaned forward. "So."

Everyone looked at him. "So…what?" Luke asked.

"This might sound a bit crass to bring up now, but

it needs to be addressed at some point. Who do you think will take Jordan's place?"

The table fell silent.

"I think that's a good question," Gavin said.

"Probably one of Jordan's brothers, I would think," Reed said. "Noah or Carter would do an excellent job. They both have been around awhile and have some seniority."

Gavin huffed a short laugh and shook his head.

"What?" Luke asked.

Sophie's gaze bounced from one to the other, landing on Gavin, who looked aggravated and hesitant to say anything all at the same time. "What is it, Gavin?" she asked.

"Nothing."

"Something," Brianne said. "What? You think you should get the job?"

Gavin shrugged, but his eyes narrowed. "If you're going by seniority, we all know that I have it."

Brianne gave a light snort. "You're just sore that Jordan beat you out for the position when you were both after it at the same time."

"Disappointed," Gavin said softly. "Not sore. There's a difference." His gaze connected with Brianne's for a moment and Sophie blinked.

Tony Knight slapped the table and they all jumped.

Sophie jerked her gaze from Gavin and Brianne and placed a hand over her heart. "Tony? You okay?"

"No. I'm not okay. Jordan's not buried an hour and you guys are quibbling over who's going to take his job. It's disrespectful…and distasteful." He lasered Gavin with a red-hot look. "Today, of all days, you can't give your ego a rest?"

Gavin sighed and shook his head. "It's not about ego, man, I just—"

"I don't think anyone meant to be disrespectful," Sophie interrupted. "Tony, I know you and Jordan were best friends and it's hard to think about him not being there in the office. Joining us here at Griffin's." She looked away and swallowed. "But the fact remains, his position will need to be filled. And quickly. As much as Jordan loved this unit and everyone in it, he would want us to think about it and make sure the unit is protected and nothing falls through the cracks."

"She's right," Luke said.

Murmured agreements swept around the table.

Tony sighed and raked a hand over his head. "You're right, Sophie, but first and foremost, I think we need to stay focused on finding Jordan's killer. Let the powers-that-be trouble themselves with a replacement while we keep our tunnel vision on this investigation."

More nods and agreeing.

Luke pulled his phone from his pocket. "I keep meaning to check on your apartment investigation and if they found any prints."

Finn frowned. "How are you doing, Sophie? We've been so focused on Jordan and Katie that I feel like we're neglecting your issues."

"You're not ignoring them at all," she said. "I'm not going to say I'm doing okay, but I'm doing as well as can be expected, I suppose." Her phone buzzed. A quick glance at the screen confirmed it was her father. "I need to answer this. Excuse me, please."

"Of course."

Sophie slipped away from the table and into the quieter area near the restrooms. "Hi, Dad."

"I'm just checking on you. How was the funeral?"

"About like what you would expect. Sad. Devastating. Hopeful in that we know we'll see him again in heaven one day."

"Yeah."

"How are things with you?" She could hear traffic in the background.

"I'm fine. Your brother called me a little while ago."

She stilled. "Okay."

"He's enlisted."

"He really did it?" So, he'd gone from buying fabric softener to enlisting in the Marines?

"Yes."

Sophie rubbed her eyes before remembering she had makeup on. She dropped her hand and let out a long, slow sigh. "Okay, well, I guess it's his life." Did those words really come out of her mouth?

"That's what he says." Her dad sounded as surprised as she felt, but she didn't have the energy to do anything about it. "But enough about him," her father said. "I want to know about you. Did anyone ever find who it was that called the house looking for you? And the person who broke into it?"

"Not yet. I think they tried to track the call, but whoever it was used a burner phone. As for whoever broke into the place, that's still being investigated. So far, they haven't found anything." She paused. "You haven't had any more trouble, have you? Something you're not telling me?" She frowned, concerned he was keeping something from her.

"Not a bit. I guess the police car on the house is an effective deterrent."

Either that or the person was keeping up with her and realized she wasn't going anywhere near her father or brother, so why bother with them?

"I'm glad."

"And no one is bothering you?"

"I'm fine." It wasn't an outright lie. Her dad didn't need to know about the man at the funeral or anything else. He'd just worry, and she didn't want to do anything to send his anxiety soaring or she'd find him camped out nearby. "I have plenty of protectors surrounding me. Even if someone wanted to try something, they'd have a very difficult time getting near me." Like the guy at the funeral.

"I can't tell you how relieved I am to hear that. All right, hon, I've got to go. Let's catch up a bit later."

"Do you still have some of those dinners I made in the freezer?"

"I do."

"And what about clothes? Do I need to have a friend come over and do a load?"

"I think I'm fine for now."

"All right, then, let me know when you start running low."

"Will do, honey."

"Okay, Dad. Bye. Love you."

"You, too."

She hung up and sighed and tried not to think about her brother's decision. Trey was a big boy. He was going to learn some things the hard way. But she'd pray for him. A lot.

When she returned to the table, Luke shot her a concerned look. "Everything okay?"

"Just my dad checking on me." She took a sip of her water.

"I got a call while you were on the phone. They didn't find any prints in your house."

"Of course not," she said.

"They did find a pair of gloves tossed in your trash can, though, which explains why he didn't have them on when he punched me. But no, there weren't any prints. And before you ask, they were cloth gloves, not latex or vinyl, so no prints on the inside either."

"Figures." She sighed. "I don't suppose it would be a good idea to return home at this point, would it?"

"You're kidding, right?" Luke asked.

She grimaced. "Pretty much."

"You've had it rough the last few days," Finn said. "First being kidnapped, being slammed in the car wreck, the threatening call to your dad, your home invasion and then the attempted attack at the funeral. It's obvious that this guy isn't giving up. I'd say you need to stay right where you are where you have trained eyes watching out for you."

Sophie nodded. "I know."

Finn looked at Luke. "And we need to be prepared for him to try again."

Luke could feel his tension rising to new levels as the conversation centered on protecting Sophie.

"We have to stay focused," Gavin said.

"Exactly, so, no arguing about who's taking Jordan's place," Tony said with a scowl in Gavin's direction. After a chorus of agreement, they fell silent to focus on their food—and thoughts.

"I said you're overdoing it and you don't need to be walking out to your car alone at night." Zach's voice came from behind him and Luke turned to see Violet standing next to Zach, hands on her hips.

"Well, I don't see how that's any of your business," she snapped. "I'm a big girl and can take care of myself."

"What's going on?" Luke asked.

Zach scowled. "She's taking a night class at the college and it's not safe."

"It's perfectly safe, Zach, I promise."

Zach's brows rose as he realized they were the center of attention in the small back room. He flushed. "So, are you taking precautions? Watching behind you? Making sure you're not being followed?"

"Come on, Zach, you're making too big a deal out of this. I have my pepper spray."

"Pepper spray! Don't you know someone can take that away from you and use it on you?"

Violet stamped a foot. "Do you really think I'm so stupid and careless? That I'm completely incompetent? Wow, you really don't think much of me at all, do you?"

"That's not what I—"

Violet spun and disappeared back into the kitchen.

Zach huffed and pinched the bridge of his nose while silence reigned for an uncomfortably long few seconds. Then he threw his napkin on the table as he stood.

"Excuse me, folks, show's over. I'm going to grovel in private."

"That's the smartest thing you've said in the last fifteen minutes," Luke murmured.

Sophie turned wide eyes on him as Zach disappeared to find Violet. "What was that all about?"

"I have my suspicions," he said.

Twenty minutes later, Luke paid the bill for both him and Sophie, left a tip on the table and stood. "Are you ready?" he asked Sophie. Bruno stood when Luke did. The dog stretched and kept his eyes on Luke, who scratched his ears.

"More than," Sophie said. "I'm exhausted. I want to check on Katie, though."

"You want to go by the house?"

She hesitated. "No. She's got Jordan's parents there and Noah, Carter and Zach will be heading that way, too, so I think I'll just text her when we get in the car."

Together, they left the restaurant and stepped into the cool night air. "I love this time of year in New York," she said. "Not too hot, not too cold—and not too humid."

"All one day of it?" Luke said with a smile. "You realize tomorrow it could be thirty degrees."

She gave a soft laugh. "I know, so let me enjoy it while it lasts."

He held her arm as they started across the street, Bruno trotting on his left side, Sophie on his right. Halfway to the other side, a loud roar reached him and when he turned, a single headlight blinded him.

Without thinking, Luke tightened his grip and

yanked Sophie away from the path of the motorcycle. Two gunshots rang out. Glass shattered behind them.

Sophie cried out and stumbled against him. Luke went to his knees in front of the car parked on the side of the street, pulling Sophie with him. His shoulder slammed into the bumper. Pain shot through him even as he rolled on top of her, shielding her.

The motorcycle zipped past so close Luke felt the heat of exhaust on his cheek. Bruno barked and bounded next to Luke. "It's okay, boy. Sophie, are you all right?" He rolled off her and ran his hands over her face. "He missed, right? You're not hit?"

"No. I'm...okay. What just happened?" Sophie croaked, clinging to him and trembling.

"Luke! Sophie! Are you two okay?" Zach yelled as he and the others tumbled out of the restaurant.

"Yeah, go after him." Luke pointed. "That way."

Finn's vehicle was closest. He and Abernathy hurried to jump in, then bolted after the disappearing motorcycle. The others soon followed after him while Luke ignored the throbbing in his knees and hauled them both to their feet. His mind raced. That could have been bad. Not that he wasn't grateful, but he almost couldn't believe the guy had missed.

"He shot at us," Sophie said. "He really did."

"Yes." He thought she might be in shock. He scanned the street, looking for anyone else who might have criminal motives on their mind. Bystanders pointed. Some held their cell phones. Others just rushed to get away from the scene. "Let's get you in the car while we wait to hear if the others managed to catch up with him."

"Did you get the plate?" she asked.

"No. Sorry. I was too busy trying to make sure you weren't hurt."

"And I appreciate it very much," she said.

He squeezed her hand and led her to the cruiser. Bruno hopped inside, and Luke helped Sophie get settled into the passenger seat. He took her hands in his and wondered if his pulse would ever slow down. "That scared me, Sophie."

Her eyes locked on his and his heart gave that funny little beat it often did whenever he was in her presence—and had a moment to acknowledge the attraction he had no business feeling.

So, knowing they were out of sight of any prying eyes thanks to the tinted windows, it made perfect sense for him to lean in and kiss her. With most of the others dealing with the motorcyclist or focused on documenting an accurate account of what had just happened, and with the danger abated for a moment, Luke was able to let his guard down a fraction and lose himself in the brief second of kissing Sophie.

And realized he might have just made a huge mistake. Not that kissing her was wrong. Quite the opposite. It felt right and good and perfectly natural. Only now, he'd never be able to go back to not kissing her. He lifted his head and gazed down at her.

She blinked, shock and bemusement stamped on her features.

"Ah, sorry," he said. "I probably shouldn't have done that." *Probably,* nothing. He *definitely* shouldn't have done that.

Her bemusement flipped into a frown. "Why not?"

"Because—" How did he explain? "Because I'm supposed to be protecting you, not—"

"Not what?"

"Not looking for romance." Okay, that wasn't helpful at all. "I mean I need to focus on this investigation and not let myself be distracted by the fact that—" He sighed and closed his eyes for a split second while he ordered his brain to start functioning. When he opened them, her face held no expression. "Can you help me out here?"

"I don't know if I want to. This is pretty entertaining."

He huffed a short laugh and, finally, she cracked a small smile. "I like you, Sophie," he said softly. "I just—"

She placed a finger on his lips. "I get it, Luke. It's okay."

With a sigh of relief that she'd let it go and didn't seem to be angry with him, he rounded the vehicle and slid into the driver's seat. He caught Bruno's gaze in the rearview mirror. Even the dog seemed to be chastising him for his bumbling awkwardness. He ignored the animal. His knees ached, and he'd have to toss his uniform pants in the trash, but at least they were still alive.

And Bruno was still staring at him.

Ducking his head and stifling a sigh, Luke cranked the vehicle and headed for home. Halfway there, the radio crackled to life and he grabbed it. "Did you get him?"

"No, he got away," Noah said. "By the time we got the chopper in the air and to the right location, he'd ditched the bike and slipped into the subway."

Luke groaned. By the time they got the security footage from the cameras, the guy would be long gone.

Sophie kept to herself during the ride home. She'd acted like everything was fine and that she hadn't been deeply affected by the kiss, but the truth was, she had been.

Every so often, she'd feel Luke's glance rest on her as though he wanted to ask her what she was thinking but wasn't quite sure if he should.

He shouldn't.

Mostly because she wasn't sure exactly what her emotions were at the moment. Part exhilaration from the kiss. Part dejection from his apologies for it.

And part anger.

An apology for kissing her?

Seriously, that should be in the *Guys Guide to Girls* handbook somewhere. If a girl is agreeable to being kissed, don't kiss her, then say you're sorry, because it won't go over well.

Luke's interest in her—and subsequent kiss—on a normal day would have sent her over the moon with happiness—and anxiety. She'd noticed him from day one, but it had been obvious he hadn't had a shred of interest in her. Which had been fine. She wasn't in the market for a boyfriend anyway.

However, when Jordan had disappeared, it had thrown them together and had apparently given Luke a different perspective of her. One she was glad of but still not sure she wanted to pursue because of her duty to her father and brother. Then again, they seemed to be doing well enough on their own. Discounting Trey's enrollment in the Marines.

Maybe once they found Jordan's killer, she would be able to consider dating someone. Okay, not someone. Dating Luke.

But what if Jordan's killer was never found?

She couldn't stand that thought, but the fact was, not all murders were solved. Like Luke's mother's. What a heavy burden for a kid to grow up with. With a sigh, she rubbed her eyes and realized they were on Luke's street.

He stopped and let the engine idle as he turned to her. "Let me come around to open the door and then we'll hurry to get inside, okay? I'll have to move my vehicle once I know you're behind locked doors with Bruno at your side."

"Sure." He didn't say he was worried about a sniper. He didn't have to.

He opened her door and she and Bruno climbed out. Luke wrapped his arm around her shoulders and tucked her against him. He dwarfed her small stature. If someone wanted to shoot her, they'd have trouble finding an opening.

Her human shield.

Some of her hurt feelings and anger faded. Some.

Once inside his apartment, he released her. "Lock the door while I move the SUV, okay?"

"Okay."

He shut the door behind him. Bruno paced in front of it for the next ten minutes until Sophie let Luke back inside. He tossed his keys onto the small table. Bruno headed to his spot near the fireplace and flopped down with a sigh.

"I guess he's glad to be home," Sophie said.

"Always."

"And glad to have you back where he can see you." She bit her lip and fatigue swept over her. While she wanted to bring up the kiss, she didn't have the energy. Everything had been said anyway, apparently. "I'm going to my room. I'll see you in the morning."

"What about dinner later?"

"I'll pass. Thanks. Tomorrow's a full day back at work and I need to get things ready."

"Of course."

She headed toward the hallway.

"Sophie—"

She turned. "Not now, Luke. We'll talk later."

He frowned and nodded, and she slipped into the bedroom that had become her safe area.

Pacing and thinking for half an hour had done nothing except give her a little exercise she didn't need. When her phone buzzed, she snatched it from the nightstand and glanced at the screen. Her brother. "Hello?"

"Sophie?"

"Hey."

"How are you? Are you okay? Dad said some psycho was looking for you."

Sophie raised a brow. "Well, I'm not sure he's psycho." Maybe desperate? "But yes, I seem to have picked up a stalker. Stay on the alert, okay? I don't think he'll bother you or Dad, but be careful anyway."

"Who is he? *Where* is he? Tell me everything and

don't leave any detail out. I'll find him and put a stop to it."

"Trey, I appreciate the protective brother thing, but the truth is, I'm surrounded by police officers. You don't have to worry about me."

"Dad's worried."

"I know. It's what he's good at." A lump formed in her throat and she pressed fingers to her suddenly burning eyes. "Look, I'm okay right now. Truly. I'd tell you if I wasn't. But I've got protection and people looking out for me. If something changes, I'll call you."

"Promise?"

"Yes."

He sighed. "Okay, as long as you're sure."

"I am." She paused. "Dad said you'd enlisted."

The line went silent.

"Trey?"

A sigh filtered to her. "I did."

"Why don't you sound happier?"

"Because while I really think it's what I'm supposed to do, I want your blessing. I need it, Sophie."

Oh. Wow. That really did show some maturity on his part, didn't it?

"Okay, Trey. Tell me why you think this is what you're supposed to do."

He huffed a short laugh. "I don't know why. Because I'm nineteen years old and a junior in college and I don't have a clue what I want to do with my life. Why keep spending money we don't have so that I can graduate with a degree I may not use?"

He kind of had a point.

"But the Marines? Why them?"

"They're cool."

"Trey…"

"Sophie…"

She groaned. "Ugh. Just keep me updated, will you? I care about you and love you and want to make sure I'm being a good big sister."

"You're a great big sister," her brother said, his voice soft. Reflective. "You've been more of a mom to me than the woman who gave birth to me. I'm blessed to have you. But it's time for me to…"

"What?"

"Grow up."

"Leaving college and joining the Marines is growing up?"

"Yeah, I think so."

Sophie couldn't deal with this right now. "You need your education, Trey. You'll lose your scholarships."

"I know, but I'll get the education I need while I'm in the service."

She swallowed. "Well, there is that."

He laughed. "I've got to go," he said. "We'll talk later. Love you, Sophie."

"Trey…"

"I'm hanging up now."

"Fine. I love you, too, but—"

"But what?"

"Don't hang up." He didn't, and she bit her lip, blinking back the rush of tears. "Trey?"

"Yeah?"

"If you think this is what you're supposed to do, then you have my blessing."

Silence.

"Really?" he finally croaked, his voice thick with his own tears.

"Really."

"Thanks, Sophie. I love you," he whispered.

"I love you, too."

She hung up with a heavy heart, feeling like her brother was making a huge mistake and she was helpless to stop him from doing it. But he was going to, so she could at least send him off with a lighter heart. She'd support him and love him. She could do that.

And she could do something else, too.

She pulled out her laptop and set it on Sam's desk. For the next four hours, she focused on catching up with emails and everything that being Jordan's administrative assistant entailed. Including fielding questions from the media—and being reminded that Stella, the Labrador from the Czech Republic, was arriving in the morning.

It would be hard going back into the office knowing Jordan wouldn't ever walk through the doors again. It would be more than hard, but her support system was there. All of the K-9 officers and the people she came into contact with on a daily basis. It would be good.

Maybe if she told herself that enough, she'd start to believe it.

She couldn't help pulling forth one niggling thought that wouldn't leave her alone.

Now that Jordan was gone, would the new chief want to bring in his own assistant? Or would he or she be willing to give Sophie a chance to prove she would do as good a job for him—or her—as she had for Jordan?

Then again, would she even live long enough for that?

If Luke and the others had anything to say about it, she would. But a killer determined to silence her was still out there and Sophie's nerves were just about shot. Wondering about her job was the least of her worries. She just wanted to stay alive.

THIRTEEN

Luke expertly flipped the pancake in the pan and set it back on the burner. While the batter bubbled, he thought. About a lot. But mostly the fact that his mind hadn't shut off since sharing that kiss with Sophie. Which had made sleeping restless. He'd decided bringing it up at breakfast would just make things more awkward.

"Do you need any help?"

He turned to find the subject of his thoughts standing in the doorway dressed in her office attire. With her hair pulled back into a bun and her black-rimmed glasses perched on her nose, she looked…intimidating. Young but professional. Capable. Faint shadows under her eyes were the only indication that she might've had a sleepless night, as well.

"No, thanks," he said. "I've got this down to a science. Of some sort." He glanced again. "Do you really need those glasses? I only see you wear them for work."

A small smile pulled at her lips. "No. I just wear them in hopes that they make me look older." He held out a cup of coffee toward her and she took it. "However," she said, "I have to admit, sometimes I wonder if it just makes me look like I'm playing dress-up."

He laughed. He couldn't help it. "You look great. Very professional and put together. Like you could do anything you set your mind to."

A flush crept into her cheeks. "Thanks."

He cleared his throat. "I'll be ready shortly. Help yourself to the pancakes."

"I've lost count of how many times you've prepared meals for me. I need to pitch in for some grocery money or something."

"Don't worry about it. If I start heading into the red, I'll holler at you." He placed the last two pancakes on a plate and handed it to her. "Those are yours. I'm going to scope the area and be right back."

"I'll just scarf these down."

While she seated herself at the table, Luke slipped out the door and scanned the area. Nothing alarmed him. Which meant nothing other than he couldn't see the danger if it was present.

"What do you think, Bruno?" he said softly. "You think anyone's out there watching?"

Bruno's ears perked at his name, but he didn't seem to be particularly interested or unnerved about anything in the vicinity. After one more careful sweep, Luke returned to the kitchen to find Sophie washing the plate in the sink.

"You actually made those pancakes?" she asked.

"Yes. Why?"

"They were fabulous. What was in the mix?"

"Ah…you'll have to ask Sam's mom that one. I just know how to pour and flip."

"I should have guessed." Bruno walked over to her and nudged her leg. She scratched the dog's ears and he settled himself across her feet. She nodded. "He's a good dog."

"He is. And apparently, incredibly smart."

"Apparently?"

"It hasn't taken him long to figure out you'll rub his ears if he asks."

A smile curved her lips, then faded as she glanced at the door. "Everything okay out there?"

"As far as I can tell, and Bruno didn't have anything bad to say. I moved the car to the front so when you're ready, we're ready."

"Well, if Bruno says it's clear, I'm ready."

"All right, then. Just like last night, okay?"

"Sure."

Luke tucked her up against his side and escorted her to the door. He had to admit, he enjoyed having her right there next to him. He'd keep that thought to himself, as he'd already hurt her with his wishy-washiness. Until he figured out what he wanted, he owed it to her not to lead her on. Not that he was intentionally doing that, but his behavior could definitely be interpreted that way.

"Luke? You okay?" she asked.

She'd buckled up and was waiting for him to shut the door. Fortunately, he was blocking any line of sight to her. "Yes. Sorry. Just thinking." He shut the door and rounded the SUV to climb behind the wheel.

"Thinking about what?"

"Just...the future," he said, "and what it may or may not hold."

"That's some deep thinking."

"Yeah. And I need to stop doing that or we're going to be late." He hated being late.

He'd been late, and his mother had died.

And they'd all been too late to save Jordan.

Clenching his jaw against the reminder, he glanced at Sophie. She was on the phone, scrolling through emails. Her laptop case rested against her leg. "You get anything done last night?"

She looked up from her phone. "Yes, actually."

"Anything I need to be brought up to date on?"

"Nothing I can think of. I was mostly making sure all of the files were organized so that someone else would be able to make sense out of them."

"What for?" He frowned.

"Just in case it's needed."

"Why would it be needed, Sophie? Are you thinking about quitting?"

She started. "No, not at all, but whoever takes over Jordan's position may want to bring in his own administrative assistant."

"That's not going to happen."

She blinked and gave a small shrug. "That's optimistic—and certainly what I'm hoping for—but you and I both know how fast things can change when there's a turnover in a high-ranking position like Jordan's."

"Well, it's out of the question this time."

He was being obstinate and pigheaded about the topic, but it scared Luke to death that she could be right. "We've already lost Jordan," he said softly. "Losing you, too, would shatter the morale around headquarters." Not to mention his heart.

You're not going there, Hathaway, remember?

She peered at him out from under those impossibly long lashes and he cleared his throat. "Seriously, we need you. You're great at the job and you have something a lot of others in the position didn't have."

"What's that?"

"You care."

"Yeah," she said, "I do."

"So, you're staying." He said it like it was up to him, but he'd certainly be very vocal in his opinion if the topic came up.

"Okay." Her word said one thing, her tone said, "We'll see."

Just like before, he parked as close to the back entrance to headquarters as he could and rushed Sophie into the building.

"I'll be at my desk if you need anything," she said.

"I'm just going to park and then I'll be in."

He waited until she was headed down the hallway before exiting and climbing back behind the wheel. Luke shook his head. "You've got to get it together, dude, or you're going to find yourself in serious trouble."

Sophie stepped from the hall into the spacious lobby area of the three-story building and found herself blocked from her office by a large crowd of officers—with the notable absence of the three Jameson brothers.

"What's going on?" she asked as she pushed her way through to the inner circle. Then came face-to-muzzle with a beautiful Labrador retriever.

Brianne Hayes knelt next to the dog. She looked up

and grinned at Sophie. "It's Stella, our gift from the Czech Republic."

The yellow Labrador retriever seemed to be relishing all of the attention. Sophie scratched the animal's silky ears. "She's beautiful."

"And fat," Gavin said.

Sophie scowled. "Never call a woman fat." But he did have a point. Why on earth would the Czech Republic gift their department such an out-of-shape animal?

He frowned back at her. "She's not a woman, she's a dog."

"She's a living creature, and she has feelings," Brianne insisted. She narrowed her gaze on Gavin. "Be nice."

He shook his head and turned, but not before Sophie caught the smile playing at the corners of his lips. Good, they needed something to smile about.

Sophie ran her hand down the animal's neck, over her back and to her hip. On her third pass, she felt something shift under her palm. "What in the world?"

"What?" Bree asked.

Sophie returned her hand to Stella's side and felt the movement again. She laughed. "Well, I guess we know why she's fat."

Brianne blew a raspberry. "She's going to develop a complex if you people keep ragging her about her weight."

"Wait a minute," Finn said, stepping forward. "Are you saying what I think you're saying?"

"Yep," Sophie said. "This is one pregnant pup. She's going to be a mama. And soon, I believe."

"You're kidding," Bree laughed. "They sent us a pregnant dog? Who does that?"

"Someone who didn't realize she was pregnant?" Sophie shrugged. "Jordan handled this whole thing personally, so I wasn't really in the loop other than to know she was coming." She dropped to her knees and looked the dog in the eye. "She's gorgeous and with the right training will make a great officer, won't you, girl?"

As if in agreement, Stella swiped Sophie's face with her tongue just as Luke walked into the fray.

Sophie giggled and stood. "It doesn't matter," she said, drying her face with a tissue she snatched from the nearest table. "Let's get her checked by the vet and see what he says."

"I'll take her down there," Bree said.

Sophie caught Luke's eye and he had the weirdest look on his face. Not a bad look, but one she couldn't decipher. If she had to guess, she'd say shell-shocked.

She raised a brow and his cheeks pinkened just before he turned away. He wasn't immune to her, that much was clear, but it was also obvious he was determined to keep a barrier up for whatever reasons he deemed important. And finding out those reasons would have to wait. She had work to do.

Bree disappeared with Stella trotting along behind her and Sophie headed for her desk.

Only when she got to her office door, she had to stop and gather her emotions, bracing herself against the wave of grief that was going to hit her when she stepped over the threshold.

"You okay?" Luke asked from behind her.

"No." She hated that the word sounded shaky. Without turning, she continued to stare at the door to her office. It wasn't entering her office that had her so emotionally paralyzed, but Jordan's space was attached to hers and she was going to have to step into that area that would no longer belong to him and yet hold his presence in a gut-wrenching way. "And I think that's going to be my answer to that question over the next few months."

"I get it. Want Bruno and me to walk in with you?"

"Yes, please."

He slid a hand down her arm and grasped her fingers. His were as cold as hers. Maybe, in this moment, he needed her as much as she needed him.

Sophie walked into her office and noted the closed door straight ahead. "Should we treat it like ripping a Band-Aid off?" she asked. "Just go over there and open the door and…"

"Face it?"

"Yes," she whispered. Face the big empty space that Jordan had seemed to make small.

Sophie led the way to the door, hyperaware of Luke's hand around hers, tightening with each step. With a shaking hand, she gripped the knob, turned it—and pushed.

The door swung in on silent hinges, just like it always did. She drew in a deep breath and entered. Jordan's desk sat in the middle of the room. The detectives also working the case had searched it and found nothing. She could see they'd tried not to leave a mess, but files were out of place, Jordan's coffee cup was on the window sill instead of on his round Yankees coaster next to his computer.

Tears welled, and she shoved them back, pulling her hand from Luke's and instantly missing his touch even while her mind desperately tried to focus on the job. "I need to go through all of this and figure out which cases take priority, which officers to remind about court appearances—and which officers can take over Jordan's for now. No one's made a decision on an interim yet."

"They will soon. I'm sure the commissioner's working on it."

Another deep breath and she was able to approach his desk to gather the files he'd been working on before he'd disappeared. "I'll just take these with me for now."

Back in her office, she set the files on the desk and Luke hovered. Bruno sat at his side. She frowned. "Did you need something else?"

"I'm worried about you."

"Oh. Well, thank you?"

"No, I mean, I'm hesitant to leave you alone. I think you should consider going into hiding."

Wanting to discount the idea outright, she opened her mouth to do so, then snapped her lips together and decided the suggestion at least deserved her consideration. "Where would I go? Some kind of safe house?"

"Yes. Exactly."

"And who would be there with me? Officers assigned to watch out for me?"

"Of course."

Sophie pursed her lips. "I can see how that might be helpful at night, but look around you, Luke. I'm surrounded by police presence all day long. He's not going to try to get to me here."

Luke rubbed his chin and sighed. "Well..."

"I just don't think that would be a very good use of our department's resources. I'd rather use that money to hunt down bad guys. Like Jordan's killer."

He started to say something, but the buzzing of his phone cut him off. He looked at the device and straightened. "We've just been called into a meeting. I've got to go."

"Of course."

"Be careful and don't go anywhere alone. If this guy will show up to a police funeral with plans to kill you, I'm not so sure he won't try something here."

She swallowed. He was right. "Okay. I'll be sure to be extra careful."

He left, and she wondered if she shouldn't have been so quick to say no to a safe house.

Because if someone could get to Jordan, he would eventually get to her.

FOURTEEN

Two hours ago, the commissioner had called a meeting and Luke now settled into the chair nearest the door around the large conference table. Bruno lay on the floor at his feet and Luke checked his email as the others filed in, cops and K-9s. When Noah Jameson entered followed by Gavin and Finn, Luke straightened. He exchanged glances with Finn, who took the seat beside him.

"You know what's going on?" Finn asked.

"No one's told me anything," Luke said. "A little surprised to see Noah here so soon."

"Yeah."

Gavin sat on the other side of Finn, and Luke saw him scowl at the sight of Noah, who stood just inside the doorway, his K-9 Rottweiler, Scotty, seated obediently at his side. Gavin's jaw tightened, but he simply sat back and placed a hand on Tommy's head. The Springer spaniel looked up at Gavin with adoring eyes, then settled at Gavin's feet, placing his nose between his paws.

Once the team was seated around the table, leaving the end spot open, the deputy commissioner entered, followed by the commissioner, Luke sat up a bit straighter.

The commissioner stood at the head of the table and pressed his hands against the tabletop podium. "Thank you all for coming so quickly and on such short notice. I had a few things to say to you and this seemed the easiest way to get it done. And—" he paused "—I wanted it to be more personal."

With his forefinger, he pushed his glasses up the bridge of his nose and blew out a low breath. "First, I want to say I'm truly sorry at the loss of Chief Jordan Jameson. He was an outstanding officer and I considered him a friend. He will be missed by all who knew him."

Silence fell for a moment. Then the commissioner continued. "I know you all have been working overtime trying to figure out the connection to Chief Jameson and anyone who might have held a grudge against him. We have detectives also working alongside of you who are anxious to make sure Jordan's killer is brought to justice. I cannot express how badly I want this person caught."

He paused. "I know I don't have to express it. I know you feel the same. I want to say that I appreciate you keeping me updated and request that you continue to do so each step of the way. Now," he said, "my staff and I have been deliberating—some might even use the word *agonizing*—over who will step into the mighty big shoes Chief Jameson left behind."

Gavin shifted, and Luke caught his laser-like gaze. He gave a small shake of his head and Gavin's scowl deepened. The room held its collective breath while the commissioner glanced at the paper in front of him. Luke suspected he didn't need it but was simply gathering his thoughts.

"Each person we looked at held extensive qualifications for the job," the commissioner finally said, looking up and letting his gaze land on each person at the table. "You are all exceptional officers. In the end, we chose Noah Jameson as interim chief until a candidate is found to fill the position on a permanent basis. I know you all will treat him with the respect you offered his brother and I know that Interim Chief Noah Jameson will do an outstanding job. Thank you. That's all for now. Do good and be safe."

No one moved, no one breathed. The commissioner nodded and exited the room.

Noah stepped to the podium and cleared his throat. "I will admit that this came as a shock when the commissioner asked me to step in as interim. I wasn't looking to do so but feel like I can honor Jordan by carrying on where he left off." He sighed. "You guys know me. You know how I work and I know how you work. I trust each of you with my life and I know Jordan did, too. Let's continue to keep each other in the loop and do our jobs."

All heads nodded in agreement. Except, Luke noted, Gavin's. The man glared, and Luke suspected he was biting his tongue raw.

"Okay," Noah said. "That's all on that matter. Just a couple of things and we can get back out there." He opened the file folder in front of him. "Luke, do we know any more about the man who kidnapped Sophie from the auditorium?"

Luke stood. "Unfortunately, no. We just know that she found herself on his radar when she caught him in the auditorium looking through Jordan's notes and called him on his presence. As near as we can figure, he knew the schedule and the people involved in the graduation ceremony, got there early and slipped the suicide note into the folder. Of course, Sophie was there early, too, and things went downhill from there. One thing that's very clear is he wants Sophie dead and will go to great lengths, including taking risky chances, to make that happen. He's also slippery as an eel and knows how to blend in with his surroundings—including a funeral with hundreds of officers in attendance."

"Then you stay with her."

"I plan to."

"Good. Anyone else have anything that might help us catch this guy before he can get close to her again?"

Gavin stood. "We've looked at the security footage from the restaurant to see if we could find any information that would lead us to the guy on the motorcycle, but so far we've come up empty. He was on camera, but he had a helmet on and there was no plate on the back of the motorcycle." Gavin dropped back into his seat and Luke couldn't read the man's expression.

"What about Snapper?" Noah asked. "Any word on him?"

Brianne stood this time. "I talked to the people in the lab just before heading over here to the meeting. They got the results back on the blood found in Jordan's SUV. It's animal blood. And while it wasn't much, it's possible that Jordan's killer killed Snapper and wrapped him in something to keep the seats…clean. Then hid his body better than he did Jordan's." She choked on the last few words, swallowed and quickly regained her composure. "Or, it could be that Snapper had a slight injury and simply left the blood behind."

"Thank you, Bree," Noah said, his voice rough. "I appreciate the update. Anyone else have anything?"

A knock on the door interrupted them and Sophie stepped inside to pass Noah a piece of paper. For a moment, her gaze locked on Luke's and the memory of their kiss blindsided him. He shot her a tight smile and looked away, but couldn't help wondering if it was at all possible to have a happy ending with Sophie. He'd admit to being halfway in love with her already. Halfway. Didn't mean he had to go head over heels. But if he didn't put some distance between them, he was going to. Their kiss had left him rattled and running a bit scared.

Part of him wanted to talk to her and get an idea of what she was feeling, yet at the same time, he wondered if he shouldn't run while he could.

Coward.

Maybe, but he had no doubt that Sophie had the power to break his heart and he didn't know how he would survive that a second time—especially if he had to see her on a daily basis.

When the door shut behind her, he ordered his heart to throw the walls back up.

At least until Jordan's killer was found. Then maybe he could revisit the idea of a relationship with Sophie.

Maybe.

* * *

The commissioner had just left, but everyone else was still in the conference room. Before stepping into the meeting, the commissioner had stopped by to inform her that Noah would be the interim. Sophie had approved his choice and he'd seemed pleased with her confirmation.

Sophie settled behind her desk once more to grab the ringing phone. If it was another reporter calling—

"K-9 Headquarters, how may I help you?"

"He can't watch you forever." Click.

The voice belonged to the man who'd kidnapped her. She'd recognize it anywhere. Sophie closed her eyes and drew in a deep breath. She would not freak out, get upset or otherwise give him the pleasure of rattling her. Not that *he* would know it if she did, but *she* would.

It took her a few seconds to get her shaking under control, then she called a friend in dispatch and asked for a trace on the number. She could get Luke to do it but didn't want to interrupt the meeting.

"I'll see what I can find out," her friend said.

"Thanks. It's probably linked to a burner, but I have to try."

"Of course. Stay tuned."

As Sophie disconnected the call, she wondered if maybe she should consider that safe house after all. She'd talk about it with Luke on the ride home.

Luke.

And that kiss.

Whew.

Thinking about that was one way to get her mind

off the fact that someone wanted her dead and had just threatened her.

A shudder ripped through her and she pushed back from the desk to stand. And pace. And think.

Until Finn entered the room. "Sophie? You okay?"

"I'm fine."

"You're a lousy liar."

She huffed a low laugh. "Thanks." She waved a hand and told him about the caller.

His brows dipped. "That's not good. Have you told Luke?"

"Not yet. I think he's still in the meeting."

"He was finished when we were."

"Oh. Well, maybe he's working on something or talking to someone and will be out in a bit."

"Probably."

Or was he avoiding her for some reason?

Surely not. Finn and Abernathy disappeared down the hall and she returned to her desk to lose herself in emails and sorting files for Noah, making notes about each one. She and he would have to sit down together, and she'd walk him through the cases, as well as the duties Jordan had assigned to her. He could decide if he wanted her to continue doing her usual or change them up. Either way, she felt better about her job security. For the time being anyway.

When her phone rang, she stretched the cramp in her neck and checked the number before answering. Her tension eased slightly when she saw that it was her friend in the dispatch office calling back. "Hi, Carol."

"Sophie, I checked the number and you were right. It was from a burner phone. There's no way to trace it exactly, but according to the towers, I can put it about five miles from you. I sent a cruiser out to the area to see if they could spot anyone fitting the description of your kidnapper, but I doubt he stuck around long after making the call. He knows we're looking for him."

"Okay, thank you." She hung up and dropped her head into her hands. When would this end? With a sigh, she went back to her notes and forced herself to concentrate.

The next time she looked up, Luke and Bruno were standing in the doorway watching her. She blinked at the frown on Luke's face. "What is it?"

"You didn't tell me you got a threatening phone call."

"Finn?"

"Yeah, he texted me and told me to check on you and make sure you didn't go anywhere alone."

She shrugged. "I was planning to tell you when I saw you."

"Did you recognize his voice?"

"Yes. It was the same guy."

Anger flashed in his eyes for a brief moment. "I'm going to stop this person if it's the last thing I do."

"How?"

"I don't know. I haven't figured that out yet. Let's see if we can come up with a plan on the way back to my place. Are you done for the day?"

"I could work another forty hours and not be done." She closed her laptop. "But I'm starving, and my eyes are burning. It's already past six so I'm ready to call it a day."

"I'll feed you," he said. "What do you want?"

The words were Luke, but the standoffish expression wasn't one he'd ever used with her before. She bit her lip, considering his features, and decided that if he was going to do his best to put distance between them, he would have to work through whatever was bugging him.

Probably that kiss.

Then again, maybe it hadn't affected him like it had her if he could so easily alter his behavior and treat her so coolly. Or maybe he was waiting on her to bring up the topic. But why should she? He was the one who'd kissed her and apologized.

Since they were alone, she started to say something about the kiss and stopped. He looked worn out. Maybe his demeanor had nothing to do with her. Maybe she was giving herself too much credit. Whatever the case, compassion stirred, and she decided to drop it. "It was a tough day, wasn't it?"

"Yeah."

She nodded. She was being selfish. They were all grieving and she was obsessing about a kiss. Later, after some time had passed, she'd bring it up. Maybe. If he regretted it, did she really want to know about it? Open herself up to the humiliation that would bring?

That was a big fat *no*.

She needed to let it go. For now.

And hope Luke would bring it up.

As strange as it may be, she had to admit that whenever she was with Luke, she felt safe. His determination to protect her allowed that. In spite of the person who seemed just as determined to kill her. She grabbed her purse. "Luke, can we talk about—?"

"Luke?"

Sophie turned to see Tony waving at Luke.

"Sorry to interrupt," Tony said, "but could I have a word? I can see you're ready to leave, but this can't wait."

"Sure." To Sophie, Luke asked, "You mind waiting?"

"Of course not."

He shot her a swift smile, then joined Tony in the small office off the hallway. The room was mostly used for storage—and private conversations. "What is it?"

Tony paced from one end of the area to the other—as much as he could pace with all the boxes stacked around the perimeter. "Reed and I were talking."

"About?"

"Gavin."

Luke leaned against one of the larger boxes and crossed his arms. "Again, about?"

"About…" Tony raked a hand over his head. "Look, I know Noah's the new chief, but I'd rather not bring him into this. Yet."

"Into what? Something's bothering you in a big way. Spill it."

"What if it was Gavin?" Tony asked, his gaze not quite meeting Luke's.

"What if…what was Gavin?" Luke didn't like where the question was taking the conversation.

Tony sighed. "What if Gavin killed Jordan because he was still mad about Jordan beating him out for the position two years ago? What if his anger has just been growing ever since and he finally snapped? There. I said it. I should be kicked off the team for even think-ing it, right?"

"No," Luke said softly. "I have to admit it crossed my mind, as well."

Tony froze for a second, then finally lifted his gaze to meet Luke's. "Really?"

"Yeah. For a brief moment, I wondered. Then felt like you. I can't believe that would even cross my mind."

"Oh man." Tony sighed. "I'm so glad you said that."

"Have you discussed this with anyone else besides Reed?"

"No. Neither one of us likes thinking it, much less discussing it, but I think…"

"What?"

"We should at least investigate and make sure he has an alibi."

Luke palmed his eyes and drew his hands down his face. He gave a slow nod. "Okay. I think that's a valid argument considering their history, but I'm going to go on record in saying that I don't believe it."

"Then let's prove it so we can defend him if it comes up with whoever winds up taking Jordan's place."

"Good idea."

"I'll get the ball rolling on that. You want to discuss this with him? He's going to be hurt and angry that we feel we even have to do this."

Luke shut his eyes and nodded. "Fine. I'll talk to him." He and Gavin seemed to have the least amount of conflict. He'd never been close to Gavin but had never had anything against the man except his attitude when it came to Jordan and his ambition. "Is he still here?"

"Yeah, I think he headed to his desk."

Tony left, and Luke joined Sophie at her desk once more.

"Everything all right?"

"Just some things I need to think about with the investigation. I have one more thing I have to take care of, then we can head out, okay?"

"Sure."

Luke left her and went in search of Gavin. He found him sitting at his desk, head in his hands. The big man looked defeated, his dark brown hair in need of a trim, his broad shoulders slumped. For a moment, Luke simply stared at the man, wondering if he was doing the right thing by bringing up the topic. He turned to leave, then stopped. No, it was probably better coming from him, because if he didn't ask, Tony would—and that would be a recipe for disaster for the whole team.

"Gavin, you got a minute?"

Gavin dropped his hands and turned. "Sure. Have a seat."

Luke settled himself in the chair next to the desk facing Gavin, and Bruno stretched out on the floor next to Luke. Gavin's dog, Tommy, shifted and crept closer to his handler, eyes on Bruno. "I need to ask you something," Luke said, "and since there's no right way to ask, I'm just going to spit it out."

With a frown, Gavin nodded.

"Do you have an alibi for the day and time Jordan went missing?"

Gavin didn't move. His eyes never left Luke's, allowing Luke to see the change as they went from friendly to frosty. "Why do I need an alibi?"

"Because it's been brought up that you and Jordan's rivalry may have escalated, and it would be a good thing for you to have it on record that you provided an alibi. Should it be questioned by anyone."

"Sounds like it's already been questioned."

"Not so much that anyone believes you had anything to do with Jordan's death, but out of the desire to protect you and have an answer if we're questioned about it."

"Questioned by whom?" Gavin flicked a glance at the others gathered near Sophie's office. "My unit members? Men and women I trust every day? People I'd die for? Them?"

"No," Luke said. "People who don't know you like we do." The statement stopped him. His own words echoed around him and he clasped his hands together as he leaned forward. "I don't think you had anything to do with Jordan's death. Not one thing. But it's well-known that you two went head-to-head occasionally and that he got a promotion that you were hoping for. For some people that would be enough to hang you right there. We want to be able to refute any such claims."

Gavin drew in a deep breath and then let it out slowly as though trying to decide whether to continue being offended or cooperate. Finally, he nodded. "I moonlight upon occasion, doing security for various events around the city." He held up a hand at Luke's start. "Only when I'm off duty and the people I work for know that I may have to bolt at a very inconvenient time. But usually, that doesn't happen. The morning of graduation, I was working a private event. Jordan had approved it."

"He gave you permission to miss the ceremony?"

"Yes. So, when you called to let me know Jordan was missing, I explained the situation to the client, then Tommy and I headed home to pick up the SUV before coming to help look for Jordan."

"Where was the event?"

"In Manhattan."

"So, your client can vouch for you?"

"Sure. And I think my neighbor could verify when I got home. But I drove my car so all you have to do is check the mileage and the GPS. I put the address in so I didn't waste time looking for it. The client also covered my parking expenses so there'd be a record of that, as well. No doubt I'm on the garage's security footage, as well, when I entered and left."

"Thanks, Gavin. I didn't want to ask, but at least we can tell anyone who brings up the subject why you're not considered a suspect."

Gavin shot him a sad smile. "But I was, even if for a short time, if you feel like you need to ask for an alibi."

"Yeah, I know. And we'll talk to your client, so leave his name and number, will you? But as far as I'm concerned, you're good."

"Thanks, man."

"Absolutely." Luke drew in a deep breath. "And now, I'm going home."

"Not without Sophie, I gather."

"No, not without Sophie." He slipped out of Gavin's cubicle and made his way to Sophie's desk, where she had packed up her bag and laptop and whatever else she needed. She stood at the window, looking out.

"You ready?"

She jerked like he'd pulled her from deep thoughts but turned and shot him a smile. "Sure."

Once they were seated in the car, Luke could feel Sophie's gaze on him. He could tell she wanted to talk about what happened between them. Specifically, the kiss. And quite frankly, even though he'd apologized and given her an explanation for why they should keep some distance between them, he was looking forward to kissing her again. Which unsettled him even further.

Completely put out with himself and his uncharacteristic behavior, he decided that instead of putting distance between them, they needed to have a heart-to-heart. If he could work up the guts to do it. First, he kissed her, then he apologized—and now he wanted to straighten things out.

Poor Sophie. She didn't deserve his indecisiveness. Although, to be truthful, if he wasn't dealing with Jordan's death and being so involved in the case, then the whole situation would be different.

He slid another glance at her. She was deep in thought, as well. He almost asked her what she was thinking about, but they were close to his apartment. His empty apartment. Sam and David were both gone. Sam out of town and David working until the wee hours of the morning. There would be plenty of time to talk.

A final glance in the mirrors reassured him that no one had followed them. Then again, whoever was after Sophie wouldn't have to follow. "Has your dad mentioned any more trouble at the house?" Luke asked.

"The guys watching the building haven't reported any, but maybe he said something to you?"

Small talk. Nice job, Hathaway.

"No, no trouble," she said, her gaze still averted.

"Good."

Could he be any more awkward? Probably, so he fell silent and pulled next to the curb. "Gavin's on his way to take a shift on watching the house. He should be here shortly. I'll walk you to the door and then go park the car."

"Okay."

"Stay put and I'll come around and get you."

"I know the drill." And she didn't sound particularly thrilled about it.

Clamping his lips on a sigh and an apology, he made his way to her door and tucked her into his side.

As he hurried her toward the front door, he knew he was lost. She was small, but she felt just right next to him—like she belonged there and he hadn't known what he was missing until he found it.

The fact that he got her safely inside almost surprised him. "I'll be back, and then we'll talk, okay?"

Sophie raised a brow, then nodded. "I'm going to get a water. Do you want one?"

"Sure."

That she was speaking to him settled his anxiety a bit as he went to search for a parking space. After finding a spot, he came back inside and opened the back door to let Bruno out into the fenced yard. The German shepherd darted out and Luke headed to the den, searching for the right words—and not finding them.

When Sophie joined him, she handed him the bottle of water and took a seat in the recliner, curling her legs beneath her.

Glad to have something to do with his hands, Luke opened the bottle and took a long swig before settling on the sofa opposite her. "Sophie, I…"

She lifted her gaze and he swallowed.

"Just say it, Luke."

She wasn't going to make it easy for him. But then, why should she?

He sighed. "I wanted to say I'm sorry."

"You've already apologized for kissing me. It's not necessary to do it again."

"What? No!" He cleared his throat. "No, that's not what I was apologizing for."

"Then what?"

"For being a wimp."

She laughed. Actually *laughed*. "Luke, you're not a wimp. And I can't stay mad at you. I've been thinking, and it's been such a crazy time for everyone that maybe we're all acting a bit out of character."

"You?"

"Of course. I'm jumping at shadows, avoiding confrontations and conflict—"

"Wait, you are?"

Another laugh, this one self-deprecating. "Yes. My brother dropped out of college to go into the military and you know what I did?"

"What?"

"Nothing."

He blinked. "What do you mean, nothing?"

"Exactly that. I did *nothing*. I've been so consumed with the kidnapping, Jordan's death, Katie's mental state…" She waved a hand. "Everything. That I completely let it go. I let my brother make a stupid decision and I said nothing."

"Why is it stupid?"

She sighed. "I don't know that it is, to be honest, but I wish he would have at least finished college before enlisting."

"Can't he finish while he serves? Or after? Then it's free."

"I suppose." She pressed fingers to her eyes before dropping her hands. "And, he's nineteen. It's not like he has to listen to me anymore anyway. Not that he ever did." She shrugged. "But maybe I don't know as much as I think I do. Maybe this is the best thing for him. Maybe he does know more than I did when I was nineteen." She paused. "Regardless, what I'm getting at is that it's okay to be a little off your game right now."

"No, it's not, because if I'm off my game, someone—"

Bruno's sudden and intense barking yanked Luke to his feet. "Stay here." He pulled his weapon and headed for the back door.

"Luke, be careful!"

He paused and looked back at Sophie then the locked door. "Don't open the door to anyone but Gavin, okay?"

"Of course."

He hesitated a fraction of a second more before Bruno's second round of frantic barks sent him out the door.

Once outside, Luke hurried to Bruno, who paced the length of the back fence. His barking had ceased, but his hackles still bristled. "What is it, boy?"

Bruno whined and trotted over to Luke, who scratched his ears. Bruno might not be trained to take down criminals, but he was an excellent watchdog and very protective of his territory. With his weapon held ready, Luke called for backup and headed for the gate.

FIFTEEN

Sophie paced while she waited for Luke and Bruno to return. She checked and rechecked the locks, made sure all of the windows were securely latched—and paced some more.

What if Luke found something? What if something found *him*? What if he was in trouble? Should she go out and check on him?

But he'd said to stay put.

But if he was in trouble, she needed to do something.

But Gavin was almost there and would help.

But what if Gavin was too late?

Pressing her fingers to her temples, she prayed for wisdom.

The doorbell rang, and she left Luke's apartment to go to the building's front door. She stopped to check the peephole. "Gavin?"

No one answered, and she couldn't see anyone through the peephole. Frowning, she glanced at Luke's apartment. Should she call for Luke?

A loud thud against the door sent her reeling back.

Another thud, then the crash and bang of the door slamming against the wall ripped a scream from her throat.

The man from the auditorium, the funeral, the one who'd kidnapped her, never stopped moving. His bloodshot eyes locked on hers as he stepped over the fallen door and bolted toward her, weapon aimed at her.

Shock at the brazen invasion held her frozen for a split second before she screamed again and turned to run. A bullet cracked into the wall beside her head and she threw herself to the floor with a jarring thud.

"Police! Freeze!" Luke stood just inside the back door, his gun aimed at the intruder.

A hard hand clamped down on her wrist and held the weapon to her head. "Back off!"

Luke's eyes never wavered, but Sophie could see her fear reflected back at her in the dark depths. "Let her go," Luke said. "You don't want to do this."

Her captor yanked her to her feet and toward the open door, keeping her between himself and Luke, using her as a shield.

"Luke!" Sophie shuddered, unable to gain any traction on the hardwood floor as the man dragged her backward. The gun moved from her neck and aimed at Luke. The tension in the man's body shouted at her. He was going to kill Luke.

"No!" She pushed his arm as he squeezed the trigger. The bullet slammed into the ceiling.

Luke dove into the kitchen, taking refuge behind the wall. Sirens sounded. Or was that the ringing in her ears from the gunshot?

Again, the man didn't hesitate. He pulled her out of the house toward his vehicle parked on the sidewalk.

The engine was running. Sophie noted the neighbors coming out of their homes to watch and point.

She struggled against his hold, but like before, he was strong and angry and once again, she found herself in the passenger seat of his car. She reached for the handle and he grabbed her by the hair, jamming the gun against her neck.

"Don't, or I'll end this here."

Blue lights flashed in the distance and Luke appeared in the doorway, his gun aimed at the vehicle. But, of course, he wouldn't shoot for fear of hitting her. "You can't kill me," she said. "You need me to get away."

"Then don't try anything and I'll let you live a few more minutes." He removed the gun from her and threw the car into gear.

"Why are you doing this?" she cried as he peeled away from the curb. She noted his shaking hands, bloodshot eyes and scruffy appearance. He was on something. Alcohol? Drugs? Did she even want to know? "Please. At least tell me why!"

"You were just in the wrong place at the wrong time." He glanced in the rearview mirror and tightened his grip on the wheel. "I've got to shake the cops." He shot her a glare. "You've messed everything up."

"Me? How?"

"It was just supposed to be a quick little job. Slip the letter in the envelope and get out. But no. You had to show up. Why couldn't you just mind your own business?"

Sophie's jaw dropped. Mind *her* business? She snapped her lips together and fought to think past the fear. He was going to kill her if she didn't escape. However, the longer he thought she would be useful as a hostage, the longer she'd have to figure out a way to escape. "What's your name?" she asked as he wheeled onto the highway. Flashing lights stayed behind them.

"Claude."

"Claude what?"

"Jenks! What's it matter to you?"

"Maybe I want to know the name of my murderer."

"I'm no killer," he said.

She let that one go. "You killed Jordan. He left behind a wife and unborn child. Why would you kill him and try to make it look like a suicide? Why?"

He let out a huff of a laugh. "I didn't kill that guy. I just told you I'm no killer."

"And yet you just said you're going to kill me." She was trying to reason with a man in an altered mental state. Add in his desperation not to get caught and it was a formula for disaster—or death. There wasn't going to be any reasoning with him. If she wanted to live, she had to get away. Period.

Once again, he shot her a dark look. "I told you, I was just supposed to slip the envelope into the folder. It was easy money. No one was supposed to get hurt. But you...you messed it up and I'm not going to go back to jail."

Back? She swallowed. "And no one has to," she said. "If you didn't kill Jordan, then you can end this before it goes any further."

He slammed on brakes and skidded across three lanes of traffic, narrowly avoiding colliding with several vehicles. Horns blared, brakes squealed and Sophie gripped the door handle in order to keep from being tossed all over the front seat. The seat belt dug into her as he got on the expressway, then the next left, then a right.

Soon, Sophie lost track of all the twists and turns. And when she looked behind her, there was no sign of blue lights. "Come on, Claude. You can go to the police station and turn yourself in. I'll tell them you didn't hurt me and you were the perfect gentleman. You won't get off scot-free, but they'll probably give you a break."

He scoffed. "I've never caught a break a day in my life."

"Maybe that can change if you do the right thing."

"And besides," he said as though she hadn't spoken, "I'm connected to a cop killer. They'll never believe anything I say."

"You know who killed Jordan?"

He glanced at her, then back at the road.

"Come on, Claude, tell me, please. Why did he want Jordan dead?"

"Because he—" He bit off the words and yanked the wheel once more.

Darkness was approaching, but she caught sight of the water straight ahead. Which body of water? She wasn't familiar with this part of Queens and her heart pulsed with dread and terror. "Because he what, Claude?"

"Enough! It doesn't matter! As soon as you're dead, I'm a free man."

"If you kill me, you'll never be free."

"Shut up, shut up, shut up!" He threw the car in Park and grabbed his weapon, bringing it up to her face.

"What are you doing?"

"I don't want to kill you, but I don't have a choice. I can't go back to prison!"

During his rant, Sophie dug behind her, latched onto the door handle and pulled. The door flew open on his last word and she fell out backward, hit the asphalt and rolled. The bullet shattered the passenger-door window. The bullet he'd meant for her head.

Claude dove across the seat, grasping for her even as she struggled to find some balance and get her feet under her. His hand latched onto her ankle, throwing her off, and she kicked out blindly with her other foot.

Her heel caught the hand with the gun and the weapon tumbled to the ground. She started to reach for it, but Claude was already coming at her fast. Her hand swiped the weapon, sending it into a nearby bush. She gave a hard yank with her captured foot and found herself free. Rolling and scrambling to get away from him, she lurched to her feet.

Only to have him catch up to her and bring her back down hard. The breath whooshed from her lungs, stunning her into stillness.

"Where is she?"

"The chopper's searching, Luke," Gavin assured him. He'd been the first one to respond to Luke's call for help, pulling up thirty seconds after Luke had watched Sophie's kidnapper peel away from the curb.

Too late. He was going to be too late once again and someone he loved was going to die. Bruno whined in the back and Gavin's Tommy barked. "I shouldn't have left her alone. So stupid. What was I thinking?"

"I should have been there when you got there," Gavin said.

"No, I shouldn't have left her alone."

"You thought someone was out in the backyard. You went to investigate—something any and all of us would have done. Quit beating yourself up about it."

Easy for him to say. "It was a distraction," he muttered. "And I fell for it."

"We're going to find her."

The radio crackled, and Luke heard chopper blades then the pilot. "Location established. Willow Lake, Flushing Meadow Park. Eyes on the vehicle."

He gave the location and Luke released a joyous breath. "Go, go. We're not too far from there."

"Suspect and victim on the ground. Victim is running." The pilot kept up the report while Gavin screamed down the highway, dodging vehicles that were slow to pull over. Other officers fell in behind them, blue lights whirling. "Run, Sophie, run."

"Victim caught. Victim is being dragged toward the lake."

He was going to drown her.

Luke's heart pounded with enough force that he thought it might rupture. Prayers whispered from his lips. *Please, God, don't let me be too late. Not this time.*

SIXTEEN

Sophie yanked against his hold but found she just didn't have the strength. "I don't want to die!"

"Too bad! I'm not going back to prison and you're the only one who can send me there!"

Water reached her ankles, then her calves.

Absently, she noted the helicopter above. The spotlight shone down, illuminating them. "Police! Let her go!"

Claude screamed and pulled her farther into the frigid water. Sophie swung her elbow and connected with his temple. He stumbled and fell with a splash.

Pulse-pounding desperation sent her stumbling away back toward shore. She allowed herself a brief flicker of hope that she might actually get away.

Only to have that hope snuffed when a hand grasped her hair and yanked her backward. She went down. Under. She flailed, kicked and caught him in the stomach. For a brief second, his grip loosened and she surfaced long enough to fill her lungs with air and note the approaching sirens before he managed to get a better grip and dunk her back under.

Help was so close, but would she be able to fight him off long enough to allow them the time to reach her?

Frantic, her mind scrambled for a way to get loose while her hands reached, grasping for anything. Her fingers pried at his, but she gave that up almost immediately. He was too strong, and she was tiring quickly.

Her lungs screamed, her limbs grew heavy, sluggish.

God! Help me!

Bright lights flashed, then everything went black.

"Sophie!" Luke threw himself out of the vehicle before Gavin brought it to a stop. Bruno loped after him. Passed him and bolted into the water. Luke caught up and flung himself into the water where he'd seen Sophie go under. The man who'd held her was scrambling out of the water along the shore. "Go after him!"

Gavin's engine roared and he took off after the fleeing man. Bruno swam in circles. Indicating that was where Sophie was?

Other cruisers pulled in as Luke dove into the cold water. Frantic, he swam down, arms reaching, while he begged God to spare her. His fingers brushed something.

Hair?

Clothing?

Then nothing.

The seconds ticked past. A minute. A minute and a half.

He surfaced, gasped in another lungful of air, noticed Bruno had moved and was swimming in circles a yard away. Luke went back down and kicked over to Bruno. Visibility was at absolute zero in the dark murkiness.

Then something bumped his leg.

He spun and shot out his hands. His palms grazed cold, smooth skin. Luke grasped hair and pulled. It had to be Sophie. He maneuvered her until he had her in a lifeguard hold and kicked to the surface.

Thankfully, the water wasn't deep and his feet hit bottom. He lifted her face and turned her toward him.

"Over here!" Zach called to him.

An ambulance was working its way toward them, but Luke wasn't about to wait on them. Sophie needed to breathe.

He stumbled out of the water and dropped to his knees, placing her on the ground. He felt for a pulse and found it, but she wasn't breathing.

Luke tilted her head and opened her mouth. He leaned down to give her the breath from his lungs. Once, twice, three times.

Nothing.

Vaguely aware of the paramedics dropping beside him, he continued to breathe for her.

Until she gasped, then choked.

Luke rolled her on her side as she gave up the water she'd inhaled. When her body calmed after one final shudder, he rolled her back, and she stared up at him. Her eyes filled with tears.

"Thank you," she whispered. "I knew you'd come." Her eyes shut, and someone nudged him aside.

"Good job," a voice said from behind him. "We've got her now."

Luke fell back and let the paramedics take over.

The shakes hit him—from the combination of crashing adrenaline and being soaking wet, no doubt—and he clasped his hands together, but he'd done it. He'd gotten to her on time. Barely. But she was alive. "Thank you, God," he whispered. "Thank you." Bruno nudged him and Luke wrapped an arm around the wet dog and slipped him his favorite toy in reward. "Good job, boy. You helped me save her."

Once the paramedics made sure she was stable, one of them tossed Luke a blanket and he wrapped it around his shoulders. He used a second blanket to rub down Bruno.

"You okay?" the guy asked.

"Yes." Luke shivered, and Bruno shook himself, spraying the remaining droplets. "Is she?"

"She will be once we get her warmed up and all of the water out of her lungs." He turned back to help his partner move her onto the gurney, then they carried her up the slight hill and loaded her into the ambulance.

Luke followed, not wanting to leave her side. He turned to Zach. "Give Bruno and me a ride?"

"Of course."

"I need to call Sophie's dad. He'll want to be there for her. I left my phone and weapon in Gavin's vehicle."

Zach handed his phone over.

It only took Luke a few seconds to get the man's number and give him a condensed version of the events that led to Sophie being taken to the hospital.

"I'm on the way," Sophie's father said. "You're sure she's all right?"

"She will be."

"Thank you." Luke heard the slamming of a car door just as he hung up.

Luke climbed in the passenger seat of Zach's Tahoe and ran a hand over his wet head and buckled up. He then used Zach's phone to make arrangements for his roommate David to take care of Bruno, grab him some clothes and meet them at the hospital. Then he dialed Gavin.

"You get him?" Luke asked when the man answered.

"No. I didn't, but a car did. He ran into the highway and got hit by a passing motorist. He's dead and the guy who hit him is a basket case." The weariness in his team member's voice said he wasn't happy. "He's the one who tried to get to Sophie the day of the funeral."

"Yes—and kidnapped her from the auditorium."

"Did he kill Jordan?"

"I don't know," Luke said. "Hopefully, Sophie can fill us in when she wakes up. The lab report came back on the content of the syringe. Let's just say if Jenks had managed to inject her, she would be dead."

"I'm glad she's okay."

"Same here."

"I'm on the way to the hospital," Gavin said.

"I think everyone is. See you there."

Zach dropped Luke at the door and Luke hurried to find Sophie. She was still in the emergency department. He flashed his badge and made his way to her side.

A man he'd never seen before sat in the chair next to her bed holding her hand. Sophie's father was his first guess. The man looked up when Luke stepped into the room. "Hi. I'm Luke Hathaway."

The man stood. "Damien Walters."

They shook hands and Luke stepped over to Sophie's side. "Has she woken up yet?"

"I think they have her on a painkiller. The guy knocked her around pretty good." Rage flashed on his features for a moment before he focused back on his daughter. "She briefly opened her eyes about a minute after I got here. Long enough to tell me not to worry," Mr. Walters said, his voice rough with emotion.

"That sounds like Sophie," Luke said. He gripped her other hand and squeezed.

Her eyes fluttered and finally opened and looked straight into his. "Luke?"

"Yeah."

"You saved me," she whispered.

His throat tightened. "Couldn't have done it without some help, but yeah."

"You weren't too late."

He gave a strangled laugh. "No, not this time." But it had definitely been close. Way too close. If he'd been only seconds later...

He shuddered as the nightmare of his mother's murder swept over him.

"Did you get him?" she whispered. "His name is Claude Jenks. He knows who killed Jordan."

Luke stilled. "It wasn't him?"

"Jenks said he didn't kill anyone. He insisted he was simply hired by someone. I got the feeling he was telling the truth."

"Who hired him?"

"I don't know. He wouldn't tell me. He said he was just supposed to put the envelope in Jordan's folder before the graduation ceremony and leave." She closed her eyes and sighed. "I'm sorry. I tried to get him to tell me once I realized he didn't actually kill Jordan himself."

"You don't have anything to apologize for," Luke said. "You just rest and focus on getting better."

"Okay." Her eyes closed and he started to leave when her grip tightened. "Don't leave me," she whispered without opening her eyes.

Luke's heart trembled, then fell over the edge right into love. He sighed as he tried to stop the acknowledgment. "I'm not going anywhere." For now. Again, memories from his childhood swept over him. His mother's bleeding body on the asphalt. Her funeral. His father's withdrawal and his brothers' accusing eyes. *You should have been on time! Why weren't you on time?*

His father's words echoed, and he kept his head down while he grappled with the memories.

When Sophie's breathing evened out, Luke looked up and his gaze connected with Mr. Walters.

The man's lips curved into a slow smile. "I think I'll go get something to eat. You'll let me know if she needs anything?"

"Of course."

"You're in love with her."

"We're…friends," Luke said with a quick glance at the, thankfully, still-sleeping Sophie.

Her father frowned, then nodded and headed for the door, stopping to clap Luke on the shoulder. "Thank you for saving my little girl." And then he was gone.

But his words lingered. *You love her.* Yes, he did. He hadn't intended to, but she'd sneaked her way into his heart and Luke clung to the fact that this incredible woman loved him. He knew she did but was afraid to admit it. He didn't blame her.

Luke pressed fingers to his weary eyes but couldn't help the small laugh of relief that broke through. Sophie was alive and her would-be killer dead.

The smile faded as reality set in. And he was going to have to figure out how to walk away from the woman he'd just admitted he loved.

SEVENTEEN

The next day when Sophie woke, she took a physical inventory and she decided her lungs were much clearer and, while she was sore, she would recover without any permanent side effects.

"Hi," Katie said.

Sophie turned to see her friend sitting in the chair. "Hi."

"How are you feeling?"

"Much better." She maneuvered herself into a sitting position. "How about you?"

"Sick, but the doctor said the baby's fine."

"I'm glad. Have you told the others?"

"No." Katie sighed. "But it's time. I've decided this baby is a huge blessing. Everyone will be excited that a little piece of Jordan will live on and…" She shook her head as tears filled her eyes.

"Sad that he won't be here to watch him grow up?"

Katie nodded and swiped her cheeks. "But," she said, "this baby will have lots of father figures in his or her life and will grow up knowing how much Jordan would have loved him. Or her."

"You're so right. And you know Ellie's going to want to be a little mama to her cousin."

Katie laughed. "Oh yes, for sure."

Sophie squeezed her friend's hand. "It's going to be okay, eventually, right?"

"Yes. Jordy would want us to be okay. So, we have to be. For him—and us, too. It's going to be a process, but I have to believe it."

"Yeah," Sophie said, "I'm believing it, too."

Fifteen minutes later, Noah, Luke, Zach and Carter gathered around her bed. After Sophie assured them she was fine and would be going home later that day, she turned the conversation to a question that burned in her mind. "You weren't able to find anything that might tell you the relationship between Claude Jenks and Jordan, were you?"

"Not yet," Zach said, "but we will."

"Did he tell you who killed Jordan?"

The brothers and Luke exchanged a look. "What?" she asked.

"When Jenks was running to get away from you, he ran into the path of a car and was killed."

Sophie gasped. "Then he couldn't tell you," she whispered.

"No, but the lab has everything that was on Jenks when he died," Luke said. "Although it looks like there wasn't anything salvageable, thanks to the water."

Carter ran a hand down his cheek. "We searched his home but found nothing to indicate who hired him to leave the note." The man shook his head. Weariness and grief were still deeply etched on his face and Sophie swallowed the lump that formed in her throat.

She had a feeling she'd be doing a lot of that over the next few months.

With a nod, she glanced at Luke, who shot her a stiff smile. Sophie's heart ached. While he'd stayed right by her side, she could feel him pulling away emotionally.

"We'll get him," she said to the brothers. "We will."

"There's no other option," Carter said. His brothers nodded, jaws like granite, eyes narrowed. They all looked so very much alike at the moment, their expressions very similar to one she'd seen on Jordan's face more than once.

"We're going to go," Katie said. She rose. "You need to rest so you can get out of here."

"Thank you." Sophie's gaze swept across them. "I would be dead without you. I want you to know how grateful I am."

Each one patted her shoulder as they left the room, with Katie swooping in for another hug. "Rest."

Sophie's eyes landed on Luke, who was edging toward the door. "I will."

Katie left, and Sophie caught Luke's hand as he passed her. He stopped and raised a brow.

"What's wrong?" she asked.

His gaze slid away. "What do you mean?"

"You've never been evasive with me before. Don't start now."

Luke sucked in a deep breath and pulled his hand from hers to pace to the window. He looked out. "I'm dealing with some pretty raw emotions right now."

"Care to share?"

He raked a hand over his hair, then spun to face her,

the torment in his eyes stabbing her heart. "I failed you, and I'm sorry."

Sophie huffed in disbelief. "*Failed* me? How can you even think that? You *saved* me."

"But I almost didn't. I let Bruno's barking distract me when I should have been on high alert."

"I'll take almost, Luke. I'm alive and very happy to be so. It wasn't your fault. Just like it wasn't your fault that someone made the choice to carjack and kill your mother. We all have choices in life. Claude Jenks made his, whoever killed Jordan made his. Now you have to make yours."

His jaw worked, and he drew in a deep breath. "I'm sorry, but I just… I don't deserve you, Sophie." He pressed his fingers to his eyes and slipped out the door just as her father stepped inside. Luke nodded a greeting but didn't stop.

Her dad raised a brow. "Am I interrupting something?"

A tear slid down her cheek, and she swiped it away. "No. Apparently not." She drew in a deep breath. "But it's probably better this way."

"What way?"

She gave a light shrug. "I don't need to make any commitments right now. Not…yet. Dating Luke would make things really hard."

"Because you think you have to take care of Trey and me? That we can't survive without you?"

Her eyes locked on his. "What do you mean? Of course I don't think that."

"I think you do."

Yes, she probably did. "I love you and Trey, Dad. I

do what I do because of that. And if I don't do it, who will?"

"Sophie, I think it's time I told you something."

She blinked. "What's that?"

"I can do laundry, honey. I can also cook."

She paused. "You can?"

"I can."

"Then why...?"

"Haven't I?"

"Um...yes."

"Because you seemed to need to do it. To heal. If you recall, I tried to get you to stop doing stuff after your mom left and it made things worse for you."

She vaguely remembered that.

"It's not that we don't need you," he said, "but we'll be okay. Besides, Trey's going to be gone in a few weeks anyway. I'm proud of him. He's reaching out and grabbing life by the horns. It's time for you to do the same." Sophie figured her jaw was inches from the mattress. He patted her leg and laughed. "I sound like I don't expect to ever see you again." A sigh slipped from him. "I just want you to be happy. Luke's a good man. I hope you two can work it out."

Tears hovered on her lashes and she blinked and shook her head. "I don't think he wants me anymore," she whispered.

"Oh, honey, I think he does. Just give him a little time to process some things."

Time. Well, she definitely had time.

Luke wasn't sure how long he stood outside of Sophie's hospital room with his eyes shut and his mind spinning. Had he just done that? He was an idiot letting his fear control him. But…he honestly believed what he said. He *didn't* deserve Sophie. She deserved better.

But there was no doubt he'd just hurt her terribly. He turned and placed a hand back on the handle and debated about apologizing. Then let go with a heavy sigh. No. He'd done the right thing.

Then why did he feel so awful?

Luke hurried to the elevator, calling himself all kinds of a coward. But he needed to think.

Outside the hospital, he climbed into the SUV and caught Bruno's gaze on him in the rearview mirror. Even the dog looked sad. Or maybe disappointed in Luke.

"Stop. It's best this way."

Bruno huffed a sigh and lay down.

Luke cranked the SUV and headed away while his heart beat heavy with regret. Without thinking about it, he drove to Griffin's. He could drown his sorrows in his coffee. Or a milkshake and a burger.

Leaving Bruno in the Tahoe, he went inside and grabbed a seat at the bar area. Violet Griffin was the only one around and she approached him with a smile. "Hi, Luke, how's it going?"

"Fine."

"You need to work on that."

"What?"

"Being convincing."

He grimaced. "I've got a lot on my mind right now."

"Jordan?"

"Among other things."

"Well, if you want to talk about it, I'm a good listener."

"That's okay, I'll work it out. Could I get a cup of coffee?"

"Black?"

"Yep."

"Coming up." A minute later, she set the steaming mug in front of him.

"Thanks."

"Sure. Could I ask you a question?"

"Go for it."

She paused, then sighed. "Do you think you'll ever figure out what happened to Jordy?"

He closed his eyes at the pain the question produced but nodded. "Yeah. I do."

"You know my parents live next door to the Jamesons, right?"

"Yes." He'd forgotten it until she just mentioned it, but he'd known that.

"My mom talks to Mrs. Jameson quite a bit. They're all blindsided and reeling."

"We all are."

"I don't think Zach's handling this very well."

"What do you mean?"

She shrugged. "Just a feeling I get. He comes in occasionally and just stares out the window. I'm worried about him."

So she'd said before. "You seem to be mostly focused on Zach. Is there something else going on?"

A flush crept into her cheeks. "No, of course not. All the Jamesons are like family. It's just… Zach seems to be taking it the hardest, that's all."

"I'll keep an eye on him," Luke said softly. He hadn't noticed, but maybe that was because he'd been so lost in his own grief and roller-coaster emotions when it came to Sophie that he just hadn't been aware.

"That would be great, Luke. Can I get you anything else? I've got to take off in a bit for a shift at the airport."

"I'm all right for now but thank you."

"Okay. Mom and Dad are both in the back if you need anything." She swept the apron over her head and disappeared into the kitchen.

Luke sipped his coffee and decided Violet wasn't completely truthful with him. When he'd first met her, he'd thought she and Zach were a couple because of the way they went back and forth with each other. Sniping about nothing, grumbling like an old married couple.

When Violet headed for the door a few minutes later, he turned. "Hey, Violet?"

She stopped at the door and glanced back at him. "Yes?"

"Why haven't you and Zach ever gotten together?"

This time the flush darkened her cheeks to a deep red. "I don't know what you're talking about." And then she was gone.

He smirked. Right.

His mirth faded immediately, and he finished his coffee as he continued to second-guess himself. His mind knew Sophie was right. It wasn't his fault his mother was dead. It wasn't his fault Claude Jenks had almost killed Sophie. And it wasn't his fault that Jordan was dead because he hadn't found him in time. His heart wanted to argue.

Luke grabbed his keys and left the diner, heading home with Bruno. When he came to his front door, he noted it had been fixed temporarily and wondered who he had to thank for that. Probably one of his unit members. Gratitude swept over him even as the empty house slapped him in the face.

Never before Sophie had he minded coming home to the emptiness. Now he wanted her here.

Bruno whined and headed and down the hall to Sam's room. "She's not here, boy."

The dog kept going. When he came back, he slumped onto his bed in front of the fireplace, eyeing Luke with the demand that he fix this.

Luke dropped onto the couch and decided to pray about the big hole in the vicinity of his heart that he had a feeling only Sophie could fill.

When Sophie walked into the office two days later, she had a smile on her face in spite of the heaviness in her heart. Her father had asked her to stay upstairs with him her first night home from the hospital and she'd agreed but couldn't stand his well-meant hovering and sad, knowing eyes.

"It's about that man who wouldn't leave your side, isn't it?" her father had asked.

"What?"

"Luke. He's the deep sadness you can't hide."

"Yes. It's about him, but I don't want to talk about it because there's nothing to say, okay? He made his choice and I'll heal. And besides, a romance wouldn't work now anyway."

"Why not?"

"Because I've just got too much going on right now."

"Meaning me and Trey?"

She'd blinked. "Well, no. I mean—"

"Honey, Trey and I love all that you do for us, but we can't be your life. You need to go after what you want. What you need. Don't let us stand in your way of a future full of happiness."

"You're not." But Luke was.

Her father had hugged her and kissed the top of her head and that had been the end of it.

Except for the *looks*.

So, she'd gone downstairs to her place to escape. And been miserably lonely with only her thoughts to keep her company.

This morning, she'd rolled out of bed after a restless sleep filled with nightmares of drowning and headed to the office, determined to get her mind off her troubles.

She walked through the lobby toward her office and waved to Zach, whose desk was closest to her door. He stood. "Hey, everyone, Sophie's back!"

A cheer went up and clapping started. Everyone was in the office today. Bree, Gavin, Reed, Tony, the Jameson brothers and Finn were on their feet.

After a long round of applause, Sophie pressed her hands to her heated cheeks. "Thanks, guys. You sure know how to embarrass a girl." But they knew she loved their show of appreciation.

However, she couldn't help but notice Luke wasn't there.

Noah stepped out of Jordan's old office. "Welcome back, Sophie. This place hasn't been the same without you." He hugged her and some of her sadness lifted. It was nice to be missed.

"I'm glad to be back, thanks."

He looked down at her, concern drawing his brows together. "You know, no one would fault you for needing to take more time. You've been through a huge trauma."

She shook her head. "I'm not going anywhere. This is my home and you guys are my family." Even if staying meant seeing Luke every day. Things would never be the same between them—and maybe that was one of the reasons she wanted to stay. She hadn't quite given up hope that he would eventually come around and realize he could love her in spite of his past.

"Good," Noah said, "I'm glad we've got that settled."

The door opened, and Katie stepped inside. Her right hand rested lightly on her abdomen and Sophie thought she caught a hint of tears in her eyes before she took a deep breath. "Hi, guys."

Everyone stopped. Noah went to his sister-in-law and gave her a hug. "What are you doing here?"

"I came to pick up some of Jordan's things, and—"

"And?"

"I also came to tell you all something since you're here."

The others gathered closer. Carter raised a brow and threw an arm across Zach's shoulders. "Everything okay?"

Katie met Sophie's gaze. Sophie smiled her encouragement.

"I've already told your parents and they told me I had to get down here ASAP and tell you."

The brothers exchanged frowns. "Katie—"

She held up a hand and Noah fell silent. "Let me finish, please." Her gaze swept the room, touching on all of them. "I just noticed Luke isn't here."

"He'll be here soon," Sophie said. "But it's okay. Go ahead."

Katie cleared her throat and Zach groaned. "Come on, Katie, spill it."

"I am, I promise. I just wanted to say how much I love all of you and how grateful I am that I got to be married to Jordan."

Sophie's throat closed and from the sudden silence, she figured hers wasn't the only one.

"Anyway," Katie said, "I know we've all been terribly sad, but I've got some good news."

The tension in the room lightened considerably.

"The day Jordan disappeared, we had an appointment that was supposed to take place after the graduation ceremony. Unfortunately, that never happened." She drew in a deep breath and blinked back the tears that surged in her pretty blue eyes. "Anyway, I just wanted to let you all know that Jordan will live on in his son or daughter." The last word slipped out on a whisper.

Sophie swiped a tear that insisted on leaking down her cheek.

Zach cleared his throat. "Aw, Katie, that's…that's…" He couldn't finish his thought due to the emotions obviously overwhelming him. Sophie stepped forward and gripped his arm.

Carter let out a whoop. "What my brother's trying

to say is that's fabulous." He hugged her, and Katie let
out a teary laugh.

One by one, the others congratulated and hugged
her and Sophie could see how much the news meant
to Jordan's brothers.

"Hey, everyone," Bree said, "not to steal Katie's
thunder, but I just got a text from Ynez. Stella's had her
puppies! I'm going to go see them. Is that okay, Noah?"

Ynez Dubois, the vet they used whenever they
needed one.

Noah shook his head and laughed. "Sure, why not?
Who can resist puppies?"

Sophie could tell he'd agreed because he knew they
all needed all the lighthearted, feel-good moments they
could get right now.

"I know it's not nearly as exciting as Katie being
pregnant," Bree said, "but babies are babies, right?"

"Right," Sophie said. Together, they walked the
short distance from the offices to the vet's.

Dr. Ynez Dubois met them at the door. "Wow, the
whole crew is here. Follow me."

Sophie held back and let the others go first. She
wanted to see the pups, but Luke's absence put a
damper on her joy.

And then it was her turn to kneel next to the sleeping bundles of yellow, brown and black. "They're so
precious."

"They're going to need homes when they're big
enough," Dr. Dubois said. Her lightly accented voice
held a world of hope. "Any of you up for fostering?"

Sophie looked up at her and smiled. "I am." She
could use the company. And if the pup eventually

was deemed able to be trained for the NYPD, then she would get to see the dog on a regular basis. If, for some reason, its temperament wasn't compatible with K-9 work, then she'd have a pet. A win-win situation in her opinion.

"Hey, everyone, I heard a rumor that we've got some new additions that'll be ready for training before too long."

Sophie froze at the sound of Luke's voice.

"Come take a look," Gavin said.

Luke stepped up next to her and Sophie's breath caught. He looked tired, but...peaceful?

"I'm surprised to see you here," he said to her as Bruno shouldered his way to her and nudged her with his snout.

She shrugged and scratched Bruno's head until he seemed satisfied with the attention and moved on to the area where the puppies were. After a brief sniff of the tiny bodies, at Stella's low growl, he turned and walked to the far corner of the room, where he lay down.

Sophie looked back at the puppies, not wanting Luke to see the hurt—and longing—in her eyes. "I've got work to do."

"Like what?"

"Like resend some emails to all the shelters and parks department staff to remind them Snapper's still missing. Gotta stay on top of things, you know?" She was babbling. Not that it wasn't true, but... She sighed. "Staying at home produces nothing but tears. I just... need to work." She stayed on her knees, hoping Luke would take the hint and move on.

EIGHTEEN

Luke swallowed hard. He'd made up his mind about what he was going to do when he saw her again, but her cold shoulder sent his anxiety soaring—along with his determination. Nope, he wasn't going to wimp out. And he wasn't going to live his life in fear or self-blame. He drew in a deep breath and knelt beside her. "Hey, would you want to take a walk?" he whispered.

This time she met his gaze, startled. "Now?"

"Yes, please?"

She gave the nearest puppy's head a gentle scratch. "Where?"

"Back to headquarters, I guess." He glanced at the others still enamored with the pups and lightheartedly arguing which ones would be trained in what specialty. "While everyone else is otherwise occupied?"

"Um…okay. Why?"

"Because I want to talk to you and I don't need a nosy audience. If we're careful, I think we can slip out without being noticed."

"They can be a nosy bunch, can't they?" She offered him a small smile.

He took her hand and breathed easier when she didn't pull away from him. He helped her to her feet, gathered Bruno's leash and led her out the door. The dog trailed along a few steps behind, content just to be with them.

"I decided to take a lesson from Bruno—and you," Luke said.

"What kind of lesson?"

"Look at him. He works hard, he's good at what he does, but he knows how to chill and enjoy life. I want to be like that."

"Okay."

He laughed and shook his head. "You're not going to make this easy, are you?"

Her eyes softened. "I'm not trying to make it difficult, Luke. I just need you to tell me what you're thinking."

"I'm thinking you were right."

A smile started to curve her lips. "About?"

"You know what about." He sighed. "I really messed things up with you and I'm sorry. I was very wishy-washy and inconsistent. You didn't deserve that."

"Thank you."

"I know what I want, Sophie, I'm just praying you want it, too."

"What's that?"

"A future together. Honestly, Sophie, every time I look at my future, you're in it. If I try to picture it without you, well, it's just not possible."

Tears flooded her eyes. "I thought you didn't want to pursue anything between us until Jordan's killer was found. What's changed?"

He gave a slow nod. "That's a fair question." He paused, wanting, needing to find the right words. "I didn't think I'd ever find someone I could trust my heart with again. Not after it took such a beating, but then you came along and the attraction I felt—and I think you felt—scared me. I think I was using the case to protect myself from my feelings for you. In other words, I was running like a coward."

"You're not a coward."

"Thanks."

"What kind of feelings?"

He huffed a short chuckle, then sucked in a deep breath. "Sophie, I'm not good at expressing myself. I never have been. After my mom was killed, I sort of locked everything up inside because I'd decided feelings were bad. Not all, of course, but you couldn't have the good without the bad, so I just decided not to feel."

"It was your coping mechanism. You were protecting yourself."

"Maybe." He sighed. "Probably. And the truth is, sometimes it worked, sometimes it didn't. With you, it didn't. I started falling in love with you the minute Jenks shoved you into my arms and we fell on the sidewalk."

She gave a breathless puff of laughter. "What?"

"And you popped up like you weren't hurting and said we needed to get back to headquarters. You were so spunky and determined and… I realized I was in trouble from that moment on."

"Trouble, hmm?"

"Well, my heart anyway. And then when you were kidnapped and I almost didn't get there in time…" He looked away and drew in yet another breath, steadying his emotions. "Walking away from you in the hospital was one of the hardest things I've ever done...and one of the dumbest."

"I'm glad you realize that last part."

He laughed. "I guess what I'm trying to say in my bumbling, awkward way is that life is short. Too short not to grab hold of something when it's right. And I think you and I together are very, very right."

Sophie couldn't stop the tears from falling any more than she could stop the tide from coming in. "You really think it's right?"

"Yes. I really do. I've come to the conclusion that age is just a number. Everyone is different and I was silly to judge you based on a number. You're so very... you. Young, but much older than I am in a lot of ways."

"Because of the way I grew up, probably. I had a lot of responsibility on my shoulders and had to grow up fast. Just like you did, if you think about it."

"Maybe. All I know is that I couldn't stand it if I lost you, Sophie."

She sniffed and swiped a hand across her cheek. "You're not going to lose me."

"But that's my point. We don't know what the future holds, and I don't want to waste another minute of it *fearing* it, being afraid to trust again and take chances. I want to live boldly and face it with you. Together. Um...you and me. Us."

"Luke?"

"Yes?"

"Could you just say it, please?"

"I love you, Sophie."

"Thank you."

He blinked. "Thank you? That's it?"

"And I love you, too. I think I have for a long time."

"What do you mean?"

"I mean, I noticed you when you weren't noticing me."

"But…you never said anything."

She scoffed. "Of course not. What was I going to do, walk up to you and ask you out and have you say, 'Who are you again?'"

"I wasn't *that* bad!"

She grinned. "Almost." Then sobered. "And I was worried about my dad and brother." She gave a short self-deprecating laugh. "Apparently, they don't need me quite as much as I thought they did."

"They need you. Just maybe not in the ways you thought."

"I know. Dad made that pretty clear." She paused. "Is it bad to be so happy while Jordan's killer is still out there?"

"What do you think?"

A slow smile slipped across her lips. "I think he'd be thrilled for us."

"Absolutely. And super mad at us if we don't cherish what we've got."

Sophie nodded, hard-pressed to get any more words past her tight throat. Jordan had lived each day with full gusto, determined to make the world a better place before he died. And he'd done that by investing in the lives of those he came into contact with.

"I don't want to be your coworker anymore," Luke said, his voice husky with emotion.

"You don't?" she squeaked. "Well, why not?"

"Because I want to be your husband. If that's okay with you."

With a squeal, Sophie launched herself into Luke's arms and planted a serious kiss on his surprised lips. He laughed when she came up for air. "Is that a yes?"

"That's a definite yes."

Cheers erupted from behind them and Luke spun, Sophie still in his arms. Sophie giggled at the sight that greeted her. Every last team member stood gawking and clapping.

"Way to go, Luke!" Zach pumped a fist in the air and Luke grinned at him. "It's about time you opened your eyes and saw the woman was crazy about you."

"He knew?"

"Everybody in the office probably did," she admitted.

"Then I'd say it's definitely about time," he murmured.

Bruno barked twice.

Luke laughed. "I guess Bruno agrees."

"I agree with Bruno," she said. "Now, kiss me again. I've been waiting a long time for you to do so without an apology attached at the end."

So, he did.

* * * * *

Dana Mentink is a national bestselling author. She has been honored to win two Carol Awards, a HOLT Medallion and an RT Reviewers' Choice Best Book Award. She's authored more than thirty novels to date for Love Inspired Suspense and Harlequin Heartwarming. Dana loves feedback from her readers. Contact her at danamentink.com.

Visit the Author Profile page
at Harlequin.com for more titles.

ACT OF VALOR

Dana Mentink

I will both lay me down in peace, and sleep:
for thou, Lord, only makest me dwell in safety.
—*Psalms* 4:8

To the brave officers of the NYPD, both canine and human, thank you for your service.

ONE

Instinct ratcheted up Violet Griffin's pulse. Something was definitely not right with the passenger who stood before her, his body stiff with impatience. The impatience part was par for the course at LaGuardia Airport in Queens. Her ticketing counter at Emerge Airline was always crazy, and passengers were not known for accepting delays with good cheer, but this guy was downright jumpy. Long and lean, with an ill-fitting canvas jacket, dark glasses and bottle-blond hair caught in a tight braid, he chewed his lip until it was his turn.

"I wanna talk to him, not you." The man pointed at her boss, Bill Oscar.

She took a moment to breathe, plaster on her "you will not fluster me" mask and flip her curtain of wheat-brown curls behind her shoulder.

"No need. I can take care of you. May I see your driver's license please?"

He shifted the strap of the bag that hung from his shoulder. "I said I want your supervisor to check me in. That guy, over there."

She gritted her teeth, trying to keep her thoughts

from coming out of her mouth. "I assure you, I can handle it, sir. I've been doing this job for a very long time."

"No," he snapped. "Him."

Shifting slightly, her fingers inched toward the security phone. If the man was about to become out of control, he'd be met with plenty of airport security.

But her boss flashed her a plump-cheeked smile. "I got this, Vi."

Insulted, she stepped aside and tended to another customer. Bill's easy grin was still in place. He must think her testiness was pure overreaction, since he did not seem the least bit nonplussed. Had he intervened to spare her aggravation, then? But she was an expert at dealing with aggravation and soothing ruffled feathers. She'd been doing it brilliantly for ten years now. She pondered her reaction to the guy as she processed a line of customers. Was her patience thinner than usual? Had her recent anguish started to show at work?

Zach Jameson's tormented blue eyes surfaced in her memory. He was in agony over the death of his older brother Jordan, the victim of a murder made to look like a suicide. She'd heard the officers gathered at her parents' diner reliving the terrible situation, trying to grapple with their grief. It had been torment for all the Jameson brothers, Noah, Zach and Carter, and for the entire NYC K-9 Command. Jordy had been the well-respected leader of their unit based in Queens. The loss was compounded by the fact that the guy who planted Jordan's fake suicide note had run into traffic and been killed while officers attempted to arrest him. The papers had run daily stories filled with more speculation than fact, but until the medical examiner's official findings were in, only Jordy's cop brothers knew for sure that their mentor had not killed himself, especially since his widow was expecting their first child.

Sadness and anger cloaked the whole NYC K-9 Command Unit in smothering grief, but it was the youngest Jameson brother who seemed to struggle most. She'd known Zach since she was a kid, and she prayed she could help him through the worst time in his life, but he was cold and distant, buried in a chill she could not penetrate no matter how hard she pressed.

Bill finished with the twitchy passenger and walked him across the busy floor to a security agent by the baggage screen. Violet relaxed. His carry-on bag would be x-rayed, and authorities alerted if anything was amiss. She was about to call out a thank-you to Bill when she saw the TSA agent usher the man through the line without putting his bag on the conveyor or walking him through the metal detector.

Agape, she hurried to her boss. "Bill, did you see that?"

He shuffled through the papers on his counter. "It's not a problem. Don't worry about it." He gave his attention to the next customer.

Not a problem? How was allowing a passenger onto a plane without proper scan not a problem? Boss or no boss, she was about to let Bill have a piece of her mind when a voice snapped her back.

"I'm in a hurry."

The next passenger's license identified him as Joe Brown. The short, barrel-chested man was a regular, flying on business, she'd always assumed. The overhead lighting gleamed off his scalp, which shone through a harsh crew cut as he pushed his suitcase onto the scale.

"Your luggage is overweight, sir. You'll have to pay a fee."

He started to argue, but she merely pointed to the digital numbers on the scale. "Take something out and put it into your carry-on or pay the fee. That's it."

With a jerk, he plopped the suitcase down, putting his body between her and the contents, and yanked the zipper. She smelled the overpowering whiff of menthol. She leaned forward.

He stared at her, eyes like wet stones. "Cold rub. I've been ill."

Cold rub? Tension slithered through her stomach. She'd heard before from Zach that smugglers had all kinds of notions about how to fool the noses of detection dogs like Zach's beagle, Eddie. Cold rub...to mask the smell of...?

When the customer yanked a rolled-up leather jacket from his bag, she saw a glimpse of something inside, lumpy, wrapped in a sock. Whatever it was had some heft to it.

Her heart stopped. Cocaine? Should she call security? But what if she was misreading the situation like she might have with the previous passenger? She forced a nonchalant smile. "Excuse me for one minute."

She walked quickly to Bill and whispered to him. "I think that guy's smuggling drugs."

Bill frowned. "I'll take it from here."

She watched, pulse pounding in her throat as her boss approached Joe. The man stood quickly, pulled on the jacket, one side hanging down lower than the other.

Whatever he'd had rolled inside must be jammed in the pocket now. She fingered her phone, ready to call for security or maybe even Zach. His work with a drug-detection dog took him all over Brooklyn and Queens as well as other boroughs, but currently he was assigned to LaGuardia Airport. She'd waved to him not an hour before, noting the slump of his shoulders, the haggard look that indicated another sleepless night.

To her utter shock, Bill Oscar pointed Joe toward the same security agent. This could not be. She grabbed at his sleeve, snapping at him. "What's going on?"

He detached himself. "Nothing at all. You need to relax. As a matter of fact, you're due for a break. I got the counter." He gently pressured her away. "Go get some coffee. You look tired."

He practically propelled her away, which only flipped on her stubborn switch. *No way. Whatever is going on here is not happening on my watch.* As Joe Brown strolled toward the TSA agent, she hurried along with her cell phone. If Bill was suddenly abdicating his job, she'd at least get a good picture of Brown and text it to Zach.

Just before she took the photo, Brown turned around.

His look brimmed with such malice, it was all she could do not to run. Her mouth went dry as she read the threat in the grim lines of his mouth. Backing away, she headed toward the employee break room, skin erupting in clammy goose bumps. The terminal was undergoing a remodel and the place where she was headed was sectioned off with cones—only employees allowed. Plastic draped the work areas and the din of an air compressor and a nail gun assaulted her eardrums.

Call Zach. Her fingers fumbled with the phone. The hairs on the back of her neck prickled, and she risked a look. Brown was striding toward her, putting himself between her and the milling crowd.

She realized her mistake at once.

Isolated corridor.

Empty break room.

And a drug smuggler bearing down on her.

She could scream, but over the din of the air compressor and construction noises no one would hear a sound.

It was time to run.

Officer Zach Jameson surveyed the throng of people congregated around the ticketing counter. Most ignored Zach and K-9 partner, Eddie, and that suited him just fine. Two months earlier he would have greeted people with a smile, or at least a polite nod while he and Eddie did their work of scanning for potential drug smugglers. These days he struggled to keep his mind on his duty while the ever-present darkness nibbled at the edges of his soul.

Jordan, his oldest brother and chief of the NYC K-9 Command Unit, was gone. Sometimes it still felt unreal to Zach. His words at his brother's funeral came back to him, when he'd promised Jordy's widow, Katie, that he and his brothers would bring her husband's killer to justice.

But they hadn't, not yet. It didn't help that his older brothers Noah and Carter, and other K-9 officers of the unit and all their collected dogs were officially off the case because of their familial connection to the victim.

Even though Noah had been appointed interim chief, he was shut firmly out of the investigation like the rest of them. A storehouse of training, intelligence, loyalty and commitment and where had it gotten them? Nowhere. The only lead so far had been killed during the attempted arrest, and Zach had not even been on scene to try and prevent it. And to add one final twist to the knife in his gut, Jordy's police dog, Snapper, was still missing.

With Jordy gone, justice and duty were the only two things Zach had left, the former seeming more unreachable every passing day. As for duty, sometimes it felt like he was going through the motions in a haze—phoning it in, as his brothers might say. The badge meant everything to him, and he despised the way that grief was dulling his edge as a cop.

Eddie plopped his bony rump on Zach's steel-toed boot and looked up into his face as if to say, "Let's do our jobs, okay?"

He stroked the dog's ears and sucked in a breath, trying to clear away the fog that had descended on him the moment he heard of his brother's death. A cop always lived with the fact that he might lose his life in the line of duty, but not this way, when Jordan and Katie had their first baby coming, and not when Zach should have been watching Jordan's back like Jordan had always done for his younger kin.

Jordan was the one who had prayed and prodded Zach through his police training, a process made more difficult by Zach's dyslexia. Everything hands-on came easy, but the written exams…taking those was like chiseling away at a mountain with a butter knife.

"Don't give up. Police force needs you, Zacho," Jordy had said during their tutoring sessions, employing the nickname Zach despised. "You're gonna be a great cop."

For all his brother's confidence, Zach hadn't had so much as a whiff of suspicion that his brother was in danger. Some cop, clueless and inept. His brain knew he should talk to somebody, somebody like Violet Griffin, his friend from childhood who'd reached out so many times. His brain knew, but his heart would not let him pass through the dark curtain. And there was no way he was talking to some department-appointed shrink who wasn't even a cop. They'd have to slap on cuffs and knock him unconscious before they dragged him into that office.

"Just get to work," he muttered to himself as his phone vibrated. Probably another text from his mom. Ivy Jameson paid no attention to the fact that he was not supposed to take personal messages while on duty. Truth be told, he'd been avoiding her calls because he could not stand to hear her cry or detect the worry in her voice when she asked him how he was doing. He'd call her later.

The phone trilled again, indicating it was a call this time. He checked the number.

Violet.

He considered ignoring it, but Violet didn't ever call unless she needed help and she rarely needed anyone. Strong enough to run a ticket counter at LaGuardia and have enough energy left over to help out at Griffin's, her family's diner. She could handle belligerent customers in both arenas and bake the best apple pie he'd ever had the privilege to chow down.

It almost made him smile as he accepted the call.

"Someone's after me, Zach."

Panic rippled through their connection. Panic, from a woman who was tough as they came. "Who? Where are you?"

Her breath was shallow as if she was running.

"I'm trying to get to the break room. I can lock myself in, but I don't... I can't..." There was a clatter.

"Violet?" he shouted.

But there was no answer.

He sprinted toward the Emerge Airline break room, Eddie racing right behind him.

TWO

Violet's phone spiraled out of her hand, clattering to the floor as Joe dropped his bag and grabbed for her arm. She wrenched herself free and lunged toward the break room door. Wild energy fueled her. When he caught up with her again, she fired a kick at his patella and heard his satisfying grunt of pain. He doubled over, grabbing at his knee, and she used the moment to thrust her ID card in its lanyard at the code reader. Her hands shook so badly it didn't work.

Why did you run here, you fool? The remodeling job left the normally bustling hallway quiet and deserted, no one to hear her scream, no one to help.

She shot a look over her shoulder. Brown loomed behind her, cheeks flushed with exertion, nostrils flared, a grimace filled with violence with no human feeling behind it. There was no question in her mind that he would kill her if she gave him the slightest chance. Were there any construction workers or painters around? A single fellow employee?

Frantically, she tried her ID again, willing her fingers to cooperate. He was only a few yards away now, closing fast. After two agonizing seconds the door clicked open. She shoved it and scrambled inside, attempting to slam it behind her.

To her horror, something prevented it closing—Brown's booted foot. With everything in her she tried to hold the door closed, her arms rigid and trembling with the effort. Inch by inch he forced it open, one hand reaching through the gap, capturing her around the wrist, digging in.

Yanking free from his grip she scratched at his face, aiming for the eyes. Surprised, he jerked back. She threw all her body weight at the door. It shuddered but did not close. He rammed his boot at it and then he was in, pushing her until she fell backward onto the floor. Crab-walking in terror she looked for something, anything she could use to defend herself. She found nothing.

Towering over her, he smiled, one front tooth sporting a tiny chip. "You stuck your nose in where you shouldn't have."

"I called the cops," she said, throat tight. "They're on the way."

"You'll be dead before they get here." Again, the smile. "A quick death is better. We could make it last much longer if we wanted to."

She opened her mouth to scream, but he was on her, rough palm pressed over her mouth. Clawing and twisting she tried to break free, to make it to the door, to knee him, poke his eye, stop her own murder however she could.

He was too strong, deflecting her efforts as though

she were a small child instead of a grown woman fighting for her life.

He reached for his pocket.

She would kick out, roll away. Maybe she'd be shot or stabbed but she would go down fighting until she had not one tiny ounce of strength left.

She heard a shrill bark, the sound of scrabbling claws and running feet. He grabbed her chin in his hand, fingers pressing into her flesh. "You butted in to my business. Not gonna leave any witnesses behind to ID me. This won't be done until you're dead." Then he released his grip and charged to the door.

Through her shuddering breaths, she heard another bark. It was Eddie, had to be, and Zach. Would they be gunned down as they sprinted toward the break room? Frantically, she tried to scramble to her feet, but her body systems were offline, legs trembling, lungs gasping for breath, terror charging every nerve and sinew. The best she could do was sit up, head whirling.

Zach slammed through the door with Eddie, gun in hand. Relief made her whimper. Brown must have gotten away without a shoot-out.

When he saw her, his blue eyes went wide and he dropped to a knee at her side. Eddie whined and poked his nose at her shin.

"Vi...how bad is it?"

"I..." she stammered. He was reaching for the radio clipped to his shoulder.

"Don't move. I'm calling an ambulance. Backup is already rolling, and Carter will be here in two minutes."

"No," she finally managed. He stopped as if he'd gotten an electric shock.

"I'm okay." She finally got the words out.

"No, you're not. I'm calling."

She forced her teeth to stop chattering. "Go after him, Zach. He goes by Joe Brown. He had drugs in his suitcase. I saw. He's wearing a brown leather jacket."

"Not leaving you."

Zach reached for the radio again, but she snatched for his wrist, pressing her fingers there and taking comfort in the steady rhythm of his pulse.

"I'm okay. Not hurt."

He raised a doubtful eyebrow. "You'd say that if you'd been sawed in half."

She shoved the hair from her face. "New York tough."

He touched her cheek with a tentative finger. "Griffin tough. You have a red mark. Here."

The touch made something ache inside, but she brushed him off. "Go do your job," she said in a voice with only the tiniest break in it, which she hoped he would not notice. "There was another guy. I don't know if they were together. He had a long braid. My boss, Bill, he escorted him to security and the TSA let him through without scanning his bags."

"Vi..." He huffed out a breath, broad chest still heaving from his run along the corridor. "Let me help you, wouldja? You could be hurt more than you think."

She flashed him a cocky smile. "Griffin tough, remember?"

She knew what he was thinking. Jordan, his hero of an older brother, had been tough, too, and now he was dead. Zach's expression said it all.

With surprising tenderness, he pressed his cheek to her palm. Warmth spread from their point of contact, up her arm, reviving and restoring. She wanted to keep him there, strong jaw, warm skin, the gesture so vulnerable. She yearned to reach out and stroke his thatch of close-cut chestnut hair and block out what had just happened.

"I'm not losing any more family. Not on my watch," he mumbled into her cupped palm.

Family. You're like a sister to him, her mind prodded. *That's all.* She sucked in a breath and tried to get hold of her glitching emotions. It took all her effort to detach herself from him. "I'm fine. Like I said. Stop babying me."

Another officer barreled in. Zach brought him up to speed and the officer relayed the info on the radio.

Zach shifted his attention from his colleague to her and back again.

"Go," she said, tone all business, tipping her chin up and daring him with her glance to disobey.

He gave her one more look, filled with emotions that a tough K-9 cop would never put into words. Concern for a longtime family friend, no doubt. Eagerness to do his job. Guilt at how he'd failed his brother. His gaze wandered her face, lips twitching for a moment with some unspoken thought. Her heart ached to see something else in his countenance, something beyond duty and childhood affection, but he turned away, in pursuit of his quarry.

Part of her prayed he would catch up to Joe Brown.

This won't be done until you're dead.

The other part prayed he wouldn't.

Fifteen frustrating minutes later Zach met his brother Carter by the ticket counter. The suspect had bolted.

Zach noted the disgruntled white shepherd, Frosty, panting at Carter's side. Fortuitous that Carter, a transit K-9 cop, was at LaGuardia for some training with the TSA employees. The command unit had dogs assigned to various departments throughout the NYPD so most of the time they were not serving in the same spot at the same time. They each had their specific unit duties, which could be preempted if a situation required a particular canine's abilities. The duties were ever changing, and it was part of the reason Zach loved his job. Even before Carter's report, Zach could tell by the dog's dejected demeanor that there had been no suspect taken into custody. Zach felt exactly the same way as the dog. He ground his teeth as his brother spun out the details.

"Witnesses saw a guy matching the description exit the airport heading west. We're on it. Still trying to work out what happened to the other guy. He didn't get on a plane, so he must have seen the cop activity and taken off, too." He cocked his head. "Vi?"

"She says she's okay. Refused an ambulance."

Carter quirked a wry smile. "Yeah. Big surprise. I'll gather Violet's boss and any other witnesses we can round up. You and Eddie gonna do a sweep?"

"Yeah. Listen, can you pull someone else to start on the statements and go sit with Violet? She's shaken up, and I want one of us with her."

His brother nodded. "Ten-four. On my way."

It made Zach feel infinitely better to know that Carter would be with Violet. For all her brave talk, there was a shadow of something in her eyes that made him wonder if she was as okay as she proclaimed to be. Not that she'd admit anything else under pain of death.

Considering the lowlife who put his hands on her made Zach's blood heat to near boiling. He forced himself to calm down. Tension was transmitted right down the leash, through the harness to Eddie, and there was no need for that. Eddie had had a difficult start in life, tied to a streetlamp as a puppy one bitter February evening and left to die. Sent to a busy shelter, he'd been rescued by a group that evaluated dogs for potential police service. Eddie's nose, even as an untrained pup, was stellar. He'd been given his name in honor of fallen NYPD officer Ed Owens. Best of all, Eddie worked for two things: affection and treats. Zach made those treats from scratch. Nothing was too good for Eddie.

Zach bent down and fondled Eddie's ears, capturing the dog's muzzle and looking at his sad brown eyes. "You're my good baby, aren't you?" he whispered in a singsong voice that he'd never allow anyone else to hear. Then, louder, "Work time."

Eddie sprang to his feet, twenty-five pounds of get-up-and-go, primed for the search. If Violet was right, maybe her attacker had ditched the drugs somewhere when he heard the cavalry arrive. If there were drugs in the vicinity, Eddie would know it, thanks to his 220 million scent receptors and a ferocious drive to do his job. All that dog talent wrapped in an adorable package. Eddie was a rock star, in Zach's view, even if he had a two-mile-wide stubborn streak. *Just like his handler*, Jordy had often said.

"Find the drugs, Eddie."

The dog put his nose to the floor as they worked their way along the corridor. There was nothing of interest immediately outside the break room. Eddie snuffled along the corridor with that signature beagle trot and tail wag. They headed to the terminal, which the cops had temporarily closed. Irate passengers huffed and complained. He ignored them, easing Eddie through the throng. Another beautiful thing about beagles: they didn't scare people like some other breeds of police dogs. Eddie was a goodwill ambassador when he wasn't taking down drug smugglers.

Carter messaged him that they had still not located the first guy who had passed through security. He'd somehow vanished, leading Zach to believe he'd been helped out of the airport by the same crooked employee and possibly Violet's boss.

Eddie sniffed, nose glued to the floor. Nothing. He shook his ears.

"Come on, boy. Anything?"

They moved on a few paces.

With a cheerful swish of his tail, Eddie waggled his way toward a cleaning cart. The custodian was about to empty a dustpan into the big plastic garbage bin.

An invisible shock went through the dog. Eddie tensed, tail erect, nostrils quivering. Zach could practically feel the animal's excitement, or maybe it was his own. He tried to keep his breathing even as Eddie circled and sat, the perfect passive response signal. He looked up at Zach.

"Sir, can you hold up a minute?" Zach called.

The custodian jerked in surprise. "Huh?"

"I need you to stop what you're doing for a moment."

The guy nodded and stepped away from the trash can. Zach peered in. "May I?" Zach said, pointing to a box of rubber gloves on the cart.

"Knock yourself out."

Zach pulled on rubber gloves and reached into the can, hauling out the brown leather jacket Violet had described and trying not to crow his triumph. Now he had physical evidence. There might be hair, prints, clues. Zach would bust the dirtbag who'd put his hands on Violet. It wasn't as good as chasing him down and cuffing him, but it was enough for now.

The custodian's mouth fell open. "Why would somebody throw away a perfectly good jacket?"

Zach put the pieces into place. Joe Brown was in a hurry, he'd heard Eddie approaching, a dog tracking the scent of the drugs, and he was desperate not to be caught. Eddie bayed long and loud. A sock peeked out of the jacket pocket, reeking with the smell of menthol rub. "He took the drugs out of his suitcase and dumped the jacket as a diversion when he ran," Zach muttered.

The custodian whistled. "Ain't that something. He figured your dog couldn't track the scent of drugs because of the cold rub?"

Zach gave Eddie one of his homemade treats from a pouch at his waist. "He figured wrong."

THREE

Zach waited impatiently for the airport officers to secure the evidence before he practically jogged with Eddie to find Violet. She looked more herself now, sitting in one corner of the employee room while Carter and the TSA supervisor interviewed her boss, Bill Oscar, in the other. He could tell by the tapping of her sleek pump on the carpeted floor that she was itching to confront the man herself. He went to her.

"Are you okay?"

"Yes, of course. He just knocked me over, that's all. Did you...?"

"He made it out of the terminal, but we've got officers looking for him, canvassing bus and subway stations, alerting the taxi cabs, et cetera. We'll get him."

"What about the other guy? Bill walked him to security. I don't know if he boarded or not."

"Looks like he ran, too. We're going over the camera footage. Don't worry."

She caught her lip between her teeth in that way that meant she was thinking. Violet was smart, so much smarter than he'd ever be. She'd been working on a college business degree in the evenings before her father broke his ankle last summer. Then she'd stepped in to help at the family restaurant, putting aside her college work for a while. Though her school was on a break for the next two weeks, she'd reenrolled in classes again, determined to finish this time. Smart, steel-tough, sassy, loyal as the day was long; that was Violet Griffin.

Bill finished with the officer and walked to them. "I am glad you're okay, Vi. I was worried."

A shower of sparks lit her eyes from coffee to caramel. "Don't bother with the pleasantries. You let the guy with the braid bypass security and you would have done the same with Joe Brown if I hadn't intervened. What gives?"

He shook his head. "Absolutely not. You misunderstood what you saw. I didn't know that TSA agent was gonna pass him through." He looked at Zach. "The guy with a long braid, acting shifty. I walked him to security personally. I figured he'd be scanned and detained if there was cause. That's a TSA responsibility."

"Just ID'd him from security footage. Roger Talmadge, goes by Roach. He's got a rap sheet—petty stuff, DUI, possession," Zach said.

Bill nodded. "I delivered him right to screening but there must have been something shady between this Roach and the TSA guy."

"Yeah," Zach said. "Agent's name is Jeb Leak. At the moment, he's missing."

"See?" Bill sighed. "On the take. New guy. I should have suspected, but…" He shrugged. "Well frankly, I was preoccupied. The wife's been sick, you know, and she's got a checkup today to see how the treatment's been working." His forehead was creased with deep grooves. "She's been in the hospital more than she's been out."

Though it looked as if her ire dulled a fraction, Violet was not about to be appeased. "What about Joe Brown? He had drugs in his suitcase. I saw it before he moved it to his pocket, and the chest rub was extra protection against the dogs."

"I agreed with you. He was probably smuggling something." Bill fixed her with a look. "Vi, you're killing me. We've worked together for ten years now, and I didn't want you involved if things were gonna get ugly, which is why I walked him there myself, just like the first guy. I was trying to protect you and you're practically accusing me of being in cahoots with a smuggler. How could you possibly think that?"

Violet didn't reply.

"Dump the guilt trip. Your behavior was suspicious," Zach said. "She was right about both men."

"I was trying to do my job and keep her out of trouble. I'd think that would garner a little appreciation." He sighed. "If you two are done interrogating me, I've got a mess of people at the ticket counter to sort through."

Violet started to follow him.

"No, no," Bill said, holding up a hand. "You go on home now. You've had a bad day and Liz is here to start her shift. Go get some rest."

Vi watched him leave, a troubled crimp on her mouth.

"You believe him?" Zach asked.

"I've known them for a long time. His wife, Rory, has been sick—breast cancer—and she hasn't responded well to treatments. He's shouldered a lot of the load with his two boys. Maybe he really was preoccupied, trying to keep me out of it." She broke off to look at Zach. "Do you trust him?"

"I'm not wired to trust people. Occupational hazard, but I do agree with him that you should go home. I'll take you."

She brushed back her hair with an impatient hand. "I don't need a chaperone. I can take the bus home or call a car service."

He braced himself for battle. "My car's faster. I have a shiny red siren."

"Your seats smell like a wet beagle, and you have a shift to finish. Go back to work."

He folded his arms. "My vehicle was detailed yesterday, and Eddie has recently been bathed with special shampoo. He practically reeks with the scent of a spring meadow. I'm walking you to my car and driving you home. You don't get to have a say in that, so grab your bag and let's go."

Her nostrils flared. "You're pushy."

"I'm right, as usual."

Vi arched an eyebrow. "Pretty high-and-mighty for a guy who can't ride a bike and breaks things on a regular basis."

"I can ride a bike, I just don't want to, and it's been two whole days since I busted anything."

"Uh-huh, but the last one at the diner was a doozy. You knocked over a wait stand and broke six dishes and a coffeepot."

"Four. Your mother said it was four dishes."

"My mother lied to make you feel better. I'm not as kind as she is."

"Get your bag, Vi," he said with a chuckle. He felt her staring at him. "What is it now?"

A gentle smile lit her face. "You laughed. I haven't heard you laugh since…" The smile faded. "I mean… for weeks."

He lifted a shoulder and grabbed for Eddie's leash. Violet had always been able to make him laugh with that combination of edgy humor and intelligence, matching him tease for tease. He knew a lot of great women—pretty, smart, ambitious—dated many of them, but none like her. There was something just…*better* about her, which he could not pin down. Probably she seemed different because he'd known her since she was a gap-toothed first-grader. Still, Violet was irreplaceable and if he and God were on speaking terms, he'd say a prayer of thanks that she was unharmed. Anger bit hard at him.

He and God weren't friends anymore. Zach deserved to encounter shipwrecks in his life, he'd probably caused most of them with his combination of impulsivity and stubbornness, but Jordy… God should have looked out for Jordy. No, he and God were no longer on speaking terms.

Shoving on his hat, he strode out of the room, grateful to have Vi clipping along in her pumps right next to him.

Violet kept her pace quick in spite of the twinges in her back and her throbbing cheekbone. She would not let Zach see her discomfort, especially the inner turmoil simmering below the surface like a monster fish ready to suck her under. She didn't want to speak of her feelings, not the real, raw, deep-down ones. Not to Zach.

He has too much on his heart already. I can't add to his burdens. Besides, they had their roles: he the jokester, overprotective big-brother type, and she the in-control, stand-up-to-anyone tough girl. She intended to keep it that way for both their sakes.

Bad enough that everyone was no doubt waiting at the diner, talking about what had happened. Her father would press for her to move into the cramped bedroom at the house in Rego Park where she'd grown up, but that would be going backward and she would not allow herself to give in to the fear. The airport attack was upsetting, traumatic, but it wasn't going to derail her progress. Her college classes were starting up again in a matter of weeks, and this time she wasn't going to take a break until she had that business degree firmly in her possession.

She was grateful that Zach did not seem to be in a talking mood as they exited the terminal and climbed on a shuttle. They made their way to the parking structure where Zach's car occupied a reserved police spot. Inside the garage the gloom felt smothering, the acrid scent of gasoline and exhaust making her stomach flip over. Eddie shook his muzzle as if to clear away the barrage of odors.

The silence grew tedious as they stepped into the garage elevator. She noticed the steely look on Zach's face. Claustrophobic, though he staunchly denied it. It brought her back to a day when the two of them, teenage rebels cutting school to go to the beach, had discovered a massive drainage pipe and stupidly gone in to explore. The deeper they'd gone into that cement tube, the sweatier and more panic-stricken Zach had become until she'd thought he was going to pass out. Grabbing his wrist, she'd led him from the pipe to a spot of sand where she'd held him around the shoulders until his breathing quieted.

"Sorry, Vi," he'd said, mortified, forehead pressed to hers.

She'd squeezed his fingers, kissed him on the cheek, made a joke and never mentioned the incident again. It was her gift to him, a secret kept, a silent pact from two childhood friends. And he'd kept her secrets, too. In eighth grade Gil Fisher had stolen her journal from her locker. Violet wasn't a writer, but inside were her sketches of the boys she'd had crushes on, complete with colored hearts around them. Gil was prepared to share her private drawings with every kid in the school until Zach got a hold of him. Whatever he'd said to Gil she would never know, but Gil had promptly handed back the journal and none of them had ever spoken of it. She wondered for the millionth time if Zach had seen the last picture in the journal, a picture she'd sketched of him.

As the elevator shuddered upward, the tight line of his jaw indicated that he was gritting out the ride. She wished she had the nerve to take his hand again and tell him she still understood, had his back through what-ever would come. She yearned to comfort him about Jordy's death. How the touch would comfort her, too, still the wobbling in her stomach and the trembling in her knees. But they had roles to play, didn't they? In-stead, she watched the buttons light the way to the third floor and stepped out next to him.

Violet sighed. "Satisfied? We made it to your car safe and sound. Box checked. The first part of your job is done."

He frowned. "You're not just a job, Vi."

He didn't look at her when he said it, and she knew the words hadn't been easy for him to get out. She gentled her tone. "I know. Thanks for everything."

"I'll get you settled in at your apartment. Make sure everything's secure."

"Not necessary."

"Did you get an alarm system or a Doberman since I was there last?"

"No."

"Then I'll check the doors and windows, since your roomie's out of town."

She threw up a hand. "Okay. You win."

"That's a first."

"It probably won't happen again anytime soon."

"Then I'll just bask in the glow."

She stopped at the rear bumper when he touched her shoulders.

"Really, Vi. Kidding aside. I want you to be careful." His hands wandered up her back, coming to rest on her neck under her hair. The blue of his eyes lulled her, his face so incredibly handsome.

A squealing of tires split the air. Zach's head jerked up. A car peeled around the curve, a flash of a familiar face behind the wheel, big, barrel-chested.

Her attacker.

Joe Brown.

Eyes slitted, ruthless, determined half smile.

The car bore down on them. Zach shoved Violet behind him.

In terror she grappled to get hold of his shirt and pull him back with her between the parked cars, but he was turning, reaching for his side arm, shouting.

The car careened on, charging toward Zach and Eddie like a heat-seeking missile until the front bumper plowed into the rear of Zach's SUV.

Glass shattered somewhere close, pinging her with tiny chips. She stumbled.

Zach leaped backward, pulling Eddie with him, crashing into the side of the vehicle. A bright drop of blood splattered the rear passenger window.

Zach lay on the ground, eyes closed, while Eddie whined and pawed at his chest.

FOUR

Zach felt pressure on his rib cage, a flash of hot pain on his cheek, followed by the clammy squelch of a probing dog nose. Cold from the cement floor seeped through his uniform shirt. The sensations coalesced all at once into a frantic need to move. He opened his eyes and jerked to a sitting position, sending Eddie into another round of high-pitched yelping. He saw himself mirrored in Violet's brown irises as she stared down at him. She pressed a hand to his sternum.

"Stay still. I'll call for an ambulance."

He ignored her, struggling to his feet while scanning the parking lot for Joe Brown. He was long gone. Zach bit back a growl of frustration, jerked his radio free and called in. The on-duty police and TSA were alerted to look for the vehicle. It was the best they could do. He declined medical help, of course. Mercifully, Violet appeared unharmed. One thing had gone right, anyway.

"How did he know you were leaving with me?" he mused. "Seems unlikely he would stick around to tail us." It wasn't coincidence, either. LaGuardia had multiple police parking areas, both outdoors as well as the garage, so it hadn't been a fortunate guess on the part of Brown. They might have been followed from the terminal, but he probably would have noticed that and no one had tracked them into the elevator.

Violet frowned and he knew what she was thinking.

"Your boss knows you left with me?"

She hesitated. "Yes."

"So it would be easy for him to pass that on to Brown…"

"He wouldn't do that," Violet said, but she didn't sound convinced. He wasn't, either.

Carter's text buzzed in his phone.

Anyone hurt?

Violet's okay.

You?

Just my pride.

He put the phone away before Carter got a chance to snap off a snarky reply.

Violet was pulling at his wrist, turning him to face her. "No matter how they found out, they're gone and you're bleeding. Stay still."

"No, I'm not hurt."

"Yes," she said in the overly controlled voice she used when he was driving her to distraction. "You are." She pointed to the side of his head.

He felt then a trickle of warmth and swiped at it, his

fist coming away with a smear of red. "I'm not hurt," he repeated, hoping he didn't sound like a cranky child.

She grabbed a tiny packet of tissues from her purse and pressed one to his temple, pulling it away to show him the blood. "Not-hurt people don't bleed on other people's clothes."

He noticed another spot on the front of her uniform.

"Sorry," he mumbled. "I must have hit the door handle on the way down. I'll wash it."

"No, you'll have it dry-cleaned, you big oaf," she said, but her smile was soft as she dabbed at his cut. "Doesn't look deep. Cops will send a unit to check on you, or an ambulance, right?"

"Told 'em not to. Need every cop out looking for Brown."

She heaved out a sigh. "And you say *I'm* stubborn."

"You are. Way more stubborn than me."

The rumble of an engine caught her attention. "Fortunately, it looks as if someone didn't listen to you, though."

Carter pulled up in his squad car, Frosty pacing in the backseat. "Get in, Zach."

Zach shook his head. "Uh-uh. I'm taking Vi back to her apartment."

Carter used the same tone he did when his young daughter Ellie was refusing to cooperate. "No, you're getting into this car until our people process this scene, and we're taking Vi to Griffin's. Everyone's there and waiting."

Violet took Zach's hand, put it over the tissue and pressed both to his head. "Do as you're told."

He wanted to snap at her and his brother, to vent

some of the tension that threatened to explode. Instead, he forced out a long, slow breath. "Fine."

Carter jerked his head. "You're sitting in the back with Frosty. Vi gets the front seat."

She cocked her head and flashed that smile again, but there was something forced about the brashness, as if she was trying a little too hard to hide her fear. It made him crazy to see it.

Don't worry, Vi. I'm gonna get these guys no matter what it takes.

Hauling himself and Eddie into the cramped back-seat of Carter's vehicle, he heard the echo of another promise, the one he'd made to Jordy's widow, the promise that he'd catch Jordy's killer no matter what it took. As the days spun into weeks with no progress from the cops working the case, his frustration was building to epic levels. At least the rabid press coverage had eased a bit, his brother's "suicide" taking backseat to various other big-city stories.

Everyone who worked with Jordy already knew it wasn't a suicide, but given the suicide note that had been planted and the lack of outward trauma to his body, that didn't keep the press from their speculations. He realized his jaw was clamped like a vise and he made an effort to relax.

Maybe it would be good to have Violet to focus on while they continued to try and unearth a lead on his brother's killer. The fatigue of many sleepless nights crowded the adrenaline from his muscles. Wearily, he stroked Eddie, threading his fingers through the fur, allowing himself just for a moment to wonder if Jordy's dog, Snapper, might still be alive. There had been blood found in Jordy's SUV, animal blood, but not a single trace of Snapper anywhere. If the German shepherd was wandering loose, lost, injured, how long could he survive?

A wave of despair washed over him. Zach used to believe there was nothing he couldn't do, that God was watching over the Jameson family and the people they loved.

I will both lay me down in peace, and sleep: for thou, Lord, only makest me dwell in safety. The psalm was inscribed inside the Bibles his mother had given each of them the day they were sworn in as cops. Now he couldn't even read the words without choking on them. With Jordy's death, there was no more peace or rest, and now with Violet facing a different threat, there would be no fairy-tale promises of safety, either.

I'll do it without You, he silently promised, the stone where his heart used to be hardening with each syllable. *I'll keep her safe.* It felt good to direct his anger at God, who'd taken the very best friend he'd ever had.

You won't take anyone else from me.

Carter shot him a look in the rearview mirror as they turned onto 94th Street and passed the K-9 headquarters, eventually pulling up in the tiny lot behind Griffin's Diner. Violet got out and beelined for the door.

Carter cut the motor and turned to stare at Zach. "You okay?"

"Yeah." He shifted Eddie on his lap. "Why?"

"Because you look like you're ready to take on an army all by yourself."

"Maybe I will."

Carter shook his head. "That's not smart. We're a team. Don't go rogue on us."

Zach didn't speak, but his gut filled in the answer. *If that's what it takes to protect Vi, bring it on.*

"Zach," Carter started again, but Zach was already out and following Violet into the comfort of the diner.

Violet breathed deeply of the familiar aromas, the rich tang of coffee, the scent of the freshly waxed floors her father insisted on, the tantalizing fragrance of simmering soup with glistening homemade noodles and shredded chicken, never diced. It was the smell of home, of comfort, of safety. The place had been unchanged for decades, obstinately resisting the pressure of the encroaching neighborhood gentrification of Jackson Heights. Her father would inevitably turn red in the face when he passed the two new luxury rental buildings and the artisanal cheese shop that had replaced the old mom-and-pop stores. Griffin's was rooted in the history of Queens, standing defiantly against the so-called progress, preserving the character of the people who had built the neighborhood brick by brick, block by block.

Sucking in a lungful of diner smells, she put the fear behind her and automatically snatched her apron from the hook by the door.

"Oh, no, you don't," her mother said. Barbara Griffin was still tall and straight-backed in spite of the lifetime of sweat and tears she'd put into the diner and raising Violet. Some silver threaded her brown hair, which she wore wound into the trademark braid. She'd never know how her mother survived losing Violet's brother at age five to meningitis, but Barbara was strong, and she'd passed that strength down to her daughter.

Sometimes you build a wall around today and you don't climb over it, her mother had told her. Violet was determined to build a wall around the frightening events of the morning and keep them behind the bricks, away from the rest of her life.

Her mother embraced her quickly, hard and tight, the contact telling her all that she couldn't say in words. After a breath, she straightened. "Carter filled me in. Are you sure you're okay?"

"Yes, Mom," she said, pulling the apron around herself. The apron made her feel safer than a suit of armor. "I'm completely fine. I'll bus table seven."

"I'd like to see you try," she said, smiling. "You'll have to get around your dad first." Violet decided that nothing would stop her, but when she made it to the dining room, the place was swimming with cops. They were collected around their favorite tables in their private room, set apart by French doors and affectionately dubbed "The Dog House," grilling Zach for the details. On the walls of the cozy room were the photos of those NYPD officers who had lost their lives in the line of duty. The K-9s were given the names of these fallen heroes to keep their memories alive. With a pang she realized that Jordy's picture would soon be added to those photos. The dogs were settled into their private porch area, and Zach led Eddie in to join them. Zach's brothers, Carter and Noah, were there with their dogs, and siblings Reed and Lani Branson along with Luke Hathaway, Brianne Hayes, Tony Knight and Gavin Sutherland. They were not all related by blood, but all were part of the K-9 unit Jordy Jameson had supervised, so that made them as close as kin could be.

She was about to grab the coffeepot and start pouring out for the cops when her father hastened up, quick though he sported a potbelly, and wrapped her in a hug that lifted her off the ground. "Baby," he said. "What is this world coming to? That airport is full of crazy people. You could have been killed. I think you should come back here and work full-time. Forget the airline job."

She squeezed him in return, furiously blinking back tears. "You always say that, Daddy."

"And I always mean it." He cupped her face and kissed her on the nose like he'd done since she could remember. One of her earliest memories was her and her little brother Bobby dressed up for Easter morning, her father presenting them each with a kiss on the nose and a basket full of goodies. Lou Griffin was a softie, through and through.

Before she could protest, he steered her to the back room into an empty chair at the table full of cops. "You're my baby, and I need you to be safe. Sit down and rest."

"I just got here."

"Rest from your ordeal. No waiting tables for you."

Her mother chuckled, carrying in pitchers of ice water. "See? I told you."

Everyone broke into a vigorous inquisition about her health and safety with a liberal amount of teasing thrown in. Holding on to her tough and independent demeanor was hard when she spoke of the attack, but she kept herself in check. She was Violet Griffin, known for her sass and wit, a strong woman who wasn't going to present anything else to her cop family, and they knew it, counted on it. When the conversation turned to shoptalk, she breathed an inward sigh.

"We got the intel back on the Joe Brown guy," Carter said. "His real name is Xavier Beck. Small-time, petty theft, some drug arrests. He may be a courier, but he's not the boss. Though there's been some street chatter that he's moving up in the ranks, trying to prove himself. We've heard the name Uno."

"You think he's the guy in charge?" Zach pressed.

Noah shrugged. "Nothing definitive, but it's telling that when we bring up the name, all our sources close up tighter than a tick on a coonhound. There's something behind this guy Uno."

"Another drug ring putting down roots here in Queens?" her father asked with a shake of his head.

"Plenty of noise that there's a drug-smuggling operation organizing," Carter said, "but we can't prove this Uno character is behind it. Malcolm Spade was running things until recently, but thanks to Declan, we got him put away."

Declan Maxwell was Zach's longtime friend and the newest K-9 officer with the elite NYPD Vapor Wake Squad. Along with the Jameson brothers, Jordan among them, Declan and his dog Storm had helped take down the drug kingpin. Thinking about it set loose a wave of sadness inside her. She had not seen Katie, Jordan's pregnant wife, at the diner in several weeks. Zach's grimace made her believe he'd been thinking about his lost brother also.

"What about the TSA guy?" Noah asked.

"No sign of him but we're looking."

Zach toyed with his coffee mug. "Bill Oscar's got to be involved. I'm going to put him under a microscope and tear his past apart until I get to the bottom of it."

Violet bit her lip. Her heart told her Bill was a good boss, a good father, a good friend, but there was no way to overlook the fact that he'd acted suspiciously at the airport. Zach's flinty expression told her she had zero chance of diverting him from that course of the investigation, anyway.

"You shouldn't go back to your apartment," Zach said, fixing her with eyes darkened to navy. "It's not safe. If Bill's involved, he can feed Beck your address."

There was universal agreement around the table.

"He wouldn't…" she started to say, until uncertainty dried up the words.

"She can move in with us," Barbara said. "Help take care of that little stinker of a puppy."

The pup's mother, Stella, was a gift from the Czech Republic to the NYPD. The yellow Lab had surprised one and all by having eight puppies shortly after her arrival, leaving the department scrambling for homes for all the pups. K-9 officer Brianne Hayes was now training mama Stella in the ways of bomb detection, but her babies were unharnessed hurricanes needing constant supervision. Latte, the precocious pup, had found a home with the Griffins. Two others had been placed with Carter and his daughter Ellie in the Jameson home. Violet figured them to be a welcome distraction in the wake of Jordy's murder.

"Yeah, you're gonna need another set of hands at least," Carter said with a groan. "The two we've got are tearing up the place. I'm down a gym bag and a Yankees cap already. Ellie is all set to keep them forever, even though they've mangled her toy sewing machine."

"So everyone agrees, then," her father said. "It's settled. Violet can work here and stay at our place. I need help keeping up with the pie demand, and everyone says that your pies are superior, Violet. Your mother's got a little birthday shindig here on Tuesday afternoon, remember. She's expecting big stuff in the pie department."

Violet steeled herself. Her father would be content if she never left their family dwelling in Rego Park, right next door to the Jamesons' shared family home. She was never sure if his overprotectiveness was due to losing his son, or the fact that she was a female, or just his natural bent, but whatever the reason, she'd fought for her independence and she wouldn't let it be stripped away because of Xavier Beck. "Hold up just one minute. As much as I adore you all, no one is going to organize my life. I am perfectly fine at my apartment, and I'm not giving up my job at the airport."

"But…" her father started.

"It's not safe," Zach said again. He got to his feet. Eddie eyed him from the porch room and stood, too, tail wagging in anticipation of a departure. "This guy Beck knows you saw the drugs in his bag. You can testify. You shouldn't be alone."

She stood. "I'm not alone. I have a roommate."

He was unmoved. "Who is away on an overseas assignment for another three weeks, correct?"

"Yes, but I live in a building with a hundred other

tenants. The guy next door is a butcher, and he knows how to handle a meat cleaver, if it comes to that."

Her father snorted. "He works practically round the clock, plus he's a Red Sox fan and that just speaks to his poor character right there." He threw up his hands as if he'd just set the universe in order.

Violet stood as tall as she could manage. Good thing she was wearing heels. Even so, she had to tip her head to look Zach in the eye. "With or without a butcher next door, I am a very competent woman, thank you very much."

"Vi…" Zach towered over her, handsome face close enough for her to reach out and touch the fatigue lines that grooved his forehead. She kept her hands clenched by her sides. "This isn't about competence," he said wearily.

The softness in his voice almost broke her resolve. Bossiness she could deal with, but tenderness… She swallowed. "I will not be forced out of my home. I'm safe and I'm not scared." She tried to believe her own brash statement.

They all stared at her. Zach folded his arms across his chest. It seemed like the entire diner went dead silent.

Noah cleared his throat. "We'll assign a detail to watch her place."

Zach shook his head. "No. It's not enough. Vi, I want you to stay with your parents."

Right next door to the home he shared with his brothers? It was part of the reason she'd been so anxious to move away. It killed her an inch at a time to see him every day, watch him bringing his girlfriends to the house for family dinners, to try and pretend she was happy for him when her own heart was protesting. In the months before Jordy was killed, she thought she'd actually achieved some level of normalcy, accepting that Zach and the Jamesons had their own lives and loves that didn't involve her. *It's the way he wants it*, she'd finally convinced herself. She thrust her chin up. "Badge or not, you don't get to tell me what to do, Zach."

His eyes sparked, narrowed, pinned her in that way he probably did when he was staring at someone he was about to arrest. She stared right back, hoping the fire in her eyes matched his.

"Okay," he said, after a breath.

She was thrilled at her victory until he continued.

"If you're going to ignore all good sense and stay at your apartment, I'm sleeping on your sofa. End of story."

Satisfaction turned to outrage. "You most certainly are not."

"Zach," Noah said. "This isn't your call. You're off shift, and you've had a long day. Go home and rest."

Zach shot him a glance. "Is that an order since you're the chief now?"

"Interim chief," Noah said, putting his coffee mug down and wiping his mouth. "But don't make it that way." The cops glanced uneasily at each other. "You're putting in full-time hours. You're exhausted. This is Violet's call, not yours."

Violet's breath caught as the seconds ticked by. She could not stand to see tension between Zach and Noah, not now, not because of her. She touched his hand, just grazing his fingertips. "Zach," she murmured, then louder. "You win. I'll go to Mom and Dad's tomorrow, after I get some things together. I'm exhausted, and I want to tell the building's superintendent in the morning so I'll stay one more night at the apartment."

Her father frowned. "But tonight would be better, really, Vi…"

She gave him the sternest look she could manage. "I've made up my mind."

He huffed out a breath. "All right. Tomorrow morning. We'll get the room ready for you."

"By *we* he means me," her mother said.

"I'm not giving up my airport job, mind you, only my living space and only temporarily."

After another long moment Zach relaxed. It seemed as though all the cops in the room did, as well. "All right, but I'm still spending the night on your sofa," Zach said.

Her nerves ignited. "That sofa is as comfortable as sleeping on a sack of potatoes."

"I'll survive."

"I don't want you to bother."

"No bother."

"Zach, you can't sleep on my sofa." Exasperation crept into her tone.

"Then I'll stretch out in your hallway and annoy the neighbors. They can step over me on the way to the elevator. The butcher will love it."

She glared. He stared. She fisted her hands on her hips. He hooked thumbs in his utility belt and gave her a slow, sassy smile, one that said, "I win and there's nothing you can do about it." She could have resisted further, but the smile was edged with something deeper, something soft that played at the edges of his mouth, tangled with the stubbornness.

"The butcher stays awake until three in the morning and plays nonstop polka music," she said in a last-ditch measure.

"Then I guess I'd better eat a hearty meal before I go off to the torture chamber." He had the audacity to wink at her.

She shook her head, biting back the retort that would not do any good, she realized.

"How about some lunch?" he said. "All these cops are starving, right, guys?"

They all broke into loud agreement, probably happy the standoff was at an end.

Zach cocked his head. "You see? Starving." He struck a plaintive expression that made him look all of ten years old. "Please feed us, Vi, before we keel over from hunger."

Violet looked from Zach to her parents, to all the other cops gathered around the table and she knew that she had lost the battle.

Fine, she resolved. *I'll do what you want, just for a while, but I'm not going to let good guys or bad guys have control over my life.*

"Lunch is coming right up," she said through gritted teeth.

FIVE

Violet whirled on her heel and marched to the kitchen. No need to ask orders of the assembled group; she'd bring them each their favorite sandwiches, which she'd memorized long ago, along with bowls of homemade soup, extra crackers on the side for Noah and a bagged chocolate chip cookie for Carter to take home to Ellie. Zach's favorite lunch was a pastrami on rye with extra spicy brown mustard, a glass of root beer, no ice, and a slice of apple pie, never à la mode. It was a meal he could devour with no guilt since he was a workout fiend and a star on the police basketball team. At least he had been known to devour all of that in one sitting before his brother was murdered. Now more often than not he'd stick to coffee or pick at his food, asking her to wrap it up for later, but she doubted he'd eat it at all. He was thinner, his face a touch on the gaunt side. She missed seeing him power down a hearty meal and sigh in pleasure at her apple pie.

"Why does your pie taste better than anyone else's?" he would ask.

She'd never tell him the answer. She prepared every

pie she made with painstaking care, because she imagined she was making them all for him. It had been that way since she was thirteen and he'd told her for the first time how much he enjoyed her pie.

Sappy, Vi. Get it together, girl.

If she couldn't salve his pain, she would follow the long-standing Griffin tradition of throwing food at the problem. *You're getting an extra-big piece of pie and you're going to eat it this time, buddy boy.*

As he took his customary place with his back to the wall, so he could track the comings and goings at the counter and front door, he kept his gaze on her every moment. Ignoring him and ladling up bowls of soup, she thought about what it would be like to have the brooding, determined Zach Jameson parked in her living room.

A year before, she'd been dating Otto, an NYPD detective. He was everything Zach wasn't: short and stocky, brilliant in math and languages, a lover of books and quiet walks. He was always there with a sweater to put around her shoulders or a bouquet of flowers to brighten her counter at Emerge. They'd had fun, but something was missing for both of them; that deep sense of "rightness" was the best way she could describe it.

They'd parted amicably, although part of her still wondered why she hadn't felt a deeper connection with Otto. He was an undeniably good man, though Zach had told her on more than one occasion he didn't think Otto was at all right for her.

You need somebody tougher, Vi, who can stand up to you, he'd said. *Somebody who can make you laugh.*

Somebody like himself? Of course, he hadn't meant

that. So why exactly was Zach front and center in her thoughts at any given moment?

Natural, in light of what happened to his brother. Thoughts were okay; it was her heart that was off-limits since she had no intention of complicating her lifelong friendship with Zach. At least she was not prone to running into him on a daily basis, since she was at the airport forty hours a week. Keep busy, was her strategy; stay away from Zach, who awakened so many contradictory feelings she could not make heads nor tails of.

He was a family friend…yet, his blue eyes made her breath quicken.

He knew her better than anyone else in the world… yet, he shut her out at the worst moment in his life. He made her laugh like no one else on the planet, but the thought of him with another woman burned like acid.

Worst of all, she felt rattled and vulnerable after the attack, and the feelings were surfacing that she desperately did not want to share with a man who was increasingly making her weak in the knees.

So how exactly is having him under my roof going to work?

It was only for one night, she told herself. Better Zach sleeping on the sofa than her being alone with a drug dealer after her. The feel of Beck's fingers grabbing at her made her skin go clammy.

Silly. She was safe, completely so, within the walls of Griffin's Diner, surrounded by cops and dogs.

But what about when she returned to her airport job? Beck's threat came back to her.

A quick death is better. We could make it last much longer if we wanted to.

Suppressing a shiver, she loaded up her tray and delivered the food. She could tell at once that the tone
had changed around the table. Zach was stiff-backed,
jaw thrust forward.

"It wouldn't have made any difference whether you
were there or not," K-9 officer Luke Hathaway said
in response to something Violet hadn't heard. "Jenks
would have bolted into traffic, anyway."

Violet knew that Claude Jenks was the man who
had left the fake suicide note at the K-9 graduation ceremony that Jordy was to have facilitated. Jenks would
have killed department secretary Sophie Walters, who'd
discovered him in the act of leaving the note, if Luke
hadn't intervened. Jenks had died denying he'd killed
Jordan Jameson, before he could reveal the name of the
murderer or the motive.

"Maybe not," Zach said. "Things might have gone
differently if you had more help."

Luke's mouth hardened. "I was saving Sophie from
drowning. You'd have done the same."

"I wasn't implying otherwise."

Luke's nostrils flared. "I think you were, Zach. Why
don't you just spit it out? You want to blame me for Jenks's death, huh?"

Noah held up a calming hand. "No one is implying
anything, Luke. Zach is just venting, and it's going to
stop." He turned a hard stare on his brother. "We are not
going to go after each other. It's bad enough with the
reporters spreading the suicide theory all over. We're
a unit and we'll stay that way. It's what Jordy would
have wanted."

Zach jerked as though he'd been slapped. He pushed

back his chair and stalked to the porch room, returning with Eddie. Violet stood frozen as he left the room and exited the restaurant.

Noah scrubbed a hand over his face and let out a long, weary breath. "Luke, don't hold it against him. He's hurting, and he doesn't know what to do about it." His look was pained as he sought Violet. "Vi, he will listen to you more than anyone. Do you think you can…?"

But she was already moving, praying God would give her the words to soothe Zach's tattered soul.

Zach leaned against the stone front of Griffin's, heart thundering in his chest.

It's what Jordy would have wanted… Noah was right. Jordy would never have tolerated him going at other members of the team, second-guessing their actions, heaping blame where it didn't belong. Shame squeezed his gut. *What's the matter with me?*

He looked at his boots when Violet approached. She stood with him, arms folded against the cold air.

"I know what you're going to say," he blurted. "Noah's right. I don't blame Luke. It wasn't his fault, it was mine. I should have been there, just like I should have sensed something was wrong, that someone was after Jordy. I should have…" He stopped abruptly as the pain closed off his throat. The back of his head banged against the hard stone behind him, and he closed his eyes. "I'm losing it."

And then she was embracing him, warm and soft, and his arms went around her as he buried his face in her neck.

"I was going to say it's okay," she whispered. "It's okay and I understand."

And with her there, he let himself hear it, clinging to her, willing her to say it again. His craving for comfort was so strong and it seemed like she was the only person who could give it to him. He didn't know how long he stayed like that, breathing in the scent of her hair, the fragrance of soup that clung to her clothes while she murmured gentle, soothing things against his cheek.

This isn't your fault.

I'm praying for you.

Praying. Lifting him up to a God whom he despised. He did not know if he could stand it, but nevertheless he grasped at the words, feeling the steady beat of her heart that somehow made his own keep on pulsing in spite of the pain that nearly crippled him. She felt like a life preserver in his arms, holding him just above the water that was trying so hard to pull him under. He wanted to lose himself in her embrace.

"I'm sorry," he mumbled against her neck. "You shouldn't have to prop me up after what you've been through today."

She pulled him away then, and put her hands on his face, stroking thumbs over his cheeks. Her eyes brimmed with emotion and strength.

"I will always be here for you, Zach, always." She kissed him where she could reach, aiming for his cheek and getting the corner of his mouth instead. Prickles formed all over and everything in him wanted to bend and capture her mouth to his properly. The thought startled him.

What are you doing? This is Violet, remember? A

longtime family friend who's just being nice because you're a complete basket case. For a moment he was paralyzed between the logic of his head and the needs of his heart. Warmth, comfort, soothing, friends, duty, honor…love?

Let her go.

With effort, he finally released her. Her cheeks were pink, probably from her work in the diner, or the cold, and a single long curl that had escaped the barrette grazed the side of her face. He used one finger to pull it away from the satin curve of her cheekbone.

"I do not deserve a friend like you," he said.

Something glimmered in those brown irises. Another few seconds and she smoothed her apron and sent him a saucy grin. "You're right. You don't."

That was the Violet he knew. Strong and sassy. A die-hard friend who would not bring up his moment of embarrassing weakness again. He sighed, cleared his throat, called to Eddie and they reentered the diner. He wasn't hungry, but he knew he'd get grief for not eating, so he made a stab at it. Noah and the others were eating, too. He waited until some of the team had gotten up to go before he caught Luke's attention.

"Sorry, man," he said. "You did the right thing. I was just blowing off some steam, but I shouldn't have directed it at you. There's no excuse for what I said."

Luke shrugged. "I get it. We're gonna figure out what happened to Jordy and someone is going to pay for it."

Carter and Noah nodded. "Copy that," Carter said.

His gaze drifted to Violet, who was cleaning up after the lunch service. For a moment he remembered the feel of her misplaced kiss, the silken caress of her wandering curl. He blinked back to reality. Jordy's case was still digging at him, but now he had another matter to attend to: keeping her safe and putting Xavier Beck behind bars.

He noticed Violet's curl, the one he'd touched, was loose again, a ribbon of brown silk against her cheek. His stomach tightened when he remembered his urge to kiss her. She did indeed represent all the things he craved…warmth, comfort, friendship, duty, honor…but love? No. Violet Griffin wasn't meant to be that for him.

No more confusion, Zach.

You have a job to do.

Don't mess this one up.

SIX

After she'd cleaned up from the dinner hour and left the kitchen spotless, Violet found Zach and Eddie waiting outside the diner. Zach drove to Violet's apartment. The more she fumed, the more cheerful he became, an annoying strategy he'd learned early on in their relationship.

"Don't mind us," Zach said, plopping down on her sofa and flipping on the TV to the sports channel. Eddie wasted no time scrambling up next to him, since he wasn't allowed on the sofa at their home. "We've stayed in much worse accommodations. We'll just catch some sports news and fix ourselves a snack later. Pretend like we aren't even here."

Like that was possible. Violet shut the bathroom door more forcefully than was strictly necessary, stripped off her soiled work uniform and showered until the hot water ran out. Marginally restored, she slid into a pair of comfortable jeans and a soft sweater. It was still only a little after eight, and the evening stretched in awkward hours before her. What was she supposed to do with Zach sitting out there?

Zach still lounged on her couch, legs sprawled out in front of him. Eddie curled up at his hip. Eddie wasn't exactly the ferocious, killer K-9. More of a lovable couch potato, she thought fondly, certainly much more easygoing than his owner.

Since she'd been too busy to eat dinner, she cooked grilled cheese and warmed up some soup for a late meal. Without asking, she set Zach a place at the table, too, happy to see him dig in with gusto. Why was it so satisfying to feed this man? Sure, she'd enjoyed preparing her best dishes for Otto, but there was something so downright fulfilling about feeding Zach Jameson. It mystified her.

"No people food for Eddie," he called, catching her in the act of treating Eddie to a leftover crust of bread.

"Says the man who bakes gourmet treats for his dog."

"Like I tell my brothers when they rag on me about it, Eddie works hard. He deserves quality rewards. I make them out of approved organic ingredients and besides, it's the only thing I know how to cook. If there really is a zombie apocalypse, Eddie and I are going to survive on gourmet dog treats and if you are very nice, we will share with you."

She laughed, enjoying the friendly teasing, the comfort of a shared meal. Remembering the peanut butter cookies she'd stowed in the freezer, she was about to try and tempt him with dessert, but he excused himself to take a call. When he returned, a frown etched his brow.

"We pulled the info for the Emerge Airline frequent fliers in the past six months. Beck showed up, Roach twice and one more guy. Do you recognize him?" He showed her a picture on his phone.

Her stomach clenched. "Yes. I've seen him several times. Is he connected with Beck and Roach?"

"Probably, but he's likely just a small-time courier. Last time they all flew to Miami. Their destinations were different this time. One was headed to Miami, and Roach to San Francisco. This third guy, Victor Jones, has got a record, but no outstanding warrants at the moment. We'll find him and ask some questions, but it's best that…"

"Don't even say it. I'm going back to work tomorrow."

He scowled. "I don't like it."

"You'll have to live with it."

He rapped his knuckles on the table. "How come you get to be irrationally stubborn and I don't?"

"Woman's prerogative," she said.

He sighed and said little for the rest of the evening.

She tried to watch her favorite home decorating show on TV, but Zach's restlessness prevented her from sticking with it. He would stroll to the window periodically and look down onto the darkened street. Then it would be back to his phone, checking messages, and several times he completed a series of pushups on the kitchen floor. Eddie's brows twitched as he took it all in from the comfort of the sofa.

"How can you stand it?" she asked the dog. "Doesn't he ever sit still?"

Eddie blew out a breath, ruffling his lips.

When Zach started in on arranging her shelf of cookbooks for the second time, she abandoned her magazine. "Zach, you're driving me bonkers."

His brows shot up in surprise. "I am?"

"Yes. Can't you relax for a couple of minutes?"

He blinked as if taking internal inventory. "I am relaxed."

"I'm sorry to be the one to break this to you, but no, you're not anywhere close to relaxed. You're like an overwound top."

"Oh. Is it the pacing?"

"The pacing, pushups, rearranging and the like. I'm afraid you're going to start busting out walls and remodeling my apartment when you run out of other things to do."

"Yeah, okay, sorry. Carter says the same thing only he doesn't use such nice words. How about I go take a shower? Sometimes that will do the trick."

"An excellent idea," she said. "Use all the hot water you want. Please."

"Yeah, Carter says that, too." Chuckling, he disappeared into the tiny bathroom.

She smiled to herself. Zach had always been like a fully wound clock, forever in motion, driven by some internal engine. At times it got on her very last nerve, but the moments when he was still and thoughtful and fully attentive were precious as pure sunlight. Violet was just settling in to her magazine when her phone buzzed with a text.

It's Nan. I'm downstairs. Purse stolen so I'm borrowing this phone. Buzz me in?

Textbook Nan. The girl in apartment 315 would probably lose her head if it wasn't fastened securely. It was a wonder to Violet how her friend kept her job as a receptionist in a dental office.

Violet texted back.

Buzzing you in.

She buzzed and opened her magazine again.

Not working, Nan texted a few minutes later.

Violet sighed. Door problems were a common occurrence in her aging apartment complex. She slipped on her animal-print flats and let herself out without disturbing Eddie, who still had eyes locked on the bathroom door, waiting for Zach to emerge.

She took the elevator down to the lobby. Through the lobby doors, she saw a car parked on the curb, probably the Uber Nan had taken. Violet did not intend to do anything stupid, considering her own precarious situation. Unless she saw her friend Nan through the glass panel of the front lobby door, she had no intention of opening it. She had not made it two steps away from the elevator when the stairwell door opened. In a matter of moments Xavier Beck had pulled her in, the door closing behind them.

She tried to scream, but he clamped a calloused hand over her mouth and jerked her tightly to his shoulder. "Hello, Violet."

He smelled of cigarettes. His stubbled chin rasped against her face. "Thought you'd ditched me for good? It was easy to wait and sneak into the building behind some oblivious tenant. Her name tag read 'Nan.' She looked about your age, so I took a chance that you knew her. I didn't think you'd actually fall for the *buzzer didn't work* trick. Dumber than you look."

Fear nearly left her immobile, but she kicked, her shoe coming loose, missing her target. There was a camera in the stairwell at the first landing, but they were not quite in view of it. Beck must have known because he pulled her in the other direction, backing into the panic bar of the basement door.

The basement...no cameras, no help, no way for Zach to know how to find her. Now she felt the full on-slaught of panic, kicking and twisting, trying to scream as Beck dragged her down the flight of stairs, pushing open the heavy door with his boot.

He shoved her inside and she fell to one knee, but only for a moment as she scrambled to get away. Beck flicked on the bare hanging bulb, which illuminated the space in a ghastly glow. The smell of mildew mixed with the sharp odor of bleach.

A labyrinth of tall shelves stretched from cement floor to dripping ceiling, cluttered with bottles and tools, plastic containers that looked as though they hadn't been opened in decades, a moldering fake Christmas tree lying like a corpse across a shelf. The opposite wall housed a set of washing machines and dryers. She jerked backward as far as she could go until her shoulders banged into a washing machine behind her.

Beck's expression was relaxed, happy, almost, as he shut the basement door, wedging a doorstop under it. "Don't you want to scream? No one would hear you, anyway, but it would make this game more fun."

She clamped her chattering teeth together. She

would never give him the satisfaction. "They'll find you. They'll arrest you," she said.

"The cops?" He laughed. "You know who wins in the end, at this game of life, I mean? The ones who don't follow the rules. Cops have to follow the rules. Me? I haven't followed any rules since I was twelve years old. Cops always lose."

She tried another tack. "I... I won't testify. I'll forget what I saw in your suitcase."

"Oh, I'm sure you wouldn't, but you don't get to the top in this business by leaving loose ends. I'm going to prove to my boss that I'm ready for bigger responsibilities." He grinned. "Your death will be a line item on my résumé." He pulled a knife from his pocket. The tip of it shone white in the dim glow. "Ready?"

Zach felt it as soon as he exited the bathroom. Violet was gone. He sprinted to her room to confirm that she was not there. He couldn't wrap his mind around it. What could have persuaded her to leave the safety of the apartment? To leave his protection? He yanked open the apartment door, but there was no sign of her in the hall.

Trying to still his rattling nerves, he shoved his gun into the waistband of his jeans and shut Eddie in the apartment with a stern admonishment. "Don't chew anything up." Then he was jogging to the elevator. He gave the button a half dozen pushes and waited for an interminable amount of time before he decided to take the stairs.

Everything was fine, he told himself. There had to be a good outcome here. No need to freak out, but his legs churned faster and faster until he reached the first floor. Sprinting into the lobby, he found the super strolling by the mailboxes, a screwdriver sticking out of his plaid pocket.

"Where's Violet Griffin?" he demanded.

"How should I know that? The tenants don't have to show me hall passes or anything." His narrow mustache quivered as he laughed at his own joke.

Zach ground his teeth. "Did you see her come down here recently?"

"No. I just came a second ago to unjam a mailbox." He squinted at Zach. "What are you doing here, by the way? You're a cop, right? The one with the dog? I've seen you in uniform before. Is there a problem?"

Oh, yeah. Big problem. His stomach clenched into a fist. Where was she? "When you came down did you take the elevator or the stairs?"

"The elevator, and it was just me, if that's your next question."

"Go look at the lobby camera footage right now. Tell me if you see where she was headed and if anyone was with her. Text me."

"What's your...?"

Zach grabbed a pen from the manager's pocket and before he could protest, Zach scrawled his cell number on the man's palm. "Do it. Now."

He left the manager gaping, texted Noah and dashed out to the sidewalk, holding open the door with a chair so he wouldn't get locked out. There was no sign of her in the bitter cold. The damp sidewalk sent shock waves through his bare feet since he'd not taken the time to put on his shoes. Doubling back he reentered the stairwell. Nothing on the landing.

He looked again and his breath caught.

A woman's shoe, Violet's animal-print flat. He put himself in the assailant's mind. He'd waited patiently until a resident had shown up and snuck into the building when they buzzed the door open. Concocting some story, he'd gotten Violet to come down, giving her an excuse she'd believed.

There was a lobby camera, but it was facing the outer doors and didn't catch the stairwell action or maybe the guy didn't care. Had they taken her out of the building via the front entrance? He didn't think they'd risk it since someone on the street might have seen them and she'd be struggling for all she was worth. Back upstairs? Why? The answer sickened him. To find a secluded place to kill her, a place where her screams would not be heard.

His phone signaled a text from the manager.

Short, muscled guy pulled her into the stairwell. Don't know if they were going up or down.

His heart slammed his ribs. Up or down? Upstairs, ignoring the cameras? Pulling an unwilling victim? No, Zach thought. He'd go down—easier, closer—to the basement laundry room. He swallowed. Soundproof.

Terror filled him as he considered. Beck would likely kill her in the basement where they wouldn't be interrupted, where it would be hours or more before anyone discovered her.

The manager texted again.

What can I do?

Cops are on their way. Go open the lobby doors. Then lock yourself in your office and wait for them to arrive.

But...

Do it.

He heaved at the basement door and found it jammed. Kicking with all the strength he could bring to bear, he succeeded in forcing it open. The wedge of wood that had secured it skidded across the floor, lost in the darkness. Dropping as low as he could, gun drawn, he made entry.

Dank air assaulted his senses as he took up a position behind a tower of crates and listened.

Voices?

A woman's, high and scared. Violet.

"Police!" Zach shouted at the top of his lungs. "Let her go."

The answer came in a scream. "Zach, he's got a knife."

"Hold on, Violet, I'm coming!" he yelled before he charged.

SEVEN

Violet could not breathe through the fear that clawed at her chest. Zach would be an easy target for Beck's knife. What could she do?

"Drop your weapon!" Zach shouted again.

She could not figure out where Beck had gotten to until she heard the creak of protesting metal. He was behind a shelving unit, circling around Zach, who could not possibly spot him in the insufficient light.

She could only think of one thing to do. She grabbed up the first item her hands could reach, an old toolbox that was almost rusted through. Flinging the top open, she began throwing the contents as fast and as hard as she could in Beck's direction. An old screwdriver, a file, a series of clamps and finally the toolbox itself. The heavy metal container crashed with a thunderous noise into the spot where she figured Beck was waiting, clipping the overhead light, shattering the lightbulb and plunging the room into complete darkness. The ink-black compounded her terror. Any moment she expected to feel a knife plunging into her back or hear Zach fall victim to Beck's ambush.

She fumbled for her phone to turn on the flashlight. The clang of metal and crash of something falling nearby almost made her scream. Was it Beck running? Going after Zach? Coming around for her again? Glass crunched only a few feet away. Finally, her shaking fingers found the light button and she was about to flick it on, until a hand reached out from the gloom.

Another hand wrapped around her mouth from behind, muffling the scream that was erupting from her lips.

"Shhhh," Zach whispered in her ear. "It's me. No light. I don't want him to see you."

Her knees went weak with relief as he released her and kept her close. His body was wire taut. He put his mouth near and spoke in her ear. "Get out, well away from here, and text my brothers with your location. They should be here any minute. I'm going to find him. He has to be in the basement still unless there's an easy exit where he wouldn't be spotted leaving."

She clutched at his forearm. "No. He'll kill you."

He pushed her firmly away a step. "Gonna get him, Vi. Do what I say. Now."

Fear flashed through her. *Cops always lose.* "Please, Zach. No."

"You're not giving orders here."

"Zach…"

This time he didn't answer, just dropped a kiss on her temple and propelled her to the threshold so fast she almost stumbled. When she turned around again, he was gone, vanishing into the shadows.

Her blood turned to ice, and a wave of fear overwhelmed her, for a moment she could not move. Beck's words assaulted her again.

You know who wins in the end...?

Zach would play by the rules—he already had, by identifying himself as a cop, making himself a target. Beck would kill Zach without a second thought.

Her fingernails cut into her palms. Desperate to run to Zach, she had to do what he said, or risk making the problem worse. *Text the Jamesons.* Stumbling over the threshold, she raced into the hallway and frantically texted Noah, but the message failed to send, thanks to her position deep in the building. She took the stairs two at a time, panic driving her. Almost at the exit to the lobby she yelped as a German shepherd dog lunged at her, barking viciously.

Carter pulled Frosty back with a sharp command. "Are you hurt?"

"No. Zach's in the basement with Beck. Beck's got a knife."

"We got his text. Keep going until you're out of here." Carter barreled by her, Frosty rigid with excitement. She continued her mindless sprint, emerging into the lobby where she found Luke Hathaway and his German shepherd, Bruno.

Luke guided her to a corner of the lobby away from the swarm of patrol cops. Noah Jameson was there, speaking into his radio. He gave her a nod, but he did not approach her. The intensity on his face aged him. She could not conceive of how he could do his job when another of his brothers could possibly lose his life at any moment. How could he calmly work the scene while Zach was in the basement with a lunatic?

Save him, she wanted to scream. *You've got to save him*.

But that was exactly what Noah and the assembled officers were trying to do, she realized. As much as she wanted to run right back down to that basement, she would do as instructed and not become another problem for the cops to deal with.

In control, strong, like she always was, but in truth, her legs felt like wet noodles. The whole thing was her fault. How could she have been so stupid to deliver herself to the lobby for Beck to abduct?

The building's super appeared at her elbow. "Zach told me to lock myself in the office until I saw the cops. Uh, er, are you okay? You're missing a shoe, and you look terrible. Did they catch the guy yet?"

Violet forced a steadying breath and gave the super a stripped-down account of what had transpired.

He shook his head. "And the worst thing I had to deal with today was a stopped-up toilet and a jammed mailbox."

Violet could not manage a reply, but she was relieved that the super went to talk to the other tenants who had begun to assemble in the lobby. The patrol cop in charge told them in no uncertain terms to clear the area but they were slow in dispersing, curious to know why there was a one-shoed tenant on the verge of hysteria holding up a wall of the building. Each breath was an effort. Would the door open to Carter's mournful face if he could not save yet another brother?

All she could do was stand there like a statue, praying like crazy that God would keep Zach safe.

A cop jogged in from outside. "Spotted Beck running as I pulled up. I pursued on foot but I lost him. He…"

"He was too quick for me, too," Zach said as he followed the cop in.

Violet's heart nearly jumped from her chest at the sight of him. It was all she could do to keep her tears from flowing and fight the urge to throw her arms around him and squeeze the breath from his lungs.

"Carter's checking the nearby shops, but I think Beck had a vehicle somewhere close by." Zach conferred with his colleagues for a moment while Violet simply stared and willed her legs to hold her up. She hunched over, trying to draw in steadying breaths. Zach came to her side.

"Hey. You okay?"

She nodded, still not looking at him. He crooked a finger under her chin and tipped her head up.

"Serious?"

"Yes," she said through chattering teeth. She wanted him to stay there, holding her arms, telling her he was all right, that the whole crazy situation was going to be okay, but she could make no sound at all.

"You lost a shoe," he said, holding her hand.

"A good excuse to get new ones."

He smiled. "Since when do you need an excuse? You've got more shoes than Bloomingdale's."

"At least I'm wearing one. You're barefoot." Violet wanted to fire back another sassy remark. Instead, she put her head on his chest to hide her face.

"You… I…when you went after him… I was… scared."

He stroked her hair. "I'm sorry you were scared, but

that's my job, Vi, and I'm gonna do it, especially if it means making sure you're safe."

Safe. She wondered if she would ever feel safe again.

"I shouldn't have gone down to the lobby. It was dumb."

He bent down to look at her, his expression stern. "This isn't your fault. None of it. You're not gonna feel that way, hear me?"

Some of her load of misery lifted. She wanted to fall into his blue eyes and float there in a sea of azure, far away from the current madness.

He tucked her into the crook of his arm. "I don't think he'll be back, but just in case, I'm taking you to your parents' house tonight and I'm sure you aren't going to argue with me this time."

"Okay," Violet said.

Zach frowned. "Okay? No arguments?"

"Uh-uh." Violet bent, both to take off her remaining shoe and conceal her fear. "You're right. I'll go. I should have listened to you in the first place."

He squeezed her around her shoulders. "I wish I could get that last bit on tape. That's not your typical comeback."

She tried for bravado. "It hasn't been a typical night. I… I mean, he could've…" The feel of Beck's arm locked around her throat shook her again. Tears gathered in her eyes, to her dismay, and she gulped them back.

Zach pulled her a bit closer and walked her to the elevator, calling over his shoulder, "Taking her upstairs to pack a bag. Be down in five."

Noah nodded, still talking to a group of officers clustered around him.

When the elevator doors closed, Zach took her in his arms. "I'm sorry this happened, Vi." He tucked her underneath his chin, his breath warm on her hair. "You don't deserve any of this."

She crushed herself to his chest and stayed there, breathing, trying to control the rampant flood of emotions. Xavier Beck's threats rang loud and clear in her ears. But she had to be strong, she told herself, calm and in control, like he expected. *Zach needs you to keep it together.*

"You know, it's...okay not to be okay," he said into her hair. "Talk about it if you need to."

It hit her like a slap. Was he really saying that she should be vulnerable with him? Asking her to spill her guts? Her self-control started to erode. She jerked away from him. "So it's fine for me to express my inner angst but not you?"

He looked startled. "Well, I mean, it's healthy to talk about it, right? That's what everybody says after a traumatic incident."

"For me, you mean, but not for a tough K-9 cop."

He offered a smile. "Right, well, that goes without saying, doesn't it?"

"No, it doesn't."

He shifted uneasily. "I don't understand why I'm in trouble here."

She goggled at him. "You can't keep your feelings locked away in a vault and expect me to share mine."

He didn't answer, just scrubbed a palm over his face.

"Where is this coming from? It's kind of out of the blue."

"It most certainly is not. It's been coming on since your brother was killed."

He flinched, but she pressed on. "It's okay that you're struggling with Jordy's death, Zach, and like you said, it's healthy to talk about it."

He did not meet her eye, but his mouth hardened into a firm line. "I don't need to talk about it. I'm dealing, Vi."

"No, you're not. You're angry and blaming God and it's making you nuts that you can't solve your own brother's murder."

He folded his arms across his chest, staring at the mirrored doors, tone hard and flat. "This isn't the time."

"Yes, it is. If you want me to share my feelings, then you can share yours."

His twitching jaw muscle told her what he thought of that idea. Without looking at her he said, "I...just want you to be all right. I'm sorry if I offended you."

Silence spooled out between them as she regarded Zach in the steel doors. So tall, strong, macho, but with his bare feet and the bemused expression and the pain that he was trying so desperately to keep sealed away, she saw his truest self: a man hurting, her best friend, whom she could have easily lost forever. She felt the anger drain out of her.

"You didn't offend me." He would not meet her eye. "And I want the same for you, Zach. I want to help you be all right, if you'll let me." Had her words been too plaintive? Too pushy? Too laced with longing that she hadn't hidden away properly?

The silence went on for a beat longer. "Why don't we talk about something else…like your baseball skills? Taking out the lights with a screwdriver, I didn't know you had it in you." His laugh was forced, tense, but the message was clear.

I don't want this.

She was changing the rules of their relationship and he wasn't ready or willing to do so. What did he want from her? Strength, wit, friendship, nothing more, nothing deeper.

Her spirit sagged. So be it. Those were the things she would give him, then. Nothing more, nothing deeper. Swallowing hard, she watched the buttons count off the floors one by one.

The silence was deafening by the time the elevator finally delivered them back to her apartment. She unlocked the door and gasped. Zach immediately pushed ahead of her, took in the surroundings and groaned. The sofa sported an eight-inch hole in the cushion, the stuffing spilling out onto the floor. Eddie was nowhere in sight.

"Officer Eddie, get your sorry self in here right now," Zach thundered.

The dog slunk from behind the couch, his face more hound dog at that moment than beagle. "What do you have to say for yourself? You're supposed to be a highly trained police K-9."

Eddie offered a half-hearted wag of his tail and a yip at his master. A bit of stuffing clung to his whiskers.

"Don't you try to make nice with me, dog. You ruined Violet's sofa. I hope you thoroughly enjoyed yourself, because you are in deep trouble. This will be reflected in your service record."

Eddie whined, ears down and then let loose with a pitiful baying.

Violet could not help the laughter that bubbled up from her mouth. Whether it was born of relief, or trauma, the giggles escalated until tears ran down her face and she doubled over.

"I'm glad you find this amusing," Zach said, glowering at her and the dog. "Now I gotta pay for a couch."

She could not restrain another peal of laughter. "At least you don't have to worry about sleeping on it."

A hint of a smile quirked his mouth and he let out a world-weary sigh. "Go pack your bag, Vi. Officer Chewsalot and I need to have a talk about behavior and life choices and the extent of his grounding."

"Yes, sir," Violet said, still giggling as she went to fetch her suitcase. *Maybe you can get the dog to open up about his feelings*, she thought, giving Eddie a little pat as she walked out.

EIGHT

Zach gave Violet an encouraging nod as she held the phone between them in the front seat of his Tahoe, dialed Bill Oscar and clicked on the speakerphone. He'd cautioned her vigorously not to mention anything about what had transpired at her apartment building. Bill might have orchestrated the whole attack, after all, and there was still a chance a cop might apprehend Beck before the night was over.

"I'm sorry for the late notice, Bill, but I am going to take your advice and not come in tomorrow. My mom really needs help with the puppy and…" She swallowed. "I'm not feeling at the top of my game, to be honest."

As close as Violet would come to admitting she was rattled. "Good job," he mouthed.

"No problem, Vi," Bill said. "I understand completely. It's about time you started to use up that mountain of vacation time you have on the books."

She thanked him again and disconnected.

Zach had listened intently and did not hear any indication of suspicion in Bill's voice. Either the guy was a great actor or he believed Violet's excuse. It gave him

some breathing room as he escorted Violet to the front
door of her parents' home.

She paused on the doorstep. The light of the
streetlamp painted her in an ethereal glow, like a por-
trait he'd seen of a woman looking down at her moonlit
garden. Was it the light that made her look so delicate
or perhaps had his vision changed since he'd come so
close to losing her in that basement?

His breathing hitched. He wanted to put his arms
around her, to feel her warm breath on his neck, to re-
assure her and himself. But he was still confused by
what had happened earlier between them in the elevator.

*If you want me to share my feelings, then you can
share yours.*

Was that what he wanted? That mutual sharing of
the deepest parts of themselves? But that was more than
friendship, wasn't it?

"Good night, Zach." As she opened the door he saw
Lou hastening toward her. Zach stepped away, wiggled
his fingers at her and left her to the comfort of her worried father.

He was satisfied as he and Eddie returned home that
at least Violet would be safe for one day and he'd have
another chance to convince her to stop working for Bill
Oscar, just until he figured out if Bill was guilty or not.
It wasn't like he was trying to force her to give up her
career or anything.

Lying in bed, he stared at the ceiling. Though his
body ached from exhaustion, his mind would not allow
him to sleep. The moment in the elevator kept poking at
him. What did Violet want him to do, flop down on her
ruined sofa and share all of his innermost feelings with

her? That wasn't the kind of relationship they had. They were friends, jovial, supportive, yes, but upbeat always. Violet was a tough lady, sure of herself and ready with a wisecrack, just like she'd always been. He couldn't imagine where she'd come up with the notion that they should cry on each other's shoulders. Then again, he'd practically cried on hers outside the diner, and for some reason it hadn't felt awkward at all.

More and more he found himself puzzling and worrying over what Violet Griffin might be thinking and yes, every so often, he felt the urge to unburden himself to her about the ravenous wolf gnawing away at his insides, the case he could not solve, the brother who was lost to him forever. There were others, a long line of people from brothers to his parents, buddies and even a cop shrink, who would listen to an emotional rant from Zach Jameson, so why could he only imagine sharing with Violet and no one else? Familiarity, it had to be. He'd known her forever.

He pictured Violet's mocha eyes and the sassy curve of her mouth, and in his mind she looked as she had on the doorstep, more tender and less tough, more wounded than wisecracking. There went the hitch in his breath again when he thought of her. He was losing it, pure and simple.

Aww, go to sleep, already, wouldja? Resolved to push Violet and everything else from his brain, he yanked up the covers and rolled onto his stomach.

After a night of fitful rest at best, he got up at dawn, pulled on a NYPD sweat suit and went out for a run in the chilly predawn of Thursday morning. Eddie, though a fairly energetic dog, was not the "jog four miles" type of animal, so he left him sleeping off his antics from the night before. Zach could only hope he had not ingested any of the sofa stuffing he'd worked so hard to disgorge. He ran long and hard, setting a pace that would drive away the angst and clear his confusion. Sweating and more relaxed, he returned to the kitchen he shared with his brothers, their families and his mom and dad, to find his six-year-old niece Ellie waiting for him.

"Hey, squirt."

"Hiya, Uncle Zach. Ready?"

"For what?"

"You forgot." Her cornflower eyes looked at him accusatorially. He scanned the counter and saw the ingredients she'd laid out: natural peanut butter, honey, wheat flour.

"No, I didn't."

"Yes, he did," Violet said, entering. "Before you lecture, an officer walked me over from next door." Her hair was caught into a loose ponytail, and she wore a shirt with greens and golds that coaxed the color of autumn leaves from her eyes. At that moment it hit him that Violet was insanely beautiful. It must have been some sort of profound idiocy that he had never noticed it before. He dropped the kitchen towel.

"No, squirt," Zach said, hastily grabbing it up again. "I remembered that it's dog-treat baking day." He grabbed a ceramic bowl and began to crack eggs into it. "Eddie's down to his last dozen or so."

The little girl nodded solemnly. "And I marked it on the calendar. See?" She pointed to a little dog bone drawn in brown marker. "That means baking day."

"Right," Zach said, whisking the eggs and slopping some over the side in the process. "Baking day, and I've got the best helper in the world. And you work cheap, too."

"One dollar," she said, but she looked troubled.

"Whatsa matter, squirt?"

Ellie squinched up her button nose and sent a side-long glance at Violet. "Violet knows how to cook more things than I do. Maybe she should be your helper."

"No way, Ellie. I only know how to make people things, not dog things," Violet said. "I'm just here to bring over some muffins, anyway." Violet kissed Ellie. He looked for signs that she was overtired, stressed from the trauma she'd endured, but she seemed in perfect control as always. "I'm heading to the diner." She held up a palm. "Carter's taking me. You two enjoy treat-baking day."

"I want to talk to you, Vi," Zach said.

"Later. Dog treats take top priority." She gave Ellie a thumbs-up and left.

Ellie watched her go. "I like Violet."

"I like her, too, even if she does argue with me."

"Why don't you marry her, then?"

He dropped an egg onto the floor. Before he could grab the paper towels, she got the salt and sprinkled it onto the smashed egg, scooping it up easily.

"Where'd you learn that trick?"

"From Violet. So why don't you marry her? She's pretty and friendly and she knows how to cook and take care of dogs and people."

He cracked another egg and got it into the bowl this

time. "'Cause we're just friends. Friends don't get married."

"Daddy said Mommy was his best friend before she died."

That one stopped him. What was the best way to answer? Distraction, he remembered. Carter always tried that when Ellie was fixated on something. "I...uh...do you want to mix?"

"No. Mixing is your job. You have bigger muscles."

"But my muscles are tired."

She tipped her head, solemnly considering in that way that made him turn to mush.

"I am the roller and the cutter," she said. "I don't do the mixing. Do you want me to get Uncle Noah to help since your muscles are tired?"

He chuckled. "I think I have enough energy to mix."

"Good. I have to do the other parts." Ellie was the one who had helped him find the dog treat recipe in the first place, sitting with him to pore over pet cookbooks, testing out several recipes until they found the perfect palate pleaser for Eddie. Ellie was great at reminding him about the next step when he forgot, and patiently setting the timer when he tried to impress her by saying he didn't need to set one. Wise beyond her years, tender and sweet, and he was proud to be her uncle. And he'd be one to Katie and Jordy's child, too, the best uncle he could possibly be. Swallowing back a tide of bittersweet emotion, he set to work.

When the dough was mixed, she rolled it out, pressing the tiny bone cookie cutter into the brown goo and loading the shapes onto the cookie trays.

"How hot do I set the...?"

"Four hundred twenty-five," she said. "For..."

"Ten minutes," he said. "I remembered that one."

"That's great. You're doing a good job, Uncle Zach."

He laughed. "Thanks. I haven't had to use the fire extinguisher in a long time, have I?"

"That's because we set the timer."

He tugged at her ponytail. "What would I do without you?"

"You would have to pay someone else a dollar to help you. Like Violet. She would help you even without the dollar."

Zach tried to forestall any more marriage suggestions by washing up the bowls and sliding the pan of baked treats out of the oven. They passed a happy half hour until Noah came in and poured coffee.

"Good morning, squirt," he said, kissing her cheek. "Your daddy said to remind you to brush your teeth."

"Can I do it later?"

Noah pretended to consider before he shook his head. "Your teeth will be sad if you wait."

"I don't think teeth get sad."

"But your daddy does, so go do it now, okay?"

"Okay." Ellie trotted off.

Noah looked at the coffeepot. "Did you make it?"

"No, Carter did."

"Excellent, then I'll have some." Noah poured himself a cup.

Zach ignored the jibe and washed the dishes. "Vi settled?"

"Yeah. All quiet at the diner. Carter made sure there's a detective outside." He fetched a water bottle and twisted off the top. "Got a tip on Victor Jones."

The third man frequenting Bill Oscar's ticket counter at Emerge Airlines. Zach perked up. "Yeah?"

"Snitch we popped says Jones hangs out at a bagel shop in Pomonok, selling drugs when he can, mostly on Thursdays, though he's been away from it for a while. We're staking it out today. I'm not even going to ask if you want in."

"Waste of breath," Zach said, sprinting for the stairs. He was showered, changed into street clothes and had Eddie secured in a civilian leash and harness by the time Noah finished his cup of coffee.

"Scotty will be sorry he's missing out," Zach said, eyeing the rottweiler's police leash hanging on a hook.

"Especially since he hates having his teeth cleaned, but I promised him a cheeseburger when I pick him up tonight." Noah paused. "I stopped in to see Katie yesterday afternoon."

His heart thunked with pain at the mention of Jordy's widow. "How's she doing? Baby okay?"

"Baby is healthy, though the doctor is concerned Katie isn't gaining enough weight. She isn't sleeping, but Sophie is plying Katie with food all the time and checking on her daily, like everybody else." Noah cleared his throat. "Katie says she keeps having dreams where Jordan and Snapper walk through the door."

A painful reminder of what she'd lost, what they'd all lost. Zach exhaled against the anguish. "Any new word on Snapper?"

"Couple more possible sightings. After the news first broke, people thought they saw German shepherds all over Queens, but nothing's panned out."

The more time that passed, the worse chance they

had of finding Snapper alive. It was possible, maybe probable, that Jordy's abductor had killed the dog, too. It wouldn't have been easy. Snapper would have fought to the death to defend Jordy. He remembered working a parade with his older brother when a guy high on drugs took a swing at Jordy. The guy had been so scared of the barking and snapping teeth he'd begged to be taken to jail.

If you're out there, Snapper, hang on, buddy. We'll find you.

Zach finished the water and slammed the bottle into the trash. There had to be something, some bit of hope in the midst of this disaster. Arresting Victor Jones might just get them some info on who was running the airport smuggling operation. Bill Oscar? The shadowy Uno?

Noah put his cup down, interrupting Zach's thoughts. "Katie said she's praying that we are all dealing with this okay."

"Praying? She can save her breath. God's not answering." He grabbed his cell phone and jammed it into his pocket.

"Yes, He is," Noah said, voice low. "We just can't hear Him right now, but we'll feel His comfort in time."

God doesn't care, he wanted to tell his brother, but he could not say such a thing, not in the house where his parents had raised them to be men of faith; not in the place Jordy would have taken him to task for railing at God.

It occurred to Zach that his brother looked tired, haggard, as if the weight of the universe rested on his shoulders. How was Noah managing to deal with his

own grief and lead the K-9 unit in that calm and rea-
soned way of his? No blowups or angry venting from
Noah. Zach admired his brother, his skills, his quiet
strength and his faith. He blew out a breath. Maybe he
would pray again someday, but it wouldn't be today.

They loaded up in their Chevy Tahoes and took off
for the bagel shop. As he drove away he peeked at the
top floor of the Griffin household, which was dark,
of course, because the whole family was busy at work
serving breakfast at the diner, which was a scant fifteen minutes from the Jameson home. Hopefully, Violet would stay put, but there was a needy puppy to be
dealt with, so she'd probably be going back and forth.
There would be a cop assigned to watch her and he felt
infinitely better knowing that during her puppy care
stints, she was right next door to a houseful of cops
and dogs, depending on the hour, instead of alone in
her apartment.

Traffic was no worse than usual, and they made it
in less than a half hour. Noah took up a position in his
car, away from the store. It would not be unusual to
see a cop car parked along a busy city block. Zach had
to prowl around for fifteen minutes before he finally
found a spot vacated by a departing delivery truck. He
began to unobtrusively stroll the street, his earpiece
hidden beneath a Yankees baseball cap, gun holstered
and concealed under his windbreaker. The tip was good
because a mousy guy in baggy clothes and a denim
jacket loitered near the dumpster that filled an alley to
the side of the deli.

"In position," Zach said into his radio.

"Ten-four," Noah replied. "I got eyes on him, too. We'll move in if Eddie alerts."

Zach and Eddie made their way to the shop window, peering in as if they were planning out a purchase. A whiff of yeast-scented steam tickled their noses. The shop was crammed with people grabbing up morning coffee and shouting out their orders for bagels to the unflappable guy behind the counter. Poppy seed, cinnamon raisin, hard salt, accompanied by dozens of different spreads from cream cheese and lox, to whitefish, to pimento-olive spread. Zach kept his peripheral vision on the alley.

He bent to scratch the dog. "Find the drugs, Eddie."

Eddie sprang into action, tail zinging as Zach walked him by the guy in the alley who was lighting a cigarette. Eddie sniffed in the direction of the man's boots, his body tensing in that way that promised a bust was going to go down. He pointed his nose at Victor's pockets, precise as a laser beam locked on target.

The man looked up, startled, just as Eddie sat down at his feet. Zach pulled his gun. "Police. Let me see your hands."

In moments Noah was there, and Gavin, too, who had been positioned a few blocks from their location. Zach patted the man down and retrieved his wallet, identifying him as Victor Jones, along with an eight ball of cocaine, three and a half grams, wrapped neatly for easy distribution. It wouldn't fetch much, probably a hundred dollars or less, but it was plenty. While Gavin cuffed Jones, Zach gave Eddie a few of the coveted treats from his pouch. The dog munched happily, celebrating a job well-done.

"You're under arrest," Gavin said, before he Mirandized Jones.

Jones grunted. "C'mon, man. I can't do jail time now. I got bills to pay and my girl's gonna dump me if I serve time now."

"Your girl should dump you, anyway, if she knows what's good for her," Zach said. "You sell drugs. She can do better." Zach waited a few beats as Victor wriggled in the handcuffs. "But I'm a softie so maybe there's something we can do, work out some kind of a deal."

Victor raised a wary eyebrow. "What kind of deal?"

"Information. You share it with me, and I can talk to the DA, maybe get you off easier."

Victor's body went tense. "Don't have any information."

"Aww, come on, Vic. Don't waste my time, man. We know you've been working with someone at LaGuardia who gets you and the drugs through security. Who is it?"

Terror sparked in Victor's eyes. He shook his head. "Dunno anything about that. I'm a homebody. I don't like airplanes."

"Not buying it, Victor. You flew on Emerge Airline three times the last month alone. You're smuggling for someone. I want the name."

"Like I said, I can't help you."

Zach stood a little closer. "Yes, you can. One name."

Victor's throat muscles worked but he remained mute.

Zach heaved an elaborate sigh. "I tried. You'll be going to jail now. You can say goodbye to your girl." He pretended to be thinking it over. "Hey, this is your second strike, so you're getting close to prison time, aren't you? Another drug charge isn't going to look good for you."

A bead of sweat slid down Victor's cheek. "Don't you have other people to hassle? I'm small-time."

Zach closed in like a shark smelling blood in the water. "But you can give me the big-time guy. Who are you smuggling for, Victor?" *Bill Oscar.* Zach was ready for Victor to spill the name. One word and he'd put Violet's boss away before he could threaten her safety any further. He stepped forward even farther, crowding Victor, and Eddie whined. Noah shot Zach a look. With an effort, Zach remained calm. "I've got things to do, Victor. We can't stand here forever. One name, that's all."

Victor chewed his lip. "Can't tell you, man."

"Why not?" Zach snapped. "If you don't, you'll go to jail for a long time."

"Better than crossing him."

"Who?" Zach demanded. "Give me the name and we'll protect you."

"Yeah, right." Victor guffawed. "'Cause the cops are so good at protecting people they want to toss in jail. Uh-uh. I don't work for anybody, and I ain't giving you nothing. Take me to jail now and let's stop wasting both our time."

Zach grunted and started to question Victor further when Noah gripped his bicep. "Let it go for now. He may be more inclined to talk after he sits in a cell for a while."

Stomach tight with fury, Zach led Eddie away. Anger coursed through him in unrelenting waves, though he tried to calm himself. He knew Victor and Beck and Roach had to be working for or through Bill Oscar. It was the perfect setup. Bill ushered them through the airport, being sure they checked in during his shift. They bypassed security via the crooked TSA guy, Jeb Leak, who had so far avoided arrest, and Bill reaped the profits. Could be Bill was working with a big-time dealer, Uno or someone else, but he was the key, Zach was certain. All he needed was confirmation from Victor…and he hadn't gotten it. He would try again after Victor cooled his heels in a cell for a couple of hours.

The flood of people exiting the store with their bagels passed by, oblivious to him and Eddie. The sun was unusually warm for May, and Eddie was basking against a brick wall, soaking in the beams after enjoying his treat. Dogs had an enviable ability to relax no matter what the circumstances. With Violet intending to return to work the next day, he felt anything but relaxed. Another chance to nail Bill Oscar had slipped right through his fingers.

Next best step. The words came to him unbidden, Jordy's favorite saying. When the wheels fell off the wagon and everything about a case was coming apart bolt by bolt, his big brother would say the only option was to take the "next best step." For the first time since Jordy's death, he was able to enjoy the memory without a stab of agony. There was pain, yes, probably always would be, but there was also a bit of gentle comfort in the replaying of his brother's wisdom. He had that to hold on to, if nothing else.

The sun was mellowing into a perfect spring morning. He felt a ferocious yearning to run along the

Vanderbilt Parkway and breathe in the sights and smells of the city like he'd done so many times with Jordy, but he knew that place would forever be ruined by the image of his dead brother, back against the tree. What had been his last thoughts as he'd died? Sadness that he was alone without a single soul to share his last moments? Zach swallowed down the anguish. There would be time for rest later, after he got Bill behind bars. Before that happened, he had another difficult mission to attend to: convincing Violet that she should take some vacation time, a leave, anything until he figured out the truth about Bill.

Violet was, above all things, loyal, so he'd have his hands full with that endeavor. Somehow he would find a way to reason with her. He looked at Eddie. "Got any good tips on how to handle a tough woman who isn't about to listen to good sense?"

Eddie opened one eye and then closed it again.

"Yeah, that's what I thought. Let's go, Eddie. Time to try and move a mountain."

NINE

Fatigue dulled Violet's senses, though it was only just past the breakfast rush. She had been awake since 3 a.m., long before her muffin drop at the Jamesons', thanks to the whining of a certain Labrador puppy. She'd finally strong-armed her parents into letting her go to the diner, promising to get a police escort when she returned to check on Latte. To her chagrin, a plain-clothes detective had been assigned to be her babysit-ter, unless Zach or another member of the K-9 unit was available.

Even without the shrill puppy whining, she would have been awake, anyway. She hadn't slept past eight o'clock more than a handful of times in her entire life. The early bird got the extra puppy shifts and she'd spent the predawn hours in between doggie playtime sessions searching her mother's cookbooks for the perfect lemon meringue pie recipe.

Now, back at home for another round of midmorn-ing puppy care, her thoughts traveled again to pie. It still irked Violet that she could not seem to master the art of making her mother's favorite pie, no matter how she went about it. Every time she attempted one, the meringue would shrink and pull away from the crust or the custard would be too loose or too firm. Her father had always said the best way to get Violet to attempt a task was to tell her she couldn't do it. He was right, and she was doggedly determined to make a perfect pie for her mother's birthday party on Tuesday. Killers and threats and fear were not going to derail her from her self-appointed mission.

Her mother's old cookbooks were yellowed and worn—obsolete, since there were millions of recipes online—but some things were better off old-school style. Violet put a sticky note on the page in the book that had belonged to her grandmother, with the hand-written, "Scrumptious!" note scrawled next to the in-gredients. If it was scrumptious enough for Grandma, it would be good enough for Mom, and maybe she could even get Zach to eat some. She closed the book as she heard Latte clamoring for attention from his pen.

Latte seemed to operate at full speed as soon as his eyes popped open. Even after three different ball-chas-ing sessions and a full-body grooming, he was alert as ever. Lying on his back in his gated area of the kitchen, he was happily chewing on his rubber bone, having upended his water since she last checked. He righted himself and leaped at the gate when he spotted her, tail zinging as if he hadn't played with her in days instead of minutes.

"You're a wild one," she said, lifting the roly-poly puppy over the gate. "I don't know how Ellie and Carter keep up with your two siblings." His pink tongue lapped her everywhere he could reach, and her problems melted away, if just for a moment. Was it humanly possible to sustain negative feelings while holding a warm puppy? She did not think so. Cuddling him and addressing him in outrageous baby talk that she'd never indulge in if others were present, she led the wriggling armful of joy outside to do his business again. Zach had admonished her in that annoying cop way of his that there was to be no taking the dog for walks in their quiet neighborhood unless he was present. Instead, she settled for playing a comical game of fetch with Latte, who would pounce on the ball eagerly, but could not be persuaded to return it to her. So far the count was five balls stored up in a pile across the yard and one left in the toy basket ready to throw.

"You're just not getting this fetch thing down, are you, Latte?"

"If only we could get the bad guys to carry around tennis balls," a voice said. "The dogs would catch them in no time."

She whirled around to find Zach leaning against the wall of the porch, arms folded, one booted ankle crossed over the other. Eddie wagged his tail and yipped at Latte. The sun lit Zach's eyes to a vivid cobalt. He was not in uniform, but his badge was clipped to his belt. Long, lean, but not entirely relaxed.

Her stomach fluttered, and she was glad she'd taken the time to shower that morning and pull her hair back into a neat ponytail. "I didn't hear you knock."

"That's 'cause I didn't. Your mother said I can let myself in the backyard anytime to let Eddie and Latte have a playdate if he isn't already booked with his puppy brothers and sisters."

"That's because she doesn't want you in the house. You break too many things."

"Nope, it's because your mother adores me, and you know it."

She did, too. Barbara Griffin loved the Jameson boys as if they were her own sons. In a way, they were, since they had spent their formative years with Violet's brother, Bobby. The hallway was lined with pictures of the six of them, Jordan, Noah, Zach, Carter, Bobby and Violet, in various stages of growing up, only Bobby's image had disappeared from the family photos too early. What would he have been like as an adult? she wondered. Would he be a cop, too? Married? A father? Again, the fuzziness of her memories of Bobby bothered her. It was as if he was fading from the pages of her mind like old photos exposed to sunlight.

Shake off those thoughts, she told herself firmly, wishing Zach did not look quite so appealing, sunlit and smiling. "You look...edgy," she said.

"Who, me? Nah."

She arched an eyebrow. "You can fool other people, but not me. You're edgy. Why?"

He shrugged, releasing Eddie to play with Latte. "We arrested Victor Jones, and I was hoping he'd roll over on his boss."

"But he didn't?"

"Not so far." Zach cleared his throat. "Threat's still out there."

She didn't answer.

"I know a guy," he said over the canine greetings. "He works at JFK and he..."

"No." There was no way she was going to transfer her job to another airport.

"But it would be…"

"Uh-uh, and we're not having this conversation again." She marched into the kitchen and poured a cup of coffee.

"Vi, why won't you see reason?"

"Because I'm not going to let anyone run me out of my job. I like it and I'm good at it."

"Your boss is likely involved with drug dealers, or he's running an operation himself."

"I just can't make myself believe it. I know he must have reasons for doing what he did, good ones."

"That's because you're loyal and stubborn and it's given you a blind spot."

She dashed milk in the coffee, splashing some over the rim. "Fine, I'll own that, but I'm not judging Bill guilty until I have proof, and if I'm working at LaGuardia I can be your eyes and ears. We can clear the whole thing up for good."

"That is a terrible idea, so get that out of your head right now. Bill's dealing with bad people like Xavier Beck."

She repressed a shiver. "I learned a lesson last night. It was stupid of me to leave the apartment, but now I'm going to keep my eyes open and not take any chances. I'll be perfectly fine in a public airport."

"What if things go bad? Beck's tough."

She recalled her fear with Beck in the dank basement. She thrust her chin up, anyway. "I'm tough."

"He's tougher."

"You're wrong."

"I'm hardly ever wrong."

She shoved the mug of coffee at him. "You say that because you are loyal and stubborn and it's given you a blind spot about me."

He shook his head and, to her surprise, actually chuckled.

"Why the laugh when I just told you off?"

"You're the only person I know who would shoot me down thoroughly with my own words and make coffee for me at the same time."

She could not stop her own smile. "I don't do that for everyone, you know. Consider yourself a blessed man."

She'd aimed for flippant, but the look he gave her was suddenly tender and thoughtful, exasperation and bemusement that resolved into a shining certainty. "I do," he said quietly. "I'm not sure how I can say that with the present circumstances of my life, but you're right. I'm blessed, where you're concerned, even though Jordy always said we fight like an old married couple."

Where you're concerned, as if she was something precious and rare that outshone the darkness cloaking him. The notion warmed her inside and eased warmth into her cheeks. *Lord, help me give him what he needs to push through the pain, to find his way back to You.*

"So what do you say, Vi? Will you consider the JFK thing? Please? For me?" It was not the little-boy-lost manner he sometimes employed to get her to agree. Sincerity teased tenderness into his tone. Oh, how tempting it was to give in, when she knew her assent would ease his strain. *Give in. Let him take care of you.* But then what would be next? Moving back in permanently with her parents? Starting over as a newbie when she'd worked hard for her seniority at LaGuardia? Worst of all, handing her independence to a man who did not love her in the way she craved? "I'm still not going to quit my job," she said. "Tomorrow I'll be back to work."

He exhaled deeply. "Yeah, I figured that's what you'd say." He drank from the mug and sighed. "You make good coffee, Vi, the best I've ever tasted."

"I know. It's in my blood. Griffins are born with coffee in their veins."

He grinned. "Cops, too."

"Otto used to say the same thing."

He looked down for a moment. "Ah, well, sorry I brought up bad memories."

"They aren't bad. Otto was a good guy, just not the one for me. The whole thing taught me that I need to take care of myself."

Zach looked at her full-on. "Violet, Otto was insane to let you go."

She offered a casual shrug, though the words thrilled her. *Keep your head, Vi. You didn't feel the right things for Otto. Like the things you feel for Zach?* Pouring herself a cup of coffee to give herself something to do, she clinked mugs with his.

Zach grinned. "You know what I found in an old box when we were packing up Jordy's stuff?"

"What?"

"A picture of that infamous Fourth of July."

She knew exactly the one. "Oh, boy. I'd forgotten about that."

"Not me. That was the best ambush in Jameson family history." His eyes twinkled with mischief. "And you were the perfect accomplice."

"I still feel guilty about it."

"No way. My brothers had it coming. They swiped the keys to my car and moved it so I thought it was stolen, remember? I ran around like an idiot for hours until they returned it just before the cops arrived, which made me look like an even bigger dummy. Oh, they had it coming and you were my wingman."

She sighed. "Yeah. I lured them all out into the backyard with the promise of chocolate chip cookies and you unleashed, what, like two dozen water balloons?"

"Oh, three dozen at least, and because I was standing on the roof at the time, they couldn't escape. It was perfect. I laughed so hard I almost slid off. That was a classic moment that I'll never forget."

"I don't know how I let you talk me into that."

"Aww—" he tugged at her sleeve "—it's because I'm irresistible and you can't say no to me, right?"

He had no idea how close he was to the truth.

Assorted barks and yips drew them to the back door, where they stood, sipping coffee and watching Eddie and Latte race merry circles around each other. It was a moment of peace to be enjoyed shoulder to shoulder. Precious seconds with a precious man. For just a fraction of a minute, she imagined what it would be like if Zach was hers, and she his…like the married couple Jordy suggested, sharing a space, sharing a life, their picture on the wall with all the others.

No good thinking that. Friends, remember?

When they finished, she took his coffee cup and rinsed it.

"I can do that," he said.

"I'm faster. I've got to secure Latte and scoot to the

diner. Mom and Dad need me for the lunch rush. Nice weather will bring people out in droves."

"I'll drive you."

"Okay, I'll let you."

He twirled her ponytail, his fingers grazing the back of her neck, teasing prickles across her skin. "Always the tough lady."

Not always, she thought, as she considered that the next day she'd be walking back into the lion's den.

But his touch, warm and reassuring, pushed the danger and every other thought to the back of her mind.

Friends, remember?

Scooping up the pup, she escaped upstairs.

"Victor Jones made bail before I finished my lunch."

Noah's words grated in Zach's gut the next afternoon as he and Eddie drove the New York streets.

Victor had been bailed out by a relative without confirming or denying that he'd been working for Bill Oscar. Now Violet was at work, against all common sense and his strongest efforts at persuasion, and he was still not a bit closer to bringing down her boss. At least he'd managed to get Victor's last known address in Queens, an illegal basement apartment on a busy intersection in Corona. Armed with a search warrant, he forced the landlord to let him into the space, which was not zoned for residential use. He'd refer that one to the housing bureau later.

Zach eased his way into the basement and flipped on the light. A futon with rumpled sheets occupied the darkest corner. A card table served as a kitchen counter, cluttered with empty Chinese-take-out containers crusted with dried noodles, a hot plate and a coffee machine, a phone-charger cord, a strip overloaded with plugs. Such was the problem with illegal apartments. One exit in case of fire, and way too many safety violations. The space also lacked appropriate ventilation, but with affordable housing so hard to come by in Queens, the temptation to rent out unsafe rooms was hard to resist. Eddie whined.

The landlord stood by the door, arms crossed defiantly. Gavin had arrived to assist, and he kept a careful eye on the man. So did Tommy, Gavin's springer spaniel, who was sitting obediently at his knee, tracking every movement.

"You have no right to come in here," the landlord snapped.

"The search warrant and the badge say otherwise," Zach said.

"My tenant has done nothing."

Zach rounded on him. "Your *tenant* is a drug dealer and if I find anything illegal in this basement you call an apartment, I'm going to find him and he'll go to prison. Would you like to join him there for interfering with an investigation? You already have enough problems, I'm thinking."

The landlord took a step forward, but Gavin raised a warning finger. "You're gonna stay out of this or I will cuff you right now, you got me?"

The landlord shot him a surly glare and retreated. Zach beamed Gavin a grateful look. "Now, where were we, Eddie?"

But Eddie was turning in agitated circles, his ears flapping.

"What do you smell?" He unclipped the dog. "Ready to work? Find the drugs, boy."

Eddie pranced into action, nosing along one wall, which was inexpertly covered with cheap wood paneling. Eddie paced back and forth along the paneling until he honed in on one particular spot. Zach's pulse thumped as Eddie's nose quivered, deciphering a thousand smells that Zach was not even aware of. Eddie finally sat and looked at him.

Gavin watched. "He got something?"

"I believe he does." Zach knelt next to him and examined the wood, rapping his knuckles every few inches. The sound echoed hollowly at the point where Eddie was most interested. Sliding on gloves, he edged a penknife in the notch between the sheets of paneling. Almost invisible to the eye, he found a tiny indentation where the wood had been filed away. Zach's gut tightened in anticipation. "Well, what do we have here?"

Using his knife as a lever, he popped the paneling loose. It came away easily. Eddie barked. Zach peered into the space where the drywall had been cut away. A stack of plastic-wrapped bricks—cocaine, no doubt—and a half dozen guns were jammed in the small alcove.

Gavin looked over his shoulder and whistled. "Dog's got a million-dollar nose, that's for sure."

"Yeah, he does. Good boy, Eddie. That's my baby," he said, doling out treats to the dog. "You did it again." The street value of the drugs was probably somewhere in the neighborhood of a half a million dollars.

Gavin radioed their findings and began taking photos. "So Victor is clearly moving product for someone," he said in between shots. "Why would he risk getting popped at the bagel store?"

Zach's thoughts spun as he turned the situation over in his mind. "He needs money. They've had to slow down their operation since Violet pointed out Beck at the airport. I think Victor was desperate for cash and kept a little to sell on the street for his own profit until he has the all-clear to start moving it again. His boss wouldn't like it, so he's kept his borrowing small."

"This supply is a lot to walk away from. Victor must intend to come back here at some point. He wouldn't abandon it, or his boss would make him pay."

Make him pay...

Just like he intended to do with Violet?

With Victor cut loose from jail and their stash discovered, would his boss order him to make another threat on Violet? Their need to keep the product moving must be growing.

He reached for his phone and left Gavin and another newly arrived officer to secure the scene and wait for the evidence to be processed. Scrambling back to his vehicle, he phoned Violet.

"Answer, answer," he said. He had to tell her that another one of the frequent fliers was involved in heavy-duty crime, probably organized by her boss. One ring, two. It went to voice mail.

He phoned Griffin's.

Barbara answered, sounding harried.

"I need to talk to Violet. Is she there?"

"No, Zach. Bill asked her to come in for an early shift today, so she left here hours ago for the airport."

His lungs struggled to do their job.

"She had a cop escort her, and she texted me that she'd arrived safely. Is there a problem?"

He forced a cheerful tone. "No, ma'am. I just…need to talk to her."

Her voice dropped low. "Zach, we're counting on you to take care of our daughter."

"Yes, ma'am. I will do that. I promise."

Barbara said goodbye and hung up, though she did not sound completely convinced.

He gunned the engine on the Tahoe and pushed out into traffic, goosing the gas and flipping on the siren.

Bill couldn't make a move to hurt Violet in the airport in front of dozens of witnesses. She was probably safe…as long as Zach could get there in time.

TEN

Violet was happy to steep herself in the madness of her ticket counter duties again. Puppy care was fun but exhausting and though her father complained about her decision, she'd kissed him and left him muttering over his vat of vegetable beef soup. As usual, her mother did not give voice to her worry, but it was evident in the tensing of her shoulders.

I've got to live my life, she wanted to say, *to take care of myself.* Killers and her burgeoning feelings for Zach aside, she really was okay on her own, and that was the way she would keep it, no matter who tried to strip it away from her.

Bill had greeted her upon her arrival with a quick hug. "Happy to see you back here, young lady. You look rested and raring to go."

"Put me in, Coach," she'd said with a smile before she was sucked into the busy whirl of airport duty.

There was nothing unusual transpiring that Violet could detect, just the typical crush of people, some anticipating a vacation trip or reunion, and those more surly, traveling on business or for some other less enjoyable reason. Bill's wife, Rory, phoned in the afternoon and asked to speak to Violet during her break.

"I am so sorry about what happened," she said. "It's horrible. Bill has been so worried about you. He's hardly sleeping, and I think he's started smoking again. He tries to hide it, but I can smell it on his clothes."

"I'll tell him to stop if I catch him with cigarettes in his pocket. We'll get him back on track." Violet pictured Rory the last time she'd seen her, the shadows that smudged Rory's eyes and her thinning hair, which had once been a thick chestnut brown. "How are you doing with the treatments? I know it's been tough."

Rory's sigh spoke of exhaustion. "Seems like the cure is worse than the disease sometimes. The doctor is optimistic. It's hard on the boys, though. I'm the one that keeps things on an even keel, normally, because Bill works such long hours. They don't quite understand how to deal with me being sick." She coughed and cleared her throat. "He doesn't, either. He tries, but it's hard for him to know what to say, how to be, so most of the time he pretends nothing is going on. And the bills, they worry him, too. He doesn't sleep hardly at all and he's lost weight."

"Have you… I mean, he's been a bit different at work. Something is definitely on his mind. Could there be something besides the treatments weighing on him?"

Rory paused a moment. "No, he's just stressed is all, and who wouldn't be?" She offered directions on some schoolwork to one of her children. "Anyway, I wanted to thank you for the flowers you sent last week and to be sure you're okay."

"Perfectly okay, thanks."

"Good. You're like family, Violet, and we'd be crushed if anything happened to you." Rory bade her goodbye. As Violet disconnected, she eyed Bill smiling at a customer. Surely Bill would not entangle himself with the drug trade. He would never do that to his wife and sons.

Bill walked around the counter and joined her after the next shift of workers arrived. He looked fatigued, twitchy. Of course he'd been off his game a little, she thought. His whole life was his family and with a thing like cancer to deal with... Guilt swelled inside her for her earlier suspicion.

I misjudged him. He couldn't have been helping Beck.

"Rory was sweet to call," she said. "She's such a thoughtful person."

"Rory's one in a million. When I married her, I won the grand prize. She's way better than I deserve."

She caught just a whiff of tobacco on his clothes. "You've been smoking again, haven't you?"

Head ducked, he sighed. "I had one or two this morning before I got here, but I'll stop, I promise. A moment of weakness."

"Why, Bill? What is worrying you, and don't say it's all Rory because you're not that good at lying."

"I'm better than you think," he said morosely.

"What does that mean?"

He shoved his hands in his pockets. "Vi, will you come have coffee with me?"

"Sure, that'd be great sometime."

"I mean now."

"Why now?"

"Your shift is done, and I'm taking the rest of the day off. I know this nice coffee shop in Astoria, a café, really, and I don't want to waste this sunny afternoon. Who knows when we'll get another one. Let me treat you before you head home."

"Some other time, maybe?"

"Please," he said, gaze drifting across the terminal. "I... There's some things I need to get off my chest."

She felt a prickle of alarm. "Why can't we talk here? We can grab some coffee in the lounge. It's terrible, I know, but it's usually hot."

He did not return her smile. "I need to speak privately with you. An hour, that's all. I promise it won't take longer than that."

Still, she hesitated.

"Vi, I've known you a long time. You know my wife, my boys. You've come to their baptisms, their school plays. You've been at our place for barbecues and my wife's jewelry-selling parties or whatever it is she arranges. You're family and it kills me to think you don't trust me anymore."

Anguish pinched the corners of his mouth. It was genuine emotion, she was sure of it. He was in desperate trouble, she could sense it. "I know you're a good man and a good father, Bill."

His smile was wan. "Well that's something, anyway. Does that warrant an hour of your time? Sixty minutes, tops? We'll stay in a public place and come right back."

She knew without a doubt that Zach would not want her going anywhere with Bill, but his expression was so downcast, she could not believe he might be the mastermind of a drug-smuggling operation. Besides, Astoria in late afternoon would be bustling, especially on such a warm day, and she did not think it would put her in any danger to have coffee with Bill. If her instincts were right, he would tell her something she could share with Zach to help him put Beck behind bars. It might be the only chance to put an end to the chaos.

"All right," she said. "Let me get my purse."

His face lit with a relieved grin. "Excellent. I'll get us a car."

Violet snatched her purse from behind the counter and sent Zach a text, noting she had a missed call from him.

Going to coffee with Bill in Astoria. Have to hear him out.

She waited, the seconds ticking by, hoping he would reply.

Bill was standing, checking his watch. Still no answer from Zach.

She made a pretense of fixing her lipstick.

"Ready?" Bill called.

Her phone screen remained blank. Doubt assailed her. She could still make an excuse, change her mind.

"Gotta get going," Bill said.

"All right." She slipped the phone into her pocket and followed him out of the terminal.

Twenty minutes later they sat on a curbside bench with their coffees since all the tables were occupied. The bench edged a wall, near the corner of two busy streets, so they sipped as a parade of pedestrians strolled by, the city bustling in all its glory.

Violet was comforted by the busyness. She relaxed just a bit in the sunshine and sipped the strong brew. It was hot and slightly bitter, not as good as Griffin's coffee, she thought Zach would say.

Bill shifted on the bench, toying with his cup but not drinking.

"What did you want to tell me, Bill?"

He grinned. "That's what I like about you, Vi. You're a 'get to the point' gal. No small talk."

"My feet are aching to be put up at home." She tried for a teasing tone but his smile had vanished, leaving his expression grim. Stomach knotted, she rested the coffee cup on her knee, tension boiling up in her stomach.

"Vi, I want to apologize in advance for what I've got to tell you."

She straightened and took a bracing breath. Whatever Bill Oscar had to confess, it wasn't going to be good.

Zach had screeched to the curb at the airport just in time to see Violet and Bill pull away in a cab. Her earlier text, the one he'd only recently read, was alarmingly short.

She had not replied to his answering string of messages that ended with "Do NOT go anywhere with him. Wait for me." Of course she hadn't waited. Violet "I can handle myself" Griffin. If it wasn't so maddening, it would make him smile, this woman who would go toe-to-toe with anyone. In their high school days, he'd actually seen her use a broom to chase away a teen who'd been intent on graffitiing the wall of the diner. She'd probably make an excellent defender if she ever had the yen to join his police basketball team. He'd jokingly asked her before, and she'd replied with a sassy, "Not in this lifetime. Your uniforms are way too ugly."

He tried to tail them, a maddening prospect in city traffic, staying far enough back in his squad car that he hoped Bill hadn't noticed. With each congested mile his pulse ticked higher. He mentally practiced the points he would make when he chewed her out. It would be helpful to prep ahead of time, since she could talk circles around him when she had a mind to, but there could be no justifying getting into a cab with Bill Oscar.

He'd lost them a few times, but finally trailed them to a coffee shop. The block was dotted with eateries, everything from Greek dolmas, Hawaiian poke, cheese blintzes, and Vietnamese noodles in rich broth. Eddie's nose twitched as he sampled the air.

"I know, I'm hungry, too. Work first, lunch later." Though he was certain Eddie questioned his priorities, he flapped his ears and continued their slow amble around the coffee shop, searching for a place to park, which had added a maddening amount of time.

He'd taken a moment to pull a plain jacket over his uniform shirt, take off his utility belt in favor of a side-arm holster and tug on a Yankees baseball cap. He put a civilian harness on Eddie and slid on a pair of sunglasses before they made their way briskly back to the café.

After completing their second casual stroll around the shop, and finding nothing amiss, he pretended to study the menu written on a chalkboard easel, keeping Bill and Violet in his sight every moment.

Bill's shoulders were tensed, knee bobbing as he

sat on the bench, close to Violet but not touching her, squinting against the sun. For her part, Violet seemed attentive, but not alarmed as far as he could tell, one elegant leg crossed over the other, peep-toed high heels adding a trademark sense of style to her navy blue airline skirt and jacket.

Bill seemed to be talking in stops and starts, nervous, clearly. Was he trying to convince her of his innocence, or confessing his guilt? Irritation and fear raked through him again. The guy could very well be a drug dealer and Violet was coolly sipping coffee with him like he was a long-lost uncle. He could have called his people to arrange a hit, or an abduction, and Violet would have no place to hide. The thought made Zach's muscles bunch into knots.

Calm down, he told himself. A tall order, even on a good day.

Zach had never been sedate. During their tutoring sessions, when Jordy helped Zach study for the police exam, they'd taken breaks every half hour, shooting hoops, doing pushups, playing with the dogs, anything to stem Zach's restlessness and frustration that came with long hours of wrestling with his dyslexia. Books made him fidgety. He'd much rather listen to them on audio while running a couple of miles.

Reining you in is like trying to saddle a wild horse, Jordy had lamented many times. Since Jordy's murder, Zach's emotions seemed to be uncontainable, breaking loose in spite of his efforts to subdue them. Embarrassing, humiliating, but the emotions would not go away no matter how hard he squashed them down.

Why had God taken away his brother?

It's okay that you're struggling with Jordy's death... it's healthy to talk about it.

No, it wasn't. Violet was wrong. Unbridling all that mess made him less of a cop, less of a man. Bill fidgeted. Zach was once again furious at the guy who'd landed Violet knee-deep in threats.

Rage threatened to gallop away with him. He had to force himself not to charge that bench and march Violet right on her sleek high heels back to his squad car. Instead, he pulled the baseball cap down and meandered closer, slouching against a nearby lamppost as if he was texting someone. Cell phones tended to trap people in bubbles of oblivion, but they could be a cop's best friend...or a killer's.

At that moment Violet looked up, riveting her brown gaze to his. She startled just a little, but to her credit, she covered it by tucking her hair back into the clip that held the mass of curls at the nape of her neck. His look no doubt telegraphed, *What exactly do you think you are doing?* but she moved her attention back to Bill. She could feel his ire, no doubt, and he figured she was going to have to bake him a whole batch of apple pies to make up for this silly stunt. He strained to hear their conversation.

"...got you into this mess," Bill was saying. The words sounded earnest enough, the body language seemed to match, but Zach didn't believe it, not one single syllable. He hoped Violet didn't, either. He scanned the crowd again. Had Bill alerted Beck? Was he snaking his way along the sunny sidewalk toward Violet? But no one seemed at all interested in the two chatting on the bench. A lady edged by him, clutching a cell

phone to one ear and toting a paper-lined basket with
a club sandwich and chips. Eddie tracked the tantalizing scent. She found a seat under one of the orange um-
brellas. A man in a business suit joined her, pressing a
kiss to her cheek before he sat. Just people out enjoying the spring sunshine, not threats. Zach bent over to
scratch Eddie, which gave him an excuse to shuffle a
few inches closer.

"Debts," Bill was saying.

The word caught Zach's attention.

"Rory's care is so expensive, and our medical ben-
efits aren't what they used to be. And the kids, I mean,
their private school costs a mint, but I can't uproot them
now, can I? Not with their mother being so sick. All
their friends are there, and Rory would be heartbroken
if we pulled them out. I'd get another job, but after forty
years with an airline, I don't know how to do anything
else. I've worked at the airport since I was sixteen."

Violet caught his wrist. "What are you saying, Bill?
Quit dancing around it."

Zach could see the coffee cup trembling in his fingers. "I… I thought it would be a quick way to earn
some money to pay for Rory's treatments and the kids'
expenses. I promise you I never wanted anyone to get
hurt."

Violet's voice was calm and measured. "Tell me the
truth, all of it."

"I can't. It's too dangerous."

"We're way past that," Violet snapped. "I almost got
killed. My house is under police watch and I can't even
sit on the front stoop."

Atta girl, Vi, Zach thought with a smile. *Stay strong. Don't fall for his sympathy act.*

Bill rubbed a palm on his jeans. "I'm so sorry, but there's no way I can fix it. You should leave things alone, Vi. Just forget the whole thing and get your cop friend to back off. Leave town, maybe. Just for a while until this all blows over."

"I'm not going anywhere, Bill, so you might as well just spit it out. What happened at the airport? What are you a part of?"

He toyed with the lid of his cup. "The guy you fingered, Xavier Beck, he's bad news. Ruthless, cunning."

No newsflash there, Zach thought.

"People who threaten him don't survive. He wants to impress his boss, and he'll go after you to clean up the mess at the airport because you're a threat. You're a witness to him smuggling drugs. You've seen his face."

What boss? Zach risked edging a few inches closer. This might be a story Bill had cooked up to protect his own skin. Or perhaps the hints about a bigger boss, Uno, were founded after all.

Violet skewered Bill with a look. "You've been allowing drugs to pass through the airport. Yes or no?"

Bill shoved his hands under his thighs. "Yes."

Violet let out a breath and sagged a little. She'd wanted so badly to believe her boss and friend was not guilty.

"Oh, Bill," she said. "I can't believe you did that."

"Me neither. Looking in the mirror now I don't even recognize myself. It was small at first. Nothing major, a few ounces to test the system. I… I worked with Jeb Leak, the TSA guy, and we let Jones through, then

Roach and Beck. As soon as I did it, I felt terrible, I wanted to stop, but Beck said he'd hurt my wife, my kids." Bill's voice caught. "What choice did I have, then? You've seen them, they're vicious."

A nice way to gain sympathy, bringing in the wife and kids, Zach thought, but the fear rang true.

Violet stared at him. "Is this the truth, Bill, or are you lying to me? Who are you working for, exactly? Who is Beck's boss?"

He shook his head, scanning the street. "I've got no idea. They never told me and to be honest, I didn't want to know. I just wanted to get away from the whole nightmare and forget it ever happened."

"You must have an idea," she pressed.

"No, I…" Bill suddenly got to his feet.

Zach tensed and put his hand on the gun hidden under his jacket.

Bill dumped his coffee in the trash. "I've said too much. I don't want you to get hurt. Please do as I say. Don't ask any more questions. Find another job. I'll write you a recommendation, whatever you need. I'm sorry I got you involved. I never wanted things to be like this."

Bill extended a hand to Violet, clasping her fingers in his. "I am truly sorry. I'll take you back now. This was a mistake."

A movement from across the street drew Bill's attention. He froze in place, hands still clasping hers, mouth open.

Zach moved forward to get a clearer view.

"No!" Bill yelled, leaping in front of Violet as gunfire erupted from across the street. Before Zach's gun cleared the holster, Bill was falling to the cement, a bullet hole punched in his right temple. He hit the sidewalk with a lifeless thud. A second and third bullet fractured the glass of the café, raining a torrent of gleaming shards.

Ambush, Zach's mind screamed as he dove for Violet.

ELEVEN

Zach had only a moment to squeeze off a shot at the assailant, a man wearing a black cap pulled down, short, barrel-chested—Xavier Beck, it had to be. Beck reeled back as Zach's shot skimmed his shoulder. Spinning, he took cover behind some parked cars.

Zach pulled Violet and Eddie inside the café. People were screaming, crying, so he had to yell to be heard. "NYPD. Everybody stay in here, and move away from the windows," he commanded. Then he radioed the dispatcher with the location, eyeing the parked cars across the street to see if he could take another shot. "Active shooter, I need backup and an ambulance." Help would be rolling in seconds.

Violet did not appear to be injured, but she was breathing hard, face pale as milk.

"Tell me what to do," she whispered.

He gently pushed her toward the tables, farther away from the fractured windows. "Take Eddie. Keep him away from the glass and see if anyone is hurt."

As he'd suspected, giving her a task seemed to break

through the shock. She nodded, accepted Eddie's leash without a word and crept from patron to patron.

He ran out into the street, crouched behind a newspaper stand, looking for the assailant. There was no sign of movement from across the street, but sirens wailed as the cavalry closed in. Would Beck flee? Or come at them in an effort to silence Violet? He'd be smart to run, but he'd already proved that there was no risk he would not take to get what he wanted. With no sign of Beck, he returned to the ruined café.

Go ahead, Beck. Make your move. I'm ready for you.

When the first officers arrived to tend to the victims, he filled them in as best he could. Violet continued her ministrations, making the rounds of the huddled diners, checking for injuries and reassuring them. The sirens were deafening now, wailing up the street, and in moments the area was awash in more cops and squad cars. It took several more moments for officers to organize and swarm the street, behind the parked cars and then into the nearby shops, clearing the spaces one by one. He joined them in the effort. With each shop they searched, his nerves hitched tighter. Where would Beck have gone? Where had he parked his motorcycle? Or had he come on foot, easily melting away into the crowd to make his escape? He could only relay his information to the arriving patrol officers and help in whatever way he could.

It was a good forty minutes before Noah arrived, followed by Brianne Hayes and Luke Hathaway.

Noah had Zach and the other canine officers regrouped in the café for a debriefing, Scotty at his side, keeping the dog away from the broken glass.

"Nothing so far," Brianne Hayes said.

Noah looked at her. "I want you in on the interviews of the victims."

"Yes, sir." Her dog in training, Stella, the Lab, could encounter similarly traumatized people in her work as a bomb-detection dog. It would aid the dog in the future to gain experience from the shooting.

"We'll continue to canvass the area and assist the lieutenant in charge of the scene," Noah said. "He's asked us to move these witnesses to the building next door, away from all this glass while Brianne gets their statements."

Brianne nodded. "I'll handle it."

"I'll help," Luke put in.

"Where's your dog?" Brianne inquired.

"I came here directly from a class. Bruno's still in the kennel."

"I want to get Violet and Eddie away from here," Zach said. "Something doesn't feel right."

"Soon as we finish the secondary sweep, put Eddie in Luke's car. Violet can go in the front seat." Noah frowned at him, speaking lower so the others wouldn't hear. "Could have had mass casualties here, Zach. You should have arranged for backup before you tailed them to the café."

"I didn't know she was meeting Bill until just before this all went down. All I could think about was tailing Bill's car. Things went bad really fast."

"One radio call was all it would have taken to loop us in." He fingered his radio, a hard edge creeping into his tone. "That's why we have these things, you know.

And safety protocols. I believe you've been trained in all that, correct? Perhaps a refresher course is needed?"

"Noah…" He fought down the adrenaline that made him want to bark at his brother. Not just his brother, his chief. He'd been brash, and he owed Noah an apology and the respect he deserved. "You're right, Chief. Sorry."

Noah quieted Scotty, who'd begun to whine. "Apology accepted, but I expect better next time. Let's do our jobs. You kept her and everybody else safe, so that's something."

But he hadn't kept Bill safe. He couldn't allow himself to mull over that at the moment. There would be plenty of time for analyzing his miscalculations later.

Violet was still walking around with Eddie in tow, talking in particular to an elderly lady until the medics took over to assess. Brianne and Luke began to herd the group from the café toward the side door that led to the next building. Noah was right. This could have been a scene of mass casualties, and Violet might have been one of them. He took her gently by the wrist and led her to a wooden chair, far away from the windows. "Wait for me here," he said to her. "Keep an eye on Eddie, okay?"

She nodded, and her meek compliance worried him.

He helped Noah and Brianne talk to witnesses that had been moved into the printing business. The manager had welcomed the victims warmly, offering bottles of water and folding chairs to the shocked patrons. New Yorkers might have the reputation for being tough-minded, but they took care of their own.

When everyone was settled as comfortably as they

could be, he returned to the café, where a few officers were taping off the glass-strewn area and taking pictures. Violet sat on a chair, bent over, her cheek pressed to the top of Eddie's head. The sight of her cuddling his dog stopped him. She looked so small, so frightened, with her escaped curls draped along Eddie's face. It was as if she'd taken off the tough-girl cape, and now the soft, vulnerable woman underneath was visible. He was not sure how to take it, this new vision of a lifelong friend, but strange feelings overtook him.

"Hey," he said softly.

She bolted to her feet, twisting the leash between her fingers.

"It's okay. I didn't mean to startle you."

"I, uh…" She swallowed. "I mean, I think they just put Bill onto a stretcher. But…" Her lower lip trembled. "He's dead, isn't he, Zach?"

The sadness and uncertainty in her face cut at him. How he wanted to comfort her, to tell her some sort of fib that would take the pain away, but he would not ever lie to Violet Griffin. Not her, not ever.

"Yes, honey. He's dead. I'm sorry."

Her face crumpled and she began to cry, quiet sobs, fists clenched to her middle as if she was trying to hold the tears inside. His heart broke one inch at a time.

Eddie whined and pawed at her shoes.

Zach took her in his arms and held her, stroking her back and pressing a kiss to her temple, rocking her gently back and forth. "Aww, Vi. It's gonna be okay." How could he even say it when he'd doubted for the past month that the world would ever look right again? God was surely against him, cruel and comfortless, but with her there, pressed against his chest, he felt something different, which made him recall the words his mother had written in his Bible.

I will both lay me down in peace, and sleep: for thou, Lord, only makest me dwell in safety. Maybe his brain didn't believe it anymore, but he made his heart recite the words because, though Zach might not deserve peace or safety, Violet surely did.

God...help me believe it again. It was all he could say, the only thing he could pray.

Someone handed him a packet of tissues and he gave one to her. She pressed it to her face and choked out a few more gulping sounds. After a few moments he felt her straighten, and she faced him, swiping the tissue under her eyes.

"I know what you're thinking. I shouldn't have come here with Bill. You were right." New tears traced glistening trails on her cheeks. "Maybe if I hadn't..." Her mouth quivered again.

He cradled her cheeks between his palms and spoke quietly. "Violet, do not go there. Bill is not dead because of you. Beck shot him. Bill didn't want to cooperate anymore, and he'd become a liability to their operation so Beck murdered him and intended to take you out, too, if Bill hadn't shielded you. That's it."

"His wife, his boys." She bit her lip and he could see her fighting for control. She would not want to lose it here, not with the cops circling around.

He dried her tears with his thumbs. "We're leaving. I'll borrow Luke's vehicle to take us to my car. It's a couple of blocks from here. Brianne can help him retrieve his when they're done with the interviews."

She didn't respond, so he picked Eddie up and tucked him under one arm to carry him past the glass. His other hand he offered to Violet. She took it. "Your hands are freezing."

She mumbled something he didn't catch. Though she'd refused any medical attention, he resolved to keep a close eye on her for signs of shock. What she'd just witnessed would probably trouble her for many years to come. They exited the café and he purposefully stayed on her right side, to block her view of the bloodstained sidewalk. She clutched his fingers in a death grip as they went by.

"Keep walking, Vi. Look straight ahead."

When Eddie was secured in Luke's backseat, he urged her toward the front passenger door. "Sit in here for just a minute while I get a blanket out of the back."

He'd just grabbed the door handle to open it for her, when a motorcycle roared up the street, ripping through the yellow caution tape.

The rider, Xavier Beck, had stripped off the cap, eyes burning like coals as he punched the motorcycle forward. Steering with one hand, he held a gun in his bloodstained other one. He bore down on them, firing wildly.

Zach had only a moment to throw himself on top of Violet and force her to the street.

The shots deafened her. Senses on overload, she could not process what was happening. Her arms and legs felt numb, her brain fuzzy. Someone, Zach, she realized, had pushed her down to the ground, shielding her with his torso as bullets peppered the asphalt around them. Sharp bits cut into her chin and the breath was squeezed out of her. Had she been shot? Had he? She could not be sure.

Then Zach pulled her to her feet, yanking her around the other side of the car, tugging her back inside the café, shouting into his radio. *We're still alive*, she told herself in disbelief. *Thank You, God*. Dimly, she heard Zach talking urgently into his radio.

"I've gotta get her out of here. I'll contact you when I can."

They sprinted out the back entrance and into an alley fetid with the smell of garbage and exhaust while cops surged all over the scene of the second shooting. She stumbled, but he helped her along. "We have to hurry, Violet. Beck made it past our guys. He's going to start tracking us if he can."

Terror made her blood run cold. Beck was coming. He'd killed Bill Oscar, her longtime friend, murdered him right on a public bench not three feet away. Now he was coming for her just like he'd promised in the airport. He wouldn't let her escape again. Icy prickles erupted along her spine. Suddenly, she could not pull any air into her lungs. She staggered to a stop, struggling against a growing dizziness.

He stopped, taking her by the arms, bending so he could look in her face. "We have to keep going."

But she couldn't. As much as she wanted to be strong, she simply could not force herself to move past the fear. It was as if her muscles and joints were paralyzed by a strange sort of inertia born of terror and helplessness.

Zach stroked her upper arms as if to warm her. "Vi, listen to me. I'm going to get you out of this. I'm going to keep you safe." He smiled. "Just like when we were kids and you got stuck in that elm I told you not to climb in the Baisley Pond Park. You wouldn't let anyone else help you down but me. Noah and Carter tried, and you screamed nonstop until I climbed up and got you. Remember that?"

She remembered. Staring into his eyes, blue as robins' eggs, she recalled that moment when he'd commanded her to release the branch and hold on to him. *Let go, Violet. I won't let you fall.*

Now she tried to catch her breath and calm her terror. He would take care of her if she let him. She knew it with every cell in her being, just like she had as a child, perched on a limb, waiting for Zach and no one else. It felt to her then as though she'd been waiting for him her whole life, waiting to step out on that fragile branch that spanned the distance between the two of them.

"You trust me, don't you, Vi?"

She could not speak so instead she nodded. No matter what happened, how scared she felt, she would always trust Zach Jameson with everything.

"That's my Vi," he said, kissing her on the forehead. He reached behind her and untied her hair, freeing it from the scarf. For one breathless second, he trailed his fingers through her curls. "So you look a little different, harder to spot," he told her with a quirked smile. "Still gorgeous, just different."

Gorgeous? She felt anything but. The cut on her shin burned and sweat dampened her brow. Grit stuck to the palms of her hands and one of her shoe heels felt wobbly. She wiped off her hands and fixed her jacket.

Zach turned his baseball cap around backward.

"We'll act casual. Head for a cab or the subway, something. You ready?"

"No, but I'll go with you, anyway."

He flashed one more grin. "Eddie will be sorry to be missing out on this adventure."

Her heart pounded as she suddenly remembered that Eddie was in the back of Luke's car. "Is he okay?" she asked as they hurried down the alley toward the sidewalk.

"Yeah, I heard him barking when we ran for the café. Luke will take care of him."

Police cars continued to pour into the area, sirens blasting. As they stepped from the alley onto the sidewalk, Violet's skin crawled. Was Beck still on his motorcycle, cruising the streets? Or was he on foot now, blending in with the pedestrians who rushed in every direction, panicked by the horrible act of violence that had occurred right around the corner?

Bill's last moments kept replaying in her mind, twisting her insides with pain. He'd been trying to fix his mistake, trying to warn her as best he could, just a man who'd fallen in with the wrong people, desperate to help his family. He'd risked his own safety to warn her, and it had cost him everything.

Zach pushed her through the agitated crowds until they were several blocks away. He radioed their location before he tucked her arm in his elbow and guided them quickly along. Her heart hammered so hard she was sure the frantic passersby could hear it. A scared woman elbowed past her and she nearly screamed, but Zach pressed her closer and sped up their pace. His expression was determined, calm. He appeared casual as he scanned the road traffic and the approaching people, but she knew he was taking in every detail. His fingers tightened around her wrist.

"There, across the street, nine o'clock."

She peeked past his shoulder and panic flooded her senses. Beck was standing across the street outside a corner grocery. He held one arm cradled to his body as he slowly perused the street.

Zach relayed Beck's location to the cops before he spoke to Violet. "He must have figured we'd ducked out the back. Keep moving. Don't speed up. We're one of the crowd," he whispered.

But Beck's perusal stopped as he fixed on them.

"He's spotted us, Zach," she said.

The aboveground subway station loomed over them. The flight of green stairs was dotted with stragglers hurrying to catch the next train. There was no time to wait for backup. Zach hesitated only a moment.

"We'll beat him to the subway."

"He'll catch us before we get there." Terror nearly blinded her.

"No, he won't." Zach grabbed her hand and they began to run.

TWELVE

He sprinted, Violet right next to him, amazingly agile even on high heels. Dodging past the crowds and earning some dirty looks, they reached the turnstiles.

"Zach," she panted, clutching at him. "I don't have my purse. I left it on the bench."

No purse meant no MetroCard. Zach wasted no time beelining to a transit official and flashing his badge. "We need to get through right now."

The heavyset officer asked no questions, just ushered them past the turnstile. They joined the people on the platform behind the yellow line, just as the train roared into the station. Zach tried to spot Beck. Had he had enough time to chase them down?

It seemed like the station was full of dark-clad men. He elbowed his way deeper into the crowd, putting his lips to her ear.

"If we get separated, make your way to this address." He mumbled it twice until she caught his collar and drew him closer.

"You're not leaving me."

"You'll get on the train and get away from here. I'll catch up with you later."

"Not going without you."

"If I spot him, I have to go after him, Vi. It's the only way to end this."

Her eyes burned and her lips tightened into a thin line. "Zach William Jameson, if you don't get onto this train with me I'll scream louder than I did from the top of that elm tree."

He wanted to laugh at her ferocious tone, but he knew it came from a place of deep fear. Would she be safer if he stayed behind and watched for Beck? But if the guy somehow managed to slip past him on the train, Violet would be completely unprotected.

He was reaching for his radio to update Noah when the people began to edge forward as the train doors slid open. Together or separate? She answered for him by grabbing his wrist and jerking him along until they were both bundled into the car. During the maneuver her high heel broke, but she hobbled along without missing a beat.

The jostling throng set his nerves firing as people crammed into the subway car. He'd never met a cop who felt comfortable in a closed space no matter what the circumstances, and he was no different. He swallowed against a wave of claustrophobia as the doors slid shut. Violet was unfazed, edging in and around the various passengers until she found an unoccupied seat on the end. She collapsed into it. Zach stood next to her, leaning on the silver pole, where he had a good view of every door, including the one to the adjoining car.

When the subway lurched out of the station, he

shifted his focus completely to that spot. If Beck was on the train, he'd be coming through that entry point.

His anger hardened like forged steel. *Let him try.*

But with a subway car full of potential victims, he could not take any chances. He took out his phone and sent a text to Noah. He was beyond relieved to hear back that no one had been injured in Beck's secondary attack and Eddie would be safely delivered to the Jamesons' and an officer would retrieve Violet's purse. His second text was in the form of a request that went to his friend, Archie Ballentine, and the positive reply came back immediately. He heaved out a sigh.

"Where are we going?" Violet whispered.

He bent to keep their conversation private. "I know a guy in Manhattan, at the address I gave you earlier. We'll go to his place. It's safe there. He just confirmed."

She didn't speak; her demeanor was outwardly composed, but he knew it was a front. The tiny tremor in her fingers betrayed her. All he could do was stay glued to her side and keep his hand free in case he needed to reach for his gun.

After the twenty-minute ride, they switched trains, watching warily for signs that Beck was following. Violet and Zach saw one person came through the adjoining cars, an older woman with a tiny white dog nestled in her purse. She sat next to Violet in a seat that had been vacated along the way.

Violet offered her a wan smile.

The woman watched them for a long while before she finally quirked a brow at Violet and then at Zach. "Not my business, young man," she said, "but you should take better care of your sweetheart. Her shoe is broken."

Violet's cheeks went red. "Oh, he's not…"

"You're right, ma'am," Zach cut in. "It's been an unusual day and I've been rushing her."

"Unusual or not," she clucked, smoothing her wrinkled hands over her dog's wiry head. "You should never rush your sweetheart. And you've spent this whole ride staring at the door or your cell phone, not even giving one speck of attention to this beautiful lady."

"She's right," the woman across the aisle piped up. Zach swiveled to acknowledge her. She was bundled in a coat and rubber boots, sporting a chic red hat.

Violet's tiny smile indicated she was enjoying his public chastisement.

The look both women shot him was pure disapproval.

"Got to step up your game," the hat lady said, "if you want to keep her."

Zach felt like an insect on a pin as he cleared his throat. "Yes, ma'am."

"Women need to be treasured, pampered, treated like jewels." The older woman eyed Violet's broken shoe. "Well, you should take her someplace where she can have that shoe repaired and then get a bite to eat. I am quite certain I heard her stomach growl. It's nearly four o'clock. Did you even bother to get her lunch? A late-afternoon snack? Anything?"

"Uh, no, ma'am. We were…"

"I haven't eaten since breakfast," Violet said, her tone melancholy.

"What has happened to the youth in our country?" Huffing out a breath, the woman reached around the dog in her bag and pulled out a chocolate bar. "Eat this, honey. You need a pick-me-up, if this fellow did not so much as get you a hot dog for lunch."

With a sweet smile, Violet accepted. "Thank you very much. It's so kind of you."

The old woman shot Zach a hostile glare. "And don't share it with him until he learns some manners."

Zach was stumbling over some sort of reply when his phone buzzed with a text from Noah.

Beck's evaded capture. Watch your back.

He blew out a breath. At least Beck wasn't on the subway train. Now, if he could just get Violet to the safe house.

He looked up to find both women watching him, frowning.

"He can't even keep his eyes off his cell phone long enough for one conversation." Hat lady sniffed. "Pathetic."

"She could definitely do better," the older one said, launching into a story about her grandfather and his courtship procedures. He was beyond relieved when the train pulled into the station. Quickly, he took Violet's hand and helped her to her feet. She staggered a bit on her broken heel.

As Violet thanked the lady again for the candy bar, the woman handed her a slip of paper, whispering loud enough for him to hear, "My grandson is an orthodontist. He's single. Here's his number."

Violet managed to keep a straight face until they were out of the train. Then she let out a mighty burst of laughter. It was a release of stress, he knew, but still. He hustled her along faster, tucking her arm under his.

"You enjoyed that, didn't you?" he said as they made their way out of the station.

She nodded. "Oh, yes. Immensely."

He sighed. He could handle being lambasted, if it took her mind off Xavier Beck, bringing back her sparkle if only for a few moments.

"Come on, Vi. Maybe I can redeem myself for my boorish behavior."

"Doubtful," she said, squeezing his hand, "but it will be amusing to see you try."

The apartment building in Manhattan was on the Upper West Side, half a block from Central Park. They'd finished the last leg of the journey in a cab. Rents here were high, and she wondered about Zach's acquaintance. Tidying her hair and straightening her jacket, she worried she looked like a vagrant with her ruined shoe. They'd already gotten stares from the taxi driver, the doorman and the lady waxing the floors, who looked pointedly at Violet's broken heel. They were buzzed through the lobby and up to a third-floor studio apartment.

"Who is Archie Ballentine?" she said.

"Friend of the family. He's at work, but he said to make ourselves at home." Zach used a key to open the door.

"Why do you have a key?"

"Friends, like I said. He's got a key to our place, too."

Must be very good friends, she thought, if he had a key to a cop's house. The interior was small, with a brick wall and hardwood floors. A neatly made queen-size bed opened onto a tiny kitchen. Another door led to the equally tiny bathroom. Zach walked to the windows that looked down onto 82nd Street. He must have been satisfied, since he drew the curtains and went to the bottom drawer of the dresser.

"Here," he said, handing her a pair of jeans and a T-shirt. "Archie's sister stays here sometimes and she left some things. Archie said to borrow what you needed and shower and change. Sorry there's no shoes, though."

"I'm okay… I…"

Zach's look went mournful. "Please, Vi. I've already been chewed up by two ladies about how I should take better care of my sweetheart. At least allow me to do this and fix you something to eat so I can salvage some shred of dignity."

"But you're not my sweetheart, so you're off the hook." Not her sweetheart, just a man she trusted with her life, who knew her better and deeper than anyone else on the planet. And why did her stomach go fluttery when she looked at him now, all strong and tender at the same time?

He pushed the bundled clothes at her. "While you shower, I need to make some calls and I'm going to fix you some eggs if there are any."

Her doubt must have shown on her face.

"Why are you giving me that look? I can cook eggs," he said defensively.

"Since when?"

"Since, like, forever."

"Last time you tried to make eggs we had to throw away the pan."

"Aww, go shower, wouldja? I need to recapture some self-esteem. You just wait. The eggs are going to be awe-inspiring. Much better than an orthodontist could make."

Taking the clothes, she squeezed into the bathroom. A narrow stand-up shower was crowded in with a pedestal sink and toilet, but to Violet it was finer than accommodations at the Four Seasons. The hot water rinsed away the grit and grime and she helped herself to a dollop of shampoo. It felt glorious to be clean, and though Archie's sister was a bigger size than Violet, she was grateful for the gentle softness of the borrowed clothes next to her skin. She used her scarf as a makeshift belt to cinch the waist of the jeans.

The mirror cast a sobering reflection back at her that took away some of her contentment. A scrape grazed the cheek that was already bruised from Beck's airport attack and there was another scratch on her forehead. But what Violet was most shocked by was the fear she saw imprinted on her own face.

Where was the independent, self-assured woman she thought she'd been hours before? Now she was nose to nose with someone small and scared, unsure, a woman who'd seen a life snuffed out right next to her. It came back in a horrifying rush. Clinging to the edge of the sink, she searched for strength. An image of Zach rose in her mind. *Zach is here, and he won't let anything happen to me.*

She didn't want to depend on someone else for her peace of mind. The very idea offended her sensibilities, but nonetheless Zach's presence was the only thing keeping the terror at bay. He was right there, in the kitchen, and his nearness meant comfort and shelter, whether she could admit it or not. Straightening her shoulders, she tucked her hair behind her ears. With her nerves bolstered a little, she pattered out of the bathroom on bare feet to find him before her confidence could evaporate.

The acrid smell of burning eggs tickled her nostrils. She found Zach staring mournfully into a blackened pan at the remnants of what had probably been his attempt at scrambled eggs.

"Oh, dear," she said.

"I don't get it." He shook his head. "I watched a YouTube video. I thought I did everything right."

"It's okay. I wasn't very hungry, anyway."

He heaved out a breath. "You know, I'm beginning to suspect I'm not very good at cooking."

The understatement of the decade. Through sheer force of will, she smothered a smile and a peal of laughter. "You just need more practice."

"I was trying to get some at the house." He groaned. "My brothers have started to call me The Incinerator. The only thing I can make is Eddie's treats and that's only because Ellie helps me. A six-year-old is a better cook than I am."

She giggled. "You can't be good at everything."

He shoved the pan in the sink, filled it with water, his back to her. Hands braced on the counter, his head dropped. "No, only one thing. I have to be good at being a cop. It's all I have," he mumbled to the soapy water.

"You are a great cop." She sensed the pain and she put her hands on his shoulders, kneading the taut muscles. He relaxed slightly, letting out a deep sigh. Her fingers massaged his neck as if she could ease away his doubt.

"I'm not sure anymore."

The vulnerability jarred her. He'd actually shared the crack in his confidence, a deeply painful thing for him to expose to anyone. "You will catch Beck," she said firmly, pressing her cheek hard to his spine. "And you will find the man who murdered Jordy and you will experience joy again, just like God wants."

He was silent for a long moment and then he turned around to face her. His eyes were thoughtful, so blue, exquisitely earnest. "Do you really still believe in me like that, Vi?"

"I really do."

"Why?" It came out as the softest whisper.

"Because I trust you, just like I did when I climbed the tree. You wouldn't let me fall then and you won't now. Jordy trusted you and you won't let him down, either."

His face was close to hers, his breath and body warm. He brushed a thumb along her cheek.

"I know you're scared," he said.

"Not me."

His touch was as gentle as the smile playing across his lips. "You're lying, Vi."

Her lip trembled. "Maybe pretending, just a little." His caress continued to connect her to him, to make a bridge past the fear to a new place that she hadn't been before.

And then his mouth was on hers and her whole world grew fuzzy around the edges. Sparks circled and danced in her spirit like fireflies on a warm spring night. He stopped for a moment, looking at her in wonder, and then he leaned in for another kiss.

THIRTEEN

Zach pressed his mouth to hers and reveled in the explosion of comfort that flooded over him. It felt like coming home. He buried his hand in her hair and held her there, her lips soft as satin. His brain could not keep up with the confusion he felt at kissing the woman who was supposed to be his friend only. Somehow with his kiss he had eased them into a new wild and thrilling territory. *This is a bad idea*, his brain blared at him.

So he stopped listening to his brain and kissed her again, letting his heart guide him toward what it wanted. When they were both breathless, she eased away a fraction, and he looked in disbelief at the brown eyes that stared from under a curtain of long lashes, reflecting his own surprise back at him. His face looked like that of a man in love.

"Zach…" she breathed.

Then the door opened and he shoved her behind him, grabbing his gun and charging the front door.

Archie Ballentine jerked to a halt with a grocery bag in one arm. He was a short plug of a man, close to seventy now, with a cap of snowy hair and a suit, custom-made, to go with his leather wing tips. "Hello, Zach. I'd raise my hands and surrender, but I don't want to drop the groceries."

Zach exhaled and holstered his weapon. "I thought you were working."

"Closed the deal early."

"You should have texted me. I could have shot you."

"I did text you." His brow hitched a fraction as he scanned Violet's face and then Zach's. "You were distracted, I guess…"

Archie had always had the uncanny ability to read Zach like a book. It didn't help that Zach's breathing was still erratic and his heart was thumping like Eddie's tail after a bust. He cleared his throat, hoping he did not still look like a lovesick puppy. "I'm sorry. Very glad to see you, we both are. Sure do appreciate your help, Archie."

"Figured you might want some food for the lady." He gave the bag to Zach along with a hug, and extended his palm to Violet.

"Vi, this is Archie Ballentine." The mundane introduction seemed ridiculous to Zach, when he was still reeling from kissing Violet. He could not tell from her face how the kiss had affected her, except for a slight petal-pink blush staining her cheeks. Ten minutes before, he would never have believed he'd have kissed Violet Griffin, not like that, anyway.

"Nice to meet you," she said. "Thank you for letting me come here."

"Sure," Archie said. "When a Jameson says he needs something, the answer is always yes. This time, however, I am a little lacking in details."

"I'll fill you in." Zach deposited the groceries on the kitchen counter as he talked. He started with the airport incident and quickly outlined events that led to his desperate text to Archie on the subway ride from Queens.

Archie nodded. "So this Xavier Beck's at large. Is he the big boss or is there someone else?"

"Bill hinted there was a bigger guy behind it all." He caught Violet's wince at the mention of her deceased boss. "I, uh… It's been a traumatic couple of hours."

Archie nodded thoughtfully. "I think I got it. What's the game plan?"

"Keep Vi here tonight, if that's okay."

Violet started to object, but Zach shook her off. "Beck's going to stick around. I want you here for a while to give our guys a chance to catch him and to set up a tighter watch schedule at your house. He's been seen by a ton of people and the cops are all over, so he won't be able to remain long out in the open. It's safer for you to stay here tonight."

She slid a look at Archie. "Is it fair to involve Mr. Ballentine in a dangerous situation?"

"Call me Archie," he said. "And offering up my apartment is a no-brainer. As far as danger goes…" He shrugged. "I can take care of myself."

"That's for sure. Always land on your feet somehow," Zach said with a laugh. "And as I recall you've beaten Carter in a judo match a time or two."

Archie grinned. "Yes, I have. More than a time or two in my younger days. His hip throw was terrible back then. Couldn't knock over a toddler."

Zach grinned. "Still can't."

"When did you two meet?" Violet asked.

Zach leaned on the kitchen counter. "Jordy and I arrested him." They both chuckled at the look of shock on Violet's face.

"All right, Miss Violet," Archie said. "Sit down at the table, if you're still willing now that you know I'm a reformed felon. I brought sandwiches because The Incinerator here can't boil water without setting something on fire."

Zach groaned. "You've been talking to my brothers."

"I check in when I can. Since my apartment smells like burned eggs, I assume you haven't changed your ways. Sit down, both of you, and I'll explain before we get ourselves a game plan." Archie passed out pastrami sandwiches and cans of soda.

Zach realized for the first time that he was starving. He'd missed both breakfast and lunch and it was well on toward the dinner hour. He ate hungrily, while Violet only managed a few bites.

"Eat, Vi," he said. "You've got to get some food down."

"That's what I've been telling you for the past two months," she said, sampling a small bite.

"I'm eating. Your turn." He wiped his mouth. "Archie was involved in a little fake taxi scam, about fifteen years ago."

"Not little," he said, chin up. "I made six grand a week as a cabbie for City Wheels Rides, the best company in all of New York City."

Zach shook his head. "Only there was no City Wheels Rides company, just a mock-up sticker on the door of his sedan, and a fake meter in the front seat."

"Hey, the important thing was I always delivered

people on time and many would request me specifically. I was their favorite driver and they'd give me Christmas gifts, family photos, even a fruit basket once. 'Give us Archie,' they all cried. I was the people's choice."

"Right up until the day we arrested you with your fake permits, license and forged insurance papers."

Archie waved a hand. "Small potatoes when you should have been chasing down real criminals. Anyway, Jordan said I was the most charismatic crook he ever busted, and he told me I should stop dithering around, go straight and get into business. I took his advice, got my license to sell real estate and now I'm doing great. All because of Jordy. Man, that guy even prayed for me, can you believe that? A cop praying for a crook he busted?"

Zach cleared a lump from his throat. "Yeah. Jordy had a way of seeing the good in people."

"Yes, he did." Archie sighed. "Boy, do I miss him."

Zach swallowed hard. "Me, too."

"Me, three," Violet added. The moment lingered there a while, and Zach thought about what Violet had said before he kissed her.

And you will find the man who murdered Jordy and you will experience joy again, just like God wants. Strange. He'd spent the past two months figuring God had to be against him, but here, crowded around this table with Violet and Archie, he had a sense that his brother was close again, cheering him on. And he'd certainly felt something very akin to joy when he'd kissed Violet in the kitchen. The warm feeling ebbed away as reality intruded.

Jordy's killer was out there, at large, just like Xavier

Beck, waiting to rob him of someone else he cared about…and loved?

Loved? Across the table, Violet pushed her plate away. Her hair was curling as it dried; he remembered the feel of it in his fingers, heavy and light at the same time. Loved…as a friend, he told himself. He'd been caught up in the moment, the emotional cascade, same as Violet. He had tugged her out onto the unfamiliar territory, testing the boundaries of a friendship he was not prepared to lose. Archie had come through the door at exactly the right moment to save him from ruining everything. She was a friend, one he had to save, and he had work to do.

Clearing his throat, he rose from the table. "I've arranged for a plainclothes detective to watch the place while I'm gone."

"I can handle it," Archie said.

"I don't doubt it, but someone eyeballing the street won't hurt."

Violet followed him to the door. "Where are you going?"

"Noah called me about a possible lead while you were showering and I was destroying the eggs. There's a furniture store near the airport that might be a front for moving drugs. Beck was spotted there earlier this afternoon. Eddie and I are going in undercover and I need to work out the details. Plus, I'm going to check every local health-care clinic and see if a guy matching Beck's description checked in since I got him with a bullet across his shoulder."

Violet played with her paper napkin uncertainly.

Archie clapped him on the back. "All right. Watch

your back and I'll watch Violet's." He carried the remaining groceries to the tiny fridge and began to unload them. Zach pulled on his jacket and headed to the door, Violet following. He stepped out into the hallway and she lingered on the threshold, looking down at her bare feet, the toenails painted a delicate pink. He could picture her curled up on her apartment sofa, surrounded by her home decorating magazines and shoe catalogs, stroking paint onto her tiny nails. It was such a girly image, so far from the businesslike woman he thought he knew inside and out. Suddenly, his thinking skills seemed to dry up in one swift stroke as the silence grew awkward between them and they both stared at the floor.

"You have cute toes," he blurted, ruing the statement as soon as it popped out of his mouth. *Smooth, Zach.*

"Thanks for noticing."

"Well, I mean, I guess I haven't seen them in a while…your toes. I just didn't realize they were, you know, cute and stuff, with the paint. So, uh, what color is that, anyway?" Why would his mouth not stop spitting out stupidity?

"Carnation Kisses."

"Ah. Er, that's nice. I mean, it looks nice."

She nodded.

More awkward silence.

"I…" They both said at once.

"I'm sorry," he said, overriding her. "About back there in the kitchen. I got caught up in everything and it just kind of happened." He scrubbed a hand over his scalp. "I shouldn't have kissed you."

She shrugged, gave him a valiant smile. "No harm, no foul."

"What I'm trying to say is, I wouldn't want to do anything to mess up our friendship."

"You didn't. You'll always be my trusty sidekick."

Relief flooded through him in a cooling tide. The ship was upright again, sailing back on the proper course. She was still his friend, his best friend. "Right." He jammed on the baseball cap. "Okay, then. I'll see if I can get your purse back, too, and your phone."

"Okay."

"So, in the meantime, Archie can reach me if you need anything. Text, or call, anytime."

"I will. Be careful, Zach."

He nodded. Then there seemed to be nothing else to say, so he walked away and she locked the door behind him.

After forty-five minutes of small talk, helping Archie unpack the groceries and scrubbing out the burned egg pan, Violet washed her face in the bathroom again and summoned up the courage she needed. She borrowed Archie's phone to call her parents. Archie excused himself to go to the lobby and retrieve his mail. She suspected he was gifting her some privacy. As the quiet of the apartment closed in around her, a trembling started up in her belly. The emptiness spread and invaded until she was half-frantic. Her fingers were clumsy on the buttons.

"Hello, Daddy, it's Violet." She got the words out, barely, before her father started in.

"Violet, this has gone too far," he said, his voice

cracking with anger and fear. "We heard about the shooting. I can't stand it. No more airport job, do you hear? You have to quit. Working for that crooked boss almost got you killed."

And whoever Bill was working for had gotten him killed. Again, the pop of the gun played in her memory, the sound of him falling to the sidewalk, his life stripped away in one cruel moment. She wanted to explain to her father what had happened with Bill, that he wasn't a bad person, just a father who'd made a grievous choice, a choice that turned out to be fatal. The words would not come. She was simply too exhausted to go into it. Instead, she heaved out a breath and swallowed. "I will see if I can find work at another airport, but for now I'm taking a leave of absence." It was a defeat. Her job, her life, everything was topsy-turvy because of what she had seen for a split second in a bad man's suitcase. How utterly ridiculous, how completely unjust.

"Good," her mother said from the other line. "You'll stay with us? Until this madman is caught? The puppy is driving me crazy. He chewed up the sofa pillows today and there is not one shrub still standing in the yard."

Violet wished Latte was there right now for her to cuddle, the soft, warm companion who would lick her chin and flop over for tummy scratches. "Yes, Mom. I will come home as soon as Zach lets me," she squeezed out.

"I'm so glad Zach was there with you." Her father's breath sounded hard and erratic over the phone. "I don't even want to think about what could have happened."

"Yes," she said quietly. "I... I wouldn't have lived through it, probably." Undoubtedly. Beck's second bullet would have been for her. The tremors grew stronger until she had to grip the phone with two hands.

"Where are you now?" her mother asked.

"With a friend of the Jamesons'. I'll be home soon, as soon as I can. There will most likely be a memorial service for Bill. I should help with the plans."

"Absolutely not," her father snapped. "You are to have nothing more to do with Bill Oscar, do you hear me?"

"He can't cause any more trouble now, Daddy." Violet gulped back a sob. "He's dead."

Her father's tone gentled. "Yes, I… I'm sorry, sweet pea. This is terrible on you, and I'm not helping. We can talk about all this tomorrow. I'd rather you were home right now, but if Zach says this is best, then I'll go along with it. You try to get some rest, okay? We love you."

"Yes," her mother echoed quietly. "We do."

She considered the amazing strength of Barbara Griffin. Having lost her only son and almost her daughter, as well, her mother remained composed, a magnificent courage she'd never appreciated fully until that moment. It made her hold the unraveling threads of her self-control long enough to say goodbye.

She barely managed to disconnect before the tears came, racking sobs and shudders. She wished she were in her own apartment where she could wail in private. Hunched into a ball on the futon with her arms around her knees, she tried to smother her outpouring. She didn't realize Archie had returned until he softly cleared his throat. There was no place to hide her condition, not in a studio apartment. Without a word, he handed her a box of tissues and led her to the bed.

"Lie down, Miss Violet. Rest awhile."

"I'm sorry," she said. "I'm not usually like this. I don't know what's wrong with me."

"You've experienced the worst the world has to offer," he said. "That's what's wrong. Time to allow yourself to be taken care of. Trust an old coot on this. Nap time for Violet."

In a fog, she allowed him to tuck the blankets around her. "But…it's your bed."

"Like I told Zach, I'm apartment-sitting for my friend next door. I'll crash on his couch after I do some work, but I'll come check on you. You sleep. I'll work. Zach will find the bad guy. Everyone's got their job, you see?"

She prayed that it would happen just like Archie said.

"Oh, and here's something that might cheer you. Zach brought this up for you while you were in the bathroom." He handed her a white box. Inside were a pair of soft leather flats with chic silver buckles, size six, and a note.

Figured you needed some workable shoes. I called the shoe store and the owner sent these over. I got the size off your busted one. Hope they fit. —Z

"He bought me shoes," she said, dumbly.

"Yes, he did. That Zach is something. Not every man has the chutzpah to tackle shoe purchasing. Heart of a lion."

She smiled, her throat suddenly thickened, heart beating fast at the memory of their kiss. What had that kiss done to her? That one moment seemed to have altered the pathways of her emotions, pathways she'd worked very hard to straighten out.

I wouldn't want to do anything to mess up our friendship.

Friendship was all it was, was all it could ever be, though her heart wanted something else altogether. She'd been vulnerable, and that attracted him for a moment, because he was a fixer, but that wasn't her. Violet Griffin was not needy, not weak and not going to offer her heart to a man who did not want her that way. If Zach broke her heart, she knew it would be a fatal blow.

Tears blurred her vision as she laid the shoes in their box carefully on the bed beside her, tucking the tissue paper around them before she closed her eyes.

FOURTEEN

The scent of coffee brought Zach out of his sprawling slumber the next morning. He cracked open a bleary eye to see a set of hairy knuckles waving a steaming mug next to his nose. Jerking upright and knocking over a pencil cup in the process, he realized he'd been sleeping on top of his desk in the K-9 office headquarters. Bunkered in his cubicle on the ground floor of the three-story building, he'd spent the night calling health clinics. The process took longer than it should have thanks to endless holds and his own fumbling, but Zach was used to that.

"Up and at 'em, sunshine," his brother Carter said, sliding the mug closer. Zach groaned, tried to stretch the stiffness out of his kinked neck and shake away the headache that had settled in his temples. Retrieving the scattered pencils, he jammed them back into the cup. Frosty regarded him with amused interest from his cushion in the corner. Zach slugged down some coffee too fast, burning his mouth. Wincing, he spilled some on his shirtfront.

"This stuff's the temperature of lava," he complained.

"The general consensus of the NYPD is that coffee is best served hot." Carter chuckled. "You look like something the dogs dug up in the park."

"You're hilarious."

"I know. Find out anything pulling an all-nighter?"

"No. No one with Beck's description sought medical help anywhere that I can find."

"Yeah, that was a long shot, anyway. He probably patched himself up. Found his bike tossed in a parking lot. Dusting it for prints and all that good stuff so we're in waiting mode, but we're pretty sure it's his."

"All right." Zach sucked down more coffee, slower this time, letting the caffeine bring him back to life. It wasn't nearly as good as Violet's. He hoped she'd been able to get some rest and that she'd liked his shoe gift. Picturing her opening them gave him a warm sensation. *Head in the game, Zach.* "Give me what you have on the furniture store. My gut says it's a front to move drugs and Beck's gotta be connected somehow. Fill me in."

"No."

Zach stared. "Whaddya mean?"

"I mean no, as in no way, I'm not going to give you any info on that."

Zach caught the gleam of stubborn enjoyment in Carter's expression. "Why not?" he asked slowly.

Carter shrugged. "We got eyes on the store. Nothing spicy so far, just normal everyday capitalism at work. Maybe when you take Eddie in you'll know more, but Noah said that's not going to happen until you come home and sleep for four hours, so he told me to give you precisely zero info about the location or stakeout details."

Zach gaped. "That's insane."

"Four hours, that's two hundred forty minutes."

He got to his feet and stalked from behind the desk and followed Carter out of his cubicle. "Carter, quit playing around."

"Not my call. Noah's the chief."

"But enforced nap time? I'm not a toddler."

"Really? 'Cause I think you drooled on your desk."

At his full height, Zach was a shade taller than his brother and he tried to take advantage. "You're gonna tell me right now what I want to know."

"I don't think so."

He glared at Carter. "The store may prove to be a connection to Beck. It's our only lead right now. Vi was shot at, almost killed by this creep yesterday after he murdered her boss, or hadn't you heard about that?"

"I'm well aware, but Noah said you're not going to do her or anyone any good if you don't sleep. He's already talked to Archie, and Violet is just fine. As a matter of fact, Luke delivered her purse and cell phone and some take-out Chinese in an unmarked car. Archie picked it up and brought it to her." He grinned. "I think it's okay to disclose it was hot and sour soup and egg rolls. We'll bring her home later this afternoon."

"I'm not going to lie around and have nappy time while we've got two cases going cold." It came out louder than he'd meant.

"Yes, you are. It's a DO."

"I don't care if it's a direct order or not. You're gonna

spit out whatever we've got on the furniture store right now."

"Actually," Carter said calmly, "I'm not."

They spent a long moment in a stare down, Jameson to Jameson. After ten seconds he knew he wasn't going to win. He might be able to beat Carter in a judo match, but his brother matched him inch for inch in toughness and determination.

"What about Jordy?" Zach demanded, hands on hips. "Do I get a status report on that at least, or do I have to nap first?"

Carter mimed zipping his lips and throwing away the key.

Zach felt like growling and putting his brother in a headlock. "You know I can take you, right?"

"In your dreams. I beat you at the hoops in our last game and if that's not enough, my dog is way tougher than your dog."

"Carter…"

"Go home, little brother, and get some sleep. If you need me to come sing you a lullaby and tuck you in, let me know." Carter turned on his heel and left Zach fuming. Frosty tossed one glance at Zach before they cleared the room that might as well have been, "Yeah, I am tougher than your measly beagle and don't you forget it."

And then he was left standing there, helpless, like a kid lost at the mall. He had half a mind to go get Eddie and storm the furniture store by himself, but he would not do that to Noah, just as he would not ever have defied Jordy's direct order.

He stared at Brianne and Gavin, who were peeking around their cubicle walls.

"And I don't suppose either of you two are going to tell me anything?"

Brianne ignored him completely, studiously avoiding eye contact, vanishing again behind her cubicle walls. Gavin gave him a sympathetic half smile, which stung worse than being ignored. It wouldn't do any good to pester any of the other K-9 unit members, either, as he was sure Noah had given his directive to all of them. Brianne and Gavin had heard every embarrassing word, of course, adding to his humiliation of being ordered to bed like a misbehaving child.

He stalked to his car, grateful that a fellow cop had driven it back from Astoria. Exceeding the speed limit and bristling with anger all the way home, he found the place deserted. Even Ellie and the puppies were gone away, getting their next vet checkup. They were probably all giving him a wide berth, knowing how he'd react to Noah's order. The whole clan was in on it, he was sure. Too angry to sleep, he took a shower, shaved, dressed and ate a container of yogurt without tasting it, followed by a peanut butter and jelly sandwich. In the process of cleaning up, he knocked a mug off the table and it smashed into three neat pieces on the kitchen tile.

Just great. He knew Violet would have laughed in that throaty way that never failed to make him join in. After he cleaned up the shards of porcelain, he flopped on his bed, overwhelmed by the irresistible urge to phone her.

But there was that kiss...and those feelings...and the stomach-dropping roller-coaster sensation when he recalled it all and the way he was having a harder and harder time thinking of her merely as a friend. Instead, he went out and retrieved Eddie and let him up on the sofa, even though they'd agreed as a family that the furniture was solely for people. "You won't tell, will you?"

Eddie wagged his tail and curled up with Zach on the couch. Again, Zach craved to hear Violet's voice.

Don't, he told himself. Not when he could still feel the sparks of their unexpected kiss. But that was behind them, a moment of insanity. It wasn't love, right? It was okay to phone a friend, wasn't it? Probably not a good idea at this juncture, but his disobedient fingers dialed anyway. She picked up on the first ring.

"Hi," he said. "Glad you got your cell phone back."

"Hi, yourself. Are you okay?"

"Yeah, just dropped a coffee mug on the kitchen floor, but fortunately, there's no one here to witness it."

She laughed, and it was a sound sweeter than the swish of a three-point shot from half-court. If a broken mug would ease her pain, he'd smash a million of them.

"That's pretty typical," she said. "At least it was only one. Why do you sound irritated?"

How could she tell over the phone? "I'm on enforced nap time, if you can believe it. Noah's got this ridiculous notion that I need rest."

"Because you pulled an all-nighter in your office?"

His jaw dropped. "How did you know that?"

"Because I know you."

Yes, she did. Better than anyone in the world. She knew him to the core, but she could not know the strange river of emotions that had begun to run through him when he thought about her. At least he hoped not.

Get it together, Zach. "Yeah, well, anyway, it's humiliating, and I don't appreciate being double-teamed by my brothers."

"Do you need me to state the obvious?"

"What?"

"That Noah loves you." She paused. "That he's taking care of you the only way he knows how."

"I can take care of myself," he said hotly, but her words quenched the flame of his anger and he sighed.

"He lost a brother, too, Zach," she said quietly. "Caring for you could be helping him heal."

Helping Noah heal? He didn't know what to say to that. It had never occurred to him that accepting coddling would help anyone else. Yet hadn't it made him feel like a superhero to arrange for shoes for Vi? And hadn't he desperately wanted to cook those eggs for her? But that wasn't coddling, just…friendliness. "I don't need any hand-holding from him," he said finally.

"Or anyone else."

"Hey, you're a fine one to talk, Miss Independence."

"Touché." She was quiet a moment. "How about a deal?"

"What deal?"

"When this…situation is all over and Beck is caught, we'll agree to let each other help with one thing."

"One thing? Like what?"

"Like… I can help you learn to scramble an egg."

"I don't need help. I just had a bad day. I'm okay at that."

"No, you're not."

"I'm insulted."

"You just need a little tweak, that's all. Five minutes of help and you'll be a pro."

He chuckled. "I'd like to see that on my apron instead of The Incinerator. All right. What do I have to help you with?"

"Perfecting a new recipe for lemon meringue pie. I've wanted to make it for my mom's birthday, and I just can't get it right. So far I've been defeated every time."

He laughed at that one. "It's more than likely going to be counterproductive to have me in the kitchen for pie building when I need a tutorial to scramble an egg."

"I just need a sous-chef and someone to stir the hot custard while I whisk in the eggs. We'll keep the fire extinguisher handy. Do we have a deal or not, Jameson?"

He sighed, a smile curving his lips as he thought about his wheeling, dealing, don't-take-no-for-an-answer Violet. As if he had the power to say no to her. "Okay. Deal."

"Excellent. I will hold you to the bargain."

"Of that, I'm certain."

Her giggle was girlish, but it died away quickly. "Um, thank you for the shoes."

"Do they fit?"

"Perfectly."

"Do you like them?"

"So much."

So much. The pleasure at having made her happy was as restorative as a full night's rest. "Good. I don't know the first thing about women's shoes." He held the phone tighter to his ear. "How are you doing, Vi? Really?"

"I slept a little."

"That isn't what I meant."

"I'm okay," she said, too quickly. "I talked to Bill's wife on the phone. That was…hard."

Excruciating, he imagined.

She continued. "I want to go home and help with Latte and the diner. When will I be allowed to?"

"Soon."

"Not soon enough. I… I need to be busy."

It was an admission that she would never have made before, a fragile offering, it seemed to him. Picturing her there, holding the phone, made him desire nothing more than to wrap her in a hug, to feel the tickle of her hair under his chin. His pulse seemed to surge into a higher rhythm.

He shifted on the sofa and added his own. "Yeah, I feel the same way. Work is the only thing that helps."

"And prayer."

Rage and prayer were not compatible. Though the rage over his brother's death had taken a back burner the past week to worrying over Vi, he did not think it would ever abate completely. It left him blind and caught in a place he did not want to be. "I can't pray right now, so maybe you can do it for us both." He'd asked her for prayer. Had it really come out of his mouth? There was some relief in it and he knew it was a step, tiny and faltering, toward healing.

"I can, and I do, every day." Her voice cracked but she quickly composed herself and added brightly, "So go get that nap, would you? And you'd better make sure Eddie is off the sofa before the family comes home."

"How did you know…?"

She laughed. "Like I said, I know you, Zach Jameson, so get some sleep."

"Yes, ma'am," he said.

FIFTEEN

The operation at the furniture store had to be postponed until afternoon, since the place was unexpectedly shut Saturday morning. "Closed until three for a family emergency," the sign taped to the door stated. Zach wondered if the family emergency had something to do with Beck's crime spree or the drug seizure at Victor's apartment, but there was no choice but to wait for afternoon to roll around. At least Violet was back, with a plainclothes cop watching her at all times plus a diner full of officers at any given moment. Beck was insane, but Zach did not think he would come after Violet with so much law enforcement around.

Then again, he'd been wrong before about Beck's boldness.

As the hours ticked away, he drove his family nuts with his incessant motion, shooting hoops, running on the treadmill, shuffling and reshuffling papers, pacing while he checked his cell phone.

Ellie approached him. "Do you want to go outside and play ball, Uncle Zach?"

He sighed. "Your father put you up to this, didn't he?"

"Yes. He told me you need someone to play with."

He laughed and tugged her pigtail. "It's okay, squirt. You don't have to babysit me."

"I like to babysit you," she said. "You're fun to play with, and you let me have ice cream. You know where Uncle Jordy hides the treats." She frowned. "I mean, where he hid them."

She stuck a finger in her mouth. He sank to one knee. "Do you feel sad right now, Ellie?"

She nodded, not looking at him.

"It's okay," he said. "It's okay to feel that way."

She sniffed and looked at him. "Do you feel sad, too? About Uncle Jordy going to Heaven?"

He fought for control. What was the right thing to say to a child when he couldn't even comfort himself? "I'm glad Uncle Jordy's in Heaven now, but I sure do feel sad that he can't be here with us."

"Do you cry sometimes?"

"Yes, I do."

"Me, too." She was thoughtful for a moment. "He was real good at playing ball."

"Yeah, the best." He waited for the razor-edged pain in his throat to subside enough for him to talk. "Your idea was super. Let's go play some catch and find the ice cream. I think there's still some in the freezer. Your uncle Jordy would want us to have some, wouldn't he?"

He'd won a smile on that precious face. *Thank You, God.* Thanking God? Why should he do that? But looking into his niece's eyes, how could he not? Jordy was gone but there was love here, still here, right before his eyes. How could he feel both love and agony at the same time? Confused, he followed her through the sliding door.

He spent some time playing in the backyard with Ellie and ate frozen ice cream treats with her. He thought Violet might have been proud of him for the way he'd handled things. It surprised him how much he hoped she would be.

Finally, three o'clock rolled around and he clipped on Eddie's civilian leash and made sure his radio transmitter was functioning. Noah and Carter and two other cops were in position as backup, monitoring from their unmarked vehicles parked in the vicinity of the furniture store.

Zach wore jeans and a baggy sweatshirt to hide the transmitter taped to his side, and his gun. If Beck was inside, he'd be recognized immediately, but so far there had been no sign of the guy. He was pleased to see that Eddie was his usual easygoing self. The dog had been upset at being separated from Zach at the shooting scene and at being brought home by someone other than Zach, and he'd hoped their couch time was enough to ease his mind. Zach could always tell when Eddie was agitated because the dog would chew relentlessly on the door to his kennel. For all his amazing law-enforcement capabilities, Eddie was a sensitive dog who had been treated cruelly in his puppy years.

While they had waited for the hours to slip by, Zach had spent a little extra time playing ball with Eddie and brushing his coat until the dog's eyes rolled with satisfaction, which restored him to normal. Now he was relaxed and eager to see what the next mission would dole out.

"All right, buddy. Here we go." Zach walked Eddie down the street and into the furniture store.

"Sir," a red-shirted man said right away. He was thin, so thin his polo shirt hung loose on his lanky frame. His name tag read Hugo. "I'm sorry, but we don't allow dogs in here," Hugo said.

Zach offered a smile. "It will only take a few minutes. Eddie is really well trained."

The man looked doubtful.

"I mean, I don't shop anywhere without my dog, and I really need to make a purchase quick."

"Well…" Hugo said. His eyes rolled in thought as he weighed the cost of breaking the rules against a potential lost commission.

"It's just that I really need a new sofa because Eddie here likes to chew, and he mangled mine. I don't have much time to find one. I was really hoping to make a purchase today."

Zach could see Hugo's eyes light up at the prospect of a quick sale. Decision made. "I guess it's all right, as long as he doesn't chew any of these sofas."

Zach made small talk, asked some questions and waited for his opportunity. When Hugo went to answer the phone, Zach bent down and patted Eddie. "Find the drugs, boy."

Then he and Eddie wandered through the displayed furniture groupings. Eddie was uninterested until they made their way closer to the back of the store, crowded with massive wardrobes, towering bookshelves and coffee tables scattered about. Eddie began to tug at the leash. Zach feigned interest in the table with oak leaves carved into the wooden legs on which Eddie was fixated.

The salesman hurried over.

"You know," Zach said. "This table would look great in my den. How much are you asking for it?"

Hugo fiddled with his pen. "I'm very sorry, sir. That piece has been purchased."

"I don't see a sold sign anywhere on it."

"An oversight on our part. It was sold a few minutes ago."

Zach noticed a bead of sweat trickle down the man's temple. "Really? I thought you just opened up shop for the day."

"Uh, well, perhaps it was yesterday, but it's sold, for sure."

Zach frowned. "But I really like this table." Eddie nosed excitedly at one of the wooden legs. "My dog does, too."

Hugo's manner became even sunnier. "We have some similar pieces that I am certain you'll like. Or I'm happy to show you a catalog. We can even have custom pieces made with enough lead time."

"Naw, it has to be this table," Zach pressed. "I'll offer more than your current buyer."

Now the man was swallowing hard, his Adam's apple bobbing up and down. Another man appeared, black-haired and clean-shaven, wearing a nice suit. He must have been listening to the conversation from the back room. His arms were muscled under the sleeves, neck thick, like he'd seen the inside of a boxing ring a time or two. Zach eased back on his feet just enough, just in case.

"Sir," the burly guy said. "I'm sorry. It would be unethical for us to resell this table to you when it's already been spoken for. I'm sure you understand." His jacket was buttoned and Zach would not have been surprised to know he had a gun hidden underneath. Casually, Zach loosened his hold on the leash, ready in case he needed to draw his own weapon. Adrenaline began to pump through his veins, but he kept his demeanor calm, relaxed. He flashed a smile. "Oh, come on. I know there has to be something you can do. Everyone has a price." Eddie tried to sniff around the big guy's legs, to get at the table behind him.

"No," the jacketed guy said coldly. "But if there's nothing else you're interested in, I'll have to ask you to leave. We don't allow animals in our store."

Eddie was oblivious to the conversation. He whined, circled three times and sat, staring at Zach.

I know, buddy. Play it cool.

Zach feigned insult. "Fine. If I can't have the table, I don't want a sofa, either. I'll take my business elsewhere. Plenty of other shops around."

"Very sorry we couldn't help you. Have a good day, sir," the nervous salesperson called as Zach left. The other man did not say a word, but Zach could feel a cold stare boring into his back.

As they headed for the entrance, Eddie whined and tugged at the leash, loath to leave his find. By sheer force of will, Zach got him out of the store and radioed Noah.

"Did you copy that? Eddie alerted."

"We're already processing a search warrant. We'll have it here within the hour," Noah said.

"Back door?"

"Covered. Carter's there with Frosty, keeping watch.

We'll eyeball the front. Nothing's gonna leave that place without us knowing."

Zach's nerves were still zinging as he guided Eddie to a quiet spot on the sidewalk and gave him a treat. Eddie accepted his prize, dropping it on the sidewalk to lick it properly before he chewed. "You did a good job, baby. We'll make the bust. Just gotta wait a while." He got a tail wag and a yip in reply.

He walked Eddie around the block, where he found Carter and Frosty in Carter's car. Without asking, he got in the front, Eddie scrambling onto his lap. Frosty barked.

"Deal with it, dog," Zach said.

Carter grinned. "Still crabby that we cut you out of the action for a while?"

"Crabby doesn't begin to describe it."

"Sorry, man."

"But not too sorry, right?"

"Well, it was fun to mess with you, I'll admit."

Carter straightened as a door opened in the back of the furniture store. "Who's that?"

Exiting the store from the rear was a figure muffled in a coat and knit cap. Zach didn't have to see the face to know the guy. "It's Victor Jones, the guy we got on airport security camera. Bill got him through security a couple of days before the thing went down with Beck. He must have been inside the store somewhere. They figured out what was going down and they're using him to move the drugs before we execute the search warrant."

Jones looked up, saw Carter and Zach staring at him and took off, sprinting down the alley between the furniture store and the warehouse to the rear. Carter called for backup and turned to Zach. "Frosty can run him down. Cut him off at the end of the alley." He leaped from the car and took off on foot, Frosty galloping along beside him.

Zach raced around to the driver's seat, slammed Carter's vehicle into gear and burned out of the parking place, sirens wailing, until he reached the other end of the alley. Braking hard, he lurched the car to a stop. Leaving Eddie inside, he pulled his weapon and charged into the alley. He surged forward, avoiding the patches slick with oil, his nerves electric with anticipation.

We got him. This time, we really got him.

Moments later he met his brother and Frosty coming from the other direction.

"Where is he?" Zach all but shouted.

Carter was breathing hard. "Dunno. He should have exited this way."

They about-faced and Frosty nosed a metal door they had not noticed before.

"Some dog," Zach groaned. "Why didn't he alert earlier?"

"He's a transit dog, not a tracking dog," Carter snapped. They counted to three and burst through the door into an abandoned warehouse, guns drawn. One look at the cavernous empty space filled them in.

Zach slammed a fist against his thigh with frustration. "He got out. Slipped through the front. They've rehearsed it before, no doubt."

"And he took the stash with him, neat as you please."

Zach could have spit nails, but he radioed in Jones's last known position, anyway.

"Our search warrant is gonna get us a big fat zero," Carter said. "Furniture store's gonna be clean as a whistle."

Another lead lost. Another chance to save Violet from harm slipped away.

From the police car, Eddie let out a heartrending howl.

He felt like doing the same.

Violet was relieved when Zach, Carter and Noah made their way into the diner. It was past their usual dinner hour and Violet was growing worried. One glance at their expressions as they led the dogs to the screened patio area told her everything. The furniture store had been a bust. Xavier Beck was more than likely still on the loose, too, judging from their slumped shoulders. She fought back a chill that rippled over her skin.

Feed them. Wordlessly, she poured bowls of clam chowder and carried them to the men. "Hard day? You must be hungry. Chowder's good."

Zach looked so downcast, she longed to put her arms around his neck and whisper comfort, but instead, she tried for a bright smile. "Saturday special is coming, fried chicken."

Zach shook his head. "Jones slipped between our fingers and we got nothing from the furniture store. Whatever they had in there was long gone. No leads on Beck, either. We got zero out of today, absolutely nothing."

"Not nothing," Noah said, checking his phone.

"What?" Zach pushed his soup away. "Did we get Beck? Victor Jones? Please tell me some good news."

"Okay, here it is, but I'm not sure it qualifies as good.

I won't sugarcoat it." Noah blinked as if fighting for control. "We've expected it, so it won't be a surprise to anyone here." He cleared his throat. "Final autopsy reports are in. Jordan died of a massive heart attack due to a cocaine overdose. It was administered via an injection into his upper arm. It wasn't a finesse job, enough to convince the coroner it wasn't self-inflicted. There was no evidence of old tracks, of course."

"We've been telling them that from the beginning," Carter said. "No way was Jordy a user."

Noah raised a palm. "Everyone in the department knew that, but the ME had to rule it out. Her official finding is the death is the result of foul play."

The room fell into a profound silence so deep that Violet could hear the water dripping in the sink.

"It's not really news, I guess," Noah said. "Just confirming what we already believed, that Jordy didn't kill himself, but now it's official enough that reporters might stop hounding us about it."

Zach's face was stark, pulled taut with extreme emotion. "No, they'll start hounding us about what we've done to catch the killer and we have nothing to say, no progress to report. It's a sizzling story, isn't it? Someone went to great lengths to make his death look like suicide and we have absolutely no idea who that someone is."

Luke Hathaway cleared his throat. "The department is working the case."

"Not hard enough or fast enough," Zach snapped.

"They have good cops on it, Zach," Brianne Hayes said. "They're doing their best and you know it."

"We should be the ones working this case, the K-9 unit. The investigators spent too much time looking at

Claude Jenks, but we know he didn't kill Jordy. We've suspected that from the beginning since Sophie caught him planting the suicide note."

"They had to be thorough. It can't be our investigation. We're too close to it," Finn Gallagher said gently. "Protocols are in place for a reason."

Zach slammed out of his chair. "I don't care about protocols, Finn. My brother was murdered, leaving a wife and child behind, and I did nothing to prevent it." His voice shook. "I'm sure as shooting not going to do nothing to solve it."

"We have to be patient," Noah said, a warning in his tone.

"No, we don't," Zach spat.

The cops looked at each other helplessly as Zach stalked into the screened room and called sharply for Eddie. The expression in his eyes, the desolation and rage when he returned, scared Violet.

"Where are you going?" Noah asked.

"To look for Snapper. If I can't find Jordan's killer, at least maybe I can find his dog."

"It's too late in the day, Zach," Noah said. "Sun's setting and you've been hard at it. Sit back down and eat your supper."

Zach's eyes flashed blue fire. "I'm off duty so I'll do what I please. Or are you giving me orders on how to spend my off-hours now, too?"

Without waiting for an answer, he stalked out.

Noah blew out a long, slow breath and closed his eyes for a moment.

Violet's stomach knotted watching him. She ached for what she understood must be his feeling of painful helplessness at days, weeks, of agony with no progress toward solving his brother's murder. Now added to that was another case that was seemingly stymieing the police. The burdens were almost too much to take for all of them.

"Do we just let him go?" Finn said. "Walk out when he's in that state of mind?"

Carter sighed. "Can't stop him. We have to hope and pray that he doesn't self-destruct or do something dumb."

Violet knew she had to act fast before her father tried to stop her. Quickly, she went to the kitchen and hung up her apron, grabbed her phone and slipped out the back door.

Hoping and praying were one thing, but she wasn't about to let Zach go off by himself.

SIXTEEN

Zach was just about to rocket out of the diner parking lot when Violet slid into the passenger seat next to him.

Eddie yipped in pleasure from the backseat.

Zach kept his gaze aimed stonily out the front windshield. "Not a good idea right now, Vi."

"Why? Because you're upset?"

"Because I'm not good company."

"Well, you're not tearing off alone, not like this."

He gripped the steering wheel. "I'm too angry, Vi. I don't want you to see me like this."

"I'm big enough to take it." She pointed a finger to the sky. "He is, too."

"Don't talk to me about God. If you insist on coming along, at least spare me that, huh? People have been telling me all about God's love since I was a kid and right now, I just don't feel it."

"All right. We'll talk about whatever you want."

"I don't want to talk at all."

"That's fine, too. Drive on, Officer."

Muttering, he put the car in gear and drove, with no particular destination in mind. His thoughts whirled and churned inside. Jordy's killer was free to roam the streets and even kill again if he wanted to, and they had not one clue as to the person's motive or identity. Nothing. Hearing the coroner confirm what they already knew burned it deeper, like slowly dripping acid. They drove in silence until he found himself at Vanderbilt Parkway, where Jordy ran almost every day and had loved taking Ellie and Snapper to play on the weekends. Zach had no doubt Jordy would have continued the practice with his own son or daughter, if he hadn't been robbed of his chance to be a father. The place was quiet, the swing still, the slides empty. A man walked by with his dog, enjoying the evening air, and Zach's worry for Snapper flared anew.

Snapper was a gorgeous German shepherd, a highly trained officer, and Jordy had been proud of that dog, devoted to him. Zach and his brothers had spent hours scouring the place in case Snapper might have somehow returned. Was he even still alive? Try as he did to believe it, the likelihood was growing slimmer with each passing hour. As Zach watched the failing sunlight, his anger shifted to a sense of heavy despair that dragged down his soul.

Violet sat quietly next to him until the thoughts finally made their way out of his mouth.

"Snapper would never have allowed anything to happen to Jordy. The dog was protective, devoted, ferocious at times. I saw a drunk guy lurch at Jordy when we were working a Knicks game and Snapper went at him. Guy needed some serious first aid."

Violet sighed. "Beautiful dog."

"Yeah. Snapper would not have given up on Jordy unless…"

She reached over and squeezed his hand, knowing the rest.

Unless the murderer killed Snapper, too.

"I keep hoping that somehow Snapper got away," he said.

"I know. Me, too."

The weight became too much. "Why keep hoping, Vi? It's just going to hurt more when we find Snapper dead, if we ever find him at all." His voice broke. He gulped and tried again. "When I wake up in the morning, for a split second I forget what happened. I think that I'll find Jordy visiting in the first-floor kitchen, laughing and bragging about his dog and joking with Katie. And then I remember, and it's like I gotta grieve it all over again. It's like a punch in the gut, you know? Every single morning."

She nodded, face sculpted like marble in the dim light. So beautiful.

"I miss my brother." He felt hot tears on his face, but he didn't have the energy to try and hide them from her, so he closed his eyes and let them flow.

He felt her fingers capture his hand between her palms and she started to pray. At first, anger flashed inside him and he wanted to pull away from her, but again, he didn't have it in him to do anything but surrender to the pain. He allowed her words to cascade over him, through him, to tangle with the rage and grief and despair. They settled into the black pit where he'd landed the moment he understood his brother truly was gone, sending ripples through the mire. He did not know how long they stayed there, praying, but when he finally opened his eyes, the sun had fully faded to nighttime and the agony inside him had lessened a degree. The pain remained intense, but for some reason he no longer felt completely alone in bearing it.

He looked at her, at the tender smile she gave him. "I'm glad God gave me you," he choked out, pulling her hand to his mouth and kissing the knuckles.

"Ditto," she said, her own eyes glittering with tears.

"You still pray for me?"

"Every day, every hour, sometimes."

"Good, because I'm still wrecked inside, and I can't talk to God about it. There's just too much pain in between us. I'm so angry."

"He'll wait until you are ready. He's amazing that way."

His feelings became too much to hold inside. "You're amazing, Vi," he said, and he meant it. "All the issues you're dealing with right now, and you come along to help me."

Something hitched in her smile then. "You'd do it for me."

"I'd try." He reached out a hand to cup her cheek and everything in him wanted to pull her close for another kiss. He pictured his cop brothers and sisters back in the diner, Violet's mom and dad, what they would say about him kissing her. And what if that kiss sent her running away, the truest friend he'd ever known? What if he drove this magnificent woman from his life? It would be the final loss, the blow that truly destroyed him. He ached to cross the inches between them, and feared what would happen if he did.

He let his arm trail away and scrubbed a hand over his face, clearing his throat. "I'll take you home."

Without waiting for an answer, he started to drive. The quiet in the car was mirrored in the scant traffic around them. New York was a city that truly never slept, but at that moment it was quieter, slower. They sat side by side in easy silence, something he shared with no other woman, no other person.

After a few blocks she sat back, cleared her throat and smoothed her jeans. "I need to go by my apartment."

"Why?"

"I could tell you, but you're not going to like it."

He heaved out a sigh and shifted in the driver's seat. Though he'd made no breakthroughs and his troubles had not eased one tiny fraction, somehow his heart felt lighter after his time with Violet. "We'll be stuck in traffic anyway, so you might as well spill it, Griffin."

"All right," she said, cocking her chin at him, "but don't say I didn't warn you."

It was good to have details to discuss. Her nerves were still tumbling after her conversation with Zach. He'd delved deep into the private place where he locked all his feelings and brought some out to lay at her feet. It was a magnificent act of trust and she was honored beyond measure. She would have been happy to stay there and listen to him for hours, but she could tell by the weary slump to his shoulders that the storm had passed temporarily, and he needed to get some rest.

Don't worry, Zach. I will pray for you until you can see the daylight again.

"So why the urgent need to go back to your apartment?" he pressed.

She figured the best way was to flat-out say it. "I need to pick up a dress."

"A dress? No way. Beck might be watching. Buy yourself a new one."

"Are you volunteering to be my personal bodyguard while I go dress shopping? Just to let you know, that usually involves several stores and a minimum four hours or so."

He rolled his eyes. "That's nuts."

"Then you'll agree it's a better choice to let me pick up the dress I already have in my closet."

His brows crimped. "May I ask why you need this garment? Sounds fancy for working in a diner and babysitting Latte."

She blew out a breath and steeled herself. "Bill Oscar's memorial ceremony is Monday."

He cut her off. "No."

"It's at a little room in the airport."

"No."

"And it will be well secured."

"No, Vi," he said, finally looking at her. "There is no way you should go to Bill's memorial service with Beck still at large."

"Come with me, then. If he makes a move, you'll be right there and you can arrest him."

"I'm not willing to risk your safety, and you shouldn't be, either. Let's be smart here."

"Zach, Bill was trying to save me." Her throat began to close and tears blurred her vision as much as she tried to keep them at bay. "He died, trying to warn me. He left behind a wife and two boys whom I have known since they were born. I have to be there for them."

Zach groaned. "Vi, you're killing me."

"I'm sorry. I don't want to make things harder, but I have to do this."

He gripped the wheel. "And I'm not going to change your mind no matter what I say?"

She shook her head.

He groaned. "At least you gave me some warning. I'll be with you every moment, of course."

Relieved, she settled back in the seat and let Zach drive back to her apartment. He looked so exhausted, eyes smudged with fatigue. Probably he was hungry, too, since he'd walked out in the middle of dinner. When they took the elevator up to her apartment, she pointed to the sofa. "You can sit on the end that isn't chewed and rest a while. It's going to take me a bit to try on the dress again. There's actually two choices, a black sheath, which is classic, but there's also…"

He waved a hand. "Right. Okay. Eddie and I will just camp out on what's left of your sofa."

She went to the kitchen and returned with a bowl of cereal, a container of milk and a spoon. "Wheat squares. Dinner of champions, since you were silly enough to walk out on my father's clam chowder."

"Silly men get wheat squares, I guess. Thanks, Vi."

"You're welcome."

She went about her task of picking out a dress, finally settling on the black sheath and leather pumps, which she put into a duffel bag, along with more clothes and toiletries since she doubted she'd get Zach to agree to bring her back anytime soon.

A low rumble sounded from the living room. Eddie was asleep and snoring, curled up in Zach's lap. Zach was also asleep, head slanted to rest on her uncomfortable, half-eaten couch. They should go, get out of that apartment and back to the safety of the diner, but her heart swelled at the sight of him there, sleeping. His face was younger in sleep, not quite so careworn, and he almost looked like the high school boy she remembered, always with a basketball in his hand, looking for mischief and rarely still. She allowed herself a moment to take in the strong planes of his face, the angular chin, before she laid a quilt gently around his shoulders.

No reason why he can't have an hour of sleep before he takes me home.

Leaving him there asleep, she curled up in her favorite chair and tried to look at a fashion magazine. Her mind kept drifting back to the car, when she thought for a thunderous moment that he might kiss her again. The problem was, she desperately wanted him to, craved it with all her being.

The truth glided in, easy as a spring breeze. Oh, how she'd loved that man, craved moments with him, stored up their fond memories like a child collects shells on the beach. She'd broken her own rules with Zach, revealed to him her soft fragile feelings and allowed him to become the most important person in her life.

Zach's lashes fluttered, and he sighed in his sleep. He was perfect for all his glaring imperfections, her heart's desire, right there on her lumpy sofa. She was fooling herself to claim anything else. She loved Zach Jameson, always had and probably always would. But that was where it had to stop, because he did not feel the same way and she could never risk losing him as a friend, her rock, her hero. If holding back her heart was the only way to preserve their friendship, then she would do it. The pain of it drove her to her feet and sent her pacing the confines of the living room.

She wandered to the window and looked down on the city street. It was dark now, but that did not completely stop the flow of New York City bustle. People traveled, even at this hour, along the sidewalks, and the parade of cars continued, along with the accompanying honking. She loved the city and it pained her as much as her father to see the little mom-and-pop shops and old brick storefronts giving way to gentrification. Why did progress have to mean losing the history and heartbeat of a community? In the glow from a streetlight, she saw a figure leaning, dark jacket, light T-shirt, the glowing tip of a cigarette poking through the gloom. It was impossible to see the face from such a distance, but the traffic headlights played over the bare head of the stranger long enough for her to catch his silhouette.

She sucked in a breath and stepped quickly out of view. Beck. He was watching the building, waiting for her and Zach to come out. Zach appeared at her elbow, rubbing his eyes. "What is it? Why did you let me sleep?"

"It's Beck, leaning against the lamppost."

Zach was instantly alert, grabbing his cell phone. "I'll get backup. Grab your stuff. We'll take the stairs out the rear exit."

Beck vanished from sight as Violet pulled back the curtain. She grabbed her bag and waited for Zach to make contact, half listening to the conversation over the rush of her own panicked breathing.

"Carter's nearby, visiting a friend," Zach said. "Local cops are responding, too."

When he finally disconnected, she asked, "Won't we be safer up here?"

Her question was answered for her when a face appeared at the fire escape and Beck's boot smashed through the window.

Zach propelled her through the door and out into the hallway. "Go. Now."

SEVENTEEN

They raced with Eddie past the elevator, which was making its way up to the third floor. Would the doors open to reveal another killer? If Violet wasn't with him, he'd take cover and wait to find out, but he couldn't risk a shoot-out, not with her close and the apartment walls so thin. Instead, he pushed her behind him as they ran to the stairwell. Clear. They scampered down two floors.

His heart was thundering the whole way. The patrol cops would be closing in on Beck as quick as they could, but traffic was impactful even for cars with sirens on the top.

One more floor and still no sign of Beck or anyone else. Heading onto the final descent, he nearly plowed into a middle-aged guy with headphones. Zach pulled his gun. The man blinked in shock and simultaneously dropped his water bottle.

"This is Mr. Gabriel," Violet said. "He walks up and down the stairs for exercise. Oh, we're terribly sorry, sir."

"Uh, no problem." Mr. Gabriel stepped aside. "People with guns and badges and dogs have the right of way."

"Did you see anyone else?" Zach said.

"No, but I didn't go outside. I just walk the stairs. It's dangerous out there."

Zach nodded grimly. He didn't know the half of it.

"This is my floor," Mr. Gabriel said.

"Get to your apartment and lock yourself in. Violet, take Eddie and go with him. If it's clear, I'll come back and get you."

Mr. Gabriel edged away. Violet hesitated.

"And if it's not safe?"

"Tell Mr. Gabriel to call the cops."

"But you're the cops."

He laughed. "Carter will tell you I'm not as good as I think I am."

"He'd be wrong."

"Thanks for the vote of confidence."

Violet stood against the wall as he went by. He pushed out into the night and crouched behind a stack of pallets while his vision adjusted. The traffic noise drifted from the street; the lot appeared empty. Nonetheless, he stayed there with his gun in his hand, listening, letting his eyes adjust to the dark. A noise pricked his ears. At first, he thought what he heard was the scuffling of claws from some rat or mouse. The sound grew more definite the longer he listened.

Then there was the tiny tapping noise, like fingers poking out a text message, from behind the hulk of a dumpster to his right. Steeling himself against the smell of rotting garbage, Zach crept around, easing into every step so he would not broadcast his presence.

When he was two feet away from the edge of the dumpster, he raised his gun to firing position and readied himself.

Slow count of three, Zach.

Silently, he ticked off the time, but as he made his move, a twig snapped under his feet. A figure took off with a cry, sprinting away from the dumpster. Zach holstered his weapon and gave chase. If he hadn't been in prime basketball shape, Zach would have lost him. As it was he barely kept pace, shouting, "Stop, police!" to no avail. They were rapidly closing in on a chain-link fence that separated the lot from the main street. The guy, clearly not Beck, didn't slow and neither did Zach. He hurtled up the chain link like a cat, Zach right behind him, grabbing a handful of the guy's sweatshirt and pulling him down to the ground. They rolled over the damp asphalt, the man wriggling, eel-like, and Zach doing his best to wrench his arms behind his back. He'd almost succeeded in doing so when a vicious bark made them both jerk.

Carter appeared at a run, holding a straining Frosty, who was yanking and tugging at the leash. Maddeningly, Violet stood a few feet away with Eddie.

"Get back, Vi. He could have a gun," Zach shouted.

"Stop resisting or I'm going to send in the dog," Carter yelled.

"No," the man said, going suddenly still. "I'm unarmed. Don't let the dog get at me. Please."

Zach kept his full body weight on the guy. "I'm going to cuff your hands. If you try to get away, you're gonna get shot or bitten. Got me?"

He nodded, eyes fastened on Frosty. Canine officers had that effect on certain suspects. Noting Frosty's laser-beam focus, Zach could understand the feeling.

Meeting no further resistance, Zach rolled the man on his stomach and cuffed his wrists behind his back. "You can sit up. Slowly. Don't do anything dumb."

The man complied and Zach got a good look at him. "You work at the furniture store. You were trying to keep me from buying a table. Name?"

"Hugo Clark."

Zach found Hugo's phone on the ground, the last text he'd been ready to send still on the screen.

In position in back.

"Who told you to watch the building?"

Hugo grimaced. "I was helping a friend."

"Who?"

Hugo didn't answer.

"A guy named Beck?"

No answer.

"You know you're going to jail?"

"What for? I didn't do anything."

"I'm going to trace the number you've been texting and find out it belongs to Xavier Beck, a wanted murderer." It was conjecture, unlikely to happen. The phones were probably all disposable, untraceable. "You're an accomplice."

"I didn't know what he was going to do. I had to help him."

"Why?"

Hugo looked at his shoes. "Same reason I follow orders at the furniture store."

"Who's your boss?"

Again no answer.

Zach took a risk. It had to be connected to the mastermind running drugs through the airport and furniture store. "Is it Uno?"

Clark's mouth dropped open, but he quickly recovered. "I don't know who you're talking about."

"I'm talking about the guy who's running a smuggling operation here in Queens. Where can I find him?"

No answer.

"You tell me, or you go to jail."

Hugo threw his head back. "I choose jail."

"So be it. Stay still and don't move or you're the dog's chew toy." When another officer arrived, Hugo was bundled off. Zach walked a few paces away to confer with Carter and Violet.

He glared at Violet. "And I'm sure you have a good reason for putting yourself at risk by coming out here?"

She looked chagrined. "I was watching out Mr. Gabriel's window. I saw Carter and I sort of followed."

He could not trust himself to reply to her so he faced Carter. "Took you a while to get here," Zach grumped.

Carter shrugged. "Traffic." He lowered his voice. "We didn't get Beck, by the way. Patrol cop said he bailed when he spotted us as your backup."

Zach groaned. "And we've got another guy who's so scared about this Uno that he will choose jail over ratting his boss out."

"Might be a good way to stay alive, plus Victor Jones was bailed out within twenty-four hours, so Hugo's probably figuring his loyalty will be rewarded."

"And he's no doubt correct," Violet said. "But it's all right. Beck didn't get to me and you weren't hurt."

He wiped the sweat from his brow and took the leash from Violet.

No, he wanted to tell her. *It's not anywhere close to being all right.*

He shot a look at Frosty, who was still staring fixedly at Hugo. "If you had released him, he would have known I was the good guy, right?"

Carter gave a nonchalant shrug and grinned. "Probably."

Zach did not say the thoughts that scrolled across his mind.

When they drove back to the diner at Violet's insistence late that evening, the team met him there, their collective brows creased in worry. He reported every detail that might be remotely helpful in catching Beck, but once again the guy had vanished.

"We've got to catch a break here sometime," Brianne said.

A smile broke over Finn Gallagher as he looked at his phone, excitement projected on his genial face. He stood up, straightening his broad shoulders. "I think we just did, but it's about another case. I have some news."

"Please let it be good this time," Brianne said. "I'm sick of the bad kind."

"Oh, yeah. I think this qualifies. Check out the picture that was sent to our tip line." Finn was a perpetual jokester, but this time Zach knew he wasn't kidding around.

They all crowded around to see Finn's screen.

Zach's nerves jumped as he peered at the grainy photo. "That's…"

"Snapper," Finn finished. "In all his big, bad, canine glory."

The image was slightly blurred, a large German shepherd caught from the side, powerful, mottled black and silver. The animal was all coiled energy, as if he was just about to sprint out of the camera view. Jordan's police dog. It had to be.

Zach pumped his fist, overflowing with sudden optimism. "Yes, he's survived somehow." The elation was almost too much to contain. "Where was the picture taken?"

"Queensbridge Park," Finn said. "We've got people there now, but I assume you'll all want to head over there on your off time and look."

"You assumed right," Carter said.

Gavin cleared his throat. "I feel like I should advise us to exercise caution here." He folded his long arms, brown eyes serious, though his tone was gentle. Zach had always appreciated Gavin's thoughtful demeanor, but at that moment it rubbed him the wrong way.

"What?" Finn said. "Why?"

"It might not be what we want it to be," Gavin said. "That's all."

Zach rounded on him. "You have something to say?"

"I don't want everyone getting their hopes up. We don't have anything definitive. There are lots of German shepherds in New York. That dog might not be Snapper."

"There's a harness in the photo…" Brianne started.

"Only part of it is visible, no NYPD markings. The photo is blurry. I'm being practical."

"You're being obstinate because you're still angry," Zach snapped.

Gavin's mouth tightened. "Wouldn't you be? If your brothers in blue accused you of murdering the chief?"

"No one accused you," Noah said.

"Might as well. You were all ready to pin me for it."

"There was bad blood between you and Jordy. He got the job you felt you were entitled to."

"The job I felt I'd earned," Gavin said. "There's a long way from professional competition to murder. I thought you all knew me better than that."

"It's over," Noah said. "We have to get past it if we're going to function as a unit and close the case."

"Easy for you to say." Gavin's expression was bitter. "You're the chief and a Jameson. You're not on the outside looking in."

"Hey," Zach said, his voice rising above the collected murmurs. "What's important here and now is my brother's dog. I am choosing to believe that Snapper's alive until I'm proven wrong."

"Me, too," Carter said.

Noah, Brianne and Finn added their approval.

"Believe it or not," Gavin said, "that's what I want to think, too. We should tread cautiously is all I'm saying."

"Fair enough," Noah said. "Cautiously."

Zach didn't say anything. He intended to search long and hard until Snapper was brought home and if that meant taking risks, so be it.

If you're alive, Snapper, we'll find you. I promise.

* * *

Violet was thrilled to listen in on Finn's good news from the kitchen as she busied herself with closing-up chores. She'd insisted on returning to the diner because there was no safer place. The comfort of pots and pans, the hum of conversation, the armor of an apron wrapped around her—somehow these things would protect her from the fear that robbed her of her self-confidence, one violent confrontation after another.

The long moments in the stairwell before Carter had arrived permeated her consciousness as she'd worried for her own safety and Zach's. Beck could have been waiting in ambush. Would she ever again live a life without fear?

Zach followed her into the kitchen.

"That's wonderful news about Snapper. When will you go out and search?"

"Brianne and Finn are going now. I'll join them once I know you're tucked in for the night."

She waited for the inevitable and it didn't take long for him to get around to the topic.

"Of course, the memorial is out of the question now."

"I'm busy, Zach. Look at this sink full of dishes. Gotta have this place in order for the breakfast service." She plunged her hands into the soapy water, surprised when he did the same, mechanically scrubbing the dishes and handing them to her for rinsing. They were up to the third dish before he started to hammer his point home again.

"After tonight you can see that Beck's got help, the furniture store people, plenty of eyes on you everywhere."

The fear balled together inside her, forming something rigid and angry. She squirted in more dish soap and slammed on the hot water. "Zach, I am going to the memorial."

"No, you're not."

"Yes, I am, and your bossiness isn't going to change that."

He clutched a soapy dish, water streaming everywhere. "Vi, knock it off."

"You're the one who should knock it off and stop dripping water all over the floor."

He lowered it quickly, smacking it on the side of the sink and chipping off a piece.

"Now, see? You broke another dish." She turned off the water with a jerk.

"With good reason. You're making me crazy." He was talking loudly now so she raised her voice over him.

"I wouldn't be forced to stand my ground if you weren't bullying me."

"I am not bullying you. I'm just trying to get you to understand…" Zach started.

The door to the kitchen swung open and her father stuck his head in. "You two are bickering so loud we can hear it the next room. We're all trying to plan out the Snapper search times. Can you keep it down to a dull roar?"

Zach blew out a breath. "Sorry, Lou."

He shook his head. "No wonder Jordy used to say you sounded like an old married couple." He took in Violet's steely glare and raised a bushy eyebrow at Zach. "You need some backup in here, son?"

"No, sir. I can handle it."

Her father smiled. "Oh, I doubt that, but I admire your pluck." Chuckling, he withdrew.

Zach waited until the door closed again. Jaw clenched, he spoke in a hard, controlled tone.

"You cannot go to that memorial, Vi. It's dangerous."

"I know that."

"Then make an excuse."

She began to stack the wet, clean dishes, one at a time, punctuating with each dish. "I will not... I can not...allow these creeps to take away my life."

"They aren't..."

The tension of the past hours, their frantic flight down her apartment stairs, began to bubble up inside her. "They are," she spat. "I have had to leave my job, my apartment, and I've had to watch you risk your safety for mine." Tears threatened but she would not let them won't let them take away my final good-bye to Bill."

"It's not worth it."

"It's worth it to me."

"You're scared. It's bringing out your stubborn side."

"Yes, I'm scared." She saw her own emotion mirrored in the blue of his eyes. She saw what he must see: a small, frightened woman, powerless, losing her world one piece at a time. It made her stand up straighter, shoulders back. "I'm scared, but I'm not a coward. I will not give up what I've worked for, what I've earned."

He blew out a breath. "I'm not asking you to give it up, just put it on the shelf for a while." The water splashes made dark patches on his shirt. "For me, Vi. Would you do it for me?"

"Zach, don't you dare." She put down the last dish so hard it cracked in two.

"Don't start breaking dishes now, too, or they'll come back and accuse us of being an old married couple again."

He was trying to jolly her, but she was too far submerged in her roiling emotions. "I'm never going to marry."

"That's not true, of course you will."

"No, I won't." Despair clattered through her along with the worry, frustration, anger at him, anger at herself and everything that had transpired since that fateful shift at the airport.

"Why not?"

Her filter failed completely, and she answered him with the truth. "Because I'll never find anyone else like you."

He stopped, stared, a dripping dish sprinkling moisture onto his steel-toed boots.

"What did you say?"

Had she said it aloud? She desperately wanted to take it back, sponge the admission away, pretend she hadn't said it, make it into a joke, but his thunderstruck expression made it clear that the damage was irreversible. She might as well have admitted aloud she was in love with Zach Jameson. A wave of nausea almost made her wretch. What had she done? She could only stand there, mute.

He blinked several times and finally looked at the plate in his hand as if it had just appeared there. Slowly and carefully he put it down. "Uh, Vi, well, I mean, I didn't really…"

She snatched up a dish towel. "Never mind. I don't know why I said that. Forget it, okay?"

"It's fine and you know, sweet, but I figured, uh, I mean, we're friends, right?"

She nodded, willing him to stop talking.

"And, uh, that will never change."

Oh, but it had. In one careless moment she'd made him see her as a love-struck teen instead of a woman, a pining lover instead of his best friend. She could not speak.

He gave her a faltering smile. "No worries. It's okay. And we can discuss the memorial thing tomorrow. I've got to talk to Noah and then I'll escort you home."

"No," she said somehow. "I want to stay. Dad will take me home later after we close."

"Okay, but I'll wait around and follow you, just to be sure." He swiped at his shirt. "So, anyway, sorry I broke the dish."

"Don't worry about it." How she'd made her mouth say the words was a mystery.

I'll never find anyone else like you.

With seven little words, she'd just ruined everything. Mercifully, she was able to contain the tears until the doors swung shut behind him.

EIGHTEEN

Monday morning Zach tapped his spoon against his cereal bowl until his brother startled him from his reverie.

"What's got you all twisted up in knots?"

Zach looked up from his uneaten cereal at Carter. "Huh?"

Carter snapped his fingers as if to rouse Zach. "You're in la-la land. You've been staring at your cereal so long it's mush. Worried about the memorial today?"

"Yeah." He was, but something else was grabbing for his attention, too—the comment from Violet that beat like a drum in his memory.

I'll never find anyone else like you.

He couldn't quite wrap his mind around Violet's bombshell from Saturday night. His tough girl had thoughts about him that were not merely friendly. The admission startled and confused him, especially when he added it together with his persistent desire to kiss her and the word *love* that continually cropped up in his mind at the drop of a hat. At Archie's apartment, he'd acted on impulse and she'd been merely surprised, not eager—hadn't she? Maybe he'd gotten it wrong. It wouldn't be the first time he'd misunderstood a woman. They were harder to read than the fine print on a medicine bottle. What if her feelings were growing as intense as his were?

"Carter, what does it mean when a woman says she'll never find anyone else like you?"

He screwed up his face in thought. "In your case, it could mean you're such a class-A dunce, she'll be hard-pressed to find anyone as clueless as you are."

"Thanks."

He slid into the chair opposite Zach. "Seriously though, who's the woman?"

Zach shrugged. "Not important."

"Uh-huh." He folded his arms and perused Zach across the table.

Zach put the spoon down. "Go ahead and say whatever it is that's on your mind. You're dying to, anyway. I can tell, so we might as well get this over with."

Carter lost the sarcastic edge. "I was just thinking that if you've got someone pining for you, it's best to go slow, huh? Our lives are completely sideways right now, and you may not be firing on all cylinders in the love department."

"Thanks for the vote of confidence."

Carter frowned. "No dig intended. We're all under a lot of stress. We may not be interpreting things exactly as we should be. I don't want you to get hurt. Not sure you could take any more of that right now. Not sure any of us could."

Zach should have been annoyed at his brother's advice, but he found he was not. Perhaps he had misconstrued Violet's utterance, with all the upheaval in his own heart and mind. More than likely, he'd heard something that wasn't there. He felt calmer, and inexplicably sad. "I hear you. Thanks."

"Anytime. Ready for today?"

They'd gone over the security details plenty of times. Zach would be in uniform with Eddie, a deterrent to anyone looking to hurt Violet in the event housed in a small room at LaGuardia. Carter, Noah and Gavin would be fanned out in the parking lot to provide eyes on the attendees to Bill's memorial along with patrol officers. The rest of the department knew about the plans, as well. Since they would be stationed at the airport, they could be there at a moment's notice if necessary. He'd not been able to get Violet to agree to wear body armor. She hadn't even replied, just given him a look that said, "You are out of your mind." She was probably right.

He passed the time before he was to pick up Violet for the eleven o'clock event by working out and doing some training exercises with Eddie in the backyard. Eddie was obliging as usual, and Zach was pleased to see he'd not dug any more holes in the yard. He was grateful that he'd not transferred any of his emotional upheaval to his dog. They sat in the buttery sunshine for a few moments and he stroked the dog's silky ears. Eddie whined with delight and offered his tummy.

As he often did, Zach contemplated the people who had abandoned Eddie as a puppy. "Wonder who you lost, huh, buddy? Did you love the people who let you down in such a big way?"

Would Jordy be let down at the way his brother had handled his death? No, Jordy loved Zach, Carter, Noah and the whole K-9 unit, and Zach knew his feelings would not have changed in spite of their inability to thwart the murder or catch the perpetrator. Jordy would have understood, and he would have had wise counsel about Zach's current maelstrom of confusion about Violet. He was not sure exactly what advice his brother would have given, but he knew it would have ended with, "Why don't you pray about it?"

Prayer. Zach didn't know how anymore. There was too much anger at God, too much sorrow, and he did not even know what to ask about his feelings for Violet. Nevertheless, the urge to pray pressed down through his reticence and he closed his eyes.

"Lord… I don't understand You and I don't think I even like You right now, but…" He swallowed. "I'll trust You. You promised peace and rest and safety, so I'm asking You to make good on that promise. Not for me, but for Vi. I'm not enough for her, or anybody else, but the Bible says You are, so I'll try to hang on to that."

When he opened his eyes, there was no change, no insight that might order his unsettled feelings, but he felt inexplicably better, lighter, somehow.

He caressed the dog sprawled across his legs. "So all we have to do is keep Violet safe, bring down Xavier Beck and whomever he's working for, find Jordy's killer and locate Snapper if he's still alive. Think we can do all that, Ed?"

The dog wagged his tail with effervescent canine optimism and beamed his soulful brown eyes at Zach.

"That's what I thought you'd say. Let's do this, Officer Eddie."

Eddie flapped his ears and followed Zach to the car.

Violet was as carefully put together as she could possibly be. Her hair was gathered into soft waves at the back of her neck thanks to several clips and a deep conditioning treatment. The black sheath was perfectly fitted, with a light sweater to cover her bare shoulders. For a touch of color, she'd gone with the silk scarf that her father had given her on her sixteenth birthday.

Because a woman should have something nice from her daddy, he'd said. The memory made her smile. Her father was probably pacing the floor at the diner right now, regardless of all her reassurance that nothing could possibly go wrong with so many safety plans in action.

"There were plenty of security people at the airport during your shift, too, and that's where all this trouble started in the first place," he'd replied.

She slipped on her black heels as Zach knocked.

"Zach and Eddie's taxi service," he called through the door. "Here for a pickup, ma'am."

Smiling, she opened it, gratified when his mouth fell open.

"Man, you look amazing."

Warmth tickled her cheeks at his flat-out admiration. "Thank you. Too bad it's for such a sad occasion."

He cocked his head. "You look perfect, Vi, except for one tiny thing. You know what would complete the outfit?"

She held up a finger. "If you say a bulletproof vest, I'm going to call for a real taxi."

He closed his mouth and sighed. "All right. It was worth a try. After you."

The private reception was held at LaGuardia, in a small room that backed the tarmac. It was an event solely for those employees who had worked with Bill. Another family ceremony would take place the following week. The roar of airplane traffic had to be dampened by extra insulation and heavy draperies on the walls. She knew, because she'd been there before, when they'd lost another coworker to a heart attack and Bill had arranged a lovely ceremony complete with a buffet luncheon. The memory made her tear up, but she tried some deep breathing. It would not help Bill's wife to have Violet fall apart at the event. She'd spoken to Rory several times on the phone, arranged for a meal to be delivered and agonized that she could not bring it personally, helped create a guest list from the airline employees who would be eager to attend the memorial.

If Beck wasn't caught, she realized, then Rory would be affected, too, perhaps never seeing justice served for her husband, her boys growing up with the knowledge that no one had been punished for taking away their father. Beck's violence had robbed them all of so much. She felt Zach's palm on the small of her back as they approached the room.

"You don't have to do this."

"Yes, I do," she said, but she was not sorry that he kept his hand there as they walked inside. The room was set up with a large photo of Bill staged on an easel. The picture captured his humble demeanor, the friendly smile. The sight of it made her breath catch. Rory looked tired and wan, but she greeted Violet with an embrace.

"The boys are at home with their grandma. They could hardly stand me leaving them today." She caught her lip between her teeth. "Actually, I'm not sure I can take it, either. I didn't sleep at all last night."

"I'm so sorry," Violet said.

Rory looked past Violet at Zach and her mouth tightened. "My husband wasn't a criminal. He just got caught up with the wrong people."

Zach tipped his head. "My condolences, ma'am. I am sorry for your loss."

She glared at him, gaze sweeping the floor. "I don't want a dog in here."

"I apologize, ma'am. I know this is a terrible time for you. Eddie will not disrupt the proceedings in any way, I promise."

"Well, at least keep him away from the food, will you?"

"Yes, ma'am."

She whirled on her heel.

"You can understand how she feels," Violet said.

"I do. I'll try to stay as unobtrusive as possible."

Not easy for a six-foot uniformed cop with a beagle sitting at his feet. Violet left him, to greet her fellow airline workers, many of whom were holding back tears. When the proceedings started, Violet listened to her colleagues talk about Bill and she tried not to let loose with her own tears. How could he be gone, yanked so abruptly away from all these people who loved him? Zach stood in the back, Eddie's nose twitching at the swirl of odors all around him.

The smell of the food, sandwiches, cheese platters and crudités set out on a skirted table, made her stomach churn. The room grew warm and she turned to slip off her sweater. She looked out the sliver of a window. Her heart stopped as she saw Beck. He pointed directly at her.

"Gotcha," he mouthed, and he smiled.

NINETEEN

Zach saw Violet's face slacken with horror. He followed her line of sight in time to see a quick glimpse of Beck's profile before he disappeared from the window. Immediately, Zach walked to Violet.

"Come with me. Now."

People looked at them, startled, but he took Violet's arm and urged her to the opposite exit, which led to the area where his car was parked. He radioed Carter, stationed at the rear, and informed him about Beck.

"I don't see him. There's something going down on the tarmac. Gavin, you copy?"

"Ten-four. Tower reports a fire on one of the runways. Sending personnel."

Zach's nerves flooded with adrenaline. "It's gotta be a diversion."

The air erupted with the wail of distant sirens as the firefighters raced to respond.

Then there was the sound of gunfire. Energy roared through Zach in a tidal wave. Though everything in him wanted to run and back up his brother and Gavin, he knew what he had to do. He burst out into the hallway, hurrying Violet, Eddie following along. They'd exited through the side, staying as far away from Beck as possible.

The radio chatter proved that Noah was rolling to assist Carter and Gavin, bringing in more reinforcements as the runways were shut down. Zach was four feet past the exit doors when a baggage truck careened up to them, pulling a canvas-sided cart behind it, Beck at the wheel. Zach froze. Beck must have used his inside man, Jeb Leak, gotten access and set the whole diversion in motion.

Zach turned and reached for his weapon when a sharp blow to the skull sent him to the ground. His radio was yanked from his grasp, his gun stripped from his holster. Sparks exploded in his skull but he forced his eyes open to see a gun pressed to Violet's temple by Xavier Beck. Eddie barked wildly, his leash tucked into the fist of Victor Jones, the one who'd hit him.

"Stupid dog. Quit your yapping." Victor rolled Zach onto his stomach, looping a length of duct tape around his wrists. Zach fought, twisting his head to keep his sights on Violet, but Jones had the leverage and he felt the weight of a boot crushing into his spine.

Beck loomed above him. "Well, if it isn't Officer Do Right. It's time to go on a little trip." Zach tried to roll over, but instead Jones yanked him by his bound wrists to his feet. Unzipping the canvas siding on the cart, he propelled him inside. The truck concealed their actions, the airport vehicle a perfect way to blend into the chaos.

"What should we do with the dog?" Jones said.

Beck snorted. "Shoot it. I hate dogs."

"No," Zach said, thrashing and kicking.

"Don't kill the dog," Violet said. He could hear her panicky breathing, but her voice was the calm tone honed from years of airline service. "If you shoot now, they'll hear. You'll have cops all over you."

The seconds ticked by with Zach shouting and kicking, until Beck came into view, the gun pressed so hard to Violet's head that he could see a red mark forming.

"If you continue to struggle, I will hurt her. You get me?"

Zach stopped, chest heaving, rage roaring like an inferno inside him. "If you hurt her, it will be the last thing you ever do."

Beck laughed. "Big words, Do Right," he said. "Move over and make room for your lady friend and the mutt."

Jones forced Violet into the cart next to him and Eddie was tossed on Violet's lap. She cradled the dog with trembling hands and worked to soothe him. Eddie whined and tried to get to Zach, but she held him.

Beck got behind the wheel. Victor climbed into the cart and partially zipped the canvas. Then he turned sideways with a gun aimed at them. "Make trouble and I start shooting," he said. "It will get really messy, really fast."

Zach stared him down. "Where are you taking us? You'll never get off the runway. Cops are everywhere. You got a flying carpet or something?"

Eyeing him in the rearview mirror, Jones answered. "You guessed, Do Right. I didn't think you had the smarts." He pointed to the end of the farthest runway. "Got ourselves a private cargo plane. No frills, but very roomy. We're leaving the country for a while until things cool down. We needed a little insurance policy to get away, what with all the cop activity you've brought down on us."

Leaving the country. A death sentence for both of them, or worse. "Take me, then," Zach said. "A cop for a hostage, not her. Let her go."

"Oh, we will take you. And when we get close to our destination, we'll toss you out, but she's coming, too. Nice to have someone around who can cook and clean."

Violet glared at him. "In your dreams."

He laughed. "Kidding. You're a witness, after all, so Beck says it will be a one-way trip for you, too."

Zach yanked at the duct tape that bound his wrists behind him. His brothers had to have seen Beck's vehicle speeding away. Were they right behind him?

"The airport is locked down. You won't make it out of here."

"No problem," Jones said. "We'll be aboard and in the air in minutes."

In the air, cut off from any help. He could not let that happen.

As they sped toward a looming cargo plane, Zach nudged Violet with his knee. She jerked a look at him and he tried to wriggle his hands while Jones studied the tarmac through the partially unzipped canvas. She understood. Since Eddie created some concealment, she snaked one arm behind Zach. With her manicured fingernails, she scratched and probed until she found the edge of the duct tape. The truck was moving fast now, the cart bumping and shimmying. Violet kept focused, prying the tape up with agonizing slowness, but she had to stop every time Jones shot a glance at them.

In the distance, he heard sirens and hope surged inside him. His brothers were on their way with plenty of units. He just needed to get free and keep Violet safe until backup arrived. The cargo plane came into view. He could not figure out how Beck had gotten weapons past security and onto the runway.

He felt the tape loosen slightly and he could barely keep still. Eddie whined as a bump jarred him from Violet's lap and sent him falling off. Violet stopped pulling at the tape and helped Eddie scramble into her protection again. Another few tugs and the tape loosened more, but she had to stop again as Beck braked to a standstill.

Beck came around and pulled Violet from the car while Jones did the same to Zach. He tied Eddie to the empty baggage cart. Eddie's shrill baying was lost in the shriek of sirens. Jones shoved them both up the ramp and onto the plane. With a brutal push, he knocked them to their knees on the floor. All around them were stacks of furniture, tied down and secure, and all no doubt filled with hidden drugs.

Zach frantically worked at the duct tape, praying that Violet had weakened the bonds. The tape began to stretch, buying him precious inches to work his wrists back and forth. He ignored the pain and the warmth of the blood caused by the abrasion. A minute more was all he needed.

"Cops have figured out our diversion. They're blocking the runway," Jones shouted.

"Take them down," Beck snapped. Jones started shooting. Bullets pounded toward the blockade of police cars, toward his brothers. Every muscle in Zach's body was wire taut. Noah's voice came out tinny and distorted over his public address channel.

"Xavier Beck, this is the NYPD. You are completely surrounded and there's no way out. Hijack protocols are in place and this airport is locked down. Release your hostages immediately and order your pilot to cut the engines."

Beck answered by firing his own weapon, too. Noah's words were lost in the barrage of bullets.

"We're taking off now," Beck yelled to the pilot through the open cockpit door.

"Air traffic control has ordered me to turn off the engines," the pilot answered, peeking out, sweat beading his forehead. "This isn't worth what you're paying me. This wasn't what I signed on for."

"If you power down," Beck snarled, "I will shoot you right now and fly this plane myself."

The pilot's lips moved but he did not speak. "Mr. Beck, there is no way...even if we get in the air..."

Beck cut him off. "I have a boss to answer to who won't settle for your death as a punishment. He'll make sure everyone you ever loved dies, too, slowly and painfully. You get me?"

Gulping, the pilot nodded and turned back to the controls.

The plane rumbled as the pilot began to ready for takeoff. Jones braced himself against the wall and kept his gun trained on them while Beck supervised the pilot. Zach yanked at the duct tape, desperate now.

If they got off the ground, they would not survive. Violet turned a terrified gaze at him, the brown of her eyes clouded in disbelief. She trusted him to keep her safe, believed in him when he did not believe in himself. And he realized in that moment that his heart would not continue to beat if hers didn't, that the cascade of confusing feelings he'd felt toward her had crystallized into one clear and shining reality: he loved her, adored her, and he was about to lose her.

The seconds ticked away as the plane began to roll down the runway.

Violet's body shook from the vibrations of the plane and her own bone-deep fear. They were trapped in a nightmare. Beck was crazy to send the plane right into the police barricade and ignore what would have to be a massive response from Homeland Security to an airport breach. Hijacking protocols in the post 9-11 days were clear. Even if the plane somehow took off, it would be tracked until it landed and met with another mountain of security personnel. Beck was insane to think they would survive.

"Victor, listen," she started. "Beck is crazy. He'll get us all killed. You'll never..."

"Close the hatch," Beck shouted from the cockpit.

Jones jerked the gun at her. "You do it. Now."

She was crouched against a crate, trying to keep her balance as the plane lurched over the tarmac. Zach faced her, on his knees. He gave her a wink. What did it mean? She thought about their childhood when such a look meant, "Keep my secret, Vi. I'm going to launch a surprise attack on my brothers."

A surprise attack? No, her mind screamed. Jones could not miss at such a distance. Zach would be killed for sure. Then she saw Zach's arm come loose from

behind him and there was no more time to stall. She
reached up as if to secure the hatch, but she pretended
to stumble and fall with a dramatic scream thrown in
for good measure.

As she'd hoped, Jones yanked a startled look at her
just as Zach surged forward, a perfect football tackle
that drove the air out of Jones's stomach.

He hurtled back, smashing into a metal edge, stunning himself. Violet grabbed up a flashlight secured
to the wall and swung it at Jones's chin. The contact
sent him toppling. His gun skittered across the floor
and behind a table shrouded in blankets. He groaned
and went still.

"Here," Zach said, gesturing with his bound hands.
She quickly unfastened the tape.

"Find the gun," Zach said, ripping the rest of the
tape from his wrists. She darted toward the stacked
furniture. The space was dark and she could not see the
gun anywhere. Dropping to hands and knees, she felt
along the grimy floor, fingers cold and shaking. Despair licked at her until she saw a corner of the weapon
poking out from underneath a plastic-wrapped pallet.

"Got it," she said, but as she reached for it, a roar of
rage stopped her.

"Get up," Beck boomed, emerging from the cockpit
with murder in his eyes.

Their time had run out.

TWENTY

"It's all falling apart, Beck," Zach said, struggling to his feet. "You can't get away. It's over."

Noah's radio command cut through the din again. "Stop the plane, Beck. There's no way out."

"He's right. You're outgunned and outnumbered."

"I'll have help when we land this bucket. All I need to do is buy some time." He aimed the gun at Zach. "I think your body bouncing across the tarmac would do the trick."

"No!" Violet yelled. He pulled the trigger. Her scream mingled with the report of the gun.

He fired just as the plane juddered, upsetting his aim. The shot zinged into the ceiling, raining sparks down on Zach. Violet darted at Beck, grabbing at his arm but he jabbed an elbow into her ribs, driving the breath from her lungs and sending her falling to the floor.

"Get out, Violet!" Zach yelled. "Jump out now."

Instead, she tried to scramble to her feet, but the impact had made her dizzy. She tried again, upright just as Beck took aim at Zach and fired a round.

Again, the bullet went wide, but Zach stumbled to one knee. Beck took aim one last time and smiled. "Trip's over."

"No!" she screamed.

There was a flash of brown and for a moment she did not realize what was happening. Eddie leaped into the plane, trailing his chewed leash. He barked with everything in him, lunging for the man who was about to murder his master.

At the same time, Zach dived for Beck's gun hand while Eddie latched on to Beck's pant leg. The combination took Beck over backward. Zach and Beck rolled on the floor, grappling for control of the gun. Another shot let loose, ricocheting off the metal door frame in a shower of sparks.

"Violet, jump off!" Zach shouted again through gritted teeth. The muscles of his neck were banded steel as he fought Beck. "Now!"

An idea sparked. She ignored the command and whipped off her scarf, pulling it around Beck's neck.

With a strength she didn't know she possessed, she held it as tight as she could until Beck began to make gagging noises. Zach hammered away at Beck's fist until the gun popped loose.

Violet continued to hold as tight as her trembling muscles would allow until Beck went unconscious. Zach rolled him onto his stomach. "Tie his hands."

She did, making a mess of the knot, but securing him nonetheless. He was breathing, body limp. Zach grabbed Beck's gun and charged into the cockpit.

"Police! Stop this plane right now," Zach commanded.

"I will, I will. Just don't shoot," came the reply.

Violet felt the plane slow until it rolled to a stop. Zach led the pilot out into the cargo area. "On your belly on the floor. Don't move." He meekly followed instructions. Zach kept the gun trained on the two.

"Violet," he said over his shoulder. "There's gonna be an army of highly amped officers swarming this plane in a matter of moments. We're going to stay really still until they can secure the scene and show them we've got everything under control in here. Okay?"

"Okay," she whispered.

Eddie snuggled up to Zach's leg, whining and pawing.

"You did great, buddy," Zach said. "And you're completely forgiven for the sofa incident." Eddie whined. Zach glanced at Violet.

"You okay, Vi?"

She nodded.

His smile was nothing short of brilliant, despite the blood smeared on his brow and grime streaking his temple. "I knew you had it in you, Vi. Never doubted my tough girl for a moment."

"New York tough," she said, and then she started to cry.

As he figured, his fellow officers had arrived with guns drawn and ready for battle. They'd arrested the pilot, and taken Victor Jones and Xavier Beck via armed guard to the hospital before their inevitable arrest. Zach figured with ten cops watching their slightest twitch, there was no way they would escape custody. Roach was still at large, but he was a small-time player to this point, and not a threat to Violet. Zach was confident they'd get him in time, too. He was tired, bruised and bloody, but buzzing with sweet satisfaction. The three of them—a cop, an airline employee and a beagle—had taken down the bad guys and kept the plane on the ground. He'd even gotten word that Jeb Leak, the crooked TSA agent, had been taken into custody. He reveled in the victory, wishing Jordy were there to share it.

Noah broke away from his duties along with Carter to out-and-out force Zach over to the paramedic unit where Violet was being checked.

"I don't need…" he started.

"I don't care what you need," Noah said. "I want you to get checked out and I'm driving the chief's car last I checked, so get your scrawny carcass over there pronto."

Carter quirked a smile. "I'd follow orders if I were you."

"Yes, sir," he said.

"When you get the all clear for you and Violet, we'll meet back at Griffin's. I've already called Lou and Barbara to tell them it's over." Noah left to talk to the airport officials.

Zach shot a look at Violet, hunched over, wrapped in a blanket and talking quietly to the medics. "You know," he said, "she would have made a great cop if she'd wanted to."

Carter considered. "That right?"

"I mean, you should have been there. She was terrified, but she came through, anyway. Went after a guy with a gun using her scarf. I've been around cops all my life and I've never seen courage like that."

Carter raised an eyebrow. "She'd probably say you're pretty good in a crisis situation, too." He paused. "Might even say she'd never find someone else like you, huh?"

Zach jerked a look at him, warmth infusing his cheeks. "I... I feel... I mean I finally realized..." He simply could not get the words out that he was in love with Violet.

His brother laughed. "I get it. I think maybe you'd be a class-A dunce not to feel that way. Go do your thing, Zach." Chuckling, Carter walked away.

Zach watched Violet for a moment. Something the medic said made her smile. That smile was worth everything they'd been through; it was priceless, breathtaking, one of a kind. The lights of the runway, the bustle of the police personnel and the sounds of the commotion all faded away as he looked at Violet, his best friend, and so much more.

With a smile of his own, he bent to talk to Eddie. "Whaddya think, Ed? A top-notch operation if I never saw one."

Eddie barked once and let loose with a jubilant beagle howl. Zach resisted the urge to bust out with one of his own.

Violet was kneading the pie crust dough when Zach came into the diner Tuesday morning. She watched surreptitiously from the kitchen as he greeted his friends in the dining room. Bruises darkened his cheekbones and there was a bandage taped up high on his left temple. What could have happened, what almost happened, made her breath catch and she looked down quickly at the floury mass in her fingers. *Keep your mouth in check, Violet.*

This would be the challenge, she thought. Now that Beck was in jail along with Jones, her world would be her work, her old airport job, the diner...and Zach, but not in the way she yearned for.

I'll never find anyone like you.

Her admission had changed the tenor of their relationship, inserted an awkwardness between them that she'd have to live with. They'd go on joking, laughing, chatting, but behind the facade, he would know that she was in love with him, and she would always be reminded that he did not feel the same.

Get used to it. Zach was beginning to heal from the grief of his brother's murder, incrementally. She would continue to pray for Jordy's killer to be caught, that Zach would open his heart to the Lord and inch by inch, he would take up the threads of his interrupted life...without her.

I hope you have peace, Zach, and rest and safety, just like the Psalm says. And that was the definition of love, she thought, wanting the best for Zach even if it couldn't be with her. Someday he would find that woman who would be a proper match for him, and Violet's heart would disintegrate, but she would never let on; she would always be the smiling, joking, tough-as-nails friend he wanted her to be.

Straightening her shoulders, she kneaded with more vigor.

"So that's how you stay in shape," Zach said as he

tied an apron around his narrow waist. "Maybe I should try baking instead of lifting weights. I'm here to be your sous-chef like I promised."

"Oh, I forgot about our deal."

"Well, I didn't. Reporting for duty, Miss Violet. Ready to slam-dunk this pie-making thing."

"You don't have to help. I can manage on my own."

"I am a man of my word when it comes to pastry. Quit stalling and show me the ropes."

Seeing that he was not about to be diverted, she retrieved a chilled disk of dough that she'd made earlier from the fridge, removed the plastic and put it on the floured stainless-steel counter in front of him. "We'll just take it one step at a time, Incinerator. Can you roll this out?"

"Of course I can. This is gonna be the best pie crust you ever tasted. People are going to line up around the block for a slice of this thing."

She sprinkled some flour on his rolling pin before she reached for the sugar and cornstarch and a saucepan to make the filling. She wished she had never made such a deal with Zach. It was too exquisitely painful to have him there, elbow to elbow with her, all jokes and banter and teasing as if they hadn't almost died together. He applied the rolling pin with enthusiasm.

"And anytime you're ready, you can show me how to do the scrambled egg thing. I am going to master that if it kills me."

"Right, as soon as there's free time," she said, intending never to initiate such a lesson unless he gave her no choice. She figured given his regular duties, his search to find Snapper and unearth Jordy's killer, combined with his natural restlessness, he would probably forget all about the egg-cooking lesson in time.

"You know, Vi," he said, working the rolling pin. "I've been thinking a lot about you."

She flipped her ponytail over her shoulder and forced a sassy reply. "Don't even start. I'm safe now. I'm going back to my job at LaGuardia on Monday, so there's no reason to bicker about that anymore."

He laughed as he continued his efforts with the pie dough. "But we're so good at bickering, you and me. We've got it down pat. Everybody thinks so...you know, old married couple, like Jordy said."

She looked up from her saucepan and eyed his progress. "Stop immediately," she blurted.

"What?" he demanded. "This rolling is perfect."

He had rolled the circle of dough into a colossal sheet of paper-thin pastry.

She could not hold back a giggle. "It's gigantic. It's supposed to fit a nine-inch pie."

He surveyed his work. "Well, you didn't tell me that."

"Do I have to tell you everything?" When she reached for the rolling pin, he surprised her by circling her waist, pulling her close and turning her away from the pastry-covered counter.

"Yes, you do. You have to tell me everything, every little thing that's on your mind, not just the stuff that you think it's okay to say."

She stared. "I don't understand. What are you talking about?"

"You're my best friend, Vi. There is no better qualification than that."

She wriggled in his arms. "Qualification for what?"

He turned her around then so she could see the engagement ring he'd placed in the middle of the dough. A white gold band set with a sparkling oval-cut diamond winked at her from its pastry background. It made not the slightest bit of sense no matter how long she ogled it. "Zach…"

He rocked her gently around so she would look at him again and away from the enigma. "I know, you think I'm stubborn and I break stuff and I don't admit when I'm wrong."

"Well, yes."

He laughed. "That's why I need a tough woman, a best friend who's not afraid to stand up to me." His smile trailed away and the expression left in its wake was tender and tremulous. "That's why I need you."

Need was the last word she'd expected from Zach Jameson. "You need me?"

He nodded. "In ways I never realized before."

"But you… I…we're friends. Aren't we?"

"Absolutely, best friends and we'll stay that way, but I finally figured out that it's not enough. I'm a really slow learner, but I get there eventually." He blew out a breath. "I love you, Vi. I want to marry you."

Something was taking place, something as monumental as an avalanche, as wide as a windswept sea, but she could not let her brain believe it. She felt desperate to back away from the dream unfolding before her. He spoke of love, for her, for them both, but she'd always loved him and he hadn't felt the same and it had been soul-crushing. She could not, must not, allow this fantasy to ruin either of them. "I… If this is about what I said, Zach…"

He grinned. "That you'd never find someone like me? Well you won't, and I'll never find anyone else like you, either."

"This is silly." She tried to push him away but he held her fast.

"You're gonna listen, Vi, so stop wiggling," he said again, a glint flashing through the sapphire of his eyes. "I'm the guy who's known you since you skinned your knees falling off your bike. I've raced you around the block, and trounced you, I might add. I helped you bandage your dolls and walked you home from school when you got sick in the lunchroom and I took care of the guy who teased you about it. And I let you bandage and splint me until I was mummified when you were working on your scout badge."

She opened her mouth to answer but he put a finger to her lips.

"And I'm the guy who knows that deep down you are a world-class lady who is beautiful, loyal and faithful and who's gonna pray for me and our future kids even when we're too stubborn or broken to do it ourselves."

"Our future kids?"

He pressed his nose to her cheek and whispered. "Yeah. I'm thinking five, but I could round up if you want."

She could only gape at him as a tingling started up in her chest and spread throughout her limbs, lovely and light, like joy itself.

When he picked up the ring and slid it onto her flour-streaked finger, she had to blink against a wash of tears.

Then he kissed her pinkie. "I'm that guy who will love you." He kissed the tip of her ring finger. "And take care of you." He kissed the next fingertip, and the next. "And drive you crazy and break your dishes." And then he kissed the top of her thumb. "And try my hardest every single day of my life to make you happy."

Dream or reality? How could it be the truth? Her pulse was thrumming so fast it radiated a frenetic pounding through her entire body, shaking her to the core, weakening the walls she'd built around her heart.

And then he sank to his knee on the floor, stirring up a cloud of flour that he'd spilled there.

"You'll ruin your clothes," she whispered.

"Oh yes, and break your crockery as we've discussed, but Vi, I will promise you right now that I will never break your heart. Will you marry me, Vi? Will you?" His expression clouded for a moment. "It won't be easy for a while, a long while, not until we catch Jordy's killer and find Snapper and even then…" He cleared his throat. "I have a lot of healing to do."

She touched a hand to his cheek, stroked a finger over the strong line of his jaw, soaked in the mingled joy and pain in his eyes. Joy and pain; there would be plenty of both ahead. This gorgeous, precious, darling man, the one whom she'd loved since she was a girl, her best friend, her defender, her love, had laid his soul bare and vulnerable at her feet. He looked at her with a love so true and pure that she knew it would last a lifetime. Finally, she allowed herself to believe, and bliss settled down on her with gossamer wings. She dropped to her knees next to him, there on the floor, and wrapped him in an embrace. "I love you, Zach. You were always the right one for me. Let's get married."

He shouted and squeezed her tight, his knees skidding on the floured floor.

"Just like Jordy always thought we would," he said, voice cracking only once as he found her mouth for the kiss she'd been waiting on her whole life long.

* * * * *